Praise for Redemption, Book One in the Buried Sunshine Trilogy

Adele Dawson is intelligent, feisty, and strong, and she emits a beam that carries this story forward, that lifts it up from the rushing current of thick Mississippi mud.
Main Street Rag

The historical aspect is spot on and the characters are either lovable or persons you have to hate. The main character is Adele and she is very close to her mother who she loses giving birth to her tenth child. Adele now takes care of her brother and sisters and she finds out that her step father had done a horrible thing and she wants to correct it herself. I highly recommend this book to who who enjoys historical fiction. – NetGalley

Courageous family saga, Carolyn Hartley's "Redemption" is a sizzling coming of age story, as heroine, Adele Dawson discovers her roots in this action-adventure, for young adult women.
Millie West, award-winning author and screenwriter
The Southern Redemption Series: The Sun Keeker, The Cast Net, and Of Sun and Rain

Redemption is a captivating story of family drama, heartache, courage, determination, and perseverance on the part of sisters trying to survive the Great Depression. – Cat Fitzgerald, award-winning Author, What If? A Seed Planted.

Characters are vivid, palpable, and develop the story in such a way that you feel you are in the midst of the story (not on the sidelines). A captivating read! – Amazon

The connection that I felt to Adelle is so like the one that I had with Scout in "To Kill a Mockingbird." In fact, "Redemption" and "TKaM" are my two most favorite books ever. That says a lot as I was an English major as well as an English teacher for many years. I look forward to the sequel. – Mimi Reese, English Instructor

Excellent story-telling! This is an era I have read little about, and I loved the strength of the main character, Adele. I have since picked up another copy to share with a friend, and highly recommend! – Amazon

This book was fantastic! I'm ready for the sequel! Hurry, please. - Amazon Highly recommend it. it's a haunting story of a young girl coming into her own. Intellectual while heartwarming - NetGalley

By Carolyn Palmer Hartley
Fiction

Redemption: One Woman's Dream to Overcome Oppression:
Find Family, Love, and Forgiveness (Book One in
the Buried Sunshine Series)

Sliding Home
A Crumble of Butterfly Wings
Madeleine Ganache

Non-Fiction
The Caregiver's Toolbox
(Amazon #1 Bestseller for nine weeks)

Working Woman's Communications Survival
Guide with Ruth Hermann Siress
and Deborah Shouse

Healthcare Professionals

HIPAA Plain & Simple, 1st 2nd, and 3rd Edition
EHR Implementation; A Step by Step Guide
for the Medical Practice
Handbook for HIPAA Security Officials
HIPAA On Demand
Field Guide to HIPAA Implementation

Reconciliation

Atone the Devil in Buried Sunshine

Book Two in the Buried Sunshine Trilogy

JMerrillPress – South Carolina

Reconciliation

Atone the Devil in Buried Sunshine

A Novel

Book Two in the Buried Sunshine Trilogy

Carolyn Palmer Hartley

Reconciliation: Atone the Devil in Buried Sunshine, is a work of fiction. Names, characters, and incidents are the product of the author's imagination. Bramwell, West Virginia, is an official historic town worthy of tourists and adventurers. Any resemblance to actual events, locals, or persons, living or dead, is entirely coincidental. Buried Sunshine references the coalification process of 300 million years ago when pressure and heat built on the peak, squeezing and drying most moisture out. West Virginia's bituminous coal is some of the cleanest burning coal on the planet.

For my husband and boat captain, Chris, whose love, ideas, and actions make my world a better place. I'm so grateful for the writer's cabin you built for me.

TABLE OF CONTENTS

Chapter 1:
All For You, Miss Know It All

Late Summer 1938

Deep in the bowels of the earth, he climbs over jagged rocks fragmented by pickaxes, knowing he's bound to trip and crack open a knee. His boots are those of a farmer, not the crusty steel-toed ones lined up on workers' lockers. He leans against the black coal wall to catch his breath, immediately feeling a shredded wall's cold, sharp edge.

The light on his helmet casts a wide glow on the bituminous pillars holding up the guts of a mountain. He turns to look down the escape tunnel built twenty years ago. As he checks to see if anyone is following, he exposes his back to the blackest black. He ponders a sudden and violent death as would any decent superstitious miner.

He has a job to do, or someone from the Familigia's members will do it for him. Stop her before she takes down a multi-million-dollar company and puts two hundred families out of work. Another world war is imminent. Big money for coal mines. She hasn't the wherewithal to bid government contracts, nor has she listened to Great Britain's increasing demand for steel. Doubtful she's ever heard how the mob might protect her. The Committee agreed to let him discourage her; send her running from a once-abundant coal mine just when it started to thrive again. Let more suitable union bosses take over, the Committee told him. Try it your way, first, they said.

His helmet light flickers. He removes it, adjusts the light, and bangs on the battery. There is no way he will trace his trail back to the entrance without light. He swore at himself for not bringing a backup battery. Cold drafts rush across his chest like a patch of fingerling shadows.

After a brief rest, he slips what he used to call his tommyknocker back on his head, picks up his gunny sack, and hoists it, groaning as its weight pinches arthritis in his shoulder. He pushes open a trap door that leads to a rough-cut stairway. Moisture made the steps slippery. One misstep, and he will tumble 600 feet. He could recite the injury totals for each year when he worked here. Injured scribbled in the book of names, families, and the young men who filled their dead father's places. Twenty years ago, he helped design and oversee the escape route construction. Anyone, he told himself, can walk out of a ground-level drift mine, but the shaft mine is accessible only by elevator. This tunneled stairway was a state engineer's idea of an escape route should electricity or a cigarette butt light up a pocket of methane gas.

His experience as a tunnel digger caught the interest of his gunny sergeant two decades ago and made him the youngest fool-hearty demolition expert in the Great War.

Midway down the chiseled stairway, he braces one leg against the slate wall while unloading the pack. Using a hand auger, he drills a hole into the wall, and places three bound sticks of dynamite into the hole, treating them like raw eggs ready to explode should they roll off the ledge. Satisfied when the blasting caps are secured, he climbs up several steps and places another bound set of sticks. The mountain will absorb the first blast, but the second will close the mine down for months.

"All for you, Miss Know-It-All," he says, smirking. "Maybe now you'll come back to me, where you belong."

Chapter 2:
The New Matriarch

August 1938

Adele Christina Dawson, the only living child born to Selma and Kenneth Dawson, sat alone. The rhythmic creak of her rocker kept a steady beat like the metronome atop Grandma Kettie's piano or the knife her stepfather shifted when he wanted to control her. Back and forth and back. She halted as if to convince the chair's pace to give her courage.

Her fingertips were still raw. Last month the mine foreman had trained her to pick shale from bituminous coal. The buried treasure of Pocahontas mines burned hotter and smokeless, making it some of the most valuable in the nation. After the day shift, the foreman accompanied her into the mine to avoid superstitious murmurs that a female, hunched over a conveyor belt, picked through contaminants. She had wrapped gauze around her fingers to keep them from bleeding, but eight-hour shifts left her fingernails filed down to the cuticle. Not the feminine image she'd hope for today, but part of the Kettie Dawson basic training program.

To steady her hands, she held a mug of warm coffee. Perhaps it would control the rapid-fire thoughts attacking her heart.

She knew what people said about her. A shame she's so young, a pitiful orphan now, and a woman to boot! Bad luck for everyone, especially the two hundred plus families that depended on the coal mines

5

to stay open. Unless they looked hard at her fingers, they wouldn't know a woman had been learning the trade. She smoothed a wrinkle on her dress to brush away a flaw before heading into town for her grandmother's funeral.

What she really wanted was a mouth-agape, full-on shoulder-shaking cry for the last ten years stolen from her. Instead, she remembered the advice her grandmother had given before a death rattle sealed her lungs for the last time.

"When I'm gone, these coal mines will be yours," her grandmother had said. "Wasn't your fault the likes of August Beck brought your mama to her knees. Your mama and daddy were the natural heirs. August Beck stole that dream from our family. All mouth and no trousers, that man; Made you a bondservant to his wicked ways. But you will never get back what he took from us.

In her eighteen years, Adele had spent her first four years as the beloved child of Kenneth and Selma Dawson before her Daddy died in a suspicious car accident. And then, there was the awful day her new stepfather pulled her out of Noona's arms and carried both her and her Momma far enough away to hide from cutthroats threatening her mother. After 15 years of living as the stepdaughter of August Beck, Adele had escaped his oppressive, scrappy poverty in the Missouri Bootheel after her mother died pushing ten babies in eleven years out of her womb.

Adele was a Dawson again, back with her daddy's family in West Virginia. She'd arrived in time to take care of her grandmother Kettie Dawson before tuberculosis stole her business firepower.

"You're home, now, where I said you should be." Kettie had said. "Emancipated young woman. No longer accountable to that sniveling thief. I know he wants you back under his control, but you and me, sweet child, are no longer bound to that reckless charlatan. From now on, you're to call me Noona. No more Nonnina. We are not tiny, powerless women." She had laughed. "As you can see by the weight I've gained."

"I have six sisters still living under his roof."

"Pity," Noona said. "That's how he played your momma. Found her vulnerable spot and filled it. Kept her down by wailing how much he needed her."

"He's a charlatan, Noona. Nothing but get-even runs in his veins. Completely unable to take care of my sisters."

"Half-sisters," Noona had corrected. "Got their goodness from your mama, Selma. Nothing but trouble from August Beck."

"I do worry about them," Adele admitted.

"Of course, you do," Noona had counseled. "Get me six feet deep, then send for them—plenty of room for them in this rambling house. But now, you and I must focus on managing the coal mines. Every day after the day shift ends, you must be at the mine. Get to know my people."

Adele felt the warmth of coffee on her lips on a warm late summer day. If she could get through the next few days, she would find a way to bring the girls to Bramwell. For good. She'd have to be exceptionally strong to stand up to the trickery of August Beck.

In Bramwell, Adele was protected by Dawson lawyers, coal mine lawyers, and Kettie's personal administrator, David Henderson, who supervised her after-hours coal mining learning curve.

She felt a connection to the families of coal miners she'd discovered on her walks along the Bluestone River. At first, they'd ignored her as the arrogant little rich girl, who come home to her million-dollar family. When she noticed children playing in the same dungarees day after day, she brought them clothes Noona had kept for years, in case she someday had more grandchildren.

Today, she felt vulnerable in the presence of so many lawyers, most of whom offered little time for her to mourn. Emotions ran high. She'd seen the worry on the lawyer's faces when they whispered August Beck's name as if he'd stolen a virtue that brought families to their knees. He should have stayed in hiding on the farm back in Missouri's New Madrid County and harvested cotton. He would slaughter hogs; field dress the neighbor's baby calves, and spear a deer's heart when they got too close to his crops. But in ten years, he'd gambled himself down to a lowly tenant farmer and lost two hundred acres that once yielded cotton and wheat. He should be prepping meat for winter, trimming fat like he did when she, Mama, and eight children lived with him. Obediently, she'd helped hide flank sections in the salt house where no neighbor could claim her stepfather had stolen livestock. Now the man, unmerciful with a scimitar knife, was hunting her. No way she would go back with him.

Liar. Thief. He should be a thousand miles away, but he'd come back for Kettie Dawson's funeral and a chunk of Adele's inheritance he thought should have been his. He was the demon behind her father's car accident; I hope someday you pay for the sorrow you've brought to this village and my family.

Rock, rock. Her feet touched the slab of native coral. Each stone was carefully dug out of the mountain and placed by a Welsh mason more than thirty years ago when her grandfather, Quillan, hand-selected immigrants from Wales to work in the coal mines. Artists, he'd called them. The artists and coal mining companies once made Bramwell Bank the wealthiest per-capita bank in America. Her grandfather paid for their passage to America, then provided the starving immigrant children and illiterate wives with daily nourishment, education, and armed protection. Fought corruption and bigotry to keep his tradesmen. In return, the craftsmen offered endurance, passion, and artistic beauty.

Focus, Adele. Focus.

A cardinal's song matched her beat each time the walnut rocker ground against the patio's floor. She braced one foot on the stones to see if the female bird's peaceful call would sweeten the void. The most loyal of all birds, Noona had said. "Protect them, Adele. A sign of love from heaven. Devoted like your mother and father, may they rest in peace."

She wrapped one foot around the rocker to stop its motion. Silence. There it was—the one thing she could control. And then there was Noona's warning. Ninety days, she'd said. After I'm gone, competing mines will lob a cannonball over the mountain. Test your worth to see if you crumble. A killing here or there? No skin off their back. Even better if the mine owners don't like the way you do business.

"You keep our miners happy, hear me, Adele?" She could hear her grandmother's coaching even now. "They'll be testing you. No doubt about it. Might be an accident that shuts you down. A lobbyist slips legislation into a popular bill for the governor's signature. But you trust your granddaddy's lawyers, you hear me? Mr. Ivan Mills, might look like a pug, but he's the best of the best. Wife's a bit smarmy, but he's the real deal. Stay close to him."

Today, her grandmother's funeral would be a showdown between her strength, the loyalty of Kettie's bodyguards, and the likes of August Beck. Kettie had already shown her strength by surviving tuberculosis for as long as she did. Five hours, and it will all be over. "No doubt about it," Adele whispered to herself.

Elijah, her grandfather's trusted butler, had coached her on the social proprieties she'd missed during the last fifteen years. "Coal miner families, they respect your beginnings," he had said. But it was her stepfather, the lawyers, circuit court judges, bankers, and hard-bitten union bosses who would test her now. *Rock. Rock.*

"You ever get too scared; you enunciate your T's and D's," Noona had said. "Men think it's their mama scolding them. You look hard at them. Let him think you are memorizing the color of their eyeballs."

Adele heard the stretched croak of the screen door behind her. She smelled moist dew from the aspen trees, the scent of mountain air welcoming a new day. Tamasin helped Adele adjust the hat's floral lace overlay around her face, enough to show respect without the netting dropping too far down her cheeks.

"It's time, ma'am," Elijah said.

Elijah and his wife, Tamsasin, were Grandma Kettie's carriage house friends. To outsiders, they were Kettie's butler and housekeeper. Both had kept Kettie alive until Adele escaped her stepfather's thieving ways to be at her grandmother's bedside. Elijah and Tamasin were free to live wherever they chose. Still, Kettie adopted them as members of the Dawson family and gave them the large carriage house to escape her demands. Before she got sick, she hired Elijah to be the home's business manager.

Adele looked at Elijah and studied the older man her grandmother loved as if he was family, the man she had come to trust. He stood tall, and walked with the authority of a college graduate. When Kettie was too sick to speak, he taught Adele how to balance the haves of being a Dawson without acting like the hoity-toity families moving to Bramwell. Elijah had coached her on the politics of coal mining leadership when Kettie was too ill to sit up. Even so, Kettie corrected him if he misspoke the loyalty of coal miners.

Behind Elijah, higher on the hill, she saw two men step out of the carriage house. One made no effort to hide the shotgun splayed across his arms. The other buttoned his black suit jacket. The bulge under his arm sent a message that troublemakers should lay low while this fragile family grieved the loss of their matriarch. Elijah nodded uphill that he approved their positions.

"You do whatever Mr. Henderson says," Elijah whispered to Adele. "He knew Miss Kettie better than anyone, 'cept me and my woman. Do as he say now. Hear?"

Repeating an order, like he did, meant Elijah was more nervous than she, but he had years of training to hide fear. She nodded, reached for his dark hand, and pressed it to her cheek.

"None a that, now, ma'am. You be right back here before the sun go down, swinging on that chair like the young lady you were meant to be."

Two of Kettie Dawson's attorneys stepped in front of the guardsmen and onto the extended stone lanai, walking confidently as lawyers going to trial. Pull yourself together; she scolded herself. Today was not a day for eloquence. Her pedigree would be tested.

"Master Henderson and Master Mills be here to escort you now," Elijah said. "Crowd already gathering at the Presbyterian church."

David Henderson buttoned his suit jacket and offered his elbow to escort her. When she curled her hand into his arm, he patted her wrist to let her know she was safe.

"We're not taking the car?" Adele asked.

"Show you strength by walking, ma'am," Elijah answered. "Comin' down the mountain like that show you got Bramwell in your heart."

Neighbors, friends, and bankers fell in line as the parade of walking mourners made its way through downtown. Workers from coal companies stood along the street, joined by dock loaders who ceased loading merchant vessels to honor the memory of a woman who brought beer for them and sandwiches for their families. Bank tellers temporarily closed their windows, joining city folk in a salute to one of its most charitable leaders. As they rounded a corner to pass the hospital, a team of nurses held up a sign, "Thank You, Kettie Dawson."

They walked past the train station, where the last of a hundred or so passengers stepped quickly onto the arrival platform and huddled together to watch the parade that now stretched nearly five blocks long. Families were traveling to Bramwell, a sign that the coal mines were sure to start hiring again.

Eventually, the line completed its rounds through town and headed up a few short blocks to Bramwell Presbyterian, where Kettie Dawson would be laid to rest next to her family: Kenneth, her son, and Adele's father, and her beloved husband, Quillan.

Adele's hat was a bit warm for the summer funeral, but the mountain air kept her from burning up. In her black satin gloved hands, she carried Mama's Bible. She needed Mama's soul and Noona's confidence entirely inside her today.

Chapter 3:
The New Doyenne

August 1938

B ent sun rays beamed through stained glass windows to warm Adele's face. She placed her hand on carved stones, the foundation for the Presbyterian church that had been a shelter for some of the nation's wealthiest coal mine owners and the families who worked for them. These stones anchored citizens of Bramwell through the Great War, floods, the Great Depression, and coalmine insurrections. She remembered her father talking about the Italian and Welsh stonemasons her grandfather brought over from Europe to build this beautiful town along the Bluestone River. That was before. *Enough*, she told herself. Take care of business. *You are a Dawson. Home again.*

She looked up at the magnificent arches where her family had worshiped. Portraits of older men hung on the wall. A brass plaque identified the years each man led the Board of Trustees. Their thick lapels and double-breasted suits created an illusion of strength and wealth.

"Do you know which one is your grandfather?" David Henderson asked. Adele studied the faces. "That's him," she said.

"He was a great benefactor. Dynamic leader," David said. "And you know this woman here," he added, pointing to a picture of women gathered on the front steps. "Everybody wanted to stand next to Miss Kettie."

"I wish I had more time with her."

"You've been in Miss Kettie's life for eighteen years," David gently corrected. "You don't remember this, but Kettie rode the train to St. Louis at least twice a year, then hired a driver to take her to New Madrid. She and Selma used to meet at a local diner. When August found out, he refused to let the children go along. Claimed it could expose Selma's whereabouts."

"Why was she in hiding?"

"Your family, Adele. Mighty as they are, they've also got plenty of skeletons buried in these hills. Some best left alone."

Outside the church, the community grew quiet, and respectful. "Come stand outside with me. Listen as friends pay respects to your grandmother," David said, escorting Adele back into the church's parking lot.

Five lawyers, stoic as soldiers, lined the driveway; their white-gloved hands crossed in front of them, standing guard over the hearse and its precious cargo. Elijah had explained how the funeral would go, but nothing prepared her for the drama of this beloved woman's celebration of life. It was up to her to listen and absorb.

Mr. Henderson excused himself from Adele's side to open the Sayers and Scoville hearse. As the line of cars inched forward, Garret Stevenson, Harold Hamburg, and Ivan Mills walked protectively beside the hearse until a black Packard filled with flowers closed the gap. Each man seemed to keep careful watch. Today, entirely in Kettie's and Quillan's world, Adele wanted everything to be a celebration for those who loved her grandmother.

"Any news?" she heard David Henderson ask.

Ivan Mills nodded toward a black and white patrol car. "Sheriff says he slipped away."

Adele knew they were talking about her stepfather. Didn't matter. Her life today would be tuned in to Kettie Dawson and the people who cherished her.

To her left, she saw the gaping hole in the church cemetery prepared for her grandmother's final resting place. Three tombstones stood proudly inside a plot of land intricately outlined in gold-painted brick. Grandpa, Daddy, and now Noona.

'Finally got what you were bellyaching for,' she could hear her stepfather scold. 'Money hungry just like your Ma.'

'This is your home, princess,' her daddy argued silently on her behalf. 'Let our friends tell you about our family. You won't like all of them. But you will love most of us if you give us a chance."

Adele clutched Mama's Bible to her chest. Voices of children nearby brought a little bit of heaven to her. She took a step forward, ready to join friends gathering in the church.

"Not yet, Miss Dawson," Frank whispered. He stood to watch while the minister and four acolytes carried candles up the colonnade and into the sanctuary. Four lawyers guarded Miss Kettie's coffin, then lifted it step by step through church doors. Two younger men at the rear kept the coffin steady.

"Ma'am? Someone is here to see you," David said. "Are you receiving?"

"Who is it?" Adele asked.

"Delly, it's us," No one in Bramwell called her Delly. "It's all of us." She immediately recognized the squeal in Elysia and Collette's voices. "How did you get from New Madrid to Bramwell? Without me?" she cried out.

"Collette?" And the B's!"

"We're here, Delly," Collette laughed. "All us girls. Miss Kettie wired money to Tommy to be sure we got here safe. You walked right by us at the train station."

"Two nights and three days, just sitting on the train," Benita whined.

She looked around at all the men in suits. "How many lawyers you got?"

"You look beautiful," Faye said.

"Faye doesn't suck her fingers anymore," Briana added. Faye held up her middle three fingers to show they were dry.

Adele opened her arms to the assortment of little women surrounding her. "You're here! You're all here!"

From behind, she heard another familiar voice. "Hello, Adele." Adele's knees buckled, loving the sound of that friend's voice.

Frank immediately stabilized her, physically blocking any space between the young man and Adele. "I'm taking you and the young ladies inside."

"Wait," Adele said. "Tommy? Your mom must be so worried about you. Does she know you're here?"

"I don't talk to my mom much anymore. Besides, I couldn't let you go through this alone," Tommy answered. "Neither could your grandmother. She made sure I could be here."

Adele released her arm from Frank. "This is my best friend, Tommy Thompson."

Frank stood nervously, watching the street to see if there were additional latecomers. "Church is filled, ma'am. Time for you to take your seat." He nodded to David as they exchanged positions, like well-drilled guardians, moving the family through the crowd.

Tommy reached for Adele and pulled her to him. "There's so much for me to tell you. Your grandmother wanted us to be here." He reached to shake David Henderson's hand. "Tom Thompson, sir. Pleased to make your acquaintance, even at such an unfortunate time as this."

Mrs. Henderson, standing behind her husband, sniffed a bit too obviously, then turned up her nose. She pulled a small bottle of Chanel No. 5 from her purse. "How about a bouquet of femininity for you, sweet child?" she asked, spraying Deirdre, Adele's nine-year-old half-sister.

Wrong girl, Adele thought. Mrs. Henderson raised the bottle of French perfume and examined how much remained. "Goodness, there are so many of you."

"Gretta, quiet," David shushed his wife, but she had opened the door for introductions.

Briana smoothed a wrinkle from her skirt and leaned in to capture a spray. "I'm Briana Marie. Our mom, she died two years ago, named us in alphabetic order so she could count to see who was missing." Briana pointed to the tall girl standing behind her. "That's Benita, and this is..."

"I'm Benita Ann," Benita cut in. "Briana Marie is my twin. I was born first. That's Collette, Deirdre, and Elysia. Faye's the wobbly one over there. We're Catholic."

"I see," Mrs. Henderson said. She slid the perfume back into her purse and pulled out a crocheted handkerchief. After giving it a quick shake, she placed it atop Benita's head. "Our church is open to all who believe."

Benita yanked the handkerchief off and plopped it on Collette's head. "Leave it," she snapped.

Mrs. Henderson cleared her throat. "My, this has been a rough time for you. Let me know how I can help."

"That's very thoughtful, ma'am," Adele said. "My sisters must be tired from their three-day train ride." She turned to Tommy, "Please come be at my side."

"Step in line behind Miss Dawson," David said to Tommy. He tucked Adele's hand into the crook of his elbow, ready to guide her down the aisle. He'd guided her through other major events, including managing the Dawson's family estate. Adele grabbed Tommy's hand but also held tightly to the arm of her grandmother's attorney and nodded that she was ready to walk together toward the chancel.

***

The organist hit the first few chords of Morning Has Broken, and the congregation stood. David Henderson looked down at Adele. "Ready?" he asked.

Instinctively, Briana took Collette's hand. The young women stood three across next to Tommy, but as slender as they were, they walked arm in arm without bumping anyone on the way to the altar. Adele looked over her shoulder to Benita.

"I got 'em," Benita offered. "Deirdre, grab Faye."

David leaned over and whispered to Adele. "You have a big family."

"Yes, sir," Adele beamed.

Kettie Dawson looked exquisite in her white satin suit, lying in the open casket. Her thick silver, well-styled hair was backlit, creating a statement of abundance. It was her mercy and grace that lifted the congregation's spirits. A few chairs along the wall remained available for latecomers. "Reserved" signs had been clipped to the front few rows.

People in the back of the church looked at David Henderson, then at Adele, and then at Tommy, who proudly held her close. All that influence passed down the generations to fall on the shoulders of young Adele Christina Dawson, nineteen years old, heir to insolvent banks, the new business owner of closed mines.

"This is your moment, Miss Dawson," David said, patting her hand. "You see church pews filled with strangers. I see a village of brothers and sisters here to welcome you home."

Halfway down the aisle, Adele smiled at the deacon who had whispered communion at Noona's bedside, serving the sacrament as he worshipped with her. Without losing her hat, she nodded at the new president of the Ladies' Aid Society. "You the new Doyenne," Elijah had instructed. "Nod like you barely notice."

Older women who brought chocolate chip cookies and warm Gruyere cheese to visitation clustered together, cupped their mouths to whisper,

"Them's Selma's daughters," and pointed at the girls. Adele could feel stories about her mother welling up. Once a debutante, her mother may have lost social status among these friends, but the recipe for love she poured into her children created an impenetrable club between sisters. Adele would forever be grateful for her beloved mother, who would have loved this parade of young women.

Adele smiled at the sight of her grandmother center stage in front of the altar, right where she should be, still leading the community, even in death. Maybe it was just Noona's emerald pin winking back against the overhead lights, but Adele thought it looked like Noona was giving her a nod of approval. Heaven's her home now next to my momma, my real daddy, and her grandfather, Quillan. All sipping Jesus wine, bragging that it was straight out of Jerusalem.

David Henderson stopped at the first reserved row and stepped aside to let the sisters walk in first. Adele waited to sit near the aisle.

Briana started to make the sign of the cross over her heart. Benita pushed her off balance. "Just go. Not that kind of church," she mumbled. Finally, after all the girls were seated, Tommy Thompson sat next to Adele. David Henderson stepped into the pew behind her. She felt a whoosh of his cologne as he touched her shoulders. Six pallbearers, all of them attorneys, whom Adele had met a few weeks earlier, came forward and stood stoic as sentries guarding Kettie's coffin. They turned and nodded to Adele as they passed her, acknowledging the pain she must indeed be suffering. Finally, they took their seats but did not remove their white gloves.

"Was your Noona a soldier?" Collette asked.

"Those men are her pallbearers," Adele whispered.

"What's a pear builder?" Faye asked.

"Shut up," Benita scolded. "All of you."

Faye slid out of her seat in the pew and stood in front of Adele. "Is that lady scared to be alone?" she asked. "What if that door comes down on her?"

Briana pulled Faye's arm and raised her onto her lap. "Come here, baby sis. Right now, we're just going to watch."

Tommy wrapped one arm around Adele and held her hand in his. "I'm glad you don't have to do this alone," he said.

"I was never alone, Tommy," Adele whispered back. "Momma was always at my side. I hear her sing every time I listen to the bells."

***

A procession of cars left the church, many of them following personal instructions to head up to the Dawson Stone House. After saying their final goodbye to Kettie at the graveside, the family would join them at the reception. Elijah and Tamasin were already at the house, ready to serve guests while waiting for the family to arrive.

Adele slid her arm around Tommy, grateful that he was at her side to say her final goodbye. Tommy leaned in to kiss her forehead. She bowed her head into his shoulder,

"You have to set her free," Tommy whispered. "The spirit of women like Kettie and your mother will always be at your side. It's their choice. Not yours."

"It's like she's already a spirit, warning me." Adele looked over her shoulder to see David and his bodyguard exchanging nods. Something was wrong. "Come with me," David said

"Is he here?" Adele asked.

"I apologize, Miss Dawson, I cannot say. Sheriff's orders."

"What orders?" Tommy asked.

David Henderson turned to face Tommy. "We've got this handled, sir."

"Not if it involves my girlfriend!" Tommy argued. "Delly, what's going on?"

"There were whispers before Noona's service."

"About what?"

"Miss Dawson," David said, introducing her, "this is Jackson Conor, my friend and bodyguard. I trust him with my life. He has a good sense of the trouble August Beck can cause."

Jackson, dressed in a black suit and loosened black tie, gave Adele a curt nod. He looked suspiciously at Tommy as if searching for concealed weapons.

"For your safety, all of you. Back inside the church."

"Wait just a minute," Tommy argued. "We haven't closed Miss Kettie's coffin."

Jackson reached up and gasped the coffin's handle. "Now it's closed. Follow me."

"Stay with the children," David instructed Jackson. "Nobody, I mean nobody, comes near the girls until I give the all-clear."

"If anyone is looking for trouble," Jackson said, patting a bulge in his chest, "he'll find it." With that, he wrapped one arm around Adele's waist and led her into the church.

"Get the girls," he said over his shoulder to Tommy.

The thought of her stepfather roaming the church grounds pushed Adele into battle mode. This wasn't the first time she'd protected her sisters against their father. What did he want?

Jackson closed the double doors and lowered the latch after escorting Adele and her sisters back inside the church. Adele went through the alphabet as she did so often to be sure all the girls were safe. The B's, Collette, Deirdre, Elysia. Faye.

"Faye?" Where's Faye?" She looked at Jackson. "Faye's not here."

Benita joined Adele. "Hey, baby sis. Jump out now, girl. No more hiding."

Adele turned to Jackson. "Open the door. I have to find Faye."

"No, ma'am. We stay inside."

"For how long?" Elysia asked, giving in to her tears. "Faye's alone!"

"Until Henderson gives the all-clear."

Obedient at first, Adele opened the grand double doors into the sanctuary, then sat on the back pew, torn between being safe inside the church and abandoning the youngest, most fragile of her sisters. The child wouldn't know a single person. She didn't think Pa would harm her, but he would certainly use her for leverage. If it came to a fight, Faye wouldn't know to step out of the way. What had she done, exchanging grasshoppers and cornfields for guns and coal mines?

She stood resolved, stepped back into the foyer, and raised the latch. Jackson was immediately beside her, holding her back. "Ma'am, I can't let you go out there."

"My baby sister is lost, Jackson." Adele blocked herself against the bodyguard, but it was like trying to move a 200-pound side of beef. For a gunslinger, Jackson was mighty muscular. He wrapped his arms around her and lifted her unceremoniously away from the door. "I'm not afraid to do that again, ma'am."

"She's alone, Jackson."

"Orders, ma'am. No one goes out these doors."

Adele glared at him. "David Henderson works for me. So, what does that make you?"

"Ma'am, I've had worse threats than yours laid on my back."

Adele glared at Jackson. "I'm not going to do nothing while she's out there."

Jackson leaned against the door and stared down at her. No nod, no movement.

"Wait," Adele said. "Tommy is still out there. Get a message to him. Tell him to find Faye and stay with her."

Jackson did not move.

She turned to Benita. "Call out to him through one of the church windows."

"And give away your position? Not a chance," Benita responded.

"Then help me."

Jackson snorted, dismissing her. Adele stepped back into the sanctuary and let the lobby doors close against her back. She remembered another exit. The choir loft, yes.

She nudged Benita. "Come with me. Quietly."

"Stop moving around," Jackson ordered. "I'm not afraid to tie you to a chair."

Adele glared at him, daring him to follow through on his threat. Then, together Adele and Benita walked up to the altar. It was like old times, the girls bonding against their father. As soon as one was on a mission, they all gathered. They stepped around the pulpit when Adele smelled her stepfather's sour breath and cheap cologne.

"Hello, Delly," August said, his voice low and husky. It was the tone he used with her mother after being gone for a week of hunting. In his arms, August Beck held his daughter, Faye Marie, to his chest. "You left your baby sister alone out there. What kind of sister does that?"

Briana stepped back and held her arms out, sheltering Deirdre, Collette, and Elysia into the back corner. Adele felt a rush of air pass by her. She didn't look to see who it was. Instead, she regarded August with the cautious intensity he demanded.

August smiled a little too wickedly and patted Faye's leg. She squirmed to get down, but August tightened his arm around her. "All those years I provided for you. The only thanks I get is you deserting me? You know better than that." By the way, he stroked Faye's hair, Adele knew he was pondering something dangerous. "Call off the henchmen," he ordered.

"Not my call to make," Adele answered.

He turned up his lip. "I gave you a roof over your head. Hunted game for you and protected you. I should have known you'd always be a Bramwell snob."

"You're not my father," she snapped.

"I treated you like my daughter. I raised you," August said.

"I wouldn't call it that." She remembered the night he locked her in the loft when the Mississippi River flooded their home. Waters rose so quickly into the attic where he had locked the door. He climbed on the first boat to get away, leaving her alone, six years old, to drown or find her way out of the rising muddy waters.

He stole a quick glance at the girls huddled in the corner. "I got unfinished business here. First you, then Benita."

"It's me you really want, isn't it?" Adele tried to console him. "Too many people here seem to think you've cheated them somehow. Whatever you've got planned, it won't work."

"You have no idea what you've stepped into," August scowled.

"What a rue," Adele scolded. "You are the one who couldn't handle seven girls. We're not your problem anymore. I'll take care of my sisters now."

Adele heard someone racking the first round into a shotgun. Whoever it was had better be prepared to shoot. She turned to see Jackson pointing his weapon at August.

August tightened his grip around Faye's legs, then pulled the child's hair, exposing Faye's neck as a target. "A few shot wads, and you'll be the one who kills this child," August sneered. "Be a damn casualty if you took her out instead of me."

"Try me," Jackson snapped.

Faye arched her back and cried out, "Delly, save me."

"Contemplate your actions, Mr. Beck." Jackson paused. "Let the girl go."

"Ain't about you, J-man," August snapped.

"You just made it about me," Jackson said, his base voice-controlled and guttural. He kept his eyes on August but took calculated, slow steps down the center aisle.

Stunned, Adele said, "J-Man? You know each other?"

Less than an hour ago, the town of Bramwell had sung Miss Kettie to heaven. Now her stepfather's anger had squared up to test Adele.

Jackson took calculated steps toward August. "My men are all jarred up for a gunfight. You won't get twenty feet outside this building."

Adele stole a glance at her younger sisters and gave them a hand signal to stay out of the way. She did the alphabet head count again. Benita was missing.

"I came in peace," August said. "Anyone gets shot; it's on you."

"Not one of us believes that," Jackson argued. "One of the Dawsons is still serving time for what you did to Selma."

Adele remembered the paragraphs in her mother's diary about her uncle Irving going to prison for killing August's father.

"No one is getting shot," Adele said. "Not me. Not Faye. Let her go. It's me you want."

August lowered Faye to the ground but kept his hands on her shoulders as he turned to Adele. "Isaac is missing."

"Your precious boy?" Adele said, emphasizing precious as a nuisance. Her mama sacrificed her life so that August could finally have a male child. "You and your new wife can't take care of a two-year-old?" She noticed shadows moving outside below the stained-glass windows. Whoever was coming, they had a piece of August Beck's hide on their minds. Had Benita slipped out to get help?

"Pa, this isn't the time or place," Adele said. "I know you believe I owe you something, but this isn't the way to get it. Leave us, now."

"Pa, is it? Well, now, that sounds more like the filly I raised."

Adele could easily spit on him. She stepped close and took Faye's hand in hers, defying her stepfather. "Girls, we are going home." She held August's glare, daring him to touch her.

"Not so fast, young lady," August sneered. "Olga says Benita knows who took Isaac."

"Olga?" Her throat tightened, just saying the woman's name. "She was supposed to tend to the children."

"I've had enough," Jackson said. "Say the word, Miss Adele, and your stepfather's a skoondog."

"I was about to say the same thing," David Henderson blurted, suddenly emerging from the choir loft. "Mighty disrespectful to shoot a man's leg off in church." David was carrying his handgun low at his side. "Let the girls go home. Auggie, you and I will take this outside."

August looked to David first, then Jackson. Finally, he looked at Adele. "I need my boy, Delly."

Her stepfather needed Isaac for leverage, depending on what political protest he had taken on. Before she escaped the farm, August pandered to his son, Isaac, his two-year-old profit and loss center, selling uninterrupted access to the boy to the highest bidder. Isaac would never grow up with any self-esteem. He would forever be damaged, thanks to Beck.

David waved his handgun. "Adele, you and the girls go on home, now. Jackson and I are going to finish up here."

Adele tugged on Faye's hand and then waved for her sisters to follow. "Come on, girls. I bet Tamasin's got warm biscuits ready for us." She sheltered them into a circle as they left the church.

"We're not done," August shouted after her. He tossed his knife between hands. She grinned ever so slightly, knowing her stepfather brought a skinning knife to a gunfight.

"I say you are," Adele heard Jackson say just before she heard a heavy thud as if someone had fallen to the ground. She wanted to watch her stepfather get the tar beat out of him, but she was desperate to get her sisters to safety.

"Briana, your twin sister will have to catch up with us later. Lead the way. We're heading up to Stone House."

If Jackson would somehow discourage August Beck from harassing her, she could begin a new happy life. Rather than worry about Faye, she now had Benita, August's protégé, to worry over.

"I know you all know the whereabouts of your sister. Where is Benita?" she asked

"I don't know," her twin sister, Briana answered. "Nita never walks from a fight. She's close. Don't worry. If no one gets hurt, she'll lose interest and come home."

***

Tommy looked defeated, the way he sat on a concrete bench outside the church. When Adele stepped out onto the front porch landing, he stood and held his arms to embrace her.

"What's with that guy? He locked me outside." Tommy kissed her forehead, then her cheek "I've been worried sick. Here I am, trying to protect your sisters. Are you okay? And how come that nut job of a gunman wouldn't let me inside?"

Adele loved the warmth of Tommy's arms around her, calming her down when he was about to explode. "Pa was secretly riding the train with you to Bramwell."

"I never saw him once, Delly. Was he inside? I would never have put you in harm's way."

Adele sat down beside him. "When I moved in with Noona, I learned some terrible secrets about this family. Mama kept a journal. My father's accident? Oh, my gosh, Tommy, she went through so many horrible nights trying to keep Daddy alive. I'm just starting to learn about the father I barely knew. Like why the Dawsons let August take mama away. Mama wrote in her journal that it wasn't just a car accident. August ran Daddy off the road."

"He what!" Tommy shouted. "August and your father knew each other, then?"

"You just got here, and I'm throwing away too many stories at you. Can we get out of here?" Adele asked.

"Yes, yes, of course." Tommy removed the light sports coat he was wearing and draped it over Adele's shoulders. Even though it was warm outside, the smell of his jacket felt familiar and comforting.

As they walked up to Stone House, Adele continued sharing what she'd learned, not only to talk it through with her best friend but also to process what she knew.

"August, my daddy, and mama went to high school together. August Beck was raised in Mingo County until my uncle adopted him and brought August to live with the Dawsons in Bramwell. Gave him new status. It seems his mother didn't like having to give up her boy, so she nagged the judge to nullify the adoption. When the judge wouldn't reopen the file, some of the Beck brothers kidnapped my mother. She was just a teenager, Tommy. Made it look like they'd had their way with her, held her hostage, hoping my uncle would give August back. Like a dog trade. But instead of giving him up, my uncle showed up with a gun and killed August's father. That's why her parents sent my mother to an all-girls boarding school, and Uncle Irving went to jail."

"And she never told you any of this before?"

"I would have remembered a story like that. Mama must have been so ashamed. I mean, the way she was able to bury so much and just focus on her children that lived."

"But she talked about your daddy all the time."

"She loved him, Tommy. So, she only talked about his goodness. It's how she wanted me to remember him."

Collette stepped beside Adele and slipped her hand into Adele's. "Is Pa going to get hurt?" Collette asked.

"I hope they beat him up," Deirdre said. She tucked her fire-red hair behind her ear. "The way he lets Olga treat us is just plain atrocious."

"Atrocious?" Tommy mimicked. "Pretty big word."

Deirdre continued. "I would call it sin! Maybe he will treat us better if he gets what Olga does to us."

Faye hopped in front of Adele's legs as if she wanted Adele to pick her up. "She hates me most. Cause I can't spell. D, whack. O, whack, G, whack. Now can you spell dog? I hate her, and I'm not going back. I'll just live out here with the D-O-Gs."

"You're all safe now," Adele said, feeling a new level of trust between her sisters.

"Just the B's," Elysia cooed, reminding Adele of the Benita-Briana club they'd formed.

"Well, one B, Benita is out somewhere still trying to make Pa proud," Briana said.

Church goers had gathered on the porch and around tables set up on the front lawn. Adele stopped the girls at the bottom of the long stone driveway. "I've been thinking. If you stay with me, I'd like this to be your new home."

"Here," Elysia asked. "It's so big."

"B-I-G," Faye squealed. "Big like mama."

"But not too big," Deirdre countered. "You'll learn your way around."

"And give up all my friends?" Briana asked.

"Yea," Collette chimed in. "Bri's got ten thousand friends."

"You don't have to decide today," Adele said. "First, we need to clean up. Change into some clothes I haven't given away."

"Deal!" Tommy said.

"You're about the same size as my father. They're a little dated," Adele said.

"I only planned to stay a few days. If I get in a bind, I might take you up on that offer. "Elijah said he'd make up a bed for me in the carriage house. I will meet you out back after you get your girl time."

Chapter 4:
Funerals Bring Out the Best

August 1938

The impenetrable fort built of stone and masonry overlooking the Bluestone River was once a social haven for nearly all Dawson family and friends. With a new matriarch, Bramwell's elite seemed cautious about making themselves too familiar with the house, remaining outside on the piazza. August Beck had already given them plenty to chatter about on the way up the mountain.

Hibiscus, lavender, hostas, and prickly pears, blossoming along the stone wall, rose like a mediator between the mountain and the long cobblestone driveway.

Cut-glass angels embedded in windows on the west side of the house reflected brilliant wings in the afternoon sun. Upon reaching the porch, four white Adirondack chairs sat around a stone firepit. Crisscrossed logs had been stacked ready to warm guests when the sun went down. Linen-covered tables would accommodate at least fifty mourners.

Adele noticed steam rising from a caged-in pie box that extended from the kitchen window. A hummingbird flitted nearby, trying to access blueberry pies, their long beaks too short to break through the screens.

Elijah stood between pillars to greet her. "Madam," he welcomed. Adele hoped she'd never get used to Elijah's loyal smile welcoming her home from church.

Adele stepped close to him. "I've never hosted a funeral party, Elijah," she whispered.

"Well, now, that's my job, Miss Dawson." He took her hand and led her into the house.

"The church doesn't provide a meal?" she asked.

"You know Ms. Kettie. She don't allow no spirits in the Presbyterian church. So, we move the b'revement reception to her porch."

Adele smiled at Elijah's use of Noona in the present tense. "You think they will still come, even after August caused so much trouble?" Adele asked.

"Mountaineer party doesn't start until someone gets a black eye," Elijah said. "Just ask your Uncle Irving."

After closing the door behind her, he adjusted the last button on his long-tailed tuxedo and then scooped a ladle of beverage from a crystal punch bowl, handing it to David as he stepped up on the portico.

Through the screen door, Adele heard David and Elijah. "Can't expect good folks to celebrate Miss Kettie if they're not sippin' a bit of her mountain dragon," David said.

In one long swallow, David finished the contents of the crystal cup. "Ahhh, she lives and breathes. Shame the governor won't put this on the market," David said. "Just keep the punchbowl full," he added. "Everybody loves Katherine Dawson's moonshine."

Adele remained inside the house, admiring both men. "You look dashing, Elijah."

Elijah's white teeth shone as he smiled at her. "Dashing," he mimicked. "Freshen up the girls. Guests just startin' to get settled in."

***

Collette, Deirdre, and Elysia had already started a game of hide and seek, running up and down the gracefully curved staircase, the centerpiece of the first floor. Its balustrade of dark scrolled walnut spindles outlined the curved steps, wide enough to have featured several hooped-skirted debutantes standing side by side back in the 1920s.

Above the landing, a great dome of stained glass honored the Dawson family's heritage. A Gregson chandelier with nearly fifty lights hung over the stairs. A polished black grand piano sat silently at the bottom of the steps, waiting to ripple sounds of music into every room.

Adele remembered the evenings her real father, Kenneth Dawson, reached his hand to receive her mother as she descended in a party gown. He would escort her into the dining room as if she was a pearl of great price. Adele stood respectfully more than a decade later, taking in the twelve-foot-high foyer and looking down the long hallway of carved library panels. Four entrances trimmed with double crown molding accented entries into the dining room, living room, library, and winter kitchen.

She thought, how will I ever get used to this home? Given enough time to learn about the Dawsons, she might come to understand what could have possibly stolen her mother away with the likes of August Beck. Marauder, impetuous investor, selfish oaf.

"You will never catch me," Collette hissed at her sisters. "I'm taller, stronger, and smarter than you." With that, Collette climbed two steps at a time.

Tamasin and her friends busied themselves in the kitchen, moving dishes and pans of food into the back-to-back butler's pantries. The pastry chef placed trays of lemon-tart puffs, passion fruit and coconut tarts, and caviar and crème Fraiche tartlets. On other trays, she had organized mini steak and ale pies, figs with bacon and chili sauce, and lobster toasts with avocado. She placed delicate spoonfuls of hot cranberry jam on mini brie bites.

An oven built into the main floor fireplace separated one of the kitchens from the long hallway. Tamasin retrieved a stone platter of tenderloin nibbles.

"This looks delicious!" Elysia said. "Is this a party?"

"I don't know, baby girl," Briana said, "We're not eating Pa's roasted rabbit for dinner."

"I'm starving," Collette said, eyeing the lobster toasts. "One bite?" she asked.

Tamasin nodded when she heard the girls' requests. "I'll bring a serving tray to your bedroom. Go now. Good to have chile' laughter back in these halls," she said.

Adele squeezed Tamasin's hand. "But they are so noisy."

"No, no," Tamasin said. "All knotted up, they was, needin' a foot tappin'."

Adele grinned. "The way you talk."

Tamasin waved her off. "Chil'ren remind us life still be good."

Adele collected her sisters, hurrying down the hallway built of herringbone mahogany wainscotting. Cabinet doors made with raised panels hid refrigeration units that pumped cold air through floor vents. Neither Faye's nor Elysia's small hands could reach around the curved baroque banister leading them up the staircase.

"Don't break anything, girls. Lord knows we can't afford to fix it."

Tamasin shook her head as she walked away. "Girl still don't know what she got," she mumbled.

Elysia and Faye grabbed the dark walnut scrolled spindles like walking sticks to help them navigate the stairs. Faye stopped at the landing to look up at the dome, but she leaned back too far and fell into Briana's arms.

Briana caught her young sister before she hit the stairs. "Nothing this big in New Madrid, is there?"

Adele guided her sisters through each bedroom when they reached the second-floor bedrooms level, pointing out Noona's Irish and Welsh design features to help them select their room. Elysia and Deidre chose the George Washington suite, filled with a four-poster queen bed; baby blue scalloped valances trimmed the top rectangular frame. Drawn curtains in the same shade wrapped around each of the bed poles. Panel doors opened into a bathroom with a separate shower and toilet.

Briana selected the Magnolia Manor room, painted bronze, a color that seemed to ground the room's floral décor, giving it a natural look. "If Nita was here, she'd claim the fireplace and haul her own firewood. Might keep me warm at night too." Briana claimed the feminine desk as her makeup cabinet and shrieked when she saw the bidet. "It's for your tush," Collette explained. "Helps get all that molasses off your butt."

"Classy," Briana scolded. "You should use it first."

Collette took the Queen Anne Suite, one of the smaller bedrooms with a dark green paisley bedspread, loads of pillows, and a desk that would convince her to stay. Faye could curl up on the trundle bed if she got tired of sleeping in Adele's room. A stand-alone claw bathtub and sink stood against a tiled wall.

Just days ago, her sisters had slept in two beds on the floor, crammed up in their shanty farmhouse with an outhouse. Gutters outside that house collected rainwater for the shower. The Bramwell house had plumbing for five full bathrooms attached to each bedroom.

The girls carried their sparse personal belongings as they followed Adele into what had been her parents' bedroom suite. Briana threw open the windows and cleared the stuffy room. "Is this where our mother used to live?"

"It is," Adele said.

"This is my room for now." Adele felt so proud of her parents and this home that was a place of joy for them.

"How come she never brought us here?" Elysia asked.

Adele knelt low to kiss Elysia's head. "She was married to a man named Kenneth Dawson back then. This house belongs to the Dawson family. Mama, Daddy, and I lived here until my daddy died."

"Why didn't mama stay here?" Elysia asked. "Must have been something terrible happened to her to make her leave a place like this."

Collette clipped Elysia on the side of her head. "She married Pa. Pa used to have money like this. You're probably too young to remember."

"Elysia, I don't know the answer to your question," Adele answered. "But I hope I find out. Faye, you will sleep with me here."

Collette leaped onto the dark green velvet bedspread, ran her fingers along with the soft satin pillows, and then jumped from the bed to open triple closet doors. "Look at the size of this room," she shouted. "Our whole family could live in a closet this big. Couldn't you just hide out here?"

"When you're four years old, you go where you're told," Adele said. "I loved our mama. I would follow her anywhere."

Tamasin knocked on the door. She stepped inside with a tray filled with bacon-wrapped figs. Briana reached for a mini chicken sandwich held together with toothpicks.

"This is what I call home," Briana giggled.

Adele sifted through closets and decided with a knot here or there; that she could dress them up for the fanciest funeral reception of their lives. After showers, the girls lined up as they did in the Bootheel shanty, ducked up to style hair, and pamper the one younger than her. It had been Adele's idea of automation so they could board the school bus on time. Adele worked on Briana's hair while Briana combed through Collette's dark wavy hair. Benita should have been in line, but she was still missing. Nothing new for the brash twin who rarely came home before dinner. Even so, Adele was worried that Benita was shaking up someone's world or just plain getting in trouble.

While they primped, Adele was surprised to hear Tommy and Jackson sparring under the bedroom balcony.

"Beating up a man twice your age doesn't solve anyone's problem," Tommy said.

Standing so close to the house, Adele couldn't see Tommy, but she had known that voice since childhood. She watched Jackson take a sip from a flask. Kneeling, Adele rested her arms on the windowsill to see whether Jackson received injuries in the fight with August. The hand that held his drink was still red and scraped, but scabs formed over his knuckles.

"Turn around," she whispered to herself, trying to see if his face was bruised.

"Where is Beck now?" Tommy asked.

Jackson held up his drink and pointed toward town.

"He's still here?" Tommy asked.

Jackson scoffed. "By the time he wakes up, he'll be close to home."

"New Madrid?" Tommy asked.

"St. Louis."

"How's he supposed to get from St. Louis to New Madrid?"

"Man's a fightin' fool. He'll figure it out." Jackson tipped the flask once more.

A group of Jackson's friends came over to greet him, but the men seemed more intent on what was inside their flasks. Adele stepped back from the window and finished combing Briana's hair. Collette was still trying to braid Deirdre's fire-red hair.

"A shame August never let Adele spend time with her grandparents," Jackson said, his voice louder than she thought necessary. Adele pulled Briana back down near the window, which upset the lineup of young women.

"Delly?" Tommy asked. "She didn't know she had family in West Virginia."

Adele stood abruptly. "What?" she gasped, not wanting to reveal she was eavesdropping but also disappointed that Tommy could not remember a time she talked about her West Virginia family. Had she thought so long and hard about them that she forgot to share this with him? As hard as she tried to get away from August Beck, how did he miss that?

"Who's talking out there?" Faye asked.

Adele lowered her voice. "Shh. Just some guests," she said. She finished off Briana's hair with a sequined comb, then searched the closet for something she could wear. Her mother's black dress with off-the-shoulder sleeves had the right balance of elegance without ruffles or frills.

For her sister, Briana, she held up a navy-blue chiffon dress with a knee-high slit, just enough to compliment Briana's sleek fifteen-year-old legs without suggesting anything but innocence. "You should wear this," she said.

From inside the closet, she heard the men quibble again. "Who's Delll-y?" She could almost see Jackson curl his upper lip as he stretched out her nickname. "You mean Adele?"

"Friends call her Delly," Tommy answered. "You'd have to know her well enough to call her that."

"Miss Kettie told me she and Adele had been apart for eleven years," Jackson responded. "By the time Adele arrived, Miss Kettie was taking breathing treatments. Never heard either of them mention a boyfriend named Tommy."

"Just a guess," Tommy snapped back. "But I doubt Delly nor her grandmother shared details of their conversations with a gunslinger."

Jackson was quiet long enough to concern Adele. Finally, he said, "How'd you and Adele meet anyway. You one of them farm boys?"

"I've known Delly since she was seven years old. She and her sisters hauled vegetable wagons down our street. Sold them to townies."

"Delly is the girl you knew on the farm," Jackson niggled. "Adele, she's an heiress. Just about everyone in Mercer County knew the Dawsons."

"Same person, different location," Tommy responded.

"Good God," Jackson said almost prayerfully. "Townies never know who is in their neighborhood. Could be a squalid farm boy or a coal-mining heiress."

"She never acted privileged," Tommy snapped.

"Course not. Adele comes from good stock. In time, I hope to get to know her better."

Adele opened the shutters and called out, "Whatever it is, gentlemen, please lower your voices or take it down the street."

Jackson stepped away from the wall and looked up to see her. He acted surprised that she had heard their squabble. "My apologies, ma'am. Not a single word was meant to dishonor you."

She saw Tommy shove his way past Jackson and away from the balcony pillars. "I'll leave you to your own devices, man. No doubt you have other people to annoy."

Adele quietly closed the window. "Hurry up, girls. We need to be outside."

***

Adele came down the steps slowly, as if she were taking her first steps on a walk meant for brides, not mourners. Deidre and Faye walked immediately in front of her. Collette slid partway down on the banister until Adele grabbed her sister's arm. "Walk."

Briana held back, choosing not to be part of her older sister's princess court. Instead, she swept aside the back of her chiffon skirt and stylishly toe-tipped down each mahogany step by herself, loving how it felt to own the grand staircase.

Adele looked over her shoulder and smiled up at Briana. She looked much older than her fifteen years, especially when she intentionally showed a peek at her ankle through the skirt's slits.

Deirdre and Faye held Adele's hands as they stepped into the courtyard. Collette curtseyed before Tommy. "It's just Tommy," Deidre said. "You don't have to bow to him."

"Hey, Punkin," he said to Collette, then turned to Adele. "If it weren't for such an unfortunate occasion, I'd say you have no right to look so gorgeous," Tommy said, closing in to kiss her cheek. "Save a few minutes for me, will you?"

"We're still in mourning," Adele said.

"Maybe you are. But the men here are into admiration." Tommy kissed her forehead. "You're nothing but stunning."

As the crowd gathered around the porch to find their table assignments, Elijah nodded at David Henderson. That's when Adele noticed David holding his arm in a sling. She feared August had used the fishing knife to defend himself and hoped David's injuries were minor.

David raised a champagne glass. "To Kettie Dawson," he said. "The most honorable, courageous woman you'll ever find in West Virginia."

As attendees shouted "Hear, hear," Adele saw Benita slide next to Jackson and shimmy her shoulders as if to share a dance move. Benita was wearing Selma's emerald green sequined flapper dress, a peacock plume flaunted out the side of her headband, belittling the intimacy Adele once had with her mother. Who wears an emerald-green flapper dress to a funeral party?

As if Tommy could sense Adele's sudden chill, he leaned in and whispered, "Nita's siding with a gunslinger. Don't let her bother you."

"She just chose the wrong side," Adele hissed.

She stepped quickly next to Benita and pinched her sister's arm. "That's Mama's dress," she hissed under her breath.

Benita shrieked as if she had just been stung by a bee. "Briana gets to wear one of Mama's dresses. Why can't I?" She spoke aloud, forcing Adele to defend herself.

"Briana didn't go snooping into something that's not hers without my permission."

"Your permission?" Benita stretched "your' to sound like a coyote's call. "I don't need your permission to wear my mother's clothes."

"You mean the clothes my father bought for her a decade ago? Oh, yes, you do."

"You can't tell me what to do, Miss Secret Keeper," Benita snapped. "You're not in charge of me." Benita adjusted the green feather in her headdress and leaned even more into Jackson.

Adele squared up next to her sister. "As long as you are a guest in my house, Benita Ann, you will put a hat on that snap."

Two women sipping Miss Kettie's signature brew placed their cups back into the saucer. One woman leaned into the other. "Who is that unruly child, and how did she get into Kettie's house?"

The other woman lifted an olive into her mouth. She removed the toothpick and pointed it back at her friend. "I could forgive Miss Dawson if she applied a willow switch to that girl."

Benita pushed away from Jackson, shoving her shoulder into Adele, causing Adele to lose her balance. Jackson immediately caught Adele's arm.

"I got you," Tommy said, deftly pushing Jackson aside. He wrapped his arm around Adele's waist to stabilize her.

Jackson released Adele but grabbed Benita's arm and pulled her against the stone wall. "Not here," he said under his breath.

"Hey!" Benita whined. "I have rights. Selma was my mom, too."

Adele noticed more people leaning in to see if they could find a trashy crack in the new Dawson regime. Bickering would give them one more reason to doubt her ability to step in as the new owner of a coal mining company. They already had a taste of August Beck. She didn't want them to think she was cut from the same cloth. She scolded herself for letting August Beck take any space in her mind today.

David Henderson excused himself from a small group of lawyers clustered around the punch bowls; the same crowd Adele had met upon her arrival. Kettie had set up a series of meetings, introducing Adele to the family's legal and financial advisors as soon as Adele finally made it back to her birth family in Bramwell. Since then, these advisors had been at her side, coaching her on Dawson business and coal mining affairs.

With his unbandaged hand, David put his arm under her elbow. "Please come with me. So many people here you'll get to know later, but let's narrow it down to two or three. I'd like you to meet the McConnell's. Mrs. McConnell and her husband own the Corner Shop, he said, then whispered, "and about half of Bramwell eats in their diner." As she leaned in to hear the McConnell's greeting, she noticed David nodding over his shoulder to Jackson.

"Understood, sir," she heard Jackson say and wondered what that exchange meant.

Adele followed David's lead as he escorted her around the back section of the porch, stopping at several tables to greet guests. Most had already selected a piece of blueberry pie to finish off their funeral banquet.

"So sorry for your loss, ma'am," one of the men said. His wife added, "We loved Miss Kettie so very much. If there is anything we can do, please let us know."

Adele smiled, grateful that David was leading her away from her loud-mouth half-sister. But when he came close to one of the farthest tables, he pulled her particularly close. It was the first time she'd felt the hard butt of a gun tucked under his suit jacket.

"Mr. Jude Radford, I'd like you to meet Adele Dawson." David paused to let the Radfords finish a bite of pie. "Quillan and Kettie's granddaughter."

"So, you're the heiress, are you?" A large balding man stood from his table. More gently than she would have expected, the man shook her hand. His palms were moist and sweaty. His teeth stained purple, making him look a bit more ghoulish than he may have liked.

"Your grandmother and I had great respect for each other," Mr. Radford said.

David coughed a bit too obvious.

"At least I had respect for her," Mr. Radford added, then paused awkwardly.

"Mr. Radford manages one of the Pocahontas minefields in Mingo County," David continued. "Adele, you may recall your grandmother telling you that Jude's father served on the General Assembly when the old teacher's college got renamed Radford University. He also was an excellent friend of your grandfather's brother, Irving."

From her mother's diary, Adele recalled Irving was the uncle who killed August's father in a heated argument over Selma. She followed David's lead and nodded, knowing she'd find more secrets about that murder somewhere in this house. Mingo, she thought. *Nothing but trouble, trouble, trouble.*

"Adele, your granddaddy helped Mr. Radford and his son move huge combines of capital into the West Virginia coal mines."

It was then that Adele also understood that Mr. Radford had access to large amounts of money, which also meant he would have a voice in how the mines operated.

"I can be much more pleasant than my son," Mr. Radford added. "Perhaps you've heard of him?"

"Not yet," Adele answered.

"Best we keep it that way."

He wiped his mouth with a white linen napkin. Mr. Radford

continued, "Kids today have everything handed to them. They think you get your way by beating, jailing, and starving your opponent. I swear he bathes himself in blood money."

Not the kind of conversation Adele expected at a funeral. "Well, then I hope you and I will become better acquainted before I meet your son."

Mr. Radford chuckled. "This generation understands new mining technology," Radford said, "now that we're using railways to move coal. Younger ones, like my boy, Chase, are naturals for change," Radford added. "But I tell you, I sure don't like the way he uses his gunmen to break up a strike. Your grandmother and I had more effective ways."

He unbuttoned his jacket and held it open a bit too conspicuous. Perhaps he'd overindulged in Tamasin's cooking, or he wanted David to see that it was well concealed if he was wearing a weapon. "Forgive me, ma'am, have you met my wife, Elizabeth?"

Adele reached across the table to shake Elizabeth's hand. "A pleasure, indeed, Mrs. Radford."

Elizabeth looked up at Adele, nodded, but folded her hands in her lap, leaving Adele to return her hand to her side.

"Oh, for goodness's sake, Liz," Mr. Radford scolded. "It's been more than twenty years."

"What's been more than twenty years?" Adele asked.

David tried to intervene. "My apologies, Mrs. Radford." David bowed humbly and tried to pull Adele back with him. "I certainly did not want to stir anything. I hope you and your husband know how much the family appreciates your attendance today."

"How did you know my mother?" Adele persisted.

"She was Besame's first choice to represent their products," Elizabeth said. "Your mother."

And she was so good at it," Adele responded, still so proud of her mama. She recalled seeing the Besame pamphlets in her parents' bedroom for the first time. Booklets she'd never seen before. "My mother was a beautiful cosmetics model," Adele said. "I wish I'd known that about her when we lived in Missouri."

"Hmmmph," Elizabeth retorted. "She had money. Money always makes women more beautiful." Adele remembered Elizabeth was in Noona's garden of friends. Still, right now, she was one of the prickly pears, brewing dislike on the inside, unforgiving about something that happened long ago.

Adele studied Elizabeth's face, her burnt orange lipstick, and the purple eyeshadow she'd chosen to wear at Noona's funeral party. A lightly powdered streak down the center of her nose minimized its size, but unfortunately, the spot was turning a deep red the more she drank.

"Perhaps you will join me for coffee someday," Adele said. Elizabeth knew something about Adele's mother, Selma Dawson Beck, and she was determined to find out what made Elizabeth Radford so churlish.

Harold Hamburg, attorney for Kettie Dawson's investments, seated at the next table, stood before Elizabeth could respond. "Miss Dawson, if I may speak? I do want to thank you for inviting my wife and me into this lovely home." He stood and stepped next to David. Between the two of them, they seemed to block Adele from Elizabeth's wrath.

Adele hadn't seen Mr. Hamburg for several weeks, though he was one of the attorneys leading Kettie Dawson's reading of the will. "Yes, Mr. Hamburg. Thank you for coming."

"Beautiful day to celebrate your grandmother's life, don't you think? We all knew Kettie had been sick, but preparations never soften the blow when a loved one passes on. You must be heartsick." Good lord, he was blathering. "Will you come and join my wife and me?" He pulled out a chair, giving Adele a chance to leave the Radford's table.

"Of course, thank you," David answered. "Adele and I were just talking about how we hadn't yet made it over to your table."

"Why does Elizabeth have such disdain for my mother?" she asked. As if Elizabeth had overheard, she stood, grabbed her cup, and smashed it onto the porch. Splinters of glass shattered beneath several tables. A cold grave of silence blanketed the room.

"None of you wants to tell her?" Elizabeth growled. "Then, I will." She turned and faced Adele. "It's about time the little hussy found out why her mother left us, I mean all of us, and married that lying hangnail."

"This is not your business anymore, Liz. No one needs to hear your story," Mr. Radford said. "Let the family celebrate Kettie's life."

"Beck the Bastard," Elizabeth laughed at her alliteration. She grabbed Jude's cup of moonshine. Some of it dribbled down her chin, leaving a dark stain on her bosom.

"Okay, that's it," Jude said. He stood and grabbed Elizabeth's hand, but she pulled away.

"You know he's a goober, don't you, child," Elizabeth said to Adele. "Even before he claimed he could protect Selma from a bitter life if they moved to the Mighty Mississippi. I spotted his slimy spots right after he ran your daddy off the road. Kenneth Dawson, God rest his soul, was on a mission to clean up Mingo county. Ever'body knows that's what happened. Your mama too broke up to see who he really was."

Adele stood beside David, embarrassed by Elizabeth's boldness.

"You know, Jude, for once, I agree with you," Harold said. "You should let the family celebrate their loved one."

"Out of the mouths of babes," Elizabeth said. "They got no bluffer. What's the word, Jude?"

"Come on, Mrs. Radford," Harold said. He leaned over to help Elizabeth to her feet. "You can leave by the back porch. Keep everything nice and private."

"Anyone touches my wife, it better be me," Jude intervened.

"You'll both feel better in the morning after a good night's rest,"

Harold continued.

Elizabeth turned to her husband. "We will not be the first to leave."

Before Jude Radford could react, David Henderson leaned forward and placed his hands on the table as if to keep the conversation private. "Listen to your friends, now, Jude. We won't ask you again."

"No need to get belligerent with me," Jude retorted. He stood abruptly and reached behind his back, fumbling with his belt. "The Radfords have never been back porch people," he growled. "Chase is going to hear about this."

Jackson was immediately at Jude Radford's side making it impossible to reach anything lurking in his belt. "No one else gets hurt today," Jackson said, calmly, slowly. He searched the back of Jude's belt with his other hand, obviously tightening Jude's pants into an uncomfortable position. "I mean you no disrespect," he said as he produced a six-shooter from Jude's belt. Jackson deftly snapped open the cylinder and dumped six bullets into Jude's cup of mountain dragon.

David and Harold stood side by side, physically blocking anyone's access to Adele. "No need for things to get ugly," Harold said. "Avoid the gossip."

Jackson added, "Man's got a right to wear a weapon, I'll give you that. But the missus is done for the night." He shoved the emptied gun into Jude's pocket, where it pointed directly at his groin. "Call it a day, Mr. Radford."

David escorted Elizabeth Radford to her car, helping her slide into the passenger seat. Jackson held Jude's arm until he was behind the wheel. "You okay to drive, Jude?"

"Course I am," Jude scoffed.

Jackson patted Jude's shoulder. "You take Mrs. Radford straight home, now, hear? Tablespoon or two of Bayer and a raw egg in the morning will help with her headache."

Adele couldn't help but admire Jackson's gentle banter. Just like that, a heat-em-up and cool down. Streaks of purple and blue painted the mountain skies as if it was just another day in the West Virginia mountains.

She watched Jackson return to the porch. He didn't stop at her table or say anything to any of the guests. David Henderson and Harold Hamburg followed Jackson into the house. Jackson waved a finger at Elijah. Elijah picked up the punch bowl and carried it into the kitchen.

As they walked away, Tommy slid into the chair beside her. He leaned close and wrapped his hands around Adele's knees. "This isn't the life you want to live," he instructed. "Everybody's got a gun hidden in their britches. How can you possibly feel safe?"

Adele smiled at him. "Guess I best get acquainted with my granddaddy's gun cabinet."

"And then what? Add assault and battery to your resume?"

"I am quickly learning who my friends are. And aren't."

Tommy sighed heavily. "You can't do this, Delly. And I can't leave you here unprotected. You and I both know you would be much happier at the University of Missouri. Your scholarship is still waiting for you."

Adele gasped. "I will never, ever go back to New Madrid."

"Not as a sharecropper's daughter, but as a college student. A great education is what you need, Del., Not this wild-west miner stuff. It's not you. You don't fit in here."

"I don't?" Adele asked. "I've never felt so alive! Lord help me, that was fun!"

"You nearly got shot, baby." He took both of her hands in his. "Don't be mad at Benita if you're just like her, putting your sisters in harm's way. You're no better than she is."

Adele pulled away. "But Tommy. You saw how many people protected my family. These are my people."

"How long will you put these men in harm's way? It's one thing when they are getting paid. That loyalty won't carry through when your family runs out of money."

"Who said we're running out of money?" Adele asked.

Tommy looked at her like he'd been caught with information not intended for him. "Not one member of the Dawson family is alive anymore, Delly. Selma, Kenneth, Quillan, Kettie. Gone. Dead. Don't you see?"

Adele shuttered. Tommy offered no evidence that the Dawson family was crumbling.

"Tommy, West Virginia is my home now."

Tommy looked straight at her. "Then I have no choice but to take your sisters back to New Madrid with me."

"You have no call to make that decision. Not about my sisters or me. That's all on me."

"No, Delly, I'm afraid not."

Adele brushed his hands away from her leg. "Then enlighten me."

"August filed a complaint before he came here, demanding the sheriff of Mercer County remand each of your sisters, Briana, Benita, Collette, Deirdre, Elysia, and Faye, into protective custody. They are still juveniles according to laws in both states. Only a matter of time until the Magistrate comes looking for you for kidnapping across state lines."

"I didn't kidnap anyone. My sisters all came with bags packed. Noona purchased train tickets. You supervised them as they traveled to Bramwell."

"The law is pretty black and white on this, Delly. August Beck can be very convincing, especially since he's married to a militant suffragette. He changed his mind once we were out of town. And since Benita knows where she hid Isaac, his back's against the wall."

"Well, then, I'll make Benita tell me," Adele snapped. "No one's taking the girls from me."

"I'm afraid only the issuing Magistrate can recall an indictment. And since I transported the girls, it looks like the US Marshall Service will be looking for me, too. His orders are to take the girls into protective custody. I'll be arrested and extradited to a federal judge in Missouri."

"How do you know this, Tommy?"

"Come on, Delly. You know my father's a lawyer. He warned me not to come."

"How long do I have?" Adele asked. "Days, weeks?"

"If you come with me now, we'll still have time to clear all this up," Tommy said. "We can leave tomorrow. I've got the train tickets in my pocket."

"Tommy, this is my home!"

Slowly, Tommy stood. "So that's it, then."

"Pa is up to no good," Adele said. "It seems he just wants Benita. What if he claims the twins? They're old enough to take care of themselves."

"You're obviously not informed. August Beck is in deep trouble with an organization chaired by his political agitator wife, Olga. Unless you can get Benita to return Isaac to his father, August Beck will make your life impossible."

***

Adele waited until the last of the guests said goodnight to let Tommy come near her. "Maybe you shouldn't have come," she said.

"I know you have something to prove," he answered. "Your grandmother gave you a great gift at the University of Missouri. Get a degree in Engineering; then you can come back and run the mine. It will still be here when you graduate."

50

Chapter 5:
Reading of the Will

Adele was still in her nightshirt when she peered out the window. Several cars had pulled up in front of the house. "The lawyers are here!" She ran to the bathroom, threw cold water on her face, pulled her hair up into a ponytail, and slipped into one of her mama's dresses.

Elijah met her on the first-floor landing. "Your appointment, ma'am? Remember? Lawyers here to read Miss Kettie's will."

"Master Henderson, Master Hamburg, Master Hemlock, and Master Stephenson await your presence in the library, ma'am. Shall I call Mr. Thomas to join you?"

"No, not yet. How do I look?"

"Sleepy, ma'am. Like you jus' lost your Noona. Come with me. Tamasin powder you up a bit."

After Tamasin pinched her cheeks a few times, Adele felt she could handle a conversation if she simply listened. Noona's standby instruction. "In the face of danger, child listen. Your lawyers will eventually show their hands."

Adele checked herself in the hall mirror just before Elijah opened the double doors. "Miss Dawson will see you now," he announced as Adele stepped into the library.

The attorneys were seated in a circle of armchairs, talking over Tamasin's coffee and sweet biscuits.

"Good morning, gentlemen," Adele greeted. Since her initial meeting with Noona's attorneys at the Bramwell Bank, she learned to expect nothing short of bowties, crisp white shirts with monogrammed cufflinks, and close shaves. Elijah closed the double doors behind her.

"My apologies for keeping you waiting," Adele greeted.

"Not a problem at all," Harold Hamburg responded first, which Adele took as a polite lie. In her mind, she recounted each attorney's stake in Dawson family money. Eugene Bolworth, her incoming accountant: a numbers guy; Frank Hemlock, her trust fund attorney. Barring any surprises, she had a relatively good idea of what Kettie had left her. Everything. Harold Hamburg, Kettie Dawson's attorney; David Henderson, Kettie's assistant; and Garrett Stephenson, her late father, Kenneth Dawson's attorney. John Clemson and Ivan Mills were the only ones missing, both representing Dawson family ownership in coal mines.

Frank Hemlock focused on Adele for a moment, then looked down into a bound legal folder. "As you recall, your grandmother appointed me to represent your interests in the Dawson estate."

"This is just a formality since Katherine and Quillan Dawson established terms for distribution of their wealth," Harold said. "As the sole living non-incarcerated heir, you have been chosen to be the beneficiary of the family's trust account."

'Non-incarcerated?" Adele asked, more to test their knowledge against what she learned reading her mother's diary and the unfortunate assault on her mother when she was not much older than Adele was today.

"Yes, we will get to Irving Dawson a bit later in this meeting," Harold continued, regaining control of the agenda.

"There are specific payouts and spendthrift clauses when you turn twenty-five so that certain people or institutions cannot access your trust fund."

"Like my stepfather," Adele asked.

"Specifically, your stepfather," David answered. "Nor are you able to withdraw unreasonable amounts without a co-signature from the estate's accountant, Mr. Eugene Bolworth. There are funds to hold you over until you are of proper age."

Adele looked over at Eugene. Greying hair, high white forehead, glasses, turtleneck sweater, penny loafers. Money done right. She wondered what they considered "proper age."

"What's unreasonable? Adele asked.

"Depends on the item and how much you wish to spend," Eugene answered. "A thousand dollars for a twin-engine plane would surely raise a flag."

Adele smiled at Eugene, trying to determine if he was serious. She decided she'd rather not get to know him just yet.

"Kettie wanted Elijah and Tamasin to remain in the carriage house until their life journey ended," Kevin continued. "Additionally, she set aside fifteen thousand a year for their personal allowances, health expenses, clothing, or similar expenses. Transportation, food, and utilities will come out of the trust's operating budget, not their account."

"They have become very dear to me. Is that enough for them?" Adele asked.

David Henderson exchanged smiles with Frank Hemlock.

"There's enough," Frank continued. "You will manage the remainder of the fund with significant and incremental payouts every ten years. For example, you will receive a lump sum when you turn twenty next month; you'll receive another large payout when you turn twenty-five, again at thirty, and the fourth upon turning forty. The condition is you remain in Bramwell and, more specifically, in this house. If you move outside of West Virginia, remaining funds will go to Kettie's charitable organizations."

"For example, move back to Missouri?" Adele asked.

"Yes, ma'am. That's a good example, one that is spelled out in the will." Frank said.

"Why would I move?" Adele asked. "I'm home."

"About your earlier inquiry. Your grandfather, Mr. Quillan, set aside two million dollars for his brother, Irving, should he ever be released from the federal prison."

"Two million?" Adele asked. "Is there any left?"

"Oh, yes, ma'am," Frank said. "There are nineteen million dollars in the family trust."

"Nineteen million?" Adele gasped. "I don't know how to count that high." She immediately felt foolish for reacting like a bumpkin.

"While it's yours to manage, with guidance from professionals," Frank added, nodding to the business team in the room with her. "it's not all in one place. Your grandfather believed the right hand should not know what the left hand is hiding behind its back. He paid each partner here to manage one portion of his wealth. Depending on how well we independently invested his money, he offered significant bonuses to any advisor who increased profits by more than ten percent over any given five-year period."

"Tough to do when the economy has been so depressed," David added. "Your team of advisors here will help guide you to manage one investment at a time. While it seems like a lot of money, Adele, your home, this house, is costly to upkeep. Kenneth was a doting father. The Dawsons are a tight-knit family. And they will do anything it takes to protect their own. Even if it means putting someone in hiding."

'Who is in hiding?" Adele asked.

"Why Irving Dawson, of course."

Chapter 6:
Creating a Haven for Sisters

Her parents whispered, laughed, kept each other warm, and loved inside the velvet burgundy, forest green bedroom. As a toddler, Adele often followed the rising steam between satin pillowcases, a place of generosity and love. She would use the bedspread as a ladder to climb on top of her father during thunderstorms. He would pull her under the covers into their steamy cave, wrapping his warm arms around her when a storm frightened her, and whisper, "You're okay. Daddy's got you."

My sisters never had this message planted in their hearts, Adele thought.

Adele had claimed this safe room, a place where she inhaled the fragrance of peace. On her bedside table, the Besame cosmetics shrine was still intact, though a bit less saintly today after Elizabeth Radford lobbed a cannon at the funeral party. Elizabeth may have grieved the loss of friends her own way, but it was Adele and Elijah who had to pick up her crystal bombs. Adele decided she must find a way to uncover Elizabeth's skeletons gently. However temperamental she was, the woman knew fragile nuggets that Selma had never shared with her daughters.

Before pulling back the sheets, Adele breathed in the cool mountain air seeping its way into the room. The cardinal's sweet tweet outside her window reminded her of the bond she had with those whom the Dawson family came to trust. If her sisters went back to live with Pa, he would never cuddle them as they needed. They wouldn't know how to act if a warm hug was comforting or treacherous. How would they know the difference? Today, she would share a fragment of Dawson family grace.

She rolled over and nearly smothered six-year-old Faye. Adele remembered the B's giggling until late at night in a bedroom three doors down. Faye barely opened her sleepy eyes, but when Adele grinned at her, Faye rolled over, begging Adele to scratch her back.

"You smell that, baby Faye? Bacon. I bet Miss Tamasin is already making up a batch of French toast. Hmmm. With molasses," Adele whispered as she ran her fingers inside Faye's nightshirt to rub her back.

"I don't wanna go home," Faye whined.

Adele wrapped her arms around Faye. "Who said anything about going home?"

"Nita. And Beena."

Adele whispered into Faye's ear. "We will talk about that this afternoon. I have a surprise for my girls."

Faye giggled and tossed the covers away. "But first, let's get food in our bellies."

***

Collette, Deidre, and Elysia were already at the table when Adele and Faye stepped into the kitchen. Collette dragged a piece of deep-fried bread through so much syrup; that it dripped on her chin before she could get it into her mouth. "Never ever had French toast like this," she said, her cheeks puffy with food.

"Don't be hurtin' Adele's feelings," Tamasin gently chided.

Deirdre lifted two pieces of bacon over her mouth. Her wiry red hair was sticky around her face from licking the plate. Adele couldn't help but grin at the freedom from her eleven-year-old sister. The sensation of fulfilling her basic existence with primal happiness.

"No one cooks like you, Tamasin," Adele responded. "Elijah and Tommy joining us?"

"Men got up early this mornin," Tamasin said. "Cleanin' up the grounds easier with plenty a hands to help. Ate down half my pantry already."

"Breakfast!" Adele yelled up the stairs, waking up the twins. "Benita, Briana. Tamasin can't wait all day."

"Just like home," Elysia said. "B's always the pokiest."

"Today, my sweet sisters, we are taking the train into Bluefield to buy school clothes."

"Shopping?" Briana asked, suddenly appearing. "There's a Salvation Army in Bluefield?"

"Nothing second-hand today," Adele said. "Miss Kettie sent money every year for us, but we never got it. This year, she handed it directly to me."

"You mean so Pa couldn't get his mitts on it first?" Benita asked, straddling a chair at the table before poking pieces of French toast into her mouth.

"You knew?" Adele asked.

Benita shrugged. "He'd tuck a few bucks in my bra."

"What!" Briana shouted. "And you never shared? You selfish hog."

"Hey, all in the past now," Adele said. "Train leaves for Bluefield every hour. If you're coming with me, we'll arrive in time to get a soda at the Apothecary."

"Take Mr. Thompson with you, chile," Tamasin said. "Man's presence calms a slippery sales lady."

***

The steam-engine train rode along the East River Mountain section of West Virginia Appalachia. Collette, Deirdre, and Elysia sat high on their knees, watching rabbits scamper away from the tracks, white-tailed deer nibbled in the meadow. A tunnel suddenly dimmed the train. Briana was the first to gasp at the lush forest greeting passengers as they emerged into a steep valley on the other side of the mountain.

Faye sat on Adele's lap. The clickety-clack of the train rails lulled her into her own peaceful place. Tommy put his arm around Adele and whispered. "You are more gorgeous today than I've seen in a long time. Let's ditch the girls." He leaned over and kissed her ear. "Briana will watch them. I haven't been alone with you since we got here."

Adele responded by leaning her head against his shoulder. "Thank you for shopping with us. Especially when you could have gone fishing with Elijah."

Tommy squeezed her shoulder. "I had no choice. Elijah insisted."

When the train stopped, Deirdre jumped first onto the platform. Together, the girls stepped through the train depot, then downtown, where they discovered a district filled with three- and four-story masonry buildings. Shoppers had already lined up in front of the Shamrock Restaurant, waiting for it to open. Briana stopped in front of the Colonial Theatre, turned sideways to see how she looked standing next to a picture of Shirley Temple. "Look there, Deidre. You look just like her except for your fire red hair."

"Keep an eye on Briana," Tommy said. "She could easily outspend us all."

After visiting several shops, the girls stepped into Elizabeth's Couturier. "I should go in first," Briana said.

Benita bumped against her sister. "No, you won't."

A sales clerk smiled at Benita and Briana. "You must be twins."

Benita said, "Nah, we just look alike. I'm older."

The clerk smiled. "School shopping?" she asked Collette. Looking at

Briana, she said, "I bet you'd like to see what's in fashion this year."

"Yes, ma'am." Briana and Collette followed the clerk to the back of the store. Tommy made himself comfortable on a settee. Adele went with Deirdre, Elysia, and Faye into the children's section.

Adele had dropped off one pile of clothes with the cashier and was holding a dress to Elysia's shoulder when the boutique door swung open, letting in a surprising burst of late summer humidity. She looked up to see Elizabeth Radford stroll in, wearing a rolled-up cloche hat that matched her beige gloves. She lifted a striped brown and beige Louis Vuitton purse over her arm, removed one of the gloves, and swiped dust away from the LV monogram. As she moved through the store, she exchanged greetings with several sales clerks.

"Faye, hold my hand," Adele said softly. "Elysia, don't touch anything." The last time she had seen Mrs. Radford, she was smashing Noona's china onto the stone patio.

"Well, well," Mrs. Radford said over the clothes racks. "Looks like Bess and the Porgys of Catfish Row have come to town."

Adele didn't understand the reference, but she caught Mrs. Radford's snippy tone.

"Yep, that's us," Benita scoffed. "We got plenty a nuttin."

Here we go, Adele thought. Benita's going to show off, and we'll all be in trouble.

"You must be the one they call Nita," Mrs. Radford said. She clutched her purse closer. "The Mensan."

"What's a mensan?" Collette giggled.

"Mrs. Bradford, is it?" Benita said over her shoulder as she held up a blue cashmere sweater. "Selma, my mother. Did you know her? She always prayed for a healthy mind."

"The name is Radford. Elizabeth Radford. And you," Elizabeth said, snapping her gloves between her fingers, "cannot afford that sweater."

Benita raised the sweater over her head and squirmed to pull it down over her shirt. "Look there. It fits. Take it out of my Yale scholarship."

Tommy lowered his head and grinned. Adele pulled Faye and Deirdre to where Benita was standing. "We'll buy it," Adele said. "Nita, add this to the clothes on the checkout counter." Under her breath, she whispered, "And stop nagging her."

"Why? It's fun. She started it with all that hoity-toity stuff."

"Outside. Now," Adele said. "Go find another store. I'll meet you after I pay for these things."

"Yes, you do that," Mrs. Radford said. She stepped behind the counter. "I'll ring up these items," she told the sales clerk.

"You work here, Mrs. Radford?" Adele asked.

"That's my name on the marquis. My, my, you must have twenty things stacked up here." She pawed through the items, then looked up at Adele. "Your total is one hundred dollars."

Adele looked at the piece of paper where she had kept track of each clothing item. "I have a list of each piece. My calculations total thirty-six dollars."

"If you cannot afford these items, step out of line so I can serve the next customer."

"Would you mind adding these again?" Adele asked. She pulled clothes back off the counter and laid them across her arm. "Let's do this together."

"Blouse," Adele said. "Half off makes it two dollars."

"Poor soul. Can't you read the price tag? It's ten dollars."

Tommy stepped up next to Adele. "What's going on here, Mrs. Radford?"

Elizabeth stood on the cashier's platform looking down at them; a sneer curled her lips upward as if she delighted in dishing out shame. "It seems Selma Dawson's daughter cannot afford my store."

Tommy picked up each garment, adding up the numbers with Adele.

Mrs. Radford shifted her feet, stomping heavily on the wooden floor. "You are standing in the way of my other customers, sir. You can see the line is backing up, can't you?"

"This won't take long, ma'am." After a moment, he looked up at Elizabeth once more.

"You're right. Adele was off by twenty-five cents. The actual amount she owes you is thirty-six dollars and twenty-five cents."

"One hundred dollars," Elizabeth repeated. "Pay or leave my store."

"Why, ma'am, I'm sure you want to treat Miss Dawson a bit kinder."

Elizabeth scoffed. "And who are you to be telling me how to treat my customers?"

Adele watched Tommy breathe like he did when he was about to start a fight with her stepfather. "When is the last time the state's attorney general paid you a visit?" Tommy asked. "My father is one of his advisors." Tommy didn't bother to add he knew the attorney general in Missouri, not West Virginia. "I'd be more than happy to write a letter and provide a few details. Of course, it would shut down your store for a good ninety days while auditors go through your books. No telling how many customers are eligible for a refund. How about you, ma'am," he asked, turning to the woman in line behind him. "Would you like a refund?"

"Fine!" Mrs. Radford said. "I don't suppose you brought any money with you."

Adele reached into her purse and produced thirty-seven dollars. "It's a little over." She looked up at Elizabeth Radford. "But keep the change," Adele smiled. "For helping Selma Dawson's daughters."

Tommy wrapped his arm around Adele, escorting her out of the boutique. "And with that, we are celebrating back to school at the Blue Mountain Apothecary."

***

Tommy and the girls caught the 4:00 train back to Bramwell, giving the girls another breathtaking trip through forests and meadows. A herd of bighorn sheep traversed down the mountain, curious to see if the train would make it through the pass. Adele thought I could make this train ride every day and never grow tired of its beauty.

"We need to get to the bottom of Elizabeth Radford's bitterness," Tommy cautioned.

"I'm sure the answer is in Kettie's closet," Adele said. "But I can't get in there for another week until it's purified. Elizabeth has been stewing for twenty years. A few more days won't hurt."

"Wait until I come back to take her on. Promise me that," Tommy said.

Adele sighed. "I promise I will try, Tommy. Mrs. Radford came out of nowhere. I have this feeling that people are holding back secrets about Mama's life."

"Don't overanalyze your mama," Tommy warned. "She was a blessed woman."

"Then how did she end up with the likes of August Beck?"

***

That evening, Tamasin prepared fresh-caught trout with cornbread, pinto beans, and gravy for dinner.

"You absolutely spoil me," Tommy said. He stood next to Tamasin as she stirred a steaming pot of beans. "How will I ever go back to eating cold cuts?"

"Good food warms the heart, feeds the soul," Tamasin replied. She tapped a spoon over the bean pot. "Go on now, have a seat with the young'uns."

"Just as soon as you and Elijah join us."

"Not the way it's s'posed to be, Mister Tommy. You eat in there. We eat in the kitchen."

"We're family here. No stations or barriers. I'll hold your chairs until you join us."

Tommy sat at the head of the table while Adele took the seat immediately to his right, mirroring the pictures she'd seen of Dawson family dinners. For once, Benita didn't complain about sitting next to her sisters. Adele considered the quiet a breath of fresh air since they usually fought over anything. Tamasin sat between Elisha and Faye.

"Mind if I bless this food?" Elijah asked but offered no room for rebuttal. "Father, God, you bring this family together. In your mercy, keep them, every one of them healthy and smart like their Selma. Bless my woman who fixed such good food from the creek. Amen."

After filling themselves with dinner and gooseberry pie, Adele said, "Tonight, I'm calling a meeting of the Bs. And I'd like Tommy to be part of it."

"Only Benita or Briana can call a meeting of the B's," Deirdre scolded. "Benita is president of the B's club."

"It's okay," Briana said. "After today's shopping trip, Delly earned the right. We're all sisters of the B's."

Each girl took a seat in the library. "Thank you, Briana, and Benita, for allowing Tommy to join us," Adele started.

Benita nodded. "Hey, it's your meeting."

Adele pulled her armchair closer to the center of the room. "Tommy is taking the train back to New Madrid the day after tomorrow. He has to be at the university in two weeks."

Benita looked over at Tommy. "Mr. Harvard."

Adele folded her hands in her lap. "I have heard you talking amongst yourselves, worried where you will live. Some of you want to go back to the farm. Others want to stay."

Briana interrupted. "You're splitting us up?" she cried. "We're sisters."

"Hear me out. I'd like each of you to move in and live here," Adele responded. "If you stay with me, we will find a way to make sure you are in school, make the honor roll, have clothes, shoes without holes in them. Respect."

"Farmers always have food, Delly," Deirdre said. "You helped build all those irrigation ditches. We sold most of the vegetables to townies, but you cooked for us. When you left, Pa made us do all the work."

"It wasn't that bad," Benita cut in.

"That's because you got all buddied up with the Olga Beast," Collette said.

"She's a strategist," Benita snapped. "Only laborers get their hands dirty."

"Oh, I know plenty of politicians with dirty hands," Briana argued.

"What do you know? You're just sixteen," Benita said.

"Nita! We are twins," Briana snapped.

"Stop," Adele scolded. "I'm trying to keep us together."

"So, let me get this straight," Benita said. "You're asking us to decide whether to live where you're in charge or choose Pa, where Olga's in charge?"

Collette stood up. "Look at this place!" She opened her arms and pointed to the wainscoting and loaded bookshelves. "Delly lives in a three-story stone house. On the farm, we all sleep in two tiny bedrooms. In a dirty shack, Pa doesn't even own. Have you seen the chandeliers here? This house has four big bedrooms just on the second floor. I haven't seen the third floor yet. Elijah won't unlock the doors until he's finished disinfectorating."

"Disinfecting," Briana corrected. "TB germs have to be dead before we move up there."

"I'm staying here with Delly," Collette continued. "I don't blame you for leaving the farm. Pa treated you like you were his servant for four years after Mama died. I just want my sister back. At least here, I've got a chance to be a real kid, not some scrounger. And that's all I have to say."

"Sit down, Collette." Benita stood to take control of the conversation. "All of you, listen. Pa and Olga have spent years building a historic event, the biggest protest in American history. Even President Roosevelt thinks it's going to change the way we live. It's like Olga says, 'Newspapers will tell our story, especially if readers think children are suffering. Together, you and I can lift the condition of American sharecroppers. A little more suffering is nothing for kids like us. Newspaper reporters are writing stories of landowners stealing subsidies from tenant farmers. Reporters are just throwing fat on the fires of injustice and inequity.'"

"There she goes again, talking like Owen Whitfield," Collette whined. "Pa says the preacher man is organizing a sharecropper roadside demonstration. First in the nation!"

"You sound like Pastor Whitfield," Elysia said. "Father MacDougal says he's the father of Sybil Disobedience."

"Civil," the word is civil," Benita said. "Forget Father MacDougal. I'm a Lutheran now."

Deirdre gasped. "No, you're not."

"It ain't that big a deal, baby sis," Benita said. "Point is, I want to have a say in how people like us get a fair shake. I'm standing up for day laborers when their families get evicted."

"People like us?" Collette asked.

Adele leaned forward in her chair. "Sounds like you have a real calling, Nita. I'm proud of you, as long as no harm comes to my sisters. You all know I want you to stay. But if you decide to leave, Tommy will escort you back to New Madrid."

"That's right," he agreed. "I'll get you back safely, just like on the ride out here."

"I hate Olga," Elysia said. "She is a fake. Sometimes she makes Isaac sleep in the horse's barn. She spanks him so hard and then puts him to bed. Without dinner."

Tommy straightened in his chair. "I've not heard that before, Elysia. I won't let her get away with that."

"By the time we find you, she's already beat the tar outa us," Deirdre added. "She says she'll smash our fingers if we misbehave."

"Yeah, how we gonna find you when you're at Harvard?" Collette added. "You're leaving tomorrow."

"Listen to me," Adele interrupted. "Neither Pa nor Olga can touch you if you are here."

Elysia swiped a defiant strand of hair from her face. "I'm staying with Delly."

"Owen Whitfield stands for justice and equality," Benita explained. "An evicted shareholder. He knows the harsh conditions we live in."

"Lived in. Especially in winter," Deirdre added. "But here, there's a fireplace in every room, Nita."

"Who do you think will chop wood for all those fireplaces?" Benita fired back. "It's not just the Beck children who need worn-out blankets in winter. Children die of starvation, cold, and diseases every year because the landowners won't pay for their tenant's work even when the government gives them money to pay us. Hoarders! We have to help our own. We can't stay in this house of luxury while my friends freeze."

"Truth be told," Adele said, "I don't always feel worthy of being in this grand house, either. I remember cold nights when the only hope of warmth came from my sisters and me cuddling in the same bed. But I will use what has been given to me to make life easier for others. So, if you decide to leave, Benita, I will make sure you have what you need."

Briana welled up in tears. "Nita, I can't go back to poverty. Not when Delly is trying to keep our family together. We're twins. Don't separate us. Who will take care of Faye?"

"Faye stays with me," Adele said. "Listen, this isn't a decision you have to make today or tomorrow."

"I'm afraid they do," Tommy argued. "I'm taking the train back to New Madrid tomorrow."

The room grew quiet.

"Take time to talk it over," Adele said. "We are sisters."

"What's to talk over?" Benita argued. "I'm building my future. And it isn't here."

***

As the girls left for their bedrooms, Benita confronted Adele. "See what you've done. You broke up the only family I've ever known. You must be so proud of yourself."

Adele grabbed Benita's arm. "Wait just one minute, Missy. You put all of us in harm's way when Pa came looking for his son. Where's Isaac?"

"Someplace safe," Benita answered and pulled her arm away from Adele's grip. "As if you ever cared."

"Isaac is the reason your father tracked you down and attacked us. Where's the boy?"

"I can tell you," Collette interrupted.

"Shut up, little weasel," Benita snapped.

"Father MacDougal put him —" but before Collette could finish, Benita slapped her face, forcing Collette to fall backward onto the floor.

"I said, shut your stupid mouth," Benita hissed.

"Hey, wait just a minute!" Tommy said. "When you hid Isaac, you put your sisters into a terrible position with the law."

"No, I didn't," Benita argued. "Pa just thinks Isaac is missing. He's mad cause he can't make any money from old men wanting to play with a baby's ding-a-ling. At least I finished what Delly should have done. Isaac is safe now."

Tommy grabbed Benita's arm. "Has August been perverting a toddler?"

"Oh, like you didn't know!" Benita snapped.

Tommy turned Benita to face him. "How would I know?"

Benita sneered at Adele. "You never told him?"

Tommy turned to Adele. "What's going on?"

"Your father and my father had this little arrangement," Benita said.

"Please, not now," Adele begged.

"No, go on," Tommy argued.

"Seems your daddy likes little boys," Benita said. "So, my father, Mr. August Righteous Beck, signed a contract giving up permanent custody of Isaac. In exchange, James Thompson would restore the deed to August's land and give it back."

Tommy cringed. His eyes grew wide with anger. "He did what?"

"You heard me," Benita scolded.

"Adele, is this true? Did you know about this?"

Adele held his gaze. "Yes."

"Do you have proof?"

Benita nodded. "Oh, yeah. I have the contract."

"Is that why you came here?" Tommy asked Adele.

"No, Tommy. I wanted to come home. After mama died, I always felt like the outsider, shouldering responsibility for seven children. I rejected my sisters for many years, always blaming them for August Beck's corruption. Pa got into so many bad things, and I had no legal authority to stop him. Mama tried to change him, but he would lock her out in the cold or slap her until she'd give in. Nine months later, another baby popped out. I talked to Father MacDougal, but he didn't do anything either. I asked Grace MacPherson for help. All this evil, right there under everyone's noses, and no one did anything to stop him. Or help Mama.

They all just turned their faces. Who does that to children?"

"You left," Benita snapped. "Isaac became my problem. So, I fixed it."

"I came to help my grandmother, Benita. She was dying."

"Old people die. Every day. But you were never planning to come home, were you?"

"I wasn't sure," Adele answered. "But after being here for a while, and now that my sisters are here, I do want all of you to live a better life. Here with me."

"All of us except Isaac," Benita snipped. "You don't care what happens to him."

After all the conniving Benita had done to Adele when they were younger, Adele could just as quickly have slammed a chair over her half-sister's head. "Benita, I'm going to be twenty years old next month. For four years, I was Pa's waitperson. I'm not doing it anymore."

"Pa's got nothing on me anymore," Benita said. "Like you, I'm making my own life."

"But you want to go back," Adele said. "Even though I have asked you to stay here."

"My calling is bigger than any stupid irrigation digging project Pa has planned for me. Olga sees that leadership in me."

"And you don't think she's manipulating you?" Tommy asked. "What's in it for her?"

"She's the big lobbyist with people in Washington. She opens doors for me."

As snippy and brash as Benita had been, Adele could see how easy it would be for Benita to fall for Olga's shenanigans. "Where does that leave Isaac?"

"Father MacDougal has him in a safe place."

"Does your father know that?" Tommy asked.

"Pa's obsessed with dirty politics, and he thinks Isaac is his ticket to getting the farm back," Benita answered. "He wants all of us to make his life easy again."

"There aren't any laws yet that stop a parent from treating a child as if he were property," Tommy said. "If what you say is true, I have a lot of work to do. Starting with my own family."

Adele stood and opened her arms for her sisters to come close. "We have so many problems to sort through. But we've worked through Pa's anger before. Maybe Noona did the right thing bringing us together. I have no idea how she thought I could make the people I love happy," she said. "But I do know that if we get some sleep, we can work out our problems tomorrow or the week after that. It's getting late. Let's call it a night."

***

After the girls settled in upstairs, Adele and Tommy sat together on her father's leather sofa, each silently processing the conversation. Adele put a record on the Victrola, intending the music to calm them both before turning in.

"Why didn't you tell me about my father?"

"Things got ugly fast," Adele answered. She sat back and listened to Summertime by George and Ira Gershwin, probably one of the last records Noona had purchased before tuberculosis quarantined her to the third floor.

"I hate knowing you have bad thoughts about my father," Tommy whispered.

Someday, she would tell him why she never wanted to see his father again if they ever got married. The trouble his father caused her and her family was too much when she needed to unwind. "Someday, I will talk about it."

"I've been your friend for a long time," Tommy said. "Far back as when you were ten years old, I'd see you walking your vegetable wagon up our street. I'd come out and walk with you."

"I remember." Adele smiled. "You were eleven. Already a fifth-grader."

"Big man," Tommy agreed. "But not wise enough to see what my father was doing to you. Or your family."

"There are some things even friends shouldn't discuss," Adele answered. "Sometime, but not now." She hoped he would never have to learn the dark side of his father's lurid behavior.

"I used to think of you like the beautiful sharecropper's daughter. And here, you were an heiress to millions. You never let on."

Adele leaned her head against Tommy's shoulder. "Some days, I didn't know who I was either. Selma's daughter, August's cook and bottle washer. Big sister. Farmhand."

"I can't remember a time I didn't love you." He leaned over to kiss her forehead. "From the moment I saw you hauling that red wagon, selling beets, carrots, celery."

Adele hummed but didn't recognize the song coming from her lips. "I understood love from a mother, but you are the one who taught me that not every man is out to control a woman. You and I will always have each other."

She could feel Tommy smile. She looked into his eyes and accepted his lips as he tenderly kissed her. Not hungrily, but tenderly, an exchange between two people who knew each other's bones, freckles, and soft spots.

"I won't let your stepfather hurt you anymore," he said. "Whatever it takes, I'm here for you."

Adele loved the intensity in his heart. She also knew that he would leave for Harvard, and it would be up to her to manage whatever August

Beck had in store for her.

Chapter 7:
Sister Love

Adele caught Collette and Briana holding hands under the breakfast table. "Don't go. Stay here," Collette had whispered. "Pa can't make us go home. Benita's the only one who can manage him."

"Who will take care of Benita?" Briana had responded, her voice so low she didn't think Adele was listening. "She and Pa will get sideways; spittin' hate at each other like a couple a bullies. Benita snuck out last night. Did you hear her fighting?"

"With whom?" Adele asked.

"Who else? Pa must have been here." Briana said. "Does he know we're not going home?"

"He might now," Adele answered. She noticed the pile of new clothes they purchased yesterday had been dropped next to the Maytag wringer as if they already expected Tamasin to wash and fold them. Ungrateful so soon, Adele thought.

"Deirdre, come look at Noona's washing machine, baby girl," Adele said. "Rollers squeeze out the water just by plugging it in."

Deirdre shook her head. "Elysia would get her hair stuck between those rolling pins."

"Tamasin has a thousand things to do today." Adele's heart was so heavy about the twins leaving; she was afraid she might step on it. The gaping hole was right there in the middle of the kitchen. Why couldn't anyone else see it? Staying busy would keep her heart from bursting.

She thought she and her sisters should do something more symbolic, like make one last trip to the Corner Shop for a parfait. She couldn't remember when she and her sisters had liked each other so much. There would be enough time later to grieve. Or not grieve. She thought three, maybe four, of the five sisters were staying with her.

"I have loved and hated these sisters of mine," she told Tamasin when she slipped into the pantry. "I swear loving hurts more than hate. You can get over hating. Loving leaves chinks the size of a mulberry tree when it leaves."

"Miss Kettie, always plantin' trees," Tamasin said. She stored up garments for the Bluefield children's home. You should give 'em to the girls."

"I like that. At least the twins will have clean clothes to take with them."

Tamasin shook her head. "Benita be traveling with a thwamper," Tamasin said.

"What's a thwamper?" Adele asked.

Tamasin made a goose egg with her hands. "Came home late last night. I put some ice on it, but she'll have a shiner tamarra."

Adele gathered all her sisters but Benita and took them to the local plant nursery. "Let's pick out a tree so we'll always remember the start of our new life together." Briana held back, her face downtrodden since Benita refused to go with them on the tree hunting excursion.

Adele drew Briana close and hugged her. "You shouldn't have to choose to stay or leave. By Christmas, this tree will have strong roots in our front yard. I'll make sure you and Benita are together for the holidays."

On the way home, Adele stopped at the Corner Shop.

"I C E C R E M," Faye spelled out.

"You forgot the A," Elysia said.

"Ice Creama?" Faye asked.

"Come on, girls," Adele giggled. "Strawberry, chocolate, vanilla. Pick your flavor."

By the time they turned onto the driveway to Stone House, Elijah had dug a hole large enough for the Mulberry tree's roots. Each of the girls knelt on the ground to pack dirt and water around the tree roots. Elysia and Deirdre sang, "Here we go round the Mulberry Tree." Faye jumped up with, "Pop goes the weasel." Except she spelled P O P," changing the rhythm with each leap. The sisters joined Faye with P O P the second time they sang the tune.

"Thank you, Delly," Briana said. "For what?"

"For being our Delly."

***

That evening, Adele stopped by each girl's room. Faye was asleep on the trundle bed in Collette's room. Adele walked down the hall to turn off the lights in Deirdre and Elysia's room. "I'm too old for you to tuck me in now," Deirdre said. "Mind Elysia. She's all snively cause Briana's leavin tomorrow."

Elysia's hair splayed across the pillow, her green eyes half-closed. Tired as she was, she raised her arms, welcoming Adele's good night hug.

"We're going to be all right," Adele comforted. "We will be lonely for a few days. But we're never going to forget our sisters. Soon enough, you'll be in school. And then snow will come. I promise I will find a way for us to stay close." She listened to Elysia's breathing calm down. "Tell you what. Tomorrow after the twins hop on the train, we're going to do some exploring in Noona's bedroom. Maybe it won't smell so much like Pine-Sol."

***

Tommy was on the porch swing when Adele stepped outside. Music wafted up from the Presbyterian church before Wednesday night Catechism classes were dismissed. As Adele stepped outside, a shooting star waved across the sky.

"See that?" Tommy asked. "Even the angels fall for your beauty."

"Gets chilly here at night. I brought a blanket."

"Oh, I like blankets," Tommy answered. "No one can see what my hands are doing." He opened one arm to welcome her.

They swung in silence, holding hands, listening to whip-poor-wills sing their nocturnal lullaby. Tommy squeezed Adele's hand. "Whip-poor-wills camouflage themselves at night while they search for their mates. Hear it? Males call females to follow their song. Keeps the competition down."

He turned Adele's face to him and then lifted her chin. "You don't have to be brave all the time," he said and kissed her neck, then the tip of her nose. When she lifted her face to his, he kissed her mouth, searching for everything precious inside her to come out and be his friend again. "You left New Madrid four months ago, but it seems like years to me." He kissed her eyebrows, her temple, then returned to her lips.

It had been more than two years since their bodies had touched belly to belly. On their first date, Tommy had turned his back on other girls wanting him to be their boyfriend. But he had chosen her. She started her first period the day after they had been together. Her stepfather, August Beck, told her she had the curse. But Tommy said cramps were her body's natural way of shedding the uterine lining. He didn't make fun of her ignorance; he knew her mother, Selma, had died before explaining feminine cycles. Tommy also protected her from her stepfather. He took more than a few punches from August Beck, trying to keep his daughter from dating. Tommy landed a few of his own when August was out of line, which was near all the time.

He kissed the nape of her neck, where she was most vulnerable. "Lean on me tonight? Come with me. I need to feel your soft skin next to mine."

He lifted her hand. "How will I ever get through college without you?" He raised her from the swing. Neither of them wanted to alarm Elijah already turned in for the night in the carriage house. Instead, Tommy walked her into the house, quietly through the kitchen, up the creaky stairs, and into the bedroom where Adele's parents shared such love for each other. Adele listened for Tamasin to close the kitchen and then head out to be with her husband.

When they were certain Tamasin was in the carriage house, Adele sat on the settee next to Tommy. "How many women since me?" she teased.

Tommy put his hand on her face. "You don't know, do you?" He kissed her lips, widening her mouth with his tongue. "Just you, baby. No one even compares."

Adele unbuttoned his shirt and tugged it down his arm, drawing circles around his muscular curves. She smiled ever so slightly as the hair on the back of his neck curled up. "Why, Mr. Thompson. You are nervous."

"Lord knows, you scare the pants off me," Tommy said. He lifted her, his hands under her legs, holding her close to him. She kissed him and locked her legs around his hips. When he lowered her to the bed, he looked deeply into her eyes. "You can stop me any time, Delly."

"I need your strength tonight," Adele answered.

"You are more woman than any man in West Virginia or Missouri can handle."

They explored each other gently at first. "Your skin, so soft. You drive me crazy," Tommy whispered. "Soft as the velvet bedspread. Your hands. I've missed you weaving them between my fingers. Your hair, falling on my face. I am the luckiest guy." She melted into his chest until he climbed on top. Then, she gently played with those dark curls curled at the base of his neck, stroking his chest as he climbed on top of her quietly to keep the bed springs from creaking.

Tommy cradled her when he had finished. "I cannot think about leaving you again. I don't know why I came to this house. Why do I put myself through this?"

Adele pressed against him, feeling his warmth, happy to be inside his arms. She raised her face to his and kissed his chin. "My one and only. Tommy Thompson."

There was a long silence as they lay together. Heat radiated from the warmth between them, just like it did when she watched her mama and daddy, Kenneth Dawson, so long ago, early in the morning.

"You left New Madrid so suddenly," Tommy said, breaking the silence.

"My grandmother was dying," Adele answered.

"She's gone, Delly. Something else is keeping you from me."

Adele didn't respond.

"You left without saying goodbye."

"Tommy, there wasn't time."

She closed her eyes, waiting for the house to creak, a sister's cough, maybe she waited for her own heart to cry out to him, "Don't go. Stay with me tonight," she begged.

Tommy took a deep breath. "AFSC got funded. Remember that cooperative you started? You wrote the grant."

"American Friends Service Committee? The money came in?"

"New Madrid town council was counting on you to help oversee funds distribution."

"Not a chance now. Noona's estate goes to charity if I leave West Virginia. There would be no way for me to help my sisters if I lose my inheritance." And there was another reason she could never go back. She hadn't told Tommy about his father's appalling assault on her before she left New Madrid. "Do you remember when you said, 'Sin runs deep in my family?'"

"You're changing the subject now?" Tommy asked. "Don't pick old wounds, please? Not when I have just a few more hours with you."

"I have been given a second chance here in Bramwell. Those wounds are why I got a one-way ticket out of New Madrid."

Tommy rolled over and raised on one elbow. His brown eyes explored her hair, her neck, then settled on her lips.

"I'm safe here, Tommy. Your father is a powerful man in New Madrid. I never told you what he did to Faye and me or how I got the money for a train."

Tommy stroked her face. "Anytime you're with me, you're safe, Delly. I know enough about my father to recognize he's a degenerate. Lawyers have to keep deep secrets."

Adele buried her face in his chest. "Pfft."

Tommy sat up. "Okay, let's open that wound. Are you still sore about my dad's contract to buy Isaac? It was August Beck's idea. He knew my mom would do anything for another son. He's the one who offered Isaac to my dad in exchange for a paid in full deed to August's farm. But that contract has been nullified. The title of your farm reverts to Isaac when he turns twenty-one. Isaac can do whatever he wants with the farm."

"Can you imagine how damaged that boy will be when he grows up?" Adele mumbled.

"It shouldn't be your burden to carry," Tommy answered. "Let me do that."

Picking old sores would cause a bloody mess. "Some memories just shouldn't see the light of day anymore," she said.

"You'll never be able to find peace if you don't talk through your conflicts. Straight on."

Adele's mind flashed like a highlight reel before the main event. Which conflict should she face first? Her stepfather trying to drown her? Together they had climbed into the attic to escape rapidly rising waters, hoping to be rescued from the Mississippi flood. But when a rescue boat came by, August slipped into the boat with baby Isaac, promising to return later that day to get her. Both knowing he wouldn't. If not for her neighbor, she would have drowned in that historic flood of 1927.

Or maybe the last conflict, when Tommy's father tried to rape her and nearly killed Faye with narcotics.

"Before I go, baby girl, face one of them. You're a walking minefield."

"Me a minefield?" Adele asked.

"I'm right here," Tommy said. He pulled her close. "You're so raw; I can see it in your eyes."

Adele rolled onto her back. "Okay, here's one. How about the day your father tried to rape me?" When Tommy didn't say anything, she kept talking. "He overdosed Faye on atropine, then pulled me out of the car when I tried to wake her." Oh, she did not want to remember this but knew she had to get it out of her head. "Faye was limp, Tommy. I thought he killed her. He just kept throwing me to the ground. Every time I pushed him away to rescue Faye, he'd hit me back onto the river rocks. I fought him, Tommy. Fought him hard. I kneed him until he couldn't move. Finally, I carried baby Faye down River Road, trying to find a doctor to help.

"Even then, he wouldn't tell me what he'd given her unless I would let him have his way with me."

Tommy rolled back onto the pillow. "So? Did you?"

"Did I what?"

"Let him, have you?"

Adele threw back the sheet covering her and grabbed her Momma's robe. "You have to ask me that?"

"I'm on your side, Delly. Tell me what happened."

"Hell, no, he did not take me. What is it with rich people, thinking Christian morals don't run through our veins cause we're poor? As hard as I punched him, he must have come home with at least one black eye."

"He's a lawyer with a lot of enemies. Sometimes he gets into bar fights," Tommy said. "Protecting clients. I remembered one night scratches on his cheek, more than the usual bad client argument. That was you?"

Adele tightened the sash around her waist and sat at the edge of the bed.

"You blame me for that?" Tommy asked.

"He found a condom on the floor of your car. Wanted his piece of cherry pie, as he put it. What's good for the son is good for the father."

Tommy stepped around the bed in front of her. He lifted her chin and studied her face. "Is that why you've been so distant from me? You thought I reminded you of my father?"

"It wasn't just because of your dad. I was nothing more than a housekeeper at home. Not a daughter. Cinderella had it better than me. I just needed to get away."

"So, all these months, you thought I was somehow in on his lurid plot?" His jaw pulsed as if he were trying to shake off something ready to rupture. Finally, not able to handle this news any longer, he punched the mattress. "Right now, I could kill my father."

"Quiet, you'll wake the girls."

"You think I care right now? Mr. High and Mighty. He's the real reason you left, isn't he? And all along, I thought my mother was the snooty one separating us."

Adele grabbed Tommy's fists and held his hands to her chest. "Listen to me. As awful as that was, I stopped being my stepfather's doormat. And it confirmed my suspicions that my kin were not in New Madrid,"

Adele said. "I needed one person, just one single person, Tommy, to know who I was."

"It's always been me," Tommy answered. "Don't you know that?"

"You knew me as the stepdaughter of a tenant farmer."

"That's what you thought? From the day you buried your momma, I knew you would arise to any challenge. But everything kept going to hell." He shook his head. "I was too ignorant to make things right."

Adele turned her face from him. "That's all gone now."

"The old Delly isn't here anymore," he said, tapping his fingertips against her heart. "You're an heiress to a coal mining dynasty now."

"Stop, Tommy. I don't know what that means yet."

"Oh, come on, Adele. I saw the lawyers schmoozing you at the funeral. How many young ladies have an attorney escorting them like a debutante? You have a bodyguard, for god's sake."

Adele wrapped her arms around him and leaned her head on his shoulder. "But you were my best friend. My man. My lover."

Tommy hugged her long enough for her to feel his chest muscles relax. "I'm still your lover,' he said. "Your best friend," he whispered, kissing her forehead. "Whatever my father did to you, I will make right when I get my hands on him. But maybe now, you'll be able to let go of one demon."

"Don't be too hard on him," Adele argued. "He did offer me a bundle of cash to get started somewhere else."

"Oh, that's the lawyer in him. Money can be a great silencer."

"I'm nineteen years old, Tommy. About to take guardianship over my sisters and a coal mine filled with men who think women are bad luck. Please don't fault me for being a little confused."

"You know I will always be here for you." He leaned his face close to hers and kissed her eyes, one at a time, then her nose, and finally her lips. "Always. Here. For. You." He stroked her hair long into the night, kissing her forehead, her eyebrows, her fingers as if he could somehow trade the legacy his father had handed her for a newer level of comfort and trust.

***

In the morning, Elijah pulled Miss Kettie's car around to the stone patio. Adele straightened her back after lifting the first two suitcases, not knowing if she was carrying the weight of overpacked bags or shoulders full of sadness.

"Strong woman, you are, Miss Adele," Elijah said. "Glad you choose to walk. Take your time getting to the train. But this old mule," he said, knocking on the car, "lightens the load. Let her carry the girls' bags. They be mighty full, now. Not like when I carried 'em up last week."

Strong wasn't the word Adele would have chosen this morning. The unmerciful monster of separation was crippling her. She had helped Briana get ready for her fall semester in New Madrid by packing her suitcases full of clothes, enough that would make her the envy of her New Madrid high school friends. She might be a farm girl, but she would board the bus with new clothes every day for a month.

Benita said she would take out what she brought in: the shirt on her back, knife in her pocket, and a batch of Tamasin's cornbread wrapped in aluminum foil. A bit of a stretch, Adele thought, because Benita was also carrying a knapsack from Elijah.

Briana held Collette's and Deirdre's hands on the eight-block walk to Bramwell's train station. "You shouldn't break us up," Collette begged Briana. "Benita can go, not you."

"I'm the only one who keeps her out of trouble," Briana answered. "And you are going to be Bramwell high school's new star cheerleader. Show everybody how you do a backflip. Introduce me to all your new friends when I come back." Her voice cracked, but she went on. "Cheerleading's not something Pa would ever let you do back home."

Benita dragged behind the family, turning her face sideways now and then to see through her puffy, swollen eyelid. No one asked how she got the black eye, and she didn't offer.

Tommy wrapped one arm around Adele's waist, guiding her across the Bluestone River bridge, then down Main Street. He slowed as they crossed onto Main Street, ensuring her foot didn't trip on loose stones. The front entrance to the Corner Shop opened, and Mr. McConnell stepped out to shake Tommy's hand.

"Don't be a stranger," Mr. McConnell said. "I'll keep that prime rib warm for you."

The clerk at Bryant's Pharmacy came outside to hug Tommy. "Come back soon, now, ya hear?" she said, reaching to embrace him.

"You've been here for a week. How did you get to know all these people?" Adele asked.

"Small town. Big heart, Miss Dawson," Tommy responded, winking at her. "Had to be sure town folk knew I was your man. You need more than that Jackson fella watching over you."

The passenger train rolled into the N&W station, and Tommy tightened his hold around Adele. "Absence, they say, makes the heart grow fonder."

"Absence anywhere is still absence," Adele moaned.

"But you'll have the girls with you. No time to feel lonely." He leaned down to kiss her. "You know the N&W has a run from Bramwell to Boston. I could meet you any time." He kissed her eyes where tears were spilling out. "Any time. Any day."

Faye wrapped her arms around Briana. "No one can un-sister us."

The conductor stretched out his leg and jumped onto the platform. "All aboard!"

Suddenly, a loud explosion rocked Adele, forcing her to lose her balance. Immediately, a cloud of black dust whipped by. She dropped to the ground as fireworks shot lightning bolts into the sky several miles away. On the heels of the blast, smoke rumbled, sounding like a high-pressure engine had just ruptured. Sound waves wobbled, making her eardrums hurt. When she tried to get up, Tommy pushed her back down, wrapping his arms around her head. His heavy breathing parted her hair.

"Collette, Deirdre, come quick," Tommy shouted. He reached out, folding the girls close to him. Benita stripped off her jacket and tossed it over Briana's head, pulling her twin sister down to the ground.

Elijah raised enough to shout to the women. "Cover you eyes!" he cried out. "Black smoke is coal dust." Adele raised enough to see women in town rush out of their mill homes. No time to button housecoats. Some were still in slippers as they ran to the top of the hill. "It's the mine! There's been an explosion."

Adele watched as the ticket agent crouched behind the window. She heard clicking as he typed a coded alert.

Four men ran out of the fire station and gripped the side handles as the pumper tanker roared up the hill. One of the men hopped beside the firetruck, holding the rail until he was on board and could pull up his suspenders.

David Henderson stepped out of his downtown law office less than a block away. He held his arm over his eyes as he ran toward the train station. When he spotted the bundle of girls on the platform, he bent low and ran towards Tommy.

"Usually more than one rupture," he said. His rapid breaths let everyone see the fear in his eyes. "Stay down until you hear the all-clear."

Even though the mines were ten or so miles away, the mountain peaks were little more than silhouettes hiding inside a smoky fog that seemed to crawl ghostlike through town. Leaves rippled through downtown, sounding like Bramwell was at the edge of a vast waterfall, leaning over a deep precipice.

Louder than the first, a second kaboom burst through the air, breaking windows at the Bramwell Bank. The boom roared through the valley like a freight train, popping windows as it passed. Tommy held Adele even tighter.

"Damn, I hope our men got out before that second trapper blew," David said. He covered his head, sheltering himself while the second hurricane-like wind passed through town.

"I have to call the governor," David said, standing halfway up.

"You go," Tommy answered.

"It will be an all-hands-on-deck until the railroad crews arrive. I'm sure they'd appreciate a strong back if you can stay another few days," David said.

"Yes, sir. Anything I can do."

"Adele, stay close," David said. "We may need your presence near the mine."

David crouched low as he rushed back to his law office. With his head down, he narrowly missed getting hit by a maroon Chevrolet sedan as it sped toward the train station.

A woman inside rolled down the window. "Hey, farm princess, get in."

"Elizabeth Radford?" Adele called out.

"Mrs. Radford to you, princess. Worst of the wounded have been taken to Welsh Community. We got us a truckload of bad cuts and gas poisons coming to the Presbyterian church. Time to get your hands dirty." Elizabeth rolled up her window and waited.

Adele looked to Elijah. "Will you take the girls home?"

"I'm coming with you," Tommy said. "Benita, Briana, take care of your sisters."

As the wave of smoke passed by them, Benita stood up to watch. "Well, B's, this train sure ain't going to St. Louis today. Pa's gonna be so mad at Delly." She stood and kicked the platform. "I'm supposed to help families pack for the protest. Reverend Whitfield said I was his favorite aid. Now he'll let someone else take my turn. And I will be left with the nobodies."

Tommy grabbed Benita's shoulder. "Look here; New Madrid is more than a thousand miles away. You are needed here. You can clean up bloody miners or take care of your sisters." He released his grip on her shoulders. "Either way, no train is leaving today, and that is not your sister's fault."

"Hey, princess. You coming?" Elizabeth yelled again.

Elijah stood and wiped a coat of black dust from his face. "I will take the ladies home. Miss Tamasin and I will clean 'em up. Go now. Miners need you more'n the missus and me."

Adele took a few steps towards Elizabeth's car, then hesitated.

"I know I've been an awful pain in the ass to you," Elizabeth shouted. "Hate that you had to get to know the bitch in me before you knew my bossy side. But you have a mighty job now, calming down this town. So, I'm asking nicely; please get in?"

Adele and Tommy jogged to Mrs. Radford's car. "Front seat, Princess. Mr. Harvard, you get in the back."

Tommy shook his head but followed Mrs. Radford's instructions.

Adele closed herself inside the Chevy. "Mrs. Radford, do you know what caused the explosion?"

"Could be anything. Bad circulation. Foreman trying to cut corners. Probably no rock dusting. Best left to the inspectors. Unions are gonna blame the owners. Get ready for a fight. Threats coming soon against your life."

Mrs. Radford put the Chevy into first gear and winked at Adele. "Don't worry. You're not the first Dawson to get threatened. I'll show you how to disarm the bullies in this town." The car jerked forward between first and second gear, then smoothed out as she drove to the church.

Chapter 8:
Make-Shift Triage Units at Church

Elizabeth Radford's Chevrolet choked from coal dust settling into the carburetor. "I could run and get there faster," Tommy sighed.

"Get out, then," Elizabeth snarled. When he climbed out of the car, she added, "Move benches to the back of the church. Soon as the Purple Beast gets me to the church. We're setting up beds." She patted the dashboard, "Getty up, girl." When Elizabeth tired of the fits and spurts, only moments later, she turned off the ignition in the middle of the Presbyterian church parking lot. "Come with me, princess, You live in a mining town. You get to know explosions. We've got blood work to do. You can take orders, right?"

Sounded like a setup to Adele. "You're a nurse?" she asked.

"No. I am not a nurse," Elizabeth spat. "But my daughter is. All mine towns have an emergency plan in place. Ours has been tested. Too many times.

Men will carry the least wounded here to the church. You and I will patch up the bloodied or burned."

She lifted a steam vaporizer from the back seat. It looked like the one Noona had at her bedside when tuberculosis had its way with her. "The worst of the worst are already at Welch Community. If we think a man's injured too badly, he will be transported to Bluefield. Pickup trucks with stretchers make hourly trips, if necessary."

Elizabeth loaded Adele's arms with several bundles of fabric. "Rip a hundred strips for bandages out of this pile."

"Tamasin and I used to tear strips for my Noona."

"Noona? Is that what you called her? Poor Kettie. Whatever happened to Grandmother?" She spat on the ground. "How quickly the bourgeoisie invades my mountain." She lifted another large basket of cloths and led Adele into the church.

Just inside the vestibule, Elizabeth dumped the fabric in the middle of volunteers. "Get to rippin' girls." Women who had rushed down the mountain to help grabbed a piece of cloth.

"This here is Miss Dawson. First timer," Elizabeth said. "All of you knew her grandmother, Kettie Dawson." She turned to Tommy, "Mr. Harvard, you come with me."

Women and teenage girls entered the church, hugging each other and asking if they'd heard anything yet.

"My husband said this would happen," one said. "Pillars cave in soon's a woman comes near."

Adele felt the crushing glares of girls younger than she, accost her as if she was the reason there had been an explosion. She suspected she would face another firing squad of glares as men were brought in for treatment.

"None of this stink eye," Elizabeth said, returning from a back room. "Best years ever when Kettie Dawson ran the mines. You will give her granddaughter respect. She needs to be just like Miss Kettie."

A young woman entered the church holding a medical bag. She stopped to help one of the women rip cloth, "Like this," she said, turning the fabric on its side. "Makes a cleaner tear." She looked over the shoulders of several other women, stopping to embrace others as they entered the church. "It'll be okay. We'll know more in an hour or two."

"I'm Cora Radford," the young woman finally said to Adele. "Hadn't expected Selma's farmhand to be pretty. We'll fix that up right away."

90

"Hello, Cora," Adele responded. "You knew my mother?"

"Everybody knew Selma and Kenny," Cora responded. "Hearts broke around town the day Selma married Kenny. I was in first grade. Cried my eyes out on their wedding day. Always thought he'd wait for me to grow up. But it wasn't to be. She was a beautiful bride, though."

Cora's chatter offered another small piece of the puzzle Adele needed to learn about her parents. "I hope we'll be friends even if he didn't wait for you."

Cora seemed to think through whether that would happen. "I'm a nurse. Elizabeth's daughter. Other nurses will be here shortly. We never know how many we need until the wounded arrive. Thank you for being here."

"I want to do anything I can to help," Adele answered.

Tommy joined other men as they moved pews against the wall. They set up Army cots in rows, allowing enough space for people to kneel next to each patient as they arrived. Two weeks ago, this sanctuary had held Bramwell's citizens to celebrate Kettie Dawson's life. But today, flowers were shoved unceremoniously into the choir loft. Their baskets now carried rolls of fabric strips. Water buckets and empty pans were stationed at the end of each row.

The smell of burnt flesh, coppery and metallic, accosted Adele as soon as men unloaded stretchers from the back of pickup trucks. They came in a steady line, stopping only long enough to let the front man be assigned to a nurse. Some could walk. Most hobbled on the arms of another man.

"Comfort these men," Cora ordered Adele. "Ask their names so we can notify their families where they've been taken." She handed Adele a thermometer and a clipboard of unprinted church bulletins. "Write their name and temperature on the back of these, then safety pin it to the cot. Anyone over 102 degrees, you call one of the nurses or me. Most of our men got burned up pretty bad." She paused while Adele examined the room. "Don't dawdle."

"Where should I start?"

"Look around.. Go to any man looks like he's about to die."

"Die?" Adele repeated.

"This is the real world. Mineworkers die in explosions. There's one right there, three pews in. Looks like he didn't fare well on the truck ride over."

If the stained-glass windows could melt, it would have been tears from weeping angels. Eighty-four men were still unaccounted for. Despite the Bureau of Mine Safety engineers' warning miners to stay away, drivers reported that those not seriously wounded were still at the tipple, pulling away at rocks, hoping to find the entombed, desperately listening for signs of life.

Firefighters and police officers, and those not injured would trace the more than 100 miles of narrow-gauge railroad lines back into the mine to find a body. Hopefully, one is still breathing.

Adele stepped over vomit buckets and bloody sheets to get to the man three pews in.

"My name is Adele Dawson, sir," she said, kneeling to his side. "I'm here to help. Can you tell me your name?"

Silence. The man didn't move. She felt for a pulse. His heart was on overload. When he finally opened his eyes, his cheeks were stained with dry salty rivers, his temples still moist.

Cora yelled, "Hey, bend near him to hear!"

"Sir?" Adele asked again, leaning close to his face.

"Your arm is severely burned, sir," Adele said. "What else hurts?"

The man raised his arm. His flesh had curled into circles of blackened skin. Adele held his hand in hers, taking in the sight of something horrific, assaulting her with a forever image. "May I ask your name?"

"Herbert."

When he opened his mouth, an odor reminding her of rotting cornfields wafted up to her face. "Where's my crew?" he asked.

"I will find out. Right now, Herbert, we are focused on you." She jotted his name on a half sheet of paper. "Who might be looking for you?"

"My wife," the man answered. "Laticia. Up Mingo County way."

Adele took notes. "May I take your temperature?"

He tried to open his mouth but coughed up phlegm. Black spittle smattered his cheeks. Adele grabbed a torn rag and wiped his lips, then his chin.

"How about I put this thermometer under your arm? What about the rest of your body?" she asked as she unbuttoned his shirt. She might as well have opened the lid to a pot of boiling water. Steam rose from his chest. She tore more strips of cotton and covered each strip with clear salve before wrapping it around his arm. Then, she grabbed a blanket and tucked it around his torso.

When she read his temperature, she called out. "Cora, can I get some cold water here?"

Kneeling next to another patient, Cora looked around until she found a volunteer who appeared to be free. "Go," Cora said to the young volunteer. "Do what she says."

Adele was holding Herbert's head up so he could catch a few sips of water when the door swung open. Another dozen injured miners hobbled into the church.

"Over there," Cora pointed.

One of the helpers brought a bucket of cool water to Adele. "Run to the Corner Shop and get me some petroleum jelly," Adele said. "And ask the pharmacist to give us all the calendula ointment they have."

Cora stepped over from the man she was helping. "Glad it's not me ordering marigolds."

"It's a derivative. And it relieves pain."

"Didn't know you flatlanders ever heard of mountain leaves," Cora whispered.

"Oh, there's more to a flatlander than meets the eye," Adele responded. "Do you want to see this man's arm before I bandage it?"

"What's his temperature?"

"103. Underarm."

"Keep a cool towel on his forehead." To one of the helpers, Cora said, "Take over for Adele. Dribble cool water on Herbert's arm, and don't pull off any loose skin." Adele scribbled Herbert's name and vitals on paper, then pinned it to his cot. She dipped a towel in cool water and placed it on his forehead. On her way to the back of the church building, she stopped at the church's ice chest and pulled out a bottle of mustard, her grandmother's quick remedy for hand burns and cuts.

She headed toward a man scratching his face, trying to pick pocks of flyrock blasted into his cheek when the door flew open again.

The sun cast a large shadow onto the church floor where the big man stood. She recognized Dr. Luttrell from when Noona was sick as soon as he stepped into the building. "Y'all are damnedest best-looking men in all of Mercer County." His smile tossed any painful moans, bloody cuts, or broken bones to the wind; men covered in black soot turned the church into a throne of jokes and heehaws. He knelt beside Herbert and whispered into his ear. "You're going to make it to the hospital, Herb. Stay alive, my friend. You'll be walking your daughter down the aisle this Christmas." With that, Dr. Luttrell ordered a stretcher and a truck to transport him to the hospital."

"Y'all aren't as bad off as everybody says," Dr. Luttrell joked as he stepped between cots.

"Let me see that hand, Billy," the doctor said, reaching for the newest dirty victims. "Rinse this off, will you, miss?" he said to Adele. She was disappointed he didn't immediately recognize her. "And then cover it with that cold mustard in your hand. Good for first or second-hand-degree burns. How'd you know mustard's healing power?"

Cora rolled her eyes.

"Pharmacy is sending down all the pain killers they got," the doctor said. "And you ordered up mustard?" He looked at her over the rim of his glasses. "You a nurse?"

"No, sir. It was cold." She thought she should remind him she had learned about mustard from Kettie Dawson, but that could stir up another round of trouble with this crew. The doctor looked at her as if he saw someone he should remember, then searched for his next patient.

"All right, Joey, Bruce, Thomas, line up here. This nurse apprentice and I are going to invoke the Holy Spirit and Robert Chesebrough," he leaned over to face Adele. "You know, the million-dollar man who invented Vaseline?" Dr. Luttrell said, adding a comedy routine into the gruesome line of burn victims. "Step up, Joey. What are you pickin' at? You get sandblasted today?"

The doctor pulled a set of tweezers from his bag and set to work removing the small rocks from the miner's arm. After several minutes, he nodded at Adele. "Miss, take a gander at that man over yonder. His name's Bruce, and he's about to pass out if we don't get him to lie down."

Adele heard the rattle in Bruce's lungs and thought immediately of Noona's chest rattle. "Come with me, Mr. Bruce," she said, suspecting the blast just blew him to a heightened state of miner's cough. Four months of treating her grandmother's tuberculosis made her aware of the deep chest cough.

All day she worked, sipped a little water to keep herself alert. By the time the sun crept partway down the mountain, she realized her hair had matted with sweat and was falling on her face. She stretched her back, then stepped up to bandage a man with a burned leg and shoulder, when another man stumbled just inside the door. When he removed his miner's helmet, he pushed back thick dark hair, exposing a nasty burn on his forehead. Work shirt torn at the shoulder, blood dripped down one arm to his shirt cuffs, brown work boots covered with coal dust, but it was what he had tucked under his arm that drew her to him. A Scottish terrier missing a chunk of his ear panted heavily for water. When the man lifted the ear back in place, the dog shivered, then whimpered in pain.

"Jackson?" Adele asked.

"Miss. Dawson," Jackson responded. "Could you help old Gunner here? Jumped out of his old man's truck when the second explosion hit. Chased everything like a crazy fool looking for Ivan."

"I'd rather take a look at your head injury," Adele said.

"Tend to Gunner first. His old man was carried up to Welch Community. If we can get Gunner fixed up, he might help Old Man Ivan stay alive."

Adele cuddled the dog's face in her hands. "I've taped plenty of doglegs, but I've never taped a dog's ears together. Who is his master?"

"Mills, ma'am. Ivan Mills."

"The mine's lawyer?"

"Yes, ma'am."

"What was he doing up at the mine?"

"You and your lawyers might want to consult him on that later. Right now, I've got to get Gunner up to the hospital."

Adele carefully cleaned out Gunner's ear, smeared Vaseline on the cut, and then taped his ear back together. "He'll have that bandage scratched off by evening."

"Not if he has a lampshade around his neck." Jackson placed Gunner on the floor. "Down, boy."

Adele rubbed Gunner's good ear, and when she stood again, she said. "Your turn, Jackson." She examined the burns on his forehead and asked Dr. Luttrell to look at his arm.

"Leave Doc Luttrell alone," Jackson responded. "Just rub a little Vaseline on it."

When Jackson unbuttoned his shirt, he struggled to get his arm free from its sleeve. The more he squirmed, the more Adele noticed the muscles that defined his arms and chest. "This wound looks more like a knife wound. Deep enough for stitches."

"Just rocks, ma'am. Methane gas will blast a home off its foundation if it doesn't get enough air," Jackson said. "Think you could hurry it up a bit? Gotta get back on search and rescue."

"I can flush this with soap and water, but you're going to need stitches."

Jackson looked into Adele's eyes as if he wanted to say, "I will do whatever you say, ma'am." Instead, he said, "Lady like you has no place near a mine."

"Too bad for you, Jackson. I worked hard to get here."

"Miners have a hard life, ma'am. Your hands were made for a kitchen."

"You don't know where I've been." She remembered cotton picking in summer's humidity, snatching blackberries before blackbirds and copperheads had their way with her, getting scratched from head to toe on brambles. Coming into the house to find Pa had fileted river bass for her to fry. Her sisters would sit outside on the porch stoop and pick cotton bolls until their bloody fingers dried from thorny cuts.

"Tell me, Jackson, why you drove such a long way for medical help."

Jackson tilted his head to study her. "Well, ma'am, I guess it's cause I was hoping the Good Shepherd would be here. Mountaineers go to the Lord's house when they need healing."

"Plenty of churches between the mines and here."

"No church with the soul of Bramwell. This here is a sacred place. Dr. Luttrell, you know, is the best damn doc in four counties." Jackson sat up straight. "Ain't that right?" he shouted. "Best damn doctor right here in Bramwell, West Virginia!"

"Hear, hear!" The men seemed to find enough strength to guffaw and raise a burned arm in honor of their beloved doctor through their moans.

"Miss Kettie loved miners. Just like you, she'd be taking care of them. Like family."

Warm pride nearly buckled her knees. Adele understood the source of her real family's honor and why she felt a powerful tug for West Virginia.

She compressed the wound on Jackson's arm holding it a bit longer than necessary to make the bleeding stop. When Cora came over to stitch Jackson back together, she rubbed his arm with alcohol, then salve before lifting the curved needle.

"Don't you have someplace else to be?" she said to Adele.

Cora and Jackson exchanged an intimate glance. Cora's eyes grew kinder when she looked at him. Aha, Adele thought. Jackson was taken, and it was time to skedaddle. Bad enough that Cora's mother, Elizabeth Radford, was just starting to like her.

She crumbled used bandages, tossed them into the trash, and then looked around the sanctuary for other patients to help. Looking outside, she watched Tommy on the back of a pickup filled with gravel and shovels, joining several men as they headed up highway 52. Amazing, she thought, how quickly he jumped in to help victims of the mine blast. She watched until the truck rolled up the hill and out of sight.

"Hey, missy," Cora bellowed. "Focus!" She pointed to men sitting on cots.

Adele stepped gingerly between temporary beds, and knelt between two men, each with blood-caked coal dust on their cheeks. One was trying to untie and remove a boot over his swollen ankle. "Why weren't you transported to Welch Community?" she asked.

"Not enough room, ma'am. If we could still walk, company foreman sent us here."

"Tell me your name. Dr. Luttrell might transport you to Bluefield."

"Knock it off, Jack," another man said. "Nothin' wrong with your leg. I've had worse infections in my eyeball."

"That's cause you're a snitch. A damn canary."

Adele arched her back. "Both of you. No battles in this church clinic."

"You tell 'em, girl," Cora belted out. "Lawyers and union jackals will pounce on us soon enough."

Adele moved to another cluster of injured men when Jackson stooped down to her. "One more thing," he said, whispering way too intimately for Cora to see. "Kettie Dawson always kept a bottle of cold mustard in her icebox. She believed nature held a cure for everything."

"You should have seen her kitchen," Adele agreed, smiling before realizing she was sharing her moment of intimacy with him.

"I did. Many times. Talk to Tamasin about your Noona's pharmacy. Everything alphabetized like the bottles hiding in her bedroom."

"And how would you know?"

Jackson smiled. "Your daddy. He and my old man shared lots of secrets."

"You knew my father?" Adele asked, suddenly alert. Jackson reached low to pick up Gunner, the wounded dog. "Oh, yeah. I knew your daddy. And your momma."

Elizabeth Radford brushed against Adele, pushing her sideways as she reached for the church's double door handles. "You were leaving, Jackson? Give Mr. Ivan my regards. Tell him how we took care of old Gunner there."

Adele said a quick prayer for her coal mining attorney, Ivan Mills. Next week, she would call a meeting of her lawyers. There was more than methane detonating this mountain.

***

By the time she made it back up to the stone house, Adele was exhausted, her face a smudge of coal dust and dried tears.

"Jus' drawd a bath for you, ma'am," Tamasin welcomed her. "Go get yourself cleaned up. I'll have you a fine suppa when you done."

"Has Tommy returned?"

"No, ma'am. Hard worker that one."

The deep claw tub was a welcome break for her tired muscles, a luxury from the carnage she'd seen today. Tamasin seemed extraordinarily excited to have the girls back home with her. She chattered and fussed over them, showing them where she stowed food in the pantry as if she might get a second chance to teach them how to cook.

After dressing for dinner, Adele came down into the living room and welcomed the flute of dry champagne Elijah handed to her. Such a contrast between the bloodied men she cared for all day. Wanting to shut out the image of bloodied men from her mind, she paused in front of the player piano, hoping to find a recording she hadn't played before. Odd that she would find "Cheek to Cheek," a song Pa used to play for Mama before their first house was destroyed in the horrible 1927 flood. Before August Beck gambled everything away and lost the farm.

"Heaven, I'm in heaven," Benita sang, suddenly beside Adele. "And my heart beats so I can hardly speak." Benita raised the champagne flute meant for Adele and drank all its contents in one swallow.

"Don't be disrespecting Miss Kettie's liquor, Adele scolded.

Benita shrugged. "Damn good moonshine, you mean," Benita corrected. "How come you're playing that?"

"I don't know. It was on the player. Thought it might be uplifting. Ask Faye to come sing with me."

Benita sang, then leaned her face against Briana's.

"What got you guys all happied up?" Collette asked halfway down the steps.

"No good reason," Benita said. "Girls gotta get happy now and then."

"Yeah, but, it's you!" Collette poked Benita in the arm and giggled. "Who told Delly what we found in the attic?"

"Shhh," Benita responded.

"What do you mean?" Adele stopped playing.

"After dinner," Benita answered. "We will blindfold you and take you somewhere."

"Ooooh, big mystery. You know something about this house that I don't?"

***

After dinner, Briana covered Adele's eyes with a towel and tied it behind her head. "Don't be afraid."

"Bring her up," Benita called from the top of the stairs. Collette and Elysia held Adele's hands while Faye and Deirdre jumped on the steps behind her. "You won't believe it," Faye sang.

They made it up to the landing, then circled Adele, leading her to the second floor. "Something in the bedroom?" Adele asked.

"Not yours," Briana chuckled.

Adele followed blindly, knowing exactly how many steps it would take to get to the girls' bedroom, but when they opened the door to Kettie's third-floor stairs, she stopped and put her hands against the door frame.

"What were you doing in Kettie's bedroom?"

"Elijah said we could."

Adele ripped the towel off her eyes. "But Dr. Luttrell hasn't given anyone permission to go inside. What if the tuberculosis is still there?"

"Dr. Luttrell informed Elijah it was safe now."

"Why wasn't I told about this?" Adele pulled away from her sisters and folded her arms. She wanted to say, "This isn't your house," but stopped herself.

"Tamasin was boiling bloody rags at the church for reuse. We asked Elijah if we could go up, and he said, Jus' stay out of ma' hair."

Elysia corrected her sister. "Elijah really said, I can't see the harm."

Adele pressed against the wall. "We are not going into Miss Kettie's private bedroom. All of you. Apologize to me."

"Just go," Deirdre begged. "There's a secret B's club up there."

"Don't be mad. We didn't break anything," Briana coaxed.

"But there is so much history in that bedroom," Adele argued. "I wanted to be the one to show you my Noona's things."

***

At the landing before the last three steps, Adele stopped the parade of sisters. "You see this portrait? It's hung at the top of the stairway since I was a little girl."

Three men in full mustaches, top hats, and overcoats stared down at the girls.

"These were some of my granddaddy's partners. Mr. Mann was the chairman of the Bank of Bramwell. The other two men owned mines inside the Pocahantas minefield. Together, these men employed about one hundred thousand people."

"Were they good to your daddy?" Elysia asked.

"I believe so. See that little guy standing out in front. Kenneth Quillan Dawson. Someday I will tell you more about him."

"Come on, Delly. You gotta see what we found," Deirdre said before she leaped up the next few steps onto the third floor.

Adele halted outside the door to listen as she always did, to hear Noona's breaths before entering. Instinctively she reached for a linen cloth to hold over her face, then remembered the room was no longer a tomb. In place of the burn pail, a bronze iron rooster held the door from closing. Faye leaned down to the rooster. "Bawk, bawk," she greeted.

Scrubbed clean, the scent of lemon and bleach replaced sulfur and decay. Noona's exquisitely quilted bedspread was gone. So were her lavender satin sheets, incinerated, no doubt. In their place, a puffy white quilted bedspread, white cotton sateen sheets with gold-trimmed pillow shams. Much too sterile, Adele thought, to feel inviting. The Mercer County Health Department had long ago picked up the warming table along with the warming lights intended to fill Kettie with artificial vitamin D.

Elysia and Deirdre ran to the chaise lounge, no longer a burgundy velvet but now covered in bright red corduroy. Gold buttons outlined the perimeter of the chair.

"Can I have this bedroom?" Collette asked.

"If anyone moves up here, it will be me," Adele said. She searched for the steamer trunk that held her grandmother's secrets, her mother's precious diary, childhood blankets, Selma's Besame cosmetics brochures, newspaper clippings of her father's run for senate, and unsettling stories of his accidental death. Kettie's eyes had lit up an azure blue when she talked of Selma.

"Okay, show me your big surprise," Adele whispered.

"It's back here," Faye chuckled. As if she could move the bed frame by herself, she began pushing against the headboard. "Help me," she begged.

"I don't suppose you knew there was a room back here?" Benita asked as if she was smarter than Adele could ever hope to be.

"I was too busy caring for my grandmother."

"Then, you are in for a big, big surprise," Benita said, pushing Faye away. "Move, baby sis. Let's show Delly the new B's Club."

Adele grabbed the bed frame and pulled it toward her, making room against the back wall. Briana and Benita angled the bed until there was enough room for Collette to open a secret door. "So much better than the B's room we had on the farm, Delly. At least you don't have to crawl up into the hayloft to get in.

"Look here," Collette continued, "this room runs to the end of the house. Don't bump your head getting in. Secret doors should never be tall enough to let anyone in. Do you think they built this room during the War of the Nations?"

"Okay, Gabby," Benita scolded.

"Tell her to stop calling me Gabby," Collette said to Adele.

"Stop talking so much," Benita responded. "Step aside. Delly has to see the treasures her grandmama has been hiding."

Chapter 9:
The Hidden Family Museum

Elysia took Adele's hand and led her through a dried flower archway that opened into the largest room she'd ever seen in this enormous home. How was Kettie able to hide this from her, she asked herself.

The first shelves contained boxes from Harrods, Bloomingdales, Saks Fifth Avenue, and Macy's. Each box had been tied with a bow matching that store's style, whether paisley, striped, or in a floral print.

"How could you not know this was here?" Benita scolded.

"I was taking care of my grandmother."

Briana stepped next to Adele and curled her fingers into Adele's hand, speaking softly. "We can never tell Pa about this room."

"Why not?" Benita belted out. "He's family."

"Not this family," Adele said louder than she intended. "Please give me a minute to take all this in."

She pulled a Bloomingdale's box from the shelf and opened it to find a tissue-wrapped blue velvet dress. Silver sequins dotted the round collar. Placed reverently on top of the gown, she found a withered floral wrist band. Perhaps worn by her mother at a political event. She remembered reading her mother's diary and ached for the life her momma would have if she hadn't married August Beck

Adele closed the Bloomingdale's box and pulled down one from Saks. She lowered it to a footstool before opening the lid. Faye and Deirdre stood over her, anticipating its contents. A large photo fell out onto the floor. Deirdre watched as Adele raised the dress to examine it. Faye pointed to the picture and cried out, "It's Olga the Witch!"

"What?" Collette was immediately beside Faye, bending over the photo. Collette pushed the photo away with her foot like a dead bug. "It's just some lady," Collette soothed.

Benita joined them near the floor and shoved the photo further under the shelves. "She doesn't have pointy boobs. Not your stepmother."

Adele reached for the photo and dusted it. "This woman is much prettier than the Olga I remember." She shoved the picture back into the designer box, closed the lid, and returned it to the shelf. She wasn't about to open more wounds about her stepfather's second wife.

Collette pulled back a green velvet drapery imploring Adele to come with her into another cordoned-off section. Behind the curtain, Adele found wooden crates with dishes wrapped in newspaper. Tarnished silver serving dishes, Waterford crystal wine glasses stuffed in cardboard wedges, place settings labeled Lenox Snow Lily, and three Flora Danica serving dishes wrapped in newsprint. She had seen several Flora Danica dishes at Tommy's mother's house in New Madrid. His mother, Catherine Thompson, would never allow Adele, a girl from the bottomland, within smelling distance of her china cabinet. "These Flora Donica pieces are for Tommy's bride," she had said, looking away, "when he marries the right girl."

"All these keepsakes," Adele whispered reverently. "It's like the Dawson Museum."

"Look at me," Faye said, modeling a black beaded hat. A bouquet of ostrich feathers perched at an angle, giving her height and sophistication.

"That's not the way you wear it," Benita snipped. She angled the hat sideways on Faye's head, then pulled a thin veil down around her little sister's face. "Now you've got the Sally Milgrim look."

"How do you know Sally Milgrim?" Adele asked.

"I read, you know," Benita said. "After you dumped us, Mrs. MacPherson brought over sappy *Saturday Evening Posts*. Said I needed to get gentrified if we were going to move in with Pa's new wife, Miss Olga blah blah."

Adele felt her heart warm, knowing Momma's friend Grace MacPherson continued to show mercy to the children. But the sound of Olga's name sent a forest of dry pine needles shimmying down Adele's back. Adele remembered pictures she'd seen of Olga's news clip in the memory chest her grandmother had saved for her. Muddy water ran deep with that one.

Faye tucked one fist against her side and sauntered like a model toward Elysia. "Go get you a H.A.T, Elysia," Faye giggled and held out another hatbox.

Adele felt joy swelling inside as she watched her sisters explore the massive room, examining place settings Selma likely helped select. She loved each one of the girls in their own way. Faye for being so innocent and fragile, a child whose precious mind was pinched during childbirth. Elysia, all girl, frilly, jeweled up with a voice that could sing songs about puppy love from the minute she saw you. Deirdre, the wild-haired redhead, born with her fists raised. Likely to be Benita's protégé. Collette, the athlete, nearly as tall as the twins and still growing. Forever talking to the extent that Benita would call her Gabby to shut her up. Collette would surely make the cheerleader's team. And then the twins, goodness, how she loved the yin and yang of those girls. Briana, the artist who stole every young man's heart but never knew she had it. Benita the brilliant attorney in the making, waiting for an ivy league school to recruit her. No filter. Opened her mouth, and fire poured out. Not many saw her tender side. Benita would leap into battle to defend her family, never thinking someday she might have to ask forgiveness for her sharp tongue or quick punch. A protester to the core. It's why Pa loved her, too. He would put a newspaper clipping of social injustice on the kitchen table, and she'd be writing an op-ed before nightfall.

Seven sisters and then the one brother she'd rather not think about. Adele had been in the bedroom with each birth, washing Mama's face as she went through delivery. Found a wet nurse out in the cornfields the year Deirdre and Elysia came too fast. Mama had said Deirdre got the wiry hair from Pa, but Elysia's voice was straight from a nightingale. Lost in thought, Adele missed noticing that Elysia and Deirdre had moved into another section where a collection of paintings hung on the wall sectioned by faded white columns.

Adele was overwhelmed by the secrecy her grandmother built. A museum of family artifacts behind her oversized bedroom suite. Perhaps Noona wanted Adele to discover this place after she was gone. Limit the number of questions she'd have to answer.

She found a portrait of her parents, Selma and Kenneth Dawson, and a baby girl sitting on her daddy's lap. "That's me," she said, stepping closer. "Mama." She touched the painting, wishing to feel her mother's soft skin. "Daddy." Her voice broke. She picked up the painting and set it aside, vowing to hang it in her bedroom. "Was this too painful for you, Noona?" she whispered. "I was just four years old when daddy died."

"You look like Mama in that picture," Briana said.

"Mama always thought Collette and I looked alike," Adele responded.

Next to the family picture hung a portrait of a red flag waving against a dark blue sky. A gold-plated sign read, "The Flag. Georgia O'Keefe. 1918." A small, faded note tucked into the frame made it difficult to read. Benita leaned close. "It says, "To Q. For your bravery."

"Who's Q?" Deirdre asked.

"My grandfather, I guess. Quillan Dawson."

"Was your grandpa shot in the war?" Benita asked.

The man Adele called Pops often talked about his service under General Pershing's command. As a young child, she had played "seize the ship" with him as he spoke of military takeovers of German warships. America was so ill-equipped to transport four million troops into Europe, he had confessed. "Never again, Jelly Delly." He winked at her when he called her that. His voice would become suddenly subdued when he talked about how quickly he commanded First Division troops of the American Expeditionary Forces through France. She remembered Pops talking about the Battle of Argonne, which she would call the Battle of All Gone because the French were so thin from Germany's battle of attrition. Pops would simply smile at her simplicity, then show her how to seize another toy ship.

"He was a commander in the Great War against Germany. And yes, he was shot, burned by a flamethrower, and got too close to the Kaiser on one occasion." She sifted through more paintings stored in the bins. "Someday, I hope to know more about the artists he loved. Noona talked about Ernst Ludwig Kirchner or Paul-Hubert Lepage. Now I can see why."

Briana held up an Otto Dix painting to her face. "And maybe someday you'll purchase a painting from me, Briana Marie Beck," she said. "Except I'll have to change my name to Beckington. Nobody buys art from a Bootheeler named Beck."

Tucked between paintings was a copy of the 18th Amendment to the Constitution, imposing federal alcohol prohibition. The 21st Amendment ratified in 1933 had been taped over the 18th Amendment, giving power to states to regulate the distribution of alcohol.

"A house divided," Benita said. "Prohibition fueled organized crime. When your daddy ran for state senator, he must have made a lot of enemies."

"He was coming home from a political rally when someone forced him off the road," Adele answered.

"That's how gangsters work," Benita answered. "At night. Olga talks about them."

Adele immediately dismissed any reference to Olga but remembered reading her mother's sorrowful diary about her father's car accident. The coroner said the car injuries might have masked some of her father's broken ribs from a beating. She would give that some thought later when the girls weren't within earshot.

Stepping away from the art collection, Adele entered another section cordoned off with red velvet rope and brass stands. In the center of the space, her grandfather's war uniform hung on a velvet-wrapped hanger. A drab olive and khaki service coat with a standing collar hung in a stiff salute. Khaki leggings with pressed pleats dangled close by. Placed on a table beside the uniform was a yellowed booklet, *Regulations for the Uniform of the United States Army, 314th REGT, Field Artillery*. Compass readings had been mapped out on the cover; the pages torn and dogeared.

She found a khaki blanket roll, ammunition belts, a partially burned canteen with a bullet hole along the lower crest, an artillery bag, and a metal cup in another canvas bag. Benita raised pieces of an old machine gun, then picked up a yellowed brochure about the Bergmann submachine gun and how the Germans developed it for trench warfare.

"This baby shoots 1200 rounds per minute," Benita said. "But it's so light. It must have mowed down anyone trying to hide from them," she said, bouncing the gun in her hand.

"Careful with that," Adele admonished.

"It's in pieces, Delly. But I can see several bullets are still in the magazine."

"How'd you get so smart about machine guns?" Adele asked.

"World History?" Benita snapped. "Remember high school libraries? We might have lived poor, but my teachers never let up on homework, just 'cause Pa was a sharecropper."

Briana picked up the rusty bayonet and slowly slid it across her hand. "Is that rust or blood on the blade? I bet it's blood." Collette pulled it from Briana's hands. "Salute your commander."

"Gabby, put that down," Benita scolded. "It was a stupid war. Some cretin assassinated the Archduke of Austria and his wife. Then the world went to hell!"

"Your language," Adele hushed. "Not in here."

"You think your commander. Pop didn't cuss a wee bit?" Benita bit back. "He would have loved me."

Deirdre picked up the canteen and held it above her face. She tried to push her finger into the bullet hole but lost interest when a gas mask got her attention. She raised it over her head.

"Stop!" Adele said. "You don't know what's been inside that mask."

"Like what?"

"Mustard gas," Benita chimed in.

"Why Pop brought that back from Germany, I'll never know," Adele added.

Adele opened a scrapbook filled with war posters with slogans that read *Take the Eat out of Wheat. Meatless Mondays. Food is Ammunition.* When she was a toddler, she remembered Noona scolding her for tossing carrots or Brussel sprouts into the trash. "Children in Europe starving, and you can't eat a few carrots? Tamasin could have made soup out of this."

Grandpa would pat Noona's arm and defend little Adele at the table. "Allies won the war five years ago. Let the child eat whatever she wants."

In the back of the room, Adele noticed hanging plants near a windowed dormer. Lemon balm, mint, basil, thyme, elderberry, and parsley, green and well-nourished. This must have been the garden Jackson spoke of yesterday when they were caring for injured miners. She placed her finger in one of the pots, checking for moisture. How would he know about this? It bothered her that Jackson might have a key to the house. Who else would get in here?

"Briana, is there another door to this room?" Adele asked.

"Why?"

"These plants are moist. Maybe this room isn't such a secret after all. Someone comes in here to water these herbs." Someone had trimmed the yellow leaves—no brown spots on the lemon balm. Emerging mint leaves looked bright green as the stems leaned toward the window for light, a window she never noticed when outside.

"Somebody knows about the attic," Adele announced. "There has to be another door."

"Probably Tamasin," Briana offered. "These are cooking herbs. Much as she likes to cook, there oughta be an entire garden up here."

"You think someone comes in here without permission?" Benita asked.

"Noona put a lot of trust in Tamasin. And Elijah," Adele answered but wondered how Jackson knew about the herb garden. She turned to see what her sisters were chatting over and caught a glimpse of Benita placing something in her pocket. Bullets? A key? Something small from the war memorabilia.

"Benita? Is there something you need?" Adele asked.

"Nope."

"But there's something in your pocket?"

"No, there isn't." Benita held out her hands. "You are always suspicious of me."

Deirdre and Elysia playfully backed away from Adele, but in doing so, Elysia tumbled into a green velvet curtain, nearly tearing the curtain from the ceiling. Adele heard her sister hit her head on a wooden cabinet tucked behind the curtain.

"You okay?" Adele bent over and kissed Elysia's head until she stopped howling.

"Look, Delly!" Deirdre said. "All these raised up wood designs. Looks like the box Father MacDougal sticks his fingers in when he's serving communion."

"It's a bank box," Benita argued. "Locked tight as a tick." She shook the cabinet door, but it would not budge. "I bet there's German gold in here."

Rosette appliques carved around the top were rubbed thin, perhaps over polished for centuries. Adele tried to tip the cabinet sideways to find a hidden key. "It's nailed to the floor. Somebody didn't want this moved."

"Shhh," Deirdre said. "Someone's here. I hear the doorbell."

"Who shows up this late?" Collette asked.

"It's getting late," Adele said. She led the girls out of the attic and held Kettie's bedroom door until her sisters filed out and down the steps.

"Help your sisters get in their jammies," she told Briana. "You girls need some sleep before I enroll you in school tomorrow."

"Not me. I'm not staying in this hick town," Benita said. "I'm going back to New Madrid."

"It's the home of millionaires," Briana argued. "Says so at the train depot."

"Still fawning for the big sis." Benita shot back. "Pa's going to come back for us before I have to sit next to some snotty brat in this town."

"Miss Adele," Tamasin called up. "Mr. Henderson come a'callin. He be waitin' for you in the library, ma'am."

"Thank you, Tamasin," Adele answered as she closed the door to Kettie's bedroom. She reached on top of the door frame for the key, then clicked the lock before stepping down the grand stairway. The library doors were slightly ajar, so Adele slipped, hopefully unnoticed, into the kitchen. "Is it just Mr. Henderson?" she whispered.

"Yes, miss."

"Got any desserts you can serve?"

"Blackberry pie just comin' out now," Tamasin answered. "'Bout done with the grow'n season. Gots to eat 'em or jelly 'em 'fore they spoil. I'll add a nice nip a' ice cream for the girls."

With David being Noona's personal lawyer, Adele wanted to ask if he knew who tended the herb garden but decided to approach that topic another day. Instead, she leaned over to smell the pie. "Why is he here this late?"

"Not my doin, ma'am. He and Mr. Quillan always talk business after the ladies settle in. Might be his way of treating you as his boss."

Adele washed her hands and rubbed some of Kettie's mint leaves between her fingers to remove the attic's molded smell. "Tamasin, the girls can eat on the outdoor porch tonight. Would you serve Mr. Henderson and me in the library?"

"Miss Adele. Dem girls got you all twisted up," Tamasin said. She wiped her hands on her apron. "Course I be servin' pie to you and Masta Henderson. You need my Elijah to pour you a brandy?"

"Make it two, will you? I hope he's got an update on the explosion."

***

"My apologies for such a late evening visit, Miss Adele," David Henderson said. He stood and held a chair for her near the fireplace, then sat at an angle on another chair, but kept a watchful eye on the door.

"With the explosion, you must be as weary as I am," Adele greeted. "Tamasin will be here in a moment with her famous blackberry pie. How can I help?" She was breathless. Damn, calm down, Adele, she scolded herself.

David had been Kettie Dawson's most loyal of all attorneys for nearly ten years. He had become a great ally of hers, frequently stopping by to check on her.

David leaned forward and put his elbows on his knees. "Mr. Ivan Mills didn't make it."

Adele lowered her head. "Dear God. I'm so sorry to hear this. How's his wife and family? And who's in charge of the mine now?"

"There's more. A lot more." David waited until Elijah closed the library doors. "Your lawyers, me included, are mighty grateful to you for helping the injured. You are a woman of character to make this your first call of duty."

"I didn't do much. Some men are still missing. That's where I'd like to put our greatest focus, David," Adele responded. She studied his tormented face. "There's more, isn't there?"

"Harold, Garrett, John, and I all recommend you make yourself seen at the Buckeye Coal tipple tomorrow. The family needs to be physically present. That someone has to be you."

She sipped her brandy and nodded. "What would Kettie have done?"

David seemed to bypass her question. "Ivan was at the mine, along with several deputies, putting down an argument with hoodlums acting like strikers. Ivan was our best negotiator, including making sure our miners were paid better than any in West Virginia. Never gave reason for a strike. Until Kettie died."

Adele lowered her brandy. "You think unions want an excuse to take over the mine?"

David continued. "It's a test, Adele. The loss of a powerful leader makes you the next target."

"Are you saying someone targeted Ivan?"

David looked straight at Adele. "That's for the deputies to decide."

"Your reaction tells me yes."

"I will say this," David answered. "We haven't had an incident this bad in six years. None of our boys ever smoke once they go into the shaft. Working the mines is an absolute adrenalin rush, but there's a brotherhood when it comes to keeping methane gas in check."

"How do I convince them that I'm not bad luck?"

"Kettie was the hammer when Quillan died. Our men respected her."

"I'm nineteen years old."

David held the brandy between his hands. "It's not your age, ma'am. It's your pedigree. Only you know your history," David said as if he was reading her mind. "Here, you're the local daughter who returned to her roots." He was quiet. Nothing moved while the grandfather clock ticked. Tock. Tick. Tock.

"Get some sleep tonight, Miss Dawson," David encouraged. "Garrett and I will pick you up tomorrow morning. 8:00. No need to say much, but your spirit must be strong. Now that's something you can offer."

Adele shook David Henderson's hand as she walked him to the door, but then she had one more horrible thought. "Do you think it's a coincidence that the explosion happened three days after August Beck barged into the church?"

David squeezed his eyes closed and shook his head. "Dear God, I hope to hell not. Whatever put that into your head?"

"Troubled history between the Dawsons and Becks. More than just mineworker issues," Adele said.

"Bad blood runs between Auggie Beck and every attorney in town. But Jackson said the bast, sorry ma'am, Auggie was on a train headed to St. Louis."

"How many stops are there between here and St. Louis? What if he got off at Bluefield?"

"He wouldn't have come to by then," David answered.

"Charleston? There's a stop in Charleston, isn't there?"

Adele remembered one more detail. "Benita came home several nights ago with a black eye. No explanation. She and my stepfather used to get into it all the time."

David leaned close to Adele and whispered. "Not a word of our suspicions over Ivan Mills' death to anyone. Not your sisters. Not Mr. Thompson. I will talk to the special agent in charge. Bad enough, our town is planning funerals for so many men."

Adele closed the front door behind him when he left, locked it, and leaned against the door in thought. Elijah stepped into the library to carry dirty dishes into the kitchen. "Everything okay, Miss?" he asked.

"Elijah, Mr. Ivan Mills was at the mine."

"Can't say I knows what you be talkin about, Miss Dawson."

"Elijah, don't be coy. Word travels fast among the Negro communities. You haven't steered me wrong since I got here. You know the history between the families. Someone is sending me a very dangerous message. Miners died." She picked up empty pie plates to help. "I don't know how August Beck pulled this off. But I know he's behind this accident."

Elijah remained silent.

"Please tell me, Elijah. What didn't Miss Kettie tell me?"

Elijah tossed a towel over his shoulder and looked straight at her. "I neva' mince words with you, ma'am. That explosion is not the way unions take ova a mine."

Adele crossed her arms to think. "That makes me believe someone is trying to shake up the board of directors' confidence in me."

"Now that about the dumbest damn thing I eva' heard. You think for a minute your daddy or your grands would approve a you thinking such nonsense? They work too hard to build a town like Bramwell only to have a jackal come in and corrupt the mine!" He stripped the towel from his shoulder and tossed it into the sink. "You start thinking like that, and I will pack up Miss Tamasin and me before sundown."

"No talk of leaving, Elijah. Tell me what to do."

"Listen to ya lawyers."

"I need more than that, Elijah. David and I will be evaluating damage to the mine tomorrow." She knew Elijah had driven Kettie Dawson to many a miners' meeting. "What would Miss Kettie wear? What would she say?"

Elijah dipped pie plates into soapy dishwater, rinsed them, and put them into a dish rack. Finally, he spoke quietly. "Can't tell you what she'd say, but--" He thought for a few moments. "You ever handle a shotgun?"

Adele stared at Elijah in disbelief. But then she recalled her stepfather teaching her how to shoot rabbits, quail, and coyotes when they broke into the chicken coop. She had killed a rabid dog when it threatened to take down their own dogs, and she had taken out more than a few rattlesnakes. If she were going to face strikers, she'd have to look like she belonged here.

"I haven't held a gun in more than a year, Elijah."

"Comes right back in no time. Miss Kettie, she never fired no gun at a dadgum union striker, 'cept once. No one bother again. But she carried. At her side, under church clothes, a nice black hat, and she carry. That what you do tomorrow. You a lot skinner than Miss Kettie, but they get the message."

"You have a gun?" Adele asked.

"Mighty Lord in heaven. Do I have a gun? You ever been up to the carriage house?"

"No, sir."

"Take my 16-gauge. Least it won't blow you ova if you have to shoot."

"What will the lawyers think if I show up with a shotgun?"

"They think you one of em. They be carryin' too."

Adele thought through the clothes she might wear. A dark suit, straight skirt, boots, and white gloves. After slipping into her nightgown, she began to process all the events of the day ahead of her. Suddenly she sat up straight. "Tommy!" she said out loud. He hadn't stopped in the house to say goodnight. Did he make it back?

Chapter 10:
The Deep Dive into Coal Mines

"You look like you are going to a barn brawl," Benita said at breakfast. She popped a bite of pomegranate pancake in her mouth and said, "I'll get my gun."

"You don't have a gun, 'Nita," Adele responded.

"You sure about that?"

"Not your business, Miss Benita," Elijah said. He poured Adele another cup of coffee. "Miss Tamasin be registerin' you girls today for fall classes."

"Take the others," Benita argued. "I know trouble when I see it."

Collette wrapped her arms around Adele. "Well, I think you look like Mama when she'd go visiting."

Adele squeezed Collette's arms. "Thank you, sweet girl. I need a whole lot of beautiful today." She studied Elijah's face when the doorbell rang. He remained stoic.

"Excuse me, ladies." Elijah excused himself from the kitchen, opened the front door, and showed David Henderson into the foyer.

Adele motioned for Tamasin to come close. "Did Mr. Thompson come back last night?"

"Not to the carriage house, ma'am."

"If you see him, please make him some breakfast. Ask him to stay put until I get back."

"Doubt you'll be back before sundown," Tamasin responded. "I'll take heed he don't go hungry if he shows."

Adele wrapped her fingers around the black woman's hand. "Thank you, Tamasin. I don't have a good feeling about today."

"You in good hands, ma'am. I'll keep the young'uns safe," Tamasin said as Adele stepped into the parlor.

"Good morning, Miss Dawson," David greeted her. "Ready for the day, I see." Official, Adele noted. Focused on her pedigree.

When she had asked Elijah what Kettie would have worn he convinced her to wear a mid-calf leather skirt, a brown suede vest, black boots, and black leather gloves. For the end of summer, she thought he had overdone her wardrobe, but Elijah had been Quillan's and Kettie's butler before managing the household. Adele picked up the loaded Winchester, just as she and Elijah had planned, and carried it barrel down to the car. Winds picked up enough to bring a fresh chill in the air.

"Keep it low and safe, Miss Adele. Jus like that."

Harold Hamburg opened the back door of a Ford slant-back sedan, brown with shiny black fenders. She stepped inside, sat on the beige leather, and raised her feet onto a footrest. Today, she was running with a band of Kettie's handpicked lawyers.

"Morning, ma'am," Harold said. He was clean-shaven, smelled of big city cologne, and wore a brown leather jacket. Her mother, Selma, had depended on Harold to negotiate her Besame Cosmetics contract.

Once they got through today's meeting, she would ask Harold to explain what was left of that agreement and why he was still on a retainer. The task of managing the Dawson estate seemed to grow each day. Adele was continually uncovering complex secrets about the Dawson family. It was enough to make her wonder why such a majestic home and complicated family had been handed down to her. Heaven with a bit of salty tears.

"Mind if I put this on the other seat?" Harold asked, gently taking the shotgun from her. "New round of bloodshed last night, Miss Dawson. I told David this was no place to bring a young lady. Sons a bitch overtook the outbuildings two nights ago. Picked off our mine guards and then tossed debris on the railroad."

"Governor Kump pissed all to hell. Flamed up by the suffering of our mine guards," David Henderson added. "Unions pick and choose where damage might do the most harm. Never did hurt our boys up near Welsh, but they sure did lay out the men here at Buckeye Tipple." He leaned back in his seat. "Anytime the Norfolk and Western VP says a blast rocked him in his bed, you can be sure the military be stepping in," he added, then closed the sedan's back door.

On the way up Highway 52 to the tipple, Harold and David coached her on the status of the disaster and the chemistry that made mines explosive.

Million years of sunshine has baked plants into peat, then into coal. *Buried sunshine, she remembered her father calling it.* Sometimes methane gas gets trapped as a byproduct of that millennial oven. Left alone and packed into the side of a mountain, methane is harmless. But when struck with an ax, ribs of coal release the gas. Something like a lit cigarette or ax spark ignites it. But good ventilation keeps the sparks from touching. And we blow limestone into the walls to keep the methane moving up and out of the mine. Geologists learned that powdering the sidewalls keeps methane below its one percent flashpoint, but when someone turns off the ventilation, oxygen and carbon dioxide create pressure so high that a match will force the air ahead of the combustion zone to compress and create a shock wave. Boom.

"That's what we think happened here."

"The fire boss's biggest job is to keep the fans running up and down the mine shaft," Howard explained. "Just mad as hell that we still don't know if it was a ventilation switch or an act of arson. But don't you worry, we've got the best engineers in the state investigating the site."

David added, "Hopefully we find our men and control the site before anything else happens here."

"No retaliation, though, until we get an official report," Howard went on. "God help the men who did this if they are found alive."

"Hell to pay," David added. "Unions have tried to bust our family-owned mines for years. Your granddaddy and Mr. Ivan Mills made Buckeye as safe as possible without any unions forcing our hand."

"That's right, Miss Dawson," Harold added. "By the book. All of it. We don't hire children to serve as breakers like they do up Pennsylvania way. No youngsters with limbs missing in these parts, at least not from slate slicing off a leg."

"What's a breaker?" Adele asked.

"Young boy, ma'am. He perches over a coal chute and picks slate from coal, like you did for a month before Miss Kettie died, except your brief apprenticeship was under very controlled circumstances. Sometimes those young'uns, though, get ahead of themselves. Conveyor belt moving too fast can chop off the boy's arm or leg. Spot a breaker boy in Pennsylvania in no time. He's smokin' a cigarette with his left hand. Right arm gone."

"Steel manufacturers pay top dollar for clean coal," David added. "Too many impurities from slate, and we lose a contract to a union shop in Pennsylvania."

"Even if it costs a boy his life?" Adele asked. She thought about the perils of living on the farm near corn conveyors. But compared to the machinery that moved coal up into the tipple, then down onto empty railroad coal cars, her mines posed a more dangerous threat trying to keep up with the country's demand for fossil fuel.

"Union's been a good thing in Pennsylvania," David offered.

"Sure, if you're a section foreman or mine foreman," Harold

countered. "Treated like vermin if not. Forced to purchase overpriced food from the company store. Quillan and Miss Kettie's family moved across the state line right after hiring Welsh immigrants. They'd take a trip up to Ellis Island to find the best. Fed them, give them a home and furnishings. Clothed and schooled the children. In return, the Welsh miners taught us how England got to be the world leader in coal. And we listened. Sometimes the hard way, but we listened."

David guffawed as if he could one-up a Quillan Dawson story. "Geez, that first ship filled with immigrants. Damn near lost Quillan. I remember my old man bailing Quillan out of jail when the train stopped in Walton. Met by blackjacks, Winchesters, and revolvers. Miss Kettie was a young bride then. Year older than you, Adele. Same bright eyes, though," David added.

"Mighty grateful to him, though." David continued. "Mr. Quillan sent me to law school. My dad died in the Great War under Quillan Dawson's command. Took shrapnel in his lungs. Your granddaddy hoisted my daddy under his arm like a bad boy up the ridge. Shame, though, all that effort. My daddy died in the field hospital, but not before your grandfather promised to send me to school. Dawsons never abandon family. It's why we're here with you."

The soldier's uniform in her grandmother's attic, Adele thought. It helped explain why her grandfather had built a military shrine. The image of the locked cabinet in the attic pinged her nerves.

She loved to hear their banter. The stories they told about her grandparents, the grueling interview processes Kettie and Quillan subjected them to, and the gift of sharp minds they exchanged with each other. Would she ever be equal to any of them?

For the next fifteen minutes, she sought the peaceful beauty of West Virginia. The Ford continued to climb a steep road, gaining higher ground as the engine's torque forced the wheels to keep moving. Harold steered into the mountains as if he'd navigated the curves and sheer drops many times. A river running beside the road slowed to a ripple over stones and fallen trees. Its banks showed layers of limestone where mighty waters from melting snow carved grooves into the banks. Unlike the Mississippi that devoured homesteads and drowned livestock, these rivers carved steppingstones for mountain climbers and snow skiers. Trees, refusing to bend into the mountain, prevailed against the slope. For a short while, a cardinal followed them, hopping through rose-colored rhododendrons until Adele recognized the gift of the bird's presence.

The noise of the V8 engine lulled her intimate conversation to a whisper. "Please be at my side, Noona," she beckoned, not intending anyone but Kettie's spirit to hear. "You keep throwing me into situations that I don't know if I can handle. You and Pops built this mine from nothing. What if I'm not bully enough to stand up to gutsy miners?"

She waited for Noona to answer. The engine groaned, climbing the last hill before Harold steered the car down the other side of the mountain.

"About five more minutes, Miss Dawson," David said. "You don't need to know all the mechanics of coal mining just yet. But you should know the basics."

"Okay, I'm ready when you are."

"Southern West Virginia has three types of mines. Drift mine is like a perpendicular road, maybe 20 feet below ground. You can drive right into it like a road tunnel. Lots of rooms between pillars where coal has been dug out decades before we got here.

"Cheapest way to mine," Harold added, "And way overdone."

"Then there's the slope mine. It slopes down into ravines, plateaus for a while, then starts to pitch down again."

"Buckeye Tipple is more of a slope mine," Harold said.

"The shaft mine," David went on, "is more like what you'll find in

Pennsylvania. Straight down, like a well."

Harold slowed the car. "Engineers believe our men may have run partway up a slope. Now they are barricaded on one of those plateaus. These were created as part of the mine's escape route in the event of an accident. Our men trained for incidents like this. For some reason, the escape tunnel was blocked, making this look like the blast was intentional."

"State Department of Mining engineers brought in several auger diggers to do some damn-fast shaft mining," David added, "straight down into where engineers believe there's a bell-shaped room."

As they rounded a bend, Adele saw the tipple, an enormous double-decker wooden bridge with trellises crisscrossed in a maze, held together with beams and steel anchors. It stood like a charred war memorial. Wooden minecarts precariously braked on the rails, some already tipped over to release coal into one of four conveyor belts. Each conveyer spilled a different size of coal: run of the mine, lump, egg, nut, slack into a rail car.

Adele was grateful to Harold and David for their quick courses in mining operations. Her grandmother's instincts would have to kick in now so she could be part of the solution.

"Why is this called a tipple?" she asked.

"As mine cars enter the upper level, its contents are dumped through a chute leading to a railroad hopper car running below. By hand, they tip the coal cars. Tipple," Harold explained.

Adele followed his fingers as he pointed out the engineering to her. To her, the tipple seemed to be in mourning, asking forgiveness for intruding its monstrosity over the river below. Running alongside the riverbank, tracks and half-full rail cars sat frozen in time, abandoned in the middle of a coal dump waiting for anyone to fill their bellies. The train seemed antsy to get back to business, annoyed, almost frustrated that it was left to languish.

"How many are missing?" Adele asked.

"Twenty-one unaccounted for, ma'am," David answered. "Nine were able to make it up into the drift mine. Bloodied, a few broken bones, but alive. Three men carried out on carts were so severely burned they didn't make it." He exchanged a disheartening glance with Harold.

"What does that look mean?"

"It means twenty-four families will be looking to sue the mine for killing the breadwinner. And that could run into the hundreds of thousands of dollars," Harold answered.

"But the twenty-one missing aren't dead yet. Right?"

Harold inched the Ford within shouting distance of the mine. He and David visually combed the surrounding field, looking for any sign of trouble. Adele saw a gigantic pile of large rocks in front of the mine's entrance, its distorted mouth cockeyed by stones looking more like broken teeth.

"That's the entrance to the drift mine?" Adele asked.

"That's the main portal. Coal seams run in several directions from here. The blast rocked several of the pillars. It will be easier to repair than the damage down in the slope," David answered. He motioned for Harold to drive on.

About a quarter of a mile away from the portal, a flurry of engineers stood around pickup trucks bearing the US Bureau of Mine's logo. Investigators gathered samples of rocks and debris while the mine foreman directed workers where to drop augers. A reciprocating piston-driver hammer drove a heavy bit into the ground. After it pounded its way into the earth, the workers pulled the borings up, reached in to pull away stones and loose rocks, and then exchanged the hammer with drills.

Dogs sniffed around the pile of rocks as they were brought up, noses so low to the ground, that they could fall between stones if they weren't so focused on a scent.

"Do we have enough workers to help?"

"Ma'am, every man, woman, and able body young boy is digging. Trying not to spark a new blast. We need the heavy equipment, but we don't want to cut off an arm or leg until we know what's buried."

"And how will you know if they are alive?" Adele asked.

"Cadaver dogs. Your grandfather, Quillan, brought a team of dogs, Leithunds, back from the war after seeing how the Germans located their missing soldiers. We've used hound dogs for years, but these Leithunds bring additional experience. The Mingo County magistrate won't ask for them. But Mercer County's Commissioner ordered those tracking dogs right after the explosion. They can smell up to twenty feet away."

"Do the dogs know they might get blown up?"

"It's a game for them. They are rewarded if they keep sniffing," David said, "A well-trained hound comes to a stand-still if he smells a wounded animal. Or man. And that's what our commissioner is banking on. Hounds speak the language of odors. You and I can't even imagine the landscapes they see colored with a man's scent."

Adele could almost hear her grandmother whisper back. *That, my dear granddaughter, is why I gave you my lawyers. To prepare you, as they have from the day you got here.*

"Your grandfather was a visionary, Adele," Harold Hamburg added. Neither lawyer made any effort to get out of the car. "You cannot imagine how many explosions Quillan lived through before he was drafted to be a soldier. Vowed he'd never lose another man to a blast, so he sneaked this breed of dogs onto a cargo plane on his way back from German.."

"Canaries, mules, and sleuthhounds," Adele mumbled. "One dies warning of low oxygen, another packs coal, and dogs search for the living. I never thought animals would be used in coal mining."

"We don't use canaries anymore," Harold said, somewhat ruffled.

"Miss Dawson, this is no place for a soft heart," David said. "Just listen and watch. You'll learn more about engineering than Miss Kettie. Workers don't want to stop digging. It's their buddies down there. They will test you."

"How do you know which workers are ours?"

"That's easy. Ours are working," David said. "Union bosses undercutting our business don't show after an explosion. They shoot from trees, not to harm anyone, just take out machinery. But if they are down below, our guys have already beat the shit out of them. My apologies, ma'am. I do hate seeing them infiltrating our workers this way."

"Is there a chance we might get picked off?" Adele asked.

"Our snipers will find them. Wasn't that long ago every mine owner hired guards after the Hatfields and McCoys tore up Mingo County. Bloody business is hard to forget."

"After we rescue the miners, I plan to rebuild," Adele stated. "I don't want to lose workers to another mine operation that's hiring."

"That's why you are here, ma'am. Both sides will be looking for your soft spot. See if they can take over a mine in trouble. Our boys know a Dawson when they see one." David turned and looked at her. "Until things settle down, let us do the talking."

Chapter 11:
Standoff at Buckeye Tipple

Cautiously, David opened the front door to the car, stepped out, and stood with his back against the Ford's front wheel. Adele stretched, alert and watching. Nothing like making a first impression with coal blasts and dead men. Let the attorneys do the talking, she reminded herself. Not her specialty yet. Taking care of sisters. Minding a dying grandmother. More her style. *Listen to your attorneys;* she heard the cardinals sing. *And focus!* Noona seemed to scold.

What kind of a leader sits in the back seat? She coached herself. She opened the back door and started to climb out.

"Not yet. On my order," David scolded. He leaned against her car door and looked around, then reached behind his back to relatch the Ford's door, shutting her back inside like a petulant schoolgirl.

Locked back inside the Ford, she looked out the window, trying to identify where a sniper might be hiding.

"Miners are superstitious," Harold said. "Keep your head straight, ma'am. Keep 'em guessing. David and I know you are here to help." He gave her a comforting smile in the rearview mirror. "When miners get spooked, they go where there's no light, except the light clipped to their helmet. Some douse themselves with water before entering a mine. Another will clap his helmet three times to get rid of evil spirits, then rub his butt before entering a mine. I saw one man touch his fingers one at a time to his heart as if counting how many children he has to feed."

While he spoke to her, Harold watched David's every move. "He knows what he's doing, Miss Dawson. David is smooth as butter, which is why Miss Kettie hired him. Softened her rough spots."

When something moved in the back of the cleared field, Harold reached inside his vest. Stealthily, he slipped a pistol down to his lap. Adele saw the movement too because it was slippery like Pa. She quickly dismissed that thought. According to Jackson, Pa was savagely beaten and, on a train, back to St. Louis. "Move that shotgun very slowly onto your lap, ma'am. Anyone with binoculars will know you're one of us. That's it. Easy now. Keep your back straight. You got your gloves on?"

"Yes, sir."

David continued taking steady steps, chatting confidently, walking toward the auger. Like the metal doughboy hats in Noona's closet, men wearing black painted hard hats kneeled next to the ground. One of them waved for quiet, then lifted a stethoscope to his ears.

"Everitt, our chief engineer, is listening for any sign of life," Harold explained softly. "We can't be hammering too hard. Firedamp can fill an air pocket down there, choke out precious oxygen. When the auger brings up a stone, it also brings up human odors. Good for the dogs."

Adele leaned closer to the window as a man tapped a hammer against a pipe, then put the stethoscope down near the ground. "We got a live one!" he shouted back.

Adele cheered, hopeful that whoever was down there knew someone topside was coming to get them. "Slow down, Miss Dawson, slow," Harold said.

Men with pickaxes and shovels ran like warriors into battle to help Everitt as he pointed where to strike. One laborer gave the sign of the cross, pulled his ear three times, then turned the auger drill down into the earth.

David stopped walking as machinery burrowed further into the ground. Down twenty or so feet, then they would pull the auger and release large buckets of stone. Men jumped to remove gravel and grit when the auger came up, then hand sharpened the blades to prevent the stone from falling below. Each dig down produced darker rock until they finally hit a coal seam. After a painfully long hour, David opened his coat and put his hands in his pockets.

Harold said, "That's our sign. I'll come around to get you. Come only as far as I say. Walk like you're hunting a deer. No heavy footsteps. Keep the Winchester at your side but pointed down. You're here to protect, not harm."

Together, they walked toward the dig site as men with rock hammers and machinery slung at the ground, desperate to get to the men buried alive. Adele felt her lungs tighten until her breath was so shallow, that she had to stretch to fill her lungs with air.

"You're doing fine, ma'am. Stand by me." Harold put his hand under her elbow, escorting her gently but slowly until he stopped and let her take a few steps forward alone, Winchester at her side, just as Elijah had instructed.

A group of men stopped hefting rocks. "What's that broad doing here?" someone shouted. "Henderson, we got enough trouble. Get that dame out of here!"

Adele almost turned to look to Harold for help. Instead, she forced her eyes to focus on the weary workers. If they inflicted any harm her way, she wanted it to be quick. "I'm here to help, gentlemen."

"Bad karma. Get the hell out of here."

Adele set the Winchester butt down at her side. She stretched the barrel at an angle to show she was at ease with her shotgun. "My name is Adele Dawson," she shouted. "I'm Kettie Dawson's granddaughter."

For a while, it was threateningly quiet at Buckeye Tipple. Even the clouds stopped moving as if the lord of bad luck would shatter the sky.

Miners stood with axes at their side. One raised his ax across his arm. Another put a hand on the man's arm, warning him to lower his weapon.

"You're not from here, are you?" one man shouted.

David raised his hands in the air like a choir director prepping schoolboys when to open their lips. "She's a Dawson. Back home where she belongs now."

"You got no right bringing her this close!" a man shouted.

"I do," David responded, "and I will."

Harold stepped close to Adele. "Mine won't last if the last of the Dawson family is taken down. Stay close now."

Adele stood with her gun at her side. "Brave men, that's what I see here. I know you're working overtime to save your buddies. I'm worried about them, too. Here to help."

"This bloody sight you see right here," one man yelled at her, "is just the beginning if you don't hike it outa here." His face was black and gritty. Several men picked up ax handles and began moving in toward her. Harold reached for her arm and tried to lead her to the car.

"You need food and water, I see." She did not move. But she also did not cup her hands to let her voice be heard.

"Who the hell are you again?"

"I'm the one who signs your checks." Adele tightened her fist around the barrel of her shotgun and brought it closer. "And I'm the one who's going to set up a camp right over there in this field. Make sure you have food every day. Take care of your families. Get your children ready for school this fall. We will rebuild this mine."

"How you gonna do that? Wave your fairy godmother's Winchester? Set up a shantytown?"

She was nervous as Pa's mules used to be at the farm, stomping the ground, waiting for the river to rise. Workers stopped digging, waiting for her to leave; she needed them back shuttling stones. So did the buried miners. The auger drill started up again as a machine operator turned away from her.

"Truth is, it's up to you whether it's a hovel or a camp. But I do know how to call the United States Army and order up about one hundred tents, all stored in a warehouse up Fort Stewart way."

She stared hard at the men, not once looking to David for affirmation.

"And I'd guess you'd need some cots for sleeping. Bring your children up here to live out the summer, 'cause it damn sure looks like this mine is going to need a rebuild." She felt the slightest release of tension from the miners.

"Ma'am, that's not possible," Harold said, low enough so that only she would hear.

"I call that bull!" a woman's voice rang out behind her.

Adele saw the shadow of the woman carrying what looked like a long-barrel rifle out in front. Quickly Adele racked her gun. What woman would be at the tipple this time of day? Somehow, she had the confidence to know Harold and David and whoever was up in the trees would protect her if she was in danger.

"You going to shoot me or what?" she heard the woman say.

Adele turned sideways to acknowledge the voice and then pointed the barrel of her gun at the ground. "Elizabeth Radford?"

"Heard you were up here," Mrs. Radford said. "Women don't live to talk about a day like this. Thought I'd see if you needed help."

"This is family business. Go back to your dress shop."

"Dress shop! Hell, half the men here are indebted for the clothes their women wear."

Adele was not going to get into an argument in the presence of an exploded mineshaft. Her stomach knotted as the hardened woman walked toward her, a 12-gauge shotgun in her arm pointed downward.

"Tell you what, boys," Mrs. Radford said. "If she's going to build a village for us, how about we all give her a hand?"

"Right after we bring up the trapped miners," Adele answered.

Elizabeth waved her shotgun in the air. "You ten over there, get back to digging. I hear my nephew calling up for help. Rest of you, open the mouth of that blown-up cave. Bound to be at least three or four more men who tried running out."

Adele thought for a moment. Elizabeth Radford carried a hell of a lot of authority. Was this the same woman who spat at the sound of Selma Beck's name? Was Adele being laughed at, challenged, or was Elizabeth genuinely trying to help? Another worker left ranks and came right up to Adele.

"Don't let her age fool you," he said over his shoulders, talking the miners. Close up; he leaned in to kiss her cheek. Adele pulled away until she saw Tommy's face through the smeared black coal dirt, his dark brown eyes smiling at her. He wrapped his arms around her waist and hugged her, leaving black soot stains on her jacket and blouse.

"Stop this," Adele scolded. "I'm trying to be tough."

"I can see that!" Tommy answered and winked at her. He turned back and waved to the men. "She raised six children by herself before she turned eighteen. And her grant to the American Friends Committee netted enough money to start the first cooperative in New Madrid County. If anyone can build a town, it's that woman. Adele Christina Dawson."

Tommy should be packing for college, Adele thought. Instead, he was dirty, coal dust on his clothes, his face dotted with dried blood.

"What are you doing out here?" she asked.

He raised his arms, questioning her as if she should know the answer. "I'm breaking coal. Getting banged up."

Not one man moved. Silence felt thick and black until Tommy kissed her cheek again.

"I absolutely adore you," she said, "dirty face and all."

"You gonna pay these guys overtime?" Tommy raised his volume as he addressed the crowd of men.

"Yes, I'm going to pay them overtime."

As Tommy lifted an ax back over his shoulder, he mouthed back, "I love you more," then stepped toward the mine where he'd been working through the night.

Adele turned to face Elizabeth. "And why are you here?"

Elizabeth took a deep breath. "Miss Dawson, I haven't been kind to you. And for that, I'm sorry. If you put up with my big mouth, I'd like to see if we could start over. My baby sis's boy is in that mine. Just a seventeen-year-old kid. Probably cold and hungry. His mama needs him after his daddy took up with another woman up Mingo way." She snickered as if there was a joke in there somewhere.

Adele remained stoic, slightly uphill from Elizabeth. With the sun just over her back, she could see Elizabeth squint from the piercing rays.

"I brought the boys some lunch," Elizabeth finally said. "But when I saw you standing there like that, I had to see if you looked like your mother."

"Why?"

Elizabeth looked at her, puzzled. "You don't know, do you?"

"I know there's something between you and my mama and that it happened before I was born. Thirty years later, and you still haven't made peace with it."

"Look, little woman. We've got us a mining disaster. My nephew's life is more important right now. Let's you and I talk later about Besame. Right now, we've got a camp to set up."

Besame? So that was it. Adele held that thought close to her chest, knowing she had to bring the subject up again if she was ever going to understand her mother's marriage to August Stupid Beck.

***

David, Harold, and Adele pulled up empty wooden barrels and sat with the US Bureau of Mines investigators for nearly two hours as the augers continued drilling.

"Sheriff Cody's already been here," Everitt, the chief engineer said. "Says he needs more hard details. Whatever happened inside was sloppy work. Doubt it was union troublers, though. This is gangster work, probably from up Wheeling way. So, the sheriff wants the evidence bags once we get our men out of the mine, fed, and bandaged up. So does the governor, by God, and the US Bureau of Mine engineers."

Adele listened intently. "How long until we can start rebuilding?"

"Ten days. Minimum. Or until we find conclusive evidence. If it's a crime scene, another forty-five days to complete the investigation. Right now, we're on a ticking bomb to find breathing bodies. So, all hands have to beat the firedamp before any more carbon monoxide gets in there."

"What do you need from us?"

"Temporary housing, ma'am," Everett said. "Blankets, first aid, hot meals."

"Lawyers will need access to employment records," David Henderson added.

Everitt nodded. "You're sixth down the line, right now. We're still in search and rescue."

As they were talking, a banged-up Studebaker pulled up to the mine, and a woman hopped out of the car. She tossed a tripod over her shoulder and carried a camera bag large enough to hold several lenses. "Zeiss" camera brand was embroidered on the side of the bag.

"Rebecca Parsons, *Bluefield Daily Telegraph*, sir," the reporter introduced herself to David Henderson first, then to Harold. "Heard there was a riot going down here. Unions against Scabs. Maybe arson. Thought I'd catch the story before it broke in the *Charleston Gazette*."

136

"Pleasure to meet you for sure," David answered. "But if you want a story, you'll need to ask for the mine owner, Adele Christina Dawson."

"A woman, huh?" the reporter responded, turning toward Adele. "Where is the old lady?"

"Right here," David said.

Rebecca Parsons looked at Elizabeth. Elizabeth pointed to Adele. "You? What's a young woman like you doing owning a coal mine?" Rebecca asked.

Adele accepted the reporter's hand. "What's a young woman like you doing reporting an explosion?" Adele looked into Rebecca's eyes, hoping to find the source of her curiosity.

"Do you think the Bureau of Mines should investigate this incident even if the mine owner opposes it?" Rebecca asked. She was holding a small spiral reporter's notebook, looking at the notebook rather than at Adele.

"Why would we oppose? We need all the help we can get."

Before Adele could say another word, David Henderson stepped between her and the reporter. "We're not taking any questions," he said. "Getting those men free is our only area of focus."

"But if an inspector had been allowed inside, don't you think he would have found the real source of the explosion? Like poor ventilation? Maybe a buildup of rock dust?"

"Miss Parsons," David responded, "we're not taking any questions right now."

Rebecca stepped in front of Adele. "Some folks up Bluefield way think it wasn't an accident. That, someone, turned off the ventilator fan. Maybe used a stick or two of dynamite to set it off."

David wrapped his arm around Adele's waist and escorted her away from the reporter. Rebecca picked up her camera bag and followed close behind.

"You know about intentional tort, don't you, Miss Dawson. Or do you think this was just a mysterious explosion so soon after your grandmother's passing?"

Adele turned to the reporter and smiled like her grandmother had taught her, letting Rebecca know she was memorizing the color of her eyeballs. Hazel, a familial blending of Irish and German. "The County Commissioner brought in a team of investigators," Adele said. "Right now, we are carefully extracting survivors. If you need a story, you'll have to wait until the investigation is complete."

"Extracting?" Rebecca raised her camera to her chest and looked down into the lens. "You're not from here, are you?" she asked.

David quickly stepped in front of Adele, but not before Rebecca had snapped several pictures. "That's all for today," David said.

Rebecca nodded and picked up her bag. "I'll just grab a few pictures and then be on my way. Those sniveling dogs make a good human-interest story."

"The hounds are my grandfather's," Adele responded. "Lifesavers, not snivelers. And I am. From here."

Rebecca picked up the camera and focused on the auger driller. "Of course you are," she mumbled.

***

Women from the Ladies Aid Society brought dinner and water up the mountain and bedding for men to sleep in the back of their Model T Runabout trucks.

"Miss Kettie wouldn't have left either," one of the women said to Adele. "Just like her, you are. Serving food and water to the men, making sure they have everything they need. Gonna be a long night. You sure you don't want to go home?"

"I'm staying here until twenty-one men are pulled out. Has anyone called a doctor? They will need treatment after we lift them out."

"Oh my, yes ma'am. Superintendent sends a message, soon as it looks like the first one is coming up and Dr. Luttrell will be on his way."

***

Sunset darkened the dig site, so workers set up gas-burning lights to illuminate the ground. Harold and David tried to convince Adele to go home, and get some rest.

"You'll never get her to budge," Tommy said, stepping out of the bath house. "Go to your families. Delly will be safe with me. I've got blankets in the truck."

David handed Tommy a handgun. "Take this. I don't think you'll need it, but if anyone poses a threat, shoot first. We will be back before sunup."

"Do you think the trapped men know we're coming for them?" Adele asked after watching the same drilling post go down, come up, and go back down again.

"It's part of training. Find a quad with air. Stay put," Tommy answered. He spread blankets over the back of the truck bed and helped her climb in.

He had borrowed Elijah's Chevy truck to come out to the rescue site. It had been Adele's grandfather, Quillan's truck before he gave it to Elijah to run errands. Kettie never learned how to drive. She either walked or Elijah drove her.

"You comfortable?" Tommy asked. The sound of auger drills reminded families that determination would not quit until we rescued all miners. "I can't quiet the drills, but if you can't sleep, we can move inside the truck," he said, climbing up to be at her side. "Just seemed more comfortable for both of us out here."

Adele couldn't rest knowing men were still breathing hundreds of feet below ground in the dark, forcing themselves to stay calm until rescue

139

teams found them. What could she do more efficiently?

"Drillers are working through the night," Tommy told her. "We'll find them."

Adele placed her hand against his cheek, now almost clean except for coal residue around his hairline. She touched the coal dust around his earlobe. "It's been more than two years since we've been in the back seat of a car," Adele said, trying to change the subject and relieve her mind of the victims below ground. "Remember our first barn dance? I was the most out-of-touch girl there."

Tommy pulled the blanket over her shoulder. "I thought you were going to say you were the most innocent girl. I'd have to challenge you on that."

"Did you ever think I'd own a coal mine?"

Tommy shook his head. "I figured you for an economics professor. That or an obstetrician, given all the babies you helped your mama deliver."

"Quite a difference, there, Mr. Thompson." Adele closed her eyes, remembering the gravesites on the hill behind her stepfather's bungalow.

"Sorry, I didn't mean to bring up old wounds," Tommy said. "You've changed so much now that you live in Bramwell. Softer, somehow. Not as ruthless."

"Is that what I was, Tommy?"

"Some people are poor, and they know it. You were poor, but you never knew it."

"Oh," Adele responded. "I knew we had nothing."

"Having nothing and yet possessing all things," Tommy quoted scripture. "You had a sense of yourself that can't be wrapped in a ribbon."

For a while, they were quiet. Adele leaned back into Tommy's stomach, spooning as they did in corn fields when he wasn't allowed to be with a poor girl from the bottomland, and she wasn't holding her breath for twenty-one live men.

He kissed her shoulder. "Since the first night we were together, I wanted to be good enough to be your husband," Tommy said. "But now? I have to leave for college soon."

Adele rolled over to face him. "Now is right here."

She looked up into his face, his firm nose that flared when she told him she was leaving New Madrid, and those lips. Those lips made the hair on her back stand up with anticipation each time he leaned in. His voice had deepened in the months she'd been gone. Or maybe she never listened to the sound of her name when he was quiet and whispery.

"Of all the places to find love, you found me in a poor man's shack."

"I would have found you if you lived in a tent. You're different, womanlier. But Delly's still inside here," he said, touching her chest.

"I never stopped loving you, Tommy. Even when your father —"

Tommy hushed her and cradled her head in his arms. "I," he said, "cannot," he continued, kissing her eyelids, "live," kissing the other eye, "without you." He finished by kissing her lips, then raised his hips to hers. "In the middle of this nightmare, I still want you, Adele."

"Tommy," whispered. "I'm scared."

"I'm here, sweetie, right here." Tommy pulled the blanket over his back and burrowed his face in her neck.

Adele wrapped her arms around him, opening her lips to let his tongue desperately find hers. When it came to diversions, Tommy knew how to calm her.

"Let me hold you until morning," he whispered.

Chapter 12:
Race to Find Survivors

Adele was still wrapped in blankets when sirens sounded the alarm that the auger had cut through to the portal nearly 500 feet below ground. She reached for Tommy, but he was already out of the truck, helping a crew build an A-frame whim gin turned by steam power over the hole's collar.

She felt rested, even though she doubted she or Tommy got much sleep. Outside the mine entrance, she found a water pump and splashed cold water on her face, the best she could do considering she'd been in the same clothes going on three days, then walked to the dig site.

Rescuers hooked several chains to a red cylinder and then hung the one-person elevator to the A-frame. Everitt, the chief engineer, tested its strength to be sure it would hold a man safely caged inside. Finally, Everitt directed workers to crank the pulley, lowering the cylinder into the ground. When the chains buckled, they knew they'd reached the bottom. Several men turned the pulley wheel at the canister's whistle, raising the cage until it crowned above ground.

Truck horns honked. Men shouted and ran to the dig site to help lift the first man out.

Reporter Rebecca Parsons came out of her Studebaker and pointed her camera, ready to be the first to capture the shot.

A woman standing by brought Adele a thermos of hot tea. "All but the waiting now," the woman said.

"Who is it?" another woman cried out, then ran in front of Adele. The woman leaned as close as rescuers would allow seeing whose husband was in the cage. A decade of pain and worry darkened the woman's bloodshot eyes.

"Miss Radford's nephew! Look at that boy," the foreman announced as if he was pulling an infant out of a woman's womb. "Brave as they come. Dirty as hell, but he's alive."

Elizabeth rushed to hug Adele. "He's alive!"

With that, Elizabeth ran to the pit, nearly knocking over one of the investigators. A rescuer opened the cage's door while a nurse placed a black cloth around the young man's eyes to protect him from the blinding sun, then wrapped blankets around him. Dr. Luttrell and two other physicians cradled the young man in their arms, lifting him to the first of several cots in the enclosed tent that would serve as a field clinic. Two nurses set up a triage unit to assist the miners as they came up, stabilizing them before transporting them to Bluefield General Hospital.

Adele felt her chest swell with pride at the team who worked through the night to deliver survivors. One man alive. Twenty to go. If only all would come up in the same or better condition. The mine owned larger five-person elevator cages. But given the emergency, the auger could dig a hole large enough for the older canister. One by painful one, they surfaced.

She ached to be at the young man's side, to ask him a thousand questions. How did he feel? How could this be prevented? Of all the questions she wanted to be answered was the one she dared not ask. The burden of shame was too great to give it up. Who did this?

As soon as Elizabeth's nephew was triaged and brought to the field clinic, rescue teams lowered the cage. Someone below set off the whistle within thirty minutes, and the men wheeled the steel capsule up again. A cloth speckled with dried blood covered the man's face, but he was breathing. His wife whispered, "Rex," and then her voice broke.

The reporter captured her face on camera, but Rex turned away from the lens. David Henderson saw Rex's response. "Stay out of the rescuers' way, ma'am. No photos of our men."

Dr. Luttrell remained in the onsite clinic to evaluate each resurrected miner. Two other doctors rotated positions at the shaft, triaging each man, and applying immediate pressure to wounds. As soon as workers folded each man in a blanket and sheltered his eyes, another physician would ask for a history of where they were most injured. Several had broken arms or legs; nearly all had second-degree burns. One burn was bad enough to expose muscle tissue.

One by one throughout the day, men emerged from the cage. Everitt stopped between loads to grease the pulley system and checked the strength of each heavy chain, then ordered the cage back into the hole.

"Can't we move any faster?" Adele asked.

"Working as fast as we can," Everitt answered. "This old cage can carry one man. No more. Or she'll break into pieces."

Early September heat and humidity wore down sweaty rescuers. Adele and the Ladies Aid Society filled water and coffee jugs to keep workers hydrated. Volunteers from the Presbyterian church tending to the injured brought another day of hot meals. Mid-afternoon, they gathered up a choir of parishioners, beat drums and sang to encourage nurses and workers hoisting and lowering the cage. The circle of families, overpowered with emotion in seeing their loved one, gradually diminished as they escorted retrieved miners to a cot.

Survivors who could stand embraced a rescuer, clapped his back for the swift recovery, but as they made their way back to the nursing station, even the grizzliest of miners would smear a cheek as an unrelenting tear sneaked from his eye. Most miners knew this was part of the adrenalin rush that kept them heading into the mine every day. That is until the rush turned vile.

Remaining wives, mothers, and sisters huddled in the background, waiting for the coveted announcement. Each time one of them stepped out of the group, the circle up on the hill closed the gap, but a growing despair darkened circles under their eyes.

Women looked at each other, then looked away for fear of seeing a luckless truth. Each hoping to be called next, worry carved into their eyes. In other mining camps, a widow had at the most, thirty days to move out, or she and her children were evicted. Kettie stopped that practice when she created a home for widows and children in Bramwell. Adele watched as their eyes closed in prayer. Hands folded, lips murmuring. "Be present, God!" she whispered. "Bring up their man."

A grey-bearded gentleman in dusty overalls stood alone, away from the women. He removed his spectacles and wiped them before dropping to his knees. Adele had just started getting to know the mining families, but her heart ached for this man isolated from the others.

A miner clothed only in his underwear emerged shivering. "The blast must have knocked his clothes off," one of the women said. "God only knows how he stayed alive down there!"

Another woman was called forward. Her husband's body fell limp as he was pulled up "Bart," she gasped. "He has emphysema," she explained as if she needed a reason for why Bart fell limp out of the cage and into the arms of a rescuer. Others stepped beside Bart and helped lift him onto a cot. "Damn, Big Bart. You gotta give up them pecan pies," a miner joked. Everyone understood, but no one laughed.

Dr. Luttrell covered the man's eyes just as he did all the others and wrapped him in a blanket. Five rescuers, along with Dr. Luttrell, carried his body into the triage area. "You're not dead," the woman prayed. Gently, she walked alongside him. "Bart, wake up."

"That's the last of them," a rescuer said. "I count nineteen."

"Twenty counting Bart," Adele heard Tommy say, his face filthy dirty except for the streaks of sweat, or perhaps tears, that created slivers of white lines down his coal black face. "Survivors said he pushed all of them free 'cuz he started hearing voices from another tunnel. Might be he had a heart attack on the way up."

Adele turned to Tommy standing near the rescue capsule. "But there were twenty-one," she said. She looked uphill where the women had gathered to see who might be left. The circle was gone. The bearded man was now on his knees; head bowed in prayer.

She walked toward him and knelt. "Can I help you find someone?" she asked.

The older gentleman looked up through filmy grey eyes. "My grandson is missing."

"He hasn't come up?" she asked.

The old man shook his head.

"Maybe he made it to another air pocket."

"Maybe." The old man raised on one knee and pressed his hand against a tree to help him stand. As he did, his cane slid out of his hand.

Adele spun around to find Tommy. "Someone had to help Bart get in. There's got to be one more person down there."

Tommy rushed back toward the rescuers. "Someone is still down there. Find him."

"Don't get your hopes up. Bart was the last one."

"That's not possible," Tommy argued. He knelt over the dig's opening and yelled, "Hey down there!" Tommy called. "Anybody?"

Rescuers leaned close to the ground, listening. Finally, they heard a faint knock. The dogs went wild with the scent of another survivor.

"We're sending the capsule down. Now!"

Tommy exchanged glances with Adele. "You have no idea how emotional these miners get when we bring a man up," he said. "This has to be so painful for them."

Elizabeth Radford squatted next to Adele and the old man. "Sounds can be disorienting, even when it's directly overhead. Who the hell did we leave behind?"

"This gentleman's grandson. His granddad's pretty frail."

"What's your grandson's name?" Elizabeth asked.

"His mama calls him J." The old man struggled to reach his cane so he could stand. "His mama and girlfriend are working the clinic. Asked if I'd come up here and pray on him a bit."

Adele stepped directly over to the old man, picked up his cane, and helped him to his feet. Elizabeth interrupted. "Wait, is your grandson Jackson Conor?"

"That's him. His mama tried to stop him from coming up here. The boy worked in the mine as a young lad. Said he knew where most of the secondary safety pockets might be."

"He's Cora's boyfriend!" Elizabeth shouted. She turned to Adele. "Jackson is Cora's boyfriend," she repeated. "If you hadn't struck up a conversation with his granddaddy, we might have left Jackson down there. Oh, my God, Adele. My daughter is forever indebted to you."

Rescuers turned the cranks and pulled the cage back up to the surface. It was empty. One man opened the cage door and looked inside to ensure the miner hadn't slipped through the bottom. They pulled the cage away from the pit and dropped to their bellies as if they could see nearly 500 feet underground.

A rescuer cupped his mouth. "You have to climb in!" he shouted, then sent the cage back down. Down to the bottom of the pit until the chains relaxed. They waited for the bounce, the siren, any indication that a man had climbed inside. Once more, the pulleys brought up an empty cylinder.

"Jackson's gotta be injured," Everitt moaned.

"What's he doing down there?" Adele asked.

Everitt shook his head. "He must have known the location of the secondary transports. Damn, I wish he would have coordinated his entrance with me."

"I'm going down there," Tommy said. "There's no reason Jackson should be injured."

"No, you're not. That's my job. I'm going down."

"Only room for one man," Everitt warned. "No place for a woman, ma'am."

"So I've heard; more than once in the last four months. It's my mine and my responsibility. Put that oxygen mask on me. Give me another one for Jackson."

Everitt reached for Adele's shoulder. "Listen to me. We don't have enough time to bring in another cage, and this one has seen its day. So, you stay put until we come back for you. Don't make any noble efforts to find another way out."

"Adele!" Tommy scolded. "You're not strong enough to lift a man into the cage."

"Got it," Adele said and closed the lock inside. She tightened the breathing mask and pointed downward for engineers to lower her into the pit.

"Not to worry," Everitt said. "I will bring her back."

She watched Tommy shake his head before she disappeared down into the hole.

She held the gas lamp against the cage walls as it descended, keeping her breathing steady. The straight tunnel down had been carefully measured to prevent the cage from banging against the walls. The few times it scraped the side, she could feel coal dust land on her hair and onto her face. She would be sure Everitt and his rotary digging team received bonuses for creating this tunnel so quickly after the explosion.

When the cage landed, she pressed the release latch and stepped down onto the ground.

"Whose executive decision was this?" she heard a man moan.

Jackson half crawled toward her.

"You're hurt."

"Seems a bit impulsive, doesn't it, coming down here." Jackson studied her, top to bottom. "Obviously, you are dressed for coal mining. Leather skirt and all. Too bad your shirt's got coal all over it."

"Show me your arm."

"How about you tear a piece of that shirt. Wrap it around my leg. That's where the bastard stabbed me."

"Who?"

"So sheltered and forgiving," Jackson said. "August Beck."

"He's down here?"

"Not anymore. He and two damn Wheeling buddies tumbled up those rocks after he and I got into it."

"What made you think he'd be down here?"

"You can see that I'm bleeding, right?" Jackson responded.

"How did you get in here, Jackson?" Adele frowned at the amount of blood on the floor. She moved the lantern closer to his body.

"Followed the coal transporters, secondary roads." Jackson tightened the grip on his arm. "Did you bring a tourniquet?"

Adele removed her vest, then unbuttoned her blouse. She remembered Tommy removing it last night as they spent the night in the truck together. Completely different reason today. If she came back with her shirt torn, what would he say?

She ripped off both sleeves, tied them into a knot when it seemed one sleeve wasn't enough to wrap around Jackson's leg. She leaned over his wound, tied the sleeves into a knot, and finally put enough pressure on his stab wound to stop the bleeding. When she looked up at him, he seemed to be enjoying an up-close look at her camisole rather than dealing with his pain.

"What was August doing down here?" Adele asked.

"Dynamite expert, that man. I'd say he's behind the blast. Damaged soul that one."

Adele guffawed. "Don't I know?" She had fifteen years of struggles living with him; four of them without a mama to soothe his rough edges. "But why is he here?"

"He wants you back," Jackson answered. "Said so. After you and your sisters left the church. It was just David and me with him. That man can create diversions." Jackson moved his leg and tried to hobble on one leg. Adele wrapped her arm around his waist to help him stand.

When he regained his balance, he looked down and wiped coal from her nose. "A little too much powder there, my sweet. You might want to put your vest back on. Boyfriends don't do well when they see their girls undressed in front of another man."

"You okay?" she heard Tommy shout down.

"We're coming up shortly," Adele answered, not sure if anyone could hear.

She finished buttoning the vest over her camisole. "He's not going to like this," she mumbled.

"I've been a total gentleman," Jackson answered. "Damnit."

"Okay, let's get you into the cage," Adele said, smiling.

She helped him hobble inside, securely fitted his oxygen mask, then pushed him against the edge before pressing the button to have the cage lifted. With that, she locked him inside. "I'll see you when I get up."

Jackson stood. "Wait, I'm not leaving you down here alone."

She raised her oxygen mask to let him know she wouldn't be without fresh air. "I've got a lamp. An hour max, and I'll be topside," she answered. As the cage began to lift, she added, "Be sure Everitt sends it back down for me."

Once the cage rose, there was nothing more that she could do but wait for it to return. Her light dimmed then brightened again, letting her know it was getting low on oil. Why August Beck? Why? It's not just about me leaving you. Do you hate me this much that you would spook the miners into thinking I'm not capable of running a coal mine? Of course, you're not, she answered herself. But she could learn from those who learned from her grandparents. She looked up into the pinhole of light, then quickly stepped away when she heard the mountain groan. "Hurry up," she whispered, then tightened the oxygen mask around her face once more.

Less than 30 minutes later, the cage was back on the bottom, along with a note. "Don't ever do that again. I love you. Tommy." She tucked the note inside her camisole, smiled, and then rang the bell to be raised from this hell hole.

She was pondering the engineering wonder of drilling a hole as fast as they did when she heard pings that sounded like gun fire raining down on her. Pieces of chain links rattled against the walls until smoking metal chunks landed at her feet inside the cage. She stomped on them to be sure they didn't start a fire.

"Hang on, Delly," she heard Tommy yell down at her. "We're taking gunfire."

She looked up at the small hole at the top of this well. "From who?"

"Not sure yet." She could hear Tommy, but when she looked up, all she could see was the top of the canister. As the next shot rang out, one of the three chains helping to lift the cage crashed against the top. She saw it fall several hundred feet until it landed almost soundlessly on the mine floor.

"Damnit! They're shooting at the cage," she heard Tommy cry. "Take cover."

"Take cover?" she repeated. "In a standing-room-only cylinder?" She pressed her hands against the edge, knowing it wouldn't stop the cage from falling, but it might keep from breaking all her bones.

"I can't hold this much longer," she heard Everitt shout.

"Hey, we've got a woman down there!" she heard Tommy shout. "Stop shooting!"

She would crash to the bottom. Of that, she was sure. The canister slipped sideways, creating sparks as the bottom scraped against the wall. The pit walls were too narrow to let her climb out. Sparks in a cave, are precisely what rescuers tried to avoid.

"Get down," she heard the engineer again, just as another ping clipped the second of three chains holding her midway up the well, one remaining chain. If she got out of this, she would damn well be sure her mines had better recovery tools. And she would hug the hell out of Everitt.

"Knock it off, you bastard," she heard Elizabeth cry out.

Adele saw nothing but coal-black walls. The canister slipped and scraped again against the wall. She didn't know if she was nearly topside or if the shooting had caused her to lose ground. "Keep my sisters safe, dear Lord. If it's my time, let them find peace in Noona's house." She reached outside the cylinder's iron walls to see if she could stop herself from slipping. Her hand was black when she brought it back.

Her lamp went dark, either from lack of oxygen or lack of fuel. Was there anyone still alive topside? Why would anyone shoot at a rescue operation unless they had reprehensible intentions? No sounds, no movement. She reached to the top of the canister to see if there might be something she could grab. Nothing. She tried to slump down into the cage, but it was so tight, her knees got stuck. She pressed down on her ankles and slowly righted herself. In the process, her skirt caught on a screw. She reached down to release the fabric when the cage bumped loose, suddenly racing to the bottom of the well. She braced for disaster, a landing that would break the cage into pieces and shatter her bones.

She felt the squeal of a pulley slow the descent, then finally, it stopped. Her knees buckled with the sudden halt. In the dark, she couldn't tell how far she had fallen. She felt a bit queasy, knowing the oxygen was running run low.

"Hang on, Delly," Tommy shouted. "We secured the chain. We're going to pull you out."

Adele thought she might never love any man more than she did right now. Thank goodness she'd left Tommy above ground. He would be bullish about getting her free from this pit. Tommy. Yes, Tommy.

***

Like a bad omen, the reporter stepped right up to the wooden braced A-frame from which the canister now dangled. As Tommy and Everitt finally pulled the cage above the pit, the reporter aimed her camera at Adele.

"This will be so good," the reporter jeered under her breath. She stared at Adele's sooty camisole and the leather skirt that had torn after the last jolt. "What the heck did Mr. Conor do to you down there?" the reporter asked.

"For God's sake, get down," Everitt shouted at the reporter. He pressed his hand against her head when another round of shots hit the ground around them. Adele saw the bullet ricochet against the pulley's wheel and dent it.

"Goddamn, you sons a bitches," Elizabeth said. She picked up her 16-gauge and took several leaps toward a band of trees at the northern edge of the field. Whatever had happened while Adele was below ground, it was enough to enrage Elizabeth to reload her shotgun. She stopped, squared herself, and pointed. "Last warning," Elizabeth shouted into the woods.

A man's laughter cut its way through the thick afternoon air. "Oh, my god," Adele breathed, recognizing the voice. She stood up and growled. "August Beck, you son of a bitch."

The reporter wrote every word in her notebook.

Workers leaned against trees, sipped water, and spat on the ground. Their gloves turned dark and moist from blood. Blisters made it difficult for them to hold on to anything. She hated that the reporter saw the carnage and wished she could grab her notepad and toss it into the pit.

"You know him, don't you," Rebecca continued. "The attacker."

Tommy put his hands on Rebecca's notebook. "You'll get more of a story if you sit back and observe."

Leaves wiggled in a far-off bend of trees as guards fired shots repeatedly into the forest. Silence. Nothing moved. No one fell to the ground, no squeal from a gunshot.

Then, another shot pinged the pulley wheel from the forest's west side, crimping more links from the splayed chain. The A-frame holding the cage bent sideways as the canister fell into the pit.

In that moment, Adele knew it was her stepfather who sabotaged the mine. But how did he manage such an enormous task? Did he act alone, or what else was in store for her? Convinced this was part of his desperate need to ruin her, Adele's mind considered a floodgate of incendiary ways she could get even with him. She had taken care of him, done all he demanded for fifteen years. And now, he was plucking away at her heritage just when she was starting to understand her birth family.

Killing innocent people had never been part of his mission; he much preferred humiliation, emotional damage, and accidental drownings. She didn't know many miner families yet, but men were devoted to their families, from what she'd seen. They did their best to make a living in coal country.

But this time, people died. That was a new low in the life of her stepfather. She'd had enough. Her back ached from the burden of shame she carried over him. Adele walked determinedly to Elijah's pickup and pulled out the shotgun. "August Beck!" Adele yelled. "Men died because of you. Now it's you and me. Old man."

Tommy was immediately beside her. "Let him go, Delly. The sheriff will catch him."

"But not before he damages my sisters," Adele said. "He's responsible for this accident. And I want him to stop."

"He'll pay," Tommy argued. "Let officers do their job."

Another spray of bullets landed around Tommy's feet.

"You still think I should let him go?" Adele asked. She racked her gun.

"Weren't my doing. I'm just picking off the pieces," Adele heard him holler back. She listened for the sound of crushed leaves, looked for tree branches that might whip as he ran. She stopped and listened. He was heading for the river.

She crossed the shotgun between her arms and ran toward a stand of trees where leaves waved a cheer revealing his location.

"Unforgiveable bastard," she said through her teeth.

A company guard rushed over to cover for her and slid in next to the engineer. "I see him." As she ran toward her stepfather, a guard fired off two shots in front of her pathway. She dropped to the ground until she heard the last bullet whiz past, amazed that her soon-to-be-fired guard would shoot while she was in his line of sight.

Rather than running into the amateur's bullets, she cut off her stepfather and followed the train tracks to the river. She heard a splash and tore down toward the bank, just as if she was navigating the mighty Mississippi, except the Bluestone River wasn't as deadly. Yet.

August was holding his shotgun over his head, wading waist-deep, slipping now and then on large rocks. She fired a round which made him duck behind a tree limb stretched over the water. Immediately she reloaded the gun, just as her stepfather had trained her.

"Why are you doing this?" she yelled.

August slowed long enough to shout over his shoulder. "Eye for an eye, isn't that what the Bible says? Man who defiles my face gets what's coming. He ain't comin' up. I seen to that."

"They both got out just fine. It was me you left down there," Adele shouted.

August shrugged. "Well, you got out, Sissy. See how hoity-toity your mine is now."

She raised her gun and pointed it at him. Through the front sight, she noticed his swollen black eye and cuts along his right arm. Not nearly enough to stop this wild animal. August finally stopped fighting the river midstream and stood straight up, daring her to shoot.

"Come home, Delly."

She kept her eye against the gunsight. "I am home."

"You don't know your enemies. They are bigger than me. I am your only family."

In disbelief, she lowered her gun. "You tried to drown me. Starve me. Remember?"

"You're a better woman for it!"

A bullet from the company security guard pinged the water. August dove under while bullets cut through the water where he'd been.

"Can't shoot for shit," Adele cussed at the guard. "You, sir, will qualify with state troopers before I let you defend this mine again." The guard stared back in disbelief.

She watched August resurface upstream. He jumped onto the riverbank and disappeared into a field of hemp. His body cut through the weeds in a straight line until she lost sight of him.

Did he need her that badly? Or was there something else he wanted? One thing was certain; he would not quit.

When she returned to the pit, she saw the extent of the damage her stepfather had caused. Rescuers were banging on the pulley's wheel to get it back in shape. But Dr. Luttrell was hunched over a cot, working on Jackson. "Got yourself mighty banged up there, I see," Dr. Luttrell said. He applied pressure to Jackson's left arm and gripped it as workers lifted him onto a stretcher, preparing to transport him to the hospital. Jackson's grandfather leaned on his cane as he accompanied Jackson. "Thank you, ma'am," he said. "You brought my grandson home to us."

Adele cradled the old man's hand. "I'm glad he's safe, now."

She wanted to gasp when she came close enough to see Jackson's bloody face. Both eyes were puffy; one was completely swollen shut. His left arm hung limp. Bright red blood dripped from his fingertips, but blood no longer dripped from his leg. Dr. Luttrell looked up to Adele and shook his head.

Adele walked beside the stretcher as long as she could. "Stay alive, Jackson Conor!" she said, squeezing his hand. "I need you." She couldn't believe she said that within Elizabeth Radford's earshot, but this was no time for apologies. She only hoped he would live.

Jackson looked up at her through his one good eye. "Trust David Henderson. And no one else."

Everitt gripped Jackson's fist. "Auggie knew where to hit," he snarled. "What gets into a man that he wants to destroy a community that badly?"

"We're going to come back stronger," Elizabeth Radford cut in. She walked alongside the stretcher as if to let Jackson know he had nothing to worry over. "Miss Dawson and I have a lot of work to build a tent community right here. The likes of August Beck won't stop us." She looked up at Adele. "Next week, we'll start rebuilding. I'll get my church folk up here and make it happen."

Adele smiled. Church folk were some of the world's best community builders. She also knew she'd have to do a better job protecting them now that she understood the depth of her stepfather's anger. She was on alert, no matter what he had in store for her or her sisters.

***

By the time the last of the injured were released, it was sundown. Adele caught a breathtaking orange hue turning the mountains into dark silhouettes. Temperatures and humidity dropped. Tommy wrapped a blanket over her shoulders and began escorting her to Elijah's truck.

Rebecca Parsons lifted her camera. "Quite a rescue operation, wouldn't you say? The new company maven goes down into the pit to pull up the last injured miner." She flipped open her journalist's notebook and started writing. "Why didn't you send someone else?"

"It's my job to be sure everyone is safe," Adele said.

"Or was it because you needed to be the hero?" Rebecca asked.

"I'm no hero," Adele answered as Tommy wrapped his arm over her shoulder and led her up the hill. "I did what any other worker would have done."

"But you inherited the mine. Shouldn't you have delegated that last trip to a man who knew what he was doing?"

"I knew what I was doing," Adele answered.

"That cage came up under a hail of gunfire. Would you say you put your engineers in danger? They might not have worked as hard if it were someone else."

Adele stopped in her tracks. "Our miners never leave anyone behind. What they did for me, they would have done for any fellow worker."

Rebecca raised her camera lens and took photos of Tommy leading Adele up the hill, photos of Adele's coal-smitten face, and of bullet dents in the cage.

"One more question, Miss Dawson," Rebecca asked. "Why does everyone blame your stepdad for the explosion?"

Tommy stepped around Adele to block Rebecca's persistent line of questioning. "If you find August Beck, I hope you'll ask the same question. Forgive us, now; I'm sure Miss Dawson wants to clean up. I'll help carry your camera equipment back in your car."

***

Guards, handpicked by David Henderson and the Sheriff of Mercer County, remained at Buckeye Tipple after rescuers went home.

David said, "You showed positive leadership today. I can't say I approve of you going into the pit. Certainly, you put a key executive in harm's way, but coal miners respect a good fighter."

Harold Hamburg added, "You showed the Dawson colors today, ma'am. Guards will need some supervision tonight. Mr. Thompson says he will stay. Can I give you a lift home?"

"One more night? I'll stay too. If August returns, I want to deal with him directly."

Harold added, "I couldn't help but overhear Elizabeth Radford's commitment to help build temporary camp up here. I caution you against getting too cozy with her. She can be a good ally, but as you know, when threatened, she's a rattlesnake."

"Then, I'd prefer you and I meet soon, so her issues don't fester," Adele said.

"I know it's a lot to take in, ma'am," Harold offered. "Given the bombshells of late. The board will reconvene end of third quarter. I'll check with your schedule before we set a date and brief you on the meeting agenda."

"Shouldn't I be involved in setting that agenda?" Adele asked.

"Old habits. So yes, it only makes sense you are involved," Harold answered.

David and Harold exchanged glances as if there might be something more about the lawyers' meeting. Whatever it was, Adele's head hurt. She needed rest and knew just the place she wanted to be.

Chapter 13:
Failure Factors

Dressed in an ankle-length duster, Chase Radford pushed open the green doors of the steak house. He nodded to the hostess.

"Good evening, Mr. Radford. The Committee is waiting for you in the back room."

Chase dragged his index finger down the hostess's neckline. "Keep this tight little bosom rosy for me, will you, doll?" Her fingertips turned white as she squeezed the reception desk. Her ruby red smile turned flat, but she did not squirm.

Chase unbuttoned his coat to cast a shadow, using the tail of his duster to unsettle tablecloths. He stepped boldly through the swing doors and into the kitchen. "My, my," he muttered, making his way to the servers' presentation station. He picked up a beef medallion from a guest's plate and dropped it into his mouth, dripping au jus onto the counter and floor.

"Damn sewer rat," the chef said. "Chew this." He held up a butcher knife.

Chase laughed and pushed his way into the back room. "Hello, father." Chase patted his dad on the back, then rested his eyes on a 40-something woman wearing a sequined red gown. One strap hung just slightly off her left shoulder. "Olga?" he greeted, conveying his surprise at seeing her. "Pardon my familiarity," he added. "Mrs. Beck."

Without looking at him, Olga Beck tossed four chips, then two more onto the table. "I'll call you, Jude, and raise you two."

Jude Radford, the only man under fifty at the table, studied Olga's face. "Call," he said, tossing chips onto the pile.

Olga placed a royal flush, king, high down on the table. Jude shook his head, then turned to his son. "You're dressed like a dick. It's the middle of summer! I swear you got twaddle for brains."

"I am my mother's son," Chase countered. He lifted one leg over a chair and plunked down at the table covered with beer bottles, poker chips, and cards. "I'll give Auggie credit. He knows how to blow up a mine. But two weeks after the explosion, she and my mom are building some damn workers' camp. Can't you control your wife?"

"She's your mother," Jude snorted.

"Always at odds with my daddy," Chase added.

"Can you not respect the players at this table?" Jude snapped.

Chase leaned over to look at his father's cards. "From my point of view, they have good reason to be happy, father."

"Fold," Jude snapped. He lowered his cards face down. "If you had arrived on time, oh competent son, you would know the demise of Flat Top."

"Fill me in," Chase responds. "The little heiress has got to go. Give me the word, and I'll carve her tombstone myself. Right next to her grandmama's."

Jude raised a long-neck beer bottle to his lips. Before taking a sip, he said, "For the benefit of my wretched son, would you please give him the highlights?"

Olga scooped chips her way. Her smile turned bland, her eyes like crystal shards ready to slice him into uneven pieces. "No one gets bumped until I say so. You got a problem with that? Take it up with Ivan."

"No problem at all," Chase nods to Ivan. "Tell me when."

Ivan's pinstriped vest did not hide his shoulder holster. "You never saw me," he growled. "Better off, everyone thinks I died in the explosion."

Olga raised a white feather boa from the base of her chair to cover her shoulder. "The family is still too close to the governor. Wait until after Little Miss Wonderful and Elizabeth get the new camp set up. I repeat. No goons to beat her up until I say so."

Jude nodded. "That doesn't mean we can't make her wish she never came to Bramwell," he said.

"What if she doesn't get the message?" Chase asked. "That coal mine will be a golden goose in two years, especially after you let the unions rebuild it. But with a lady at the helm of the mines, Pittsburgh doubts we can deliver."

"We will be ready," Olga scolded. "The Secretary of State is counting on us for bituminous."

"You and I both know Pittsburgh is shipping to Britain even now. I say that Dumb Dora will slow us down," Chase complained.

"We're not doing anything until President Roosevelt gets his majority vote in Congress," Olga argued. "US is not planning to send warships to Europe. We're merely protecting British merchant vessels."

"Maybe we should send a special delivery envelope to... what did you call her? Little Miss Wonderful? Draw a black hand on the envelope, let her know she's on her last breath."

"Do not stir up anything with the Vagabonda Famiglia," Ivan said. "Took ten years to settle a truce."

Olga added, "American businesses still enjoy shipping to belligerent countries. Besides, Miss Dawson has protection."

Chase leaned back in his chair. "Oh, you mean all those loyal family and business mouthpieces her granddaddy hired."

"Quillan was a decorated warrior," Ivan chastened. "Don't ever underestimate a man who schemed his way through British trenches. Your Dumb Dora comes from royal stock."

"I always felt she was out of place on August's farm," Olga said. "Never confronted an opponent directly. She confounded and strategized. Her sisters are her weakness."

"Pft," Chase snapped. "That dame will never know what hit her."

Within a flash, Ivan withdrew his pistol and pointed it directly at Chase's head. "No one touches her. Not one hair, you understand?"

Chase leaned in and put his forehead against the gun barrel. "You intend to use that?"

Ivan and Jude exchanged looks. Jude shook his head in disgust.

"I do," Ivan said. He pointed the gun down to Chase's foot and pulled the trigger.

Chase leaped from the table, tipping over as he cried out, "He shot me! He shot me, Daddy!" Chase fell to the ground at the base of his father's chair. "What are you going to do?"

"Not a damn thing," Jude responded. He nodded over at one of the henchmen guarding the door. "Take him out the back door. And clean up this blood." To his son, Jude said, "I hear about you coming 100 miles of Adele Dawson and I'll be the one putting a bullet in your head."

Jude and Ivan busied themselves, resetting the table. "I suppose you have a backup plan?" Olga asked when Jude shuffled the cards for another poker round.

"I do."

"Will I recognize him?"

"You won't. Better that way. My boy never graduated from Sundance Canyon," Jude answered. "His senior year might last a couple extra semesters by the time the schoolmaster lets him out."

"What about Elizabeth? She was a close family friend," Olga asks Jude. "What does she know?"

Jude gave Olga a harsh look. "Elizabeth served time for the crap you put her through. She'll bend to my wishes, but don't push her. Adele is Kettie's granddaughter, but Quillan's blood is fire in her veins."

Chapter 14:
Respite at the Bluefield Inn

An orange glow rose slowly over the mountain's brow, a heavenly kindling that would warm the day. It cast a glow making even the worst of the blast remains golden. Adele walked the mine perimeter, analyzing where they might build the temporary community and foreman shops. The explosion had taken out so much of the adit, the drift mine's entrance, it might be better to rebuild than repair the mine. She added that to the list of questions she planned to discuss with engineers.

Excavators, auger drills, and hand shovels had been moved away from the dig site, leaving the A-frame pillar a skeleton, a reminder of the chaos in the last three days. The damaged cage lay over the collar to discourage anyone from accidentally stepping into the well.

Adele's arms were still sore from shoving Jackson into the cage. Two hundred pounds of near-dead weight had tested her strength. She thought about Rebecca Parson's question last night. Why you? Why not a worker who knew what he was doing? If she saw Miss Parsons again, she would be prepared for a better answer.

"You're up early!" Tommy greeted her. He tightened the blankets over his shoulders as he sat up in the back of Elijah's truck. Adele put her clipboard down on the tailgate and climbed up next to him.

She leaned down to kiss his cheek. "I thought being a coal mine owner would be balancing accounting books and making sure we had enough sales to feed families."

Tommy shrugged. "You took on a mighty big job last night, rescuing Jackson. Did you see the tears on his grandfather's face?"

"The way he hugged his boy. Stole my heart," Adele answered. "I didn't know you talked in your sleep."

"Only when I'm exhausted. What did I say?"

"Nope. Nope. She's not doing that," Adele answered. "That was between bountiful lip slurps and a smattering of cuss words. Are you still angry with me that I helped rescue Jackson?"

Tommy sat up and reached for her hand. "You're trying too hard to prove yourself."

"All that banter at Noona's funeral. I thought you'd think I was paying him too much attention."

"Good Lord, Delly. He was wounded badly. He knows you're my girl."

A quick shiver spiked across her back. What was that about, she asked herself.

Tommy rubbed the back of her hand. "I love the fighter in you. When you were in the pit, all I could think about was where I should spend my last night with Adele, And then I remembered the beautiful Bluefield Inn. We're going there tonight."

"First, the guards have to break down the make-shift hospital. They can line up the cots near that stand of trees," she said, pointing. "I don't know Elizabeth's plan for building a temporary community, but what I do know is that we need to get back to the business of mining. Darn quick."

***

Turning from the Jefferson Street steep hill onto the Bluefield Inn driveway, Tommy maneuvered the truck between tall stone pillars on either side of the narrow driveway. The house stood proudly encased in two stories of white verandas, well-lit with gas lanterns. The plantation porch with six sets of pillars, sparkling windowpanes set inside European doors made her feel like she had entered a place where magic boldly sat on a silver platter. Several gatherings of wicker chairs and tables spread out on the enormous first-floor veranda as if preparing for a wedding reception. Tommy parked next to the carriage house. He stepped around the truck to open the door and took her hand to escort her into the inn.

As dirty as Tommy was, the owner greeted them like local millionaires. People married young in this town. The owner's wife looked at Adele's muddy and smelly clothes and said, "I have just the suite for you. It looks like you've been working so very hard, and your husband must want you to feel like royalty. Let me take you to the Queen Anne room.

Tommy leaned over to her and said, "That coal dust under your nose makes you even more beautiful."

She wiped the back of her hand against her nose, then wiped the slack onto a black towel the owner offered her. Tommy and Adele stepped through the library, where the owner pointed out the exquisite wine bar. Leave a few coins in the brass jar if you wish for a nightcap. Breakfast will be served at 9:00 or in your room. "Which do you choose?" she asked.

"In our room," Tommy answered. "Is there a local pub where we can get some dinner? We've been quite distracted the last few days."

"Our kitchen is closed for the day," the owner said, "but I could bring up some mini beef tourtieres and some marinated olives if you wish. Why don't you take this nice bottle of French rivesaltes up with you and settle in? I'll ring your bell before I bring up the appetizers."

Adele smiled at the owner. "I don't even know what that is, but it sounds delightful."

"Any luggage we can get for you?" the owner continued.

"I'm afraid we've just come from a nasty mine explosion," Adele said. "We've both been there for several days."

"You mean that terrible incident at Buckeye Tipple? It's all the talk in town. Were you there?"

"We were," Tommy answered. He held the bottle of wine and two glasses in his hand. Adele knew all they wanted was a hot shower.

"Dear hearts," the owner said, "Your nerves must be in a tizzy. Everyone in town needs that coal mine back up and running. If you need a change of clothes, I will call the shop owner on Franklin street to bring clothes over."

"That wouldn't be Elizabeth Radford's boutique?" Tommy asked.

"Lord, no. She marks up all her prices much beyond what any Bluefielder can afford." For a moment, Tommy and Adele exchanged knowing glances. "Okay, then. I will ring the bell when I bring up your appetizers."

***

"Tommy! Even the Queen of England would love this room," Adele said. "The four-poster bed, toile fabrics, and look at this Persian rug." She stepped inside the room dreamily, as she did the first time she saw her deceased mother and father's bedroom in Bramwell. "Only millionaires could afford a house this luxurious. Do you think we'll ever be rich?"

"Um, you are rich," Tommy said.

"I don't feel rich," she answered. "I feel tired and sore."

Tommy closed and locked the outer door before helping Adele roll up and remove her coal-slacked clothes. "Right now, I want to climb into that gold plated bathroom and get clean."

"Verily, I smell like a raccoon," Adele teased.

"You'll always be mine, even if you smell like a raccoon," Tommy said as he kissed her shoulder, "or a bear," he added, then tenderly kissed the nape of her neck.

Adele pulled back the thick curtain panel and stepped down into the sunken shower with multiple heads forcing hot water against her sore muscles. At first, she let the water run layers of black dust off her face, then turned sideways watching the black coal float down the drain, washing away the dirtiest of family memories.

"I've missed you already," Tommy whispered. He stepped into the shower behind her, opened a bottle of shampoo, and ran his fingers through her hair as he scrubbed her scalp. He rinsed her hair and then stood close behind her, lathering her again; this time, his fingers massaged her scalp, releasing endorphins that made her quiver.

Using a cloth, he washed the black soot from her eyes, the back of her ears, and the soft lines around her chin. There had never been a time when anyone nurtured her so completely, so childlike, and so respectful of her femininity. She felt her stepfather's humiliation fall away like dead skin cells. Mama and Noona, the two women who had meant the world to her, embraced her spirit as he scrubbed. She passed from the violence of her young adult years, where her skin remembered everything, to a place of beauty and security. She leaned her head against Tommy's shoulder and knew she could safely lose control. When he wrapped his arms around her, she felt convulsive sobs blurt out demons that had tucked their spears into her spirit.

"Cry it out," Tommy coached. "You can't hold this in any longer. That's it, baby. Cry it out."

Muscles in her back loosened. Her legs felt wobbly as Tommy rinsed the last of the coal dust away. He grabbed a large bath towel and wrapped her tightly, holding her up. When her legs stopped quivering, he wrapped another towel turban-style around her head, stepped out of the shower, and lifted her into his arm. She wrapped her arms around his neck, letting herself be carried to the intimacy of their square four-poster bed.

"How long I have waited for you to trust me," Tommy whispered. "I'm not your father, and I'm sure not like my father." He wiped her eyes dry, then wiped her back, even as she failed to regain her composure.

"I'm not usually wimpy," Adele apologized for her behavior.

"Don't I know that."

"You are headed to college. You will change."

"Can't get rid of me that easily," Tommy answered.

"Then, we're not being honest with each other." She looked into his eyes and held his gaze. "I want you tonight so very much, and yet I have nothing left inside me to give."

Tommy nodded. "Maybe tonight, we just talk about you and me and the worlds we're about to take on."

The bell rang, and the owner knocked on the door. "I'll leave everything out here, Mr. Thompson. There's a fresh change of clothes for the morning, as well."

"Thank you, ma'am," he said.

When they heard her walk down the steps, Tommy wrapped himself in a towel, then opened the door. "Oh my," he said as he brought in a room service table filled with pastries and meats. On the shelf below the table, the owner had folded clothes for both. In a separate pile, a lace nightie for Adele and silk boxers for Tommy.

"This is a little more service than I expected," Tommy said. "Not complaining." He opened the French white wine, poured drinks for both he and Adele, and laid down beside her. "A toast. To the reckoning of Adele Christina Dawson to her rightful coal company, and to us as we learn new things about each other, together."

"Yet apart," Adele added.

"Yet apart," Tommy agreed. "What does that mean to you?"

Adele sipped her wine. "This is exquisite," she said and took a bite of pastry before answering. "We write to each other." The turban leaned sideways. She removed it and let her brown locks float down to her shoulders as she leaned up against the headboard. "I want to know all the courses you are taking at Harvard. What you are learning, your professors, whether you hate them or like them. Your roommate's name and what foods they give you."

"Whoa! That's more than a letter."

"Then you'll have to come to West Virginia. One weekend a month."

"As for me?" Tommy started. "I want you to promise you'll register for college."

"Tamasin has already said she'd take care of the girls while I'm in school. But it's going to be a bit of a challenge," she said, taking another small bite of meat, "to run a mining company while I'm in classes."

Tommy rolled over and laid his head on her lap, pondering before he spoke again. "My father was a scoundrel, but he also taught me a few important business lessons."

"Like what?"

"Management runs the company. But senior management runs the managers. I want you to consider one more promise."

Adele sipped her wine. "I'll consider anything."

"Hire Jackson Conor as your mining supervisor."

Adele choked on her wine. "What!" She thought Tommy would be jealous of any affiliation she had with Jackson.

"Hear me out." Tommy sat up and sipped his wine, then leaned back on his side. "Jackson is a smart guy, and he's tough. Miners won't give him any crap."

"Aren't you worried about having a guy like Jackson working day to day with me?"

"What I know about you, Missy, is that you never cross the line between work and play. I already know Jackson wants a role in your life. So, I say give him a job title with clear direction. By the end of the day, you'll both be so tired you won't have time for any shenanigans."

Adele slipped into the lace nightie while Tommy put on the silk boxers. "Such a shame to waste such glorious lingerie on our last night together," he said.

She slipped under the covers and held the sheets for him to crawl in beside her. "My skin right next to yours, all night," Adele said. "The night isn't over, Mr. Thompson."

"I'm counting on that, Miss Dawson." Tommy pulled her close and wrapped his arms around her as they spooned into the night. "People will say you are a beautiful woman. I have seen your soul, and it's designed by angels."

Angels, she thought as she fell deeply into sleep.

***

Thick fabric draperies blocked out the orange hue of dawn, except for a pinprick of sun that fought its way into the bedroom. It was enough for Tommy to notice Adele had wrapped herself around his chest, her hair splayed warmly as a blanket across his torso. He raised her face to his lips and curled deeper under the blanket to face her.

"Good morning, Mrs. Thompson."

"Did we marry last night?"

"In my heart, we did." He cupped her breasts and stroked her cheek gently, then drew circles with his tongue around the tips of her nipples until she groaned. "You are a delicate piece of art this morning. Exquisite detail here. And here." He lifted her hand away from his face and kissed the palm. "Your graceful hands are a bit scuffed this morning, my sweet, but you have been blessed with young tight skin," he added as he stroked the inside of her thigh.

Adele kissed his neck, knowing exactly where the soft pressure points sent shock waves down his back. "The first time we were together, I was barely fifteen. So awkward. Do you think you sort of took advantage of me, given you lured me with that flask of vodka into the back seat? You only knew me as the poor girl from the bottomland."

"You don't know? Every guy in high school wanted you?" Tommy whispered. "I was, I am your friend. But that night I saw them looking at you. You were a filly with those long bewitching legs."

"So, you were protecting me?" Adele teased. She gasped as he found her most tender spot, the place she called her love button.

"Was I?" he asked. Tommy's lips were on hers now, his tongue searching her tongue. He climbed on top of her and looked down at her. "Dancing like that? I was claiming you."

He laid down on her stomach, looked at her face and ears, then kissed her eyes. "Two nights ago, I didn't ask if I could be inside you. This time, I want to honor everything delicate and delightful about you. We can stop right now, and I will be a happy man."

Adele smiled at the man who had been her friend long before he became her lover. Tomorrow morning, he would be on a train heading back to New Madrid to say goodbye to his mother before he left for college. But this morning, she wanted to claim him as hers. "You will always be my first and last love, Mr. Thompson. No matter what happens to us, you are my beloved. Please be my man."

Tommy was gentle. He called her his precious Delly. They connected lustfully. Sweat and fluids passed between them. Then he was tender as if there was a reason why she should feel so deliciously beautiful.

Chapter 15:
Benita Makes a Stand

On the way back from Bluefield Inn, Adele and Tommy stopped along the side of the road to pick fresh turmeric roots and red sassafras bark. Adele acknowledged it was an excuse to spend more time with him but also bring Tamasin a gift since she brewed Elijah's arthritis roots. Wild persimmons would be ripe in a few weeks, but Adele couldn't resist stopping at a grove of bushes to pluck low-hanging blackberries. Tamasin had promised to take her with her this fall when Elijah and Tamasin went on their persimmon search for "the fruit of the gods," she called them.

Adele snuggled next to Tommy as he drove Elijah's truck up the long driveway to Stone House. Kettie's car was parked outside the huge porch. "Something's not right," Tommy said. 'Elijah isn't standing in front of the car."

Tommy clung to Adele's waist as they walked toward the front door. Before opening the door, he stepped in front of her, protecting her from something neither of them yet understood.

She stepped inside the house and dropped the persimmons into the sink.

"Where have you been?" Briana scolded.

"Briana, I am exhausted. Can we talk about this later?"

Briana blinked back tears. "If you had been here, my sister wouldn't have run away." "What?" Adele spun around. "Which sister?"

"Benita. She's gone."

Collette rushed into the kitchen. "And she took —"

"Hush," Briana warned. She stomped out of the kitchen and into the main hall. "Nobody cares that half of me has been ripped apart."

Adele followed Briana into the hallway, where she found the girls huddled together on the grand stairway. "Oh, my goodness, such downcast faces. What happened?"

"You've been gone for four days," Collette said. "What have you been doing all that time?"

Adele squeezed in and sat between them. "Hey, wait a minute. I've been managing an explosion. People were hurt. I had to stay there."

"But not for four days," Elysia said. "We helped at the church, and we came home."

Deirdre scooted closer to Elysia. "You should have told us you'd be gone that long."

Adele reached for Deirdre's hands. "Deirdre, you're right. I am sorry you felt alone." She could see the sadness in her sister's eyes. But something else was nagging them.

"Did Mr. Henderson stop by to check on you?" Adele asked. "He told me he spoke with Tamasin and Elijah to let them know I'd be delayed a few days. Tamasin and Elijah were with you, right?"

"Elijah got hurt," Deirdre blurted.

"And it's your fault," Elysia added. "'Cause you weren't here."

Collette, Elysia, and Deirdre looked at each other to see who would break the silence. Finally, Collette took a deep breath. Her voice was subdued as she spoke. "Elijah tried to stop Benita from leaving. And she stole stuff before she left."

"Stole things? From where?" Adele blurted.

"From the attic."

"How did she get in?" Adele asked. "I hid the key."

"She watched Elijah go in and water the plants, then followed him out through the cellar," Collette said. "When Benita came out with three suitcases, Elijah tried to stop her. Nita swung a candlestick at him and knocked him down the basement steps."

Faye came down and sidled next to Adele. She was sucking on her three fingers, a reminder of her worst days.

"Come here, baby girl," Adele said. "Did you see what happened?"

Faye nodded.

"Can you talk about it?"

"'Nita said I couldn't go with her. 'Cause I'm D U M."

Adele wanted more than anything to slap her halfsister right then and there. Or, bolt up into the attic to see what Benita had stolen, but right now, her sisters needed her.

"Where is Elijah now?"

"Up at the carriage house. Tamasin and I bandaged him up," Briana said.

"Shall we go check on him? We might feel better."

Tommy leaned over to kiss Adele. "The train. Doesn't look like the twins will be accompanying me. It will be here in an hour."

"I will take you down to the station," Adele said. "It's too far to carry your clothes."

"Delly, baby. I will be fine. It's just one duffle bag."

"No and no. I will deal with Benita when I get back from the station. She will not get in my way for my final goodbye."

Tommy and Adele arrived at the railroad station just as the train came down the mountain. Its brakes squeaked as the conductor slowed for passengers.

"I already miss you," Tommy said. "Don't watch me leave. I can't bear to see you standing alone."

"Write to me," Adele encouraged. "Tell me everything. And I will do the same."

"The first letter is already in my head. It begins with memories of last night." He pulled a suitcase of dirty clothes from the back of the pickup and leaned in to kiss her. "You know I cherish you, right?" Tommy said.

Adele choked on the lump in her throat and forced herself to swallow her sadness. "Harvard better take good care of you, my love. You will make such as difference in people's lives. And I love you for it."

"And you! Get your application in for the fall semester. Tell me what Benita did to Elijah."

Adele sat in Elijah's truck until the train rolled out of the station before heading back up to the stone house on River Street. She hated Benita for robbing her of sorrowful moments where she could focus on Tommy's departure. "Whatever have you done now, Nita?"

Her sisters were already banded together on the porch waiting for her. "Did he get off okay?" Briana asked as if it might offer a sisterly transition into their latest set of problems.

"He did. Now let's go see Elijah." Adele and her sisters banded together on the short walk to the carriage house, knocked, and waited for an answer. "Mr. Elijah restin'," Tamasin hissed through the closed screen door. Her bloodshot eyes told Adele more than she wanted to know.

"Tamasin, shall I call Dr. Luttrell?"

"Doctor been here already. Nothin' broken. Jus' bruised. Fought real hard, my man did, against that awful girl. Elijah, he ashamed he couldn't protect Miss Kettie's things."

From the porch, Adele heard Elijah call for his wife. "Tamasin, let it be."

"Please tell him how much we love him," Adele said.

Tamasin waved Adele closer. "Tell him you'self. He here makin' a ruckus."

When Elijah stepped out on the porch, Adele pressed her fist to her lips. His right eye was the color of an eggplant. Red scratches dotted his scalp. He wobbled to the porch railings to secure his footing.

"I surely tried to stop her, ma'am. Thought about drivin' Miss Kettie's car after her. But old Elijah just can't keep up." He looked down at the ground. "Your granddaddy's war treasures. They be gone. Your mama's gowns all strewn about like she be fightin' a band a devils."

Adele put her hand on her heart to keep it from falling out. Why would she be so concerned over Mama's gowns when she should be more worried about her grandfather's war weapons and Elijah's injuries?

"Hornet's nest in that one," Tamasin said. "Sheriff McKinley says don't touch nothin' until he gets ova here to record the damage."

"It's that bad?" Adele questioned.

"Miss Kettie woulda never stood for such impertinence. Not from a white girl who know better," Tamasin answered. "Not many sheriffs take damage to a colored man seriously," she added. She tucked her arm around Elijah to help him back inside. Over her shoulder, she added, "Miss Kettie and Sheriff McKinley was schoolmates. Gonna be hell to pay if you aks me."

"Miss Benita took the Express to Louisville. Headed to St. Louis," Elijah added. "Sheriff made a call to Louisville station to intercept her."

"Crossing state lines with stolen goods," Adele said. She turned to go back to the house. "My sisters and I want to help you while you're on the mend," she called back to Elijah. "I'm home now. And I'm just so sorry this happened to you."

"Is Benita going to get arrested?" Elysia asked, skipping alongside Adele. "She hurt Elijah! She should pay. I thought she was gonna kill him."

Adele wrapped her arm around Elysia and joined hands with the other sisters. "Come on, girls. Show me what Benita did to the attic."

Elysia slid under Adele's elbow and took her sister's hand as they ducked inside the attic door. "I told you. You can always tell when 'Nita's mad."

In place of the gardens of memorabilia, Adele stooped to pick up one empty box after another, each gaped open and tossed into a heap of hateful resignation. Ribbons that once tied a lover's memories inside the Bloomingdales and Sachs Fifth Avenue boxes, now knotted into a ball. Petals from a dried floral wrist band had broken off when Benita tossed them against the wall. Adele picked up a lavender satin button that had fallen out of a box.

More than gowns, these were physical reminders of the love between Adele's mother, Selma, and her father, Kenneth. She felt the pain her mother must have known when she tenderly tied the boxes in ribbons after her husband's death. Her heart felt dark and empty. Saying goodbye to a lover just moments ago made her even rawer.

The room had been a woman's shrine to a departed loved one, an attempt to rekindle precious memories. Her father, Kenneth, must have taken Selma to state dinners, and ballrooms where they waltzed like Rudolph Valentino. But now, her mama's ode to love had become a battlefield. Adele seethed with disgust that Benita would steal these memories from the sisters who never really knew the loveliest side of their mother. Stories Adele wanted to tell her sisters vanished into a black veil.

As she walked further into this great disaster of a museum, she saw three of the four Flora Danika plates were gone; just one unbroken dish left behind. Its hand-painted Danish flower no longer represented an artist's expression; now, a shattered symbol of disrespect. Adele held the broken pieces, imagining how she might be able to piece them together. If only it weren't a symbol for her separation.

The Sally Milgrim hat display sat empty. Benita had to have smashed the hats into a ball to fit in her suitcase. The insensible furry of having to move so quickly and intentionally tore at Adele's heart. Why hadn't she expected this from Benita? This destruction of Adele's legacy?

Deirdre stood next to Quillan's war display. "The Browning, that's what Nita called it. I heard her tell Elijah she wanted it. Now it's gone. So are the bullets. Delly, I should have been here to stop her."

All but three scattered coins on her grandfather's war memorial remained. The Deutsch's Reich German coins, priceless, the gun he must have brought back from The Great War, all stolen. Adele leaned down over the table, folded her hands as tears welled in her eyes. "Pop-Pop, I'm so sorry."

"I wanted her gone," Elysia said, stomping her foot. "She's always so mad. Mad at you. Mad at Tamasin. Mad at Pa."

"You can't control someone when they are determined to destroy," Adele said. "It's not the time."

There were fresh scratches around the wooden cabinet's artwork, a sign that Benita had tried but failed to open the bank vault. On a floor-length mirror, Benita had written in shaming red lipstick, "You're not the only one who writes letters."

Adele stared at the letters, then ran her finger through the red word, Letters, smearing it as she remembered how Benita intercepted Adele's attempts to find her grandmother—even stealing Adele's precious pennies to keep her from purchasing a stamp. So great was Benita's fear that she might have to take over Adele's chores.

Adele caught herself lost in sad thoughts until she recognized the sound of Faye's slurping. When she looked down, she saw the agony on her youngest sister's face. Adele slid down to the floor and brought Faye onto her lap. Deirdre leaned into hug Faye. "Don't cry, sissy."

Collette, Elysia, and Briana sat beside Adele and leaned in to hug her. "You're right, Deirdre. We already have great memories of our mama," Adele said. "And you, Briana, you must be broken-hearted, missing your twin sister."

Briana sniffed and said, "The B's Club is a little broken, isn't it, Delly?"

***

After eight in the morning, Sheriff McKinley drove Bramwell's only Wolseley patrol car up the long driveway to Stone House. With Elijah still in the carriage house, Tamasin came over to the big house and answered the doorbell.

"About time you shows up," Tamasin whispered. "These chilen and my man mighty troubled."

"I'm here to help, Tamasin," the Sheriff answered, loud enough for Adele to hear. Tamasin opened the door for the officer to enter, then left him standing in the foyer.

"Mister Sheriff here to see you, ma'am."

"That was fast," Adele mumbled to Tamasin, but Tamasin merely harrumphed. "He all yours now, Miss Adele. Elijah needs me."

"Is this a good time?" Sheriff McKinley asked. He held his police campaign hat in his hand as he stood in the hallway. A belt holster worn on his left hip carried a Colt .38 handgun, one of the guns Adele and her stepfather used for target practice at the farm. Sheriff McKinley was a trim, battle-scarred trooper with well-groomed gray hair who looked like he could run down a criminal, even one with a fifty-yard head start.

"Please, come in, Sheriff," Adele answered. She cleared away the morning's dishes into the sink and offered a chair at the large kitchen table. "We're kind of fending for ourselves while Tamasin is helping Elijah recover."

"I've been inside many a home, ma'am. Dirty dishes are a sign of healthy kids."

Collette took a seat at the table beside Sheriff McKinley. "Oh, this is going to be good," she said. Sheriff McKinley seemed to dismiss Collette's comment, choosing instead to focus on Adele.

"Ma'am, I'm following up on a complaint of a theft at your home."

Adele was tormented by how much she should share. What if Benita claimed she had a right to Selma's things? How many times had she reminded Adele that all the sisters shared the same mother, even though Adele knew Selma in a way that none of the others would ever understand? And then there was the criminal record the Sheriff would likely file against her sister. Benita would never get into Harvard or any law school with a criminal record.

Collette shoved her elbow into Adele. "Did you hear Sheriff McKinley? He wants to see the attic."

"There's just one way into the attic that I know of, sir," Adele answered. "And I don't have a key to unlock the door."

"Yes, you do," Collette said. "It's above the door trim. Come with me, Sheriff McKinley," she added. "I'll let you in."

A sudden fear that Benita might not make it into college crushed her heart. As cruel as Benita could be, Adele still wanted to protect her. "Collette, that room is under construction," Adele argued.

"No, it isn't," her sister argued.

Sheriff McKinley studied Adele, then lowered his eyes and tapped his pen against the notebook. "Why don't you ladies work things out here while I go check on Mr. Elijah. I do need to follow up on the assault charges."

"Assault? Will Benita have to serve time in jail?" Adele asked.

"Can't say until I see what happened."

"But she's just sixteen years old."

To your knowledge, is this your sister's first offense?"

"Yes," Adele tutted. She didn't dare mention Benita's late-night roaming. She didn't know where Benita had gone. This was not the time to look like she wasn't in charge of her sisters.

"Family court keeps disputes confidential as long as the abuser is a minor. Unless you feel your sister is a continuous threat to your home, property, or personal safety, I don't see why her records would be reopened. But my personal experience, ma'am, is that if you let incidents like this go without any repercussions, you are fostering a repeat criminal."

"So, if my sister applied for college, her juvenile record wouldn't stop her from being accepted?"

"Juvenile records remain sealed if the offender is under eighteen years old," Sheriff McKinley said. "A court order can reopen them if the minor is a repeat offender. But she needs to be brought to justice, even if she is a juvenile. She used international coins," he looked at his notebooks, "from Germany, it appears, to purchase a train ticket. Norfolk and Western says they'll press charges unless that debt is paid in US currency."

"I will take care of that fee today," Adele responded.

Collette folded her hands on top of the table. "So, Sheriff McKinley looks like you can follow me into the attic."

"Only with your sister's permission," Sheriff answered. "You are a minor, too."

"Of course. Do you mind climbing a few flights up to the third floor?" Adele asked.

"Ma'am, Miss Kettie and I go way back to school days. I helped your grandmother move a few collections into the attic, protecting them from being sold. Before that, I was here the day we arrested your Uncle Irving. Quillan said if Irving was going to turn himself in, we would have to face the family lawyers standing together. I knew Irving had shot old man Beck, but sometimes law enforcement has to see the better picture."

Adele stopped at the top of the second-story stairs. "You knew my father?"

"Mighty fine family you come from, Miss Adele. You weren't even a twinkle in your Daddy's eye yet. Kenneth was still in high school when we took Irving to court."

"Who is Irving?" Collette asked, even as Adele was trying to recall the stories Noona had told her.

"Finest hot head you'll ever meet," Sheriff McKinley said. "Man loved his family, A Marine who fought our country's battles here and abroad. Shame he ended up serving time, but he's up for parole next month. I believe he will get it this time, long as none of the Beck family protests. His wife died while Irving was in prison. Thirty years is a long time."

"Wait, wait," Collette said. "I have more family in West Virginia?"

Sheriff McKinley stopped in the middle of the hallway. "There I go rerunning my mouth. I apologize, Miss Dawson."

"We're all trying to catch up," Adele said. "I guess that's why it hurts to have Noona's attic destroyed. That room is a family treasure."

"It surely is," he answered. "Here you are all trying to learn what being a Dawson really means." Sheriff McKinley held the door to the third-floor stairway as Adele and Collette climbed the steps. The sheriff stopped at the third-floor landing and looked up at the portrait still watching over Miss Kettie's bedroom. "Best men in all of Bramwell," the trooper said. "Quillan Senior, Pop Myers, and Isaac T. Mann. All of 'em stood up for West Virginia like no other."

Sheriff McKinley stood at attention and placed his hand over his heart in tribute. "You ever decide to sell that portrait, call me first. Promise me, will you? I was just a tyke when Isaac T ran the Bank of Bramwell. But I've heard enough stories about him and Pop Myers that will keep Bramwell famous for generations to come. If you hear when Irving is released, I'd like to shake his hand. Man's nigh unto seventies years by now. Heard his mind is still sharp as always."

"I'd like to hear his stories, too," Adele said. "It's hard to learn about family when so many of them are no longer with us."

"Or stolen from you," the trooper added.

"Hmm," Adele agreed. She led the Sheriff up the last three steps and then into Miss Kettie's bedroom.

"Odd seeing this room again without the warming lights or her apothecary," Sheriff McKinley said. He ducked inside the attic door and followed Adele into the enormous room. "I remember when Quillan built this hideout for Kettie. He was about to be shipped to Great Britain. She used it as her painting studio for a while. She'd sit right there by the nook overlooking the street and watch people when she wasn't running a company or volunteering." He pointed across the room to the plants. "I see Elijah is keeping her plants alive. Used to think she'd get well if she'd only take a few more teaspoons of cod liver oil. She swore by Pinus and Phytolacca. Hear tell Tamasin packages them for the Negro children, keeping them healthy."

Sheriff McKinley took in the sights of gown boxes strewn unceremoniously onto the floor. "Well, I'll give her this. She can sure turn a museum into a mess. Can you tell me what was stolen?" He removed the pen from his uniform pocket and prepared to take notes. "Good lord, I can see it right here. Quillan's coveted coin collection."

Collette took him on a tour of the museum carnage. "Plus, she stole plates, except this one that she probably broke. And over here, some paintings are missing. And oh, gosh, Delly, she took the bayonet, too."

Sheriff McKinley scratched his head. "You wouldn't happen to know whether Benita had an accomplice?"

"An accomplice?" Adele asked.

"She couldn't have taken all she did without help."

Adele wondered how Benita could have shoved so many stolen items into three suitcases. Had she let August into this room? Why would she expose so many precious Dawson memories to the likes of that disgusting man?

"You heard that my stepfather was here?"

"You mean for the funeral?" Sheriff McKinley asked. "I heard about that. I also heard Mr. Henderson encouraged him to jump on a train back to Missouri."

"He must have jumped off between here and St. Louis. He was at the explosion."

"Well, that's not good news," the sheriff answered. "The FBI is overseeing the investigation now, taking over but collaborating with state police and the US Bureau of Mines investigators. Explosions are a present fear for any mining family. But these seemed to be too controlled, like a nasty message. Miss Kettie is looking down on you with a grand smile."

"Thank you, Sheriff McKinley," Adele answered. "And you'll let me know when Irving is released? I'd like to welcome him home."

Collette popped back in front of the sheriff before he walked out the door. "Will you come back and tell us stories about the Beck family? They are the bad guys, right?"

"Collette, some stories are best left for the judge."

"Why? I'm family, too," Collette argued. "I cannot figure out why my Pa keeps coming back here. Maybe you will help me understand."

"Mighty wise for a fifteen-year-old. Tell you what. You and Miss Adele, let me know a good time, and we will make it a date."

Chapter 16: First day of school

September 1938

On the first day of school, Tamasin fixed a pot of oatmeal and cooked pork sausage links for the girls. "Gotta keep your minds on books, not you bellies," she said.

Briana exchanged glances with Adele when Tamasin included a place for Benita. "She be back," Tamasin chattered. "Runaway one day. Back the next. Maybe the Good Lord convicts her this time, and she come a'runnin' back with all the stuff she stole."

Briana leaned her head down on her crossed arms. After several moments her sisters stood over her to provide comfort. Suddenly, Briana leaped from her chair. She moved Benita's chair into the pantry and moved her own into the place Benita once occupied.

"I know it's hard," Adele said.

"I can deal with it," Briana answered. She wiped the back of her hand against her cheek. "I have the bedroom to myself now. Can't hear Benita snoring all night."

Adele touched her sister's shoulder, trying to acknowledge the pain Briana must be feeling now that her womb buddy had walked out on the family.

"Tamasin packed a nice lunch for all of you today. I tucked milk money into your coin purses. Books are on the shelf, ready for you to dig in for a brand-new year."

Collette seemed to have grown two inches in the last three weeks. Her ankles exposed from the hem of her pants." After school, let's see if we can dig up any pants from the general store."

"Why? This is what everyone's wearing now. They're called lounge pants, Delly. At least I don't have to wear a skirt every day like Briana."

"Why aren't you dressed yet, Delly?" Deirdre asked. "Aren't you supposed to be in college?"

"I'm going to check on the mining village. Winter's coming in sooner than we thought. We're going to need supplies," Adele answered.

Elijah stepped into the kitchen, limping only slightly from his ordeal with Benita. "Shall I drive you, ladies, to school?"

Elysia jumped up. "Yeah, Elijah! Can he?" she asked Adele.

"You need your exercise. It's less than eight blocks away. Besides, today is a beautiful sunny day," Adele answered. "Save the drives for when it's cold and rainy."

Each girl picked up several books and a lunch bag, then headed out the door. Elysia and Deirdre held hands as they walked down the stone drive, then across the Bluestone River Bridge. Adele stood on the veranda watching that they turned left onto Main Street while Collette and Briana turned right onto North River Street. Each sister headed towards their respective schools until they disappeared into the side streets.

"Never easy seeing the babies off to school," Tamasin said.

"They need a normal life again," Adele responded. "It's been one event after another since they arrived. Maybe school will offer some stability."

Elijah poured hot water over a tea ball while Tamasin spooned molasses into his hot oatmeal. "Eat now, husband. Miss Adele needing you to drive her up to the Bluefield College."

"I am?"

"Yes, ma'am. I promise Mr. Thompson, and I promise Miss Kettie that you will be in college before the first freeze. Too many spirits again' me if I don't make good on my word."

"But it's nearly ten miles from here!" Adele argued. "I can't have Elijah taking all-day driving me there and back."

Elijah sipped his tea. "You could drive yourself. Get your West Virginia driver's license.'

"I didn't need a license in Missouri." Adele looked to Tamasin for guidance.

Elijah put his teacup on the counter. "Roads all the same, no matter what state. Some just a bit curvier. I got nothing better today than to teach Miss Adele the West Virginia ways. I'll bring the car around front."

Tamasin shrugged her shoulders. "Listen to my man." She pounded her fist into a bowl of fresh bread dough. "He help you navigate all them loop de loops."

Elijah tucked his black derby down over his head and kissed Tamasin, ignoring Adele, before stepping out to the garage. Within a few moments, he drove Miss Kettie's black Buick around to the front door.

"Well, damn," Adele said. She waited on the portico for him to open the back seat door.

"Can't reach the steering wheel from back there, Miss," Elijah instructed. "Sit up here."

"I'd feel better if Briana was in the car with me."

"Briana in school." Elijah waved his hand into the driver's seat, waiting for her to come around. Finally, Adele walked around the front of the car. "Easy as pie. You was drivin' on the Missouri mud fields. Today you learn West Virginia rules."

Adele eased herself into the front seat. It was so low and worn she couldn't see the road except through the steering wheel.

Elijah shook his head, stepped out of the car, and walked up to the carriage house. When he returned, he was carrying an orange paisley pillow. "Sit on this. You are tall enough now."

"I drove a truck, Elijah. The gearshift was on the floor."

"About the same." Elijah acted out the three gears, showing her how to move from one to another, then drew a diagram of the three-speed transmission in her hand. "You go up here, then down, then ova' there," he said. "Just like a truck, you put your left foot on the clutch and your right foot on the brake."

The transmission gears ground when Adele put the car into first gear. "It lived through Miss Kettie. It'll live through you."

"My grandmother drove this car?"

"Up until she got sick."

"But she was much taller than I am."

"Quit your bellyaching, Miss Adelle," Elijah said. "Right foot on the brake. Left foot on the clutch. Now move your right foot over to the gas pedal. One come up while the other go down. That's it."

After she'd practiced several times, Elijah said, "Now let's see if we can get somewheres. Down the driveway, then. Keep your eyes on the bottom of the hill, not on the stonewall."

Elijah guided her to the road. "Turn right. Practice going up the hill before we take Kettie's demon downtown."

The next day, Elijah brought the Buick around to the front. "Today, we be going to Bluefield College. Miss Kettie's friend, the Academic Dean, been asking about you."

"Maybe I can drive some of the ways?"

Elijah laughed. "No driving out of Bramwell until you get a license. Already got more than enough Dawsons in jail."

***

When the girls came home from school, Faye greeted them with the biggest smile. She held out chilled apple juice and fresh bread.

"Tamasin and I baked everything," Faye said. "I'm going to be a B A

194

K E R when I grow up." Faye looked to Tamasin to be sure she had spelled the word correctly.

Tamasin nodded her approval. "Keep your portions down, now," she advised the girls. "Suppa coming in a few hours. Miss Faye and me got some pork ribs in the smoker."

"Where's Delly?" Collette asked. She dropped her books on the grand staircase.

"Don't be clutterin' my steps," Tamasin said. "Them books go in the library or your bedroom. Miss Adele, she'll be here soon. Registered herself up at the Bluefield College. All you girls got stories to tell once you gets your homework done." To Elysia and Deirdre, she said, "Set the dining room table. We all gonna celebrate your first day of lessons."

Tamasin stirred beet greens while Faye used claws to pull tender pork sections away from the hog's shoulder. Faye raised the claws high into the air when Adele walked in.

"Look, Delly! I fixed dinner."

Adele hugged Faye and kissed her forehead. "I can see you did! Miss Tamasin has you all dolled up like a chef."

"Not a chef. I'm going to be a B A K E R. Bakers don't suck their fingers, do they Tamasin?" Faye bragged. "That's what Tamasin said. No finger sucking in my kitchen."

Adele mouthed, "Thank you," to Tamasin before she leaned to kiss Tamasin's cheek.

Dinner that night may have been the most joyful meal Adele could remember. All the girls were seated around the table, eager to tell stories of new friends, how straight they had to walk in the hallway without talking. "My teacher said I should be a mathematician," Elysia said. "Or a chemist." Deirdre added, "My teacher wanted to know where I got my red curly hair. I told her I got struck by lightning when I was a baby and all my new girlfriends laughed. So, she made us kneel beside our desks for fifteen minutes."

Collette broke away a piece of fresh bread and dragged it through warm butter. "I'm going to try out for the basketball team."

"Are girls allowed to play basketball here?" Adele asked.

"First year," Collette answered. "We're called the Basquettes 'cause we throw balls into an apple basket. The coach came to gym class and watched us dribble balls. She said I had big hands and long legs."

Adele stopped eating for a moment and looked at her sisters with great pride. "We are off to a good start, aren't we, girls?"

Briana ate in silence, picking away at her food. "I miss Nita," she said. "She's not there to change seats with me and fool the teachers."

***

After dinner, Elijah brought the mail to Adele while the girls did their homework in the library. She pressed the letter from Tommy against her chest before opening it.

> Sweet Delly,
>
> I can hardly believe it's been two weeks since I left you. You've been in my heart every day, my love. I think about you when I'm in English Literature and find I have to sit with my legs close together when reading Percy Bysshe Shelley. Beauty in the world, he says, is worthless without a kiss from you. You drive me crazy, but in such a good way. I think about you in world history. You make my own history worth creating. Lord knows you are on my mind in calculus. You make me want to be a better student. I hope to graduate in three years if only so I can be with you sooner. That means year-round school, but I will find weekends and holidays to visit you. Be healthy and happy, my sweet.

All my love,

Tom

Adele pulled out a piece of stationery and sat at the desk to reply. She wrote four pages in less than an hour, letting him know how happy she was enrolled in college. She hadn't yet claimed a major, but she was still very interested in agriculture. She told him Benita had run away, perhaps back to Missouri, and how much Briana missed her twin sister. Elijah had taught her how to drive a three-on-the-column and that she would sit for the West Virginia driver's license exam next week. She told him that thirty families had moved into the temporary mining camp and that Elizabeth Radford corralled wives to create a competition bake-off to see who made the best deer chili. The children are in class every day, and wouldn't Mama be proud of them for keeping school a big part of their life, just like she did in the floods of 1927. She also told him the FBI officially declared arson to be the reason for the mine explosion, but Sheriff McKinley said they had enough evidence now that could rebuild the mine. Sheriff McKinley and Collette had become good friends. He and his son came over a few times to teach Collette how to play basketball. She closed the letter with an apology for not being as poetic as he, but how very deeply she missed and loved him.

Fortunately, her beloved Tommy included his return address. She licked the envelope's seal and the postage stamp and asked Elijah to take it with him to the post office.

"You got a board meeting coming up, ma'am. Mr. Henderson sent a letter, too."

"Thank you, Elijah."

"Right here waiting for you," Elijah said as he offered it to her.

"What did it say?"

"Not my place to read your mail, ma'am,' Elijah answered. "I just knows it's that time a year for Miss Kettie to be prepping for the board."

"I'll be in the library, then."

"Shall I invite the lawyers ova for afternoon tea?" Elijah asked. "Talk through the agenda? If they have not called you yet, they might be forgetting their place."

"It's a lot to remember, Elijah. College, taking care of the girls. Overseeing the mine. And now, preparing for an annual meeting? Maybe I should postpone college right now. At least until the mine gets back in business."

Elijah pulled a handful of silverware from the cabinet and spread them on the table. "Each one of these has a job. All of them can lift. But a spoon cannot hold a piece of meat. A knife shouldn't lift spinach to your mouth. But you, ma'am, hold all of them in your hands at once. You gots to tell each of them what to do."

Elijah scooped the silverware and held them in his hand. Without looking at her, he said, "Master Jackson just about fully recovered."

"Tommy wanted me to recommend him for mine's superintendent. That will take board approval."

"You buildin' the agenda already," Elijah praised her. He held the silverware in front of her. "Which a these does the best job?"

"The fork."

Elijah nodded. "Miss Adele, you way ready. Shall I drive you to his house? Or do you know the way?"

"I should be trying to get into your Negro college instead of Bluefield," Adele said.

"You can't get in," Elijah said and smiled.

"Why not?"

"You white."

***

Jackson was outside his mother's home chopping and stacking wood for the winter. Adele recognized his grandfather on the porch and waved to him. The old man nodded.

"He doesn't see much anymore," Jackson hollered to her. The sleeves on his flannel shirt had been rolled up. His gloves form fitted to his hands. Jackson buried the axe bit into a tree stump, fragmenting the log into quarters, and then stacked wood into his arms. "Step on up to the door and wish him a good morning."

Adele stood near the Buick, trying to remember the brilliant words she wanted to say that would convince Jackson to lead the mine's reconstruction. She stood far enough away from him to avoid letting him see that she had begun to perspire. She pretended to wave a strand of hair away from her eyes as she mopped her brow.

"I could use a hand," Jackson said. "Winter's coming early this year."

Adele brushed her hands against her skirt. "I'm not exactly dressed for chopping wood." Goodness, she was confused as to why she sounded out of breath.

Jackson stacked wood chunks into a single row out of the shade to ensure enough air would pass underneath to keep the wood dry. Each row was crisscrossed, creating a pillar at the end for stability. His flannel shirt expanded a bit too deliciously around his arm. He swiped the back of his hand against his forehead to remove beads of sweat. "Say your peace, woman, or get some gloves. My granddad has an extra pair."

"You look like you've healed up fairly well," Adele finally managed to babble. Don't be so coy; she scolded herself. Jackson is making a business call. Do not be overcome with his manliness.

"Nothing like a knife fight with your old man to motivate me."

"He's not my father."

Jackson picked up the ax and sliced another block of wood in half. "Glad we got that straightened out. So why are you here?"

Adele stepped within a few feet of his wood pile. "I'd like you to help rebuild the mine."

"No, ma'am. I am done with that place." Jackson squared his jaw.

"Not as a miner, but as a leader. You're the only one I trust to be the new superintendent."

Adele thought she saw a slight mound of dirt bounce from the ground as Jackson dropped the ax head near his feet. His gloved hand remained firmly locked around the handle. She feared he caught her watching his hands. "Now, what makes you think I can do something like that?"

"The men respect you, Jackson."

"The men, you say."

Good lord, he was going to force her to admit she wanted him too. And here she was, acting like a flirty pubescent when she was a coal mine owner. Give him direction. Be the fork!

"You have what it takes to be a great leader. You know your way around the mines, you helped develop its safety programs, and you stood up to defend it when it was under attack."

Jackson picked up the half-round of wood, raised the ax and quartered the log. She watched as pieces fell away from the chopping bench.

At least he was thinking. Or was he still ignoring her?

"I can stay here all day. Not leaving until you give me an answer," she finally said.

"You're going to have to seal the adit. Build another drift mine portal, a quarter-mile away. Inland Steel is the biggest buyer right now. Unions hold that monopoly since they already sell coal to Great Britain."

This was a good sign. "Okay," Adele said.

"You sure you got all the dead bodies out? Men start seeing ghosts if they think there's a man's soul down there."

Dead bodies? She was sure all missing had been found. What was Jackson saying?

"The Bureau of Mines and the inspectors say all men have been accounted for. We're trying to do all we can for the families, Jackson. Too many of them live 20 miles away, and we need foremen close to the job site. We built a temporary mining community so the workers can go home at night to their families."

"Who's in charge of that?"

"Elizabeth Radford."

"Battle Axe, that one," Jackson said.

"She gets the job done," Adele answered.

Jackson picked up two more slices of timber and tucked them under his arm. He reached into the cut pile of wood and gripped the third piece of wood with one hand. He's playing you, girl, Adele told herself. Trying to outthink you. Those fingers around the wood. She noticed him looking at her and caught his slight grin. Stay focused, Adele Christina Dawson.

"What's the going rate for a supervisor these days?"

"You would know better than I."

"It's your company."

"What do you want?" Adele asked.

"We're not playing that game, Miss Dawson. You lay it down, and I'll think about it."

She mentioned a number that she thought would be fair.

Jackson snickered. "I can make that working as a scab in Mingo County."

"Ten percent annual revenues if no one is fatally injured."

"Twelve percent every six months. And no one dies on my watch. Ever."

Adele did some calculations in her mind while also considering how she would present this counteroffer to the board of directors. It was her company, but she had plenty of board members, investors, government officials, and families to answer to.

While she pondered, Jackson stood the chunk of wood in place, raised the ax, and cut the timber into four pieces.

"I want the families to be well treated," Adele said. "And you attend board meetings."

"Do I have to sit next to you?"

Adele studied his face to see whether he was joking with her. "No."

Jackson raised his ax again to slice another piece of wood. "One more thing," he said. She stood waiting for the chop. Instead, he lowered his ax and stepped close to her. "Have dinner with me, and I'll think about it."

She wasn't prepared for Jackson to get personal with her. Cora Radford, his girlfriend, would be furious if she learned he was dining with another woman. There would be no end to the wrath from Elizabeth Radford, just when she and Adele saw eye to eye. And how would she explain dinner to Tommy?

Adele despised herself for not looking directly at him. "You know I cannot do that."

Jackson stepped a few inches closer and smiled down at her, not evocatively or dominating. There was trust in his eyes. "I'm not asking you to make love to me. Dinner. That's all." He stepped back and returned to the chopping block. "Sooner the better, the way I hear."

"Your word, Jackson. Just dinner."

There he was, back in front of her again. "If you didn't think I was a man of my word, you wouldn't be here."

"I'll take that as a yes," Adele answered.

"To what?"

"You are the coalmine's new supervisor."

"And I name the location for dinner."

She returned to the car. The Buick sputtered a bit, and jerked when she put it in reverse, but Adele took a deep breath before putting her foot on the gas pedal. She could drive as smooth as butter if only Jackson did not smile at her like that, ever again.

Chapter 17:
Adele Discovers More Enemies on Her Board

October 1938

Tamasin covered the dining room table with a satin tablecloth and then set out some of her favorite hors d'oeuvres that she and Faye had worked on for days: crème Fraiche tartlets, caramelized figs with bacon and chili, and bacon-wrapped parsnips.

Elijah reminded Adele to sip her wine only enough to appear to be social. Her challenge was to remember everything that each man said without writing a single word. "That's your board secretary's job. Miss Kettie always sat near the secretary."

During the social hour, Elijah meandered among board members, keeping their glasses filled with white wine. When Adele invited all ten board members into the library, Elijah switched to red wine and cognac. Five attorneys, three bankers, two certified public accountants, all males, and one female owner. Elizabeth Radford attended to report on the mining camp, but she would be asked to leave when the board went into executive session.

David stood next to Adele and subtly sipped his wine. "You ready for this?" he asked.

"If you hadn't helped me walk through each scenario, I would have let these men overrun the meeting," Adele said.

"We don't like to make our CEOs look bad," David said. "Any time you feel picked on, you look at me."

David Henderson called the meeting to order, leaving Elizabeth to wait in the parlor until summoned to give her report. He announced each member's full name for the secretary's notes, then called a quorum. Adele thought, who wouldn't attend? Each man could check out the youngest of all Dawsons coal company, and a young female at that! They could also judge her social capabilities and have something to gossip about at church gatherings or at the Corner Café. Lord knows she'd given the town enough to talk about with the explosion, mining village, and her plan for restoring the mines.

Thanks to Tamasin and Elijah, she seemed to be relatively well accepted this evening. Board members had come to one of the largest homes in Bramwell and received free food and drink on this crisp early October evening. Hard life being a board member, she told herself, and counted on Noona to have selected the right minds into this very private circle.

David called the meeting to order while Garrett Stephenson invoked the Holy Spirit to be present with them this evening and with the departed soul of Ivan Mills and our blessed Kettie Dawson. Garrett, she recalled, was her grandfather's estate attorney and the closest friend to Mr. Mills.

"Let's get right down to business," David said. "We all want to know what happened at the mine. What caused the explosion, and what's our timeline for rebuilding?" David pulled folded sheets of paper from his coat jacket and began to read.

"Arson," he read, removed his glasses, and addressed the group.

"Comes as no shock to us, but what you will find surprising is that the explosion happened the same day Irving Dawson received a compassionate release from prison. Irving more than paid his debt for killing Jacob Beck, but he saved Selma Cassidy's life."

"Oh, my Lord, Irving killed Jacob Beck in self-defense," Frank cut in, stating the facts as if everyone in the room should know better than to inquire. "The way those boys dishonored the Dawson family." He looked to Adele. "I'm sorry, ma'am, but the best thing that ever happened to your family was when Kenneth took Selma as his wife. Of course, we're all looking for a repeat of that nurturing as you lead us forward.

"Much as we want to pin this accident on August, it was his cousins who should have been on trial. I'm not saying Auggie didn't have a hand in making it worse. But the payouts Quillan established after acquiring the Pocahontas Mine. Good Lord. The Cassidy's grandsons confessed they didn't want to trade what they already had for a new contract. Irving would get his share, and they would leave it at that."

It had been a long time since Adele had heard the Cassidy name. She'd always thought of her mother as Selma Dawson, forgetting that her mother's maiden name was Cassidy. Selma Cassidy always sounded like a movie star's name, not her mother.

Garrett added, "The Lord works in mysterious ways." He looked to Adele as if he wanted to add color to the corporate history lesson Frank and David had initiated. "When Irving saved Selma's life, there wasn't much Giles Cassidy could do to pay off law enforcement. But he could make sure Irving's finances were in good order when he got out of prison. So, Giles Cassidy and Quillan Dawson agreed to merge their coal companies. Irving would be a silent partner until he got out of the penitentiary. When Kenneth Dawson married Selma Cassidy, that more than secured the relationship. Until Kenny and Selma both died, making Adele Dawson the only heir from two families to take over the Flat Top Coal and Pocahontas Coal Mine companies."

A stillness so toxic filled the room that Adele could hardly breathe. What had just happened that caused such friction? Frank Hemlock cleared his throat. Each of the bankers looked down at the floor. Jude Radford,

Elizabeth's husband, looked at Adele, then tapped a pen against his notebook.

"It's more than that," Jude said. "You know my wife, Elizabeth, has tried several times to open the door for what needs to be said here."

"And what is that?" David asked.

"Do we plan to discuss financials tonight?" Jude asked.

"We do." David looked to Jude to fill the void. "Say your peace."

Jude looked straight at Adele as if he could not wait to take her down. "Miss Dawson, you haven't met my son, Chase, yet, but you know Kettie had something against him. She never wanted him managing the chart of accounts. But Chase's financial statements indicate large sums have been withdrawn to build this little temporary community of yours up near Buckeye Tipple. The mining company will be bankrupt in the next three months if you continue."

"Why haven't I been informed about these large withdrawals?"

Jude looked to one of the bankers, who cleared his throat. "I've got withdrawal signatures right here from Ivan Mills," the banker responded.

"Ivan Mills died in the explosion," Adele snapped. She felt fire swelling in her throat. "Why would you be accepting signatures from a dead man?"

"His signature was on file, ma'am," Jude answered. "And until this board meeting, he was the only one authorized to distribute such large sums of money."

"How much?" Adele asked.

"Gentlemen, we're getting a little ahead of ourselves," David interrupted and held up a copy of the agenda. Our CPA is working on financial statements," he said. "We haven't had time to present it to Adele for review."

"Why not?"

David studied her as if she had forgotten her role in this meeting.

"Miss Dawson, if you'll allow us to continue?"

"Agenda or no agenda," Adele said. "We're trying to keep our miners from going to work elsewhere. At least until we reopen," she explained.

"Then, let me state the obvious," Jude broke in. "You cannot continue to operate a missionary camp near Buckeye Tipple and feed families day and night. We run a business here. Have you discussed your plan to pay my wife? Any of the laborers? How will you fund the recovery efforts with any members of this board?"

The board secretary stopped taking notes. Quillan's library collection of literary and poetry authors seemed to lean closer to hear her response. The grandmother's clock ticked. Outside, a cardinal hopped onto an oak branch.

"I will do whatever it takes to pay them," Adele said. "It's been a little crazy here. The explosion, attending classes, getting my sisters in school."

"My point exactly," Jude said. "You're too young, and frankly, Miss Dawson, you have no experience running a coal mining company. Not like my son, Chase does. And especially not one this large. You have no financial or leadership experience, no vision of how coal is bought or sold. Look at you; you're a child. I'm not analyzing your potential. But right now, you are not suited for this job. In time, perhaps, but this is not your time. And you're a ..."

"A woman!" Adele spat.

So, now it was out in the open. Her greatest fear. Youth, no experience. And a woman. Adele couldn't decide whether to fire back assaults at Jude or excuse herself from the room, grab her sisters and get out of Bramwell. Jude had revealed her greatest weakness, the one that would heal if she had more time to mature. She could be on the next train headed to St. Louis. Give the girls back to their father. They were his, to begin with. She would attend the University of Missouri, where she'd already been accepted. And wanted! She'd have to pull some strings to get back in school. After all, she'd authored several grants to create an agricultural co-op in New Madrid. Maybe that's where she belonged. Your secret is out, Adele, a voice screamed at her. Too young. Get out. And run. She could hear her stepfather's laughter. He was winning.

She sat in her chair. Nothing could be worse. Every adult in Bramwell who ever meant anything to her waited for her to run from the room. Denounce her inheritance. They would invoke some smarmy lawyer to strip her of her experience. Find her in the bottom of the pit. Pa had shamed her once more. She couldn't even bury herself in Tommy's arms. He was in Cambridge, nearly 500 miles away. Even the clothes she wore were borrowed. She wasn't smart enough to stop her teenage sister from stealing artifacts from her deceased grandfather. How in the world would she run a million-dollar mining company? She prayed to her Lord and Savior if she could just get out of this room, she would never again, ever try to be something she was not.

Everything Jude said was correct. Nothing about the ten years she spent taking care of her family counted for anything. Suddenly Jude was posturing for board president. President of her company. She felt a chill as the library doors opened, and everyone, except her, stepped out.

She heard David call her name several times. "Adele. You're shaking." The library was empty. "Adele, it's not as bad as you think. You must get ahold of yourself. Everything we talked about just happened."

Adele shook her head. "I can leave tomorrow. What was I thinking?"

David grabbed her and held her against his chest. "This is what got your mother in trouble. Attacks from so many powerful people, she was too embarrassed to stand her ground."

Adele looked at David. "I have no idea what you are talking about. My mother was the best person I've ever known."

"She left unfinished business here in Bramwell. You don't know why she ran away. Don't give up now. I'm going to reconvene the board back from recess. Elijah has some coffee ready for you. You tell me when you're ready."

"I'm not ready," Adele said.

"Yes, you are. Of all the Dawsons, you are the strongest. You saved a mine. Now you're going to rebuild it. And we're going to help. We will find a way to fund the reconstruction. If you surrender on me now, you'll have nothing."

Elijah stood in the doorway with a cup of coffee. When he placed his hands around hers, she felt a strength unlike anything she'd felt before. Tamasin, Elijah, Faye, Briana, Collette, Deirdre, Elysia, Tommy, and Jackson in her corner. She had to fight back. But first, she had to listen.

"You, Miss Kettie's granddaughter," Elijah said. His deep brown eyes soothed her. "You got what it takes to be a boss lady. You stand your ground, hear? Everybody else gets fresh sniff of cognac. Calms the nerves. Even yours."

David called the meeting back into session. "We are not going to fault Adele for not knowing the history of Pocahontas Mine. At this time, I move we go into executive session so we can freely discuss what's driving Jude's fear."

Upon unanimous agreement, David turned the meeting over to Frank Hemlock.

"Seventeen years ago, Mingo County was the site of the bloodiest three-day war between coal miners and strikers."

Adele recalled sitting on her grandfather's lap in this library; her grandparents prevailed upon the governor to impose martial law. Adele was about four years old then. Strike breakers were intent on forcing families out of their homes owned by the mining company. But strikers had set up tent colonies along the Tug River to protect their jobs and protect the mine.

"Those were scary times for us," Garrett added. "Every coal mine owner from Pittsburg to the Cumberland Gap hired their own militia. Property destroyed, riots, and bloodshed rampant. Even the presses were banned from publishing under martial law. During the night, families hid in the mines. Striking fathers and sons lived in tent villages along the river. Hoping to fight back against coal mine owners who brought in immigrants, blacks, Jews, and Irish scabs.

"Conditions were that bad for coal miners," Garrett said. "But your grandfather believed we needed to change how we treated workers. It's when he sought out Governor Morgan to intervene."

The governor was caught between corporate mine owners and swaggering shooters. So, he prohibited all assemblages within the strike zone unless they lived in the tent colony. Strikers kept a lonesome distance from each other. More than one hundred people jammed up in the county jail for violating his orders."

Jude seemed to soften his tone a bit. "When you and Elizabeth started talking up a temporary mining camp up at Buckeye Tipple, amid a possible striker's attack, you stirred up a hornet's nest."

"You feared August Beck would incite another war?" Adele asked.

"He's a protestor, born and bred," Jude answered. "Loves nothing more than a riot, something we cannot afford now that the mines are recovering from the Depression."

"Doesn't matter the cause. Rioting is big business," Garrett answered. "He honed that skill when he was running for state auditor."

David continued while Garrett sipped his cognac. "At the time, Adele, your family owned the Flat Top Coal Company. Quillan and Kettie feared the Flat Top colliery stood too close to the War on the Tug, so Quillan offered military protection to your future father-in-law, Giles Cassidy. Just before Selma and Kenny married, Quillan and Giles consummated the business merger. Ultimately the minefield became the Flat Top Pocahontas Coal Mine."

"Jude," Adele said, "do you think my youthfulness might set off another strike?"

"It certainly sets the stage for that," Jude answered. "Knowing how to delegate is one skill, but your stepfather knows how to pollinate fear and then spin it to his financial advantage. As I understand, he's still chasing after another protest back in Missouri."

Adele held the warm coffee in her hands and finally sipped it, smelling the orange spice from Elijah's shot of cognac. She appreciated the history lesson, but it was time for them also to know a bit more about her.

"For fourteen years, August Beck and I have been fierce opponents. During the great Mississippi flood of 1927, he nearly drowned me. I was ten years old. For years before then, he locked me away from my mother by forcing my twin sisters and me to live in a locked attic, released only to work the cotton fields and eat dinner. When the last of ten babies were born, he told me to quit high school and raise them. Two of the babies never made it beyond a couple of days. Isaac, the last baby … August sold him to our landowner in exchange for getting parcels of land he bartered away. He did this in secret, discovered after my sisters found the contract. You may think I'm a child, but I also know August Beck so much better than any of you. I know his smell, slippery laughter, and conniving temper, and I know he has big protester ambitions in Missouri. West Virginia is not his battleground. There is much more money to be made from tenant farmers. His goal here was to shame me."

She waited for a response but witnessed little more than bankers and lawyers sipping cognac as if it was communion Sunday. It was time for her to share some business concepts she learned from Mr. Fullerman, her high school history teacher and former assistant to the Under-Secretary of Agriculture. She'd also learned a few things from Jackson about the sale of coal.

"Inland Steel is our only real buyer, "Adele continued. "Not much is sold without their nod because they hold the monopoly. If we let Inland overrun us, we sell our livelihood to a company that tells us how much we will earn, where we work, and cheat us on every pound of coal. Right now, they are turning to our competitors because we can't meet demand. Great Britain is the world's biggest buyer of steel, building up its forces against another German invasion. If we aren't producing coal for Inland Steel, they will go elsewhere. So, with your permission, I will entertain a motion to get out of executive session and talk about how we will rebuild Buckeye Tipple."

Jude didn't bend his head, but his eyes looked sideways to Frank Hemlock, then across the room to the bankers. She caught the bankers give him a nod.

"That should set us straight, then,' David said.

Adele's heart warmed knowing her parent's companies would continue making a significant contribution to the economy, but she still had several loose ends. "In moving forward," she asked, "Ivan Mills is dead. His signature no longer holds authority. I plan to hire Jackson Conor as our new mine superintendent."

Adele suspected it would make Jude happy since it would ultimately pave the way for Jude's son, Chase, to be an accountant if Jude and a majority of the board members approved of him. It also would give employment to their daughter's boyfriend. Enough of the gunslinging.

She presented a document with job responsibilities, salary, and incremental incentives, pending safety measures are met. Then, she waited for her board to review her proposal.

"He's worked his way up from underground miner to heavy equipment driver and fire boss," David said. "The men respect him."

"I don't know," Frank said. "He can be a hot head."

"I trust him with my life," David argued. "His principles are in the right place."

Jude called for a vote, which passed with a majority.

"Do you want to inform him of the board's decision, Miss Dawson?" David asked.

Adele thought about the dinner requirement Jackson had imposed on her and opted for a strong ally. "I prefer we do this together. Next week?"

In the next thirty minutes, the board invited Elizabeth Radford into the meeting, where she unfolded blueprints for the temporary mining community, nutritional needs, and water hookups, as long as tents would be retired in four months. Families must be taken off the corporate teat to buy their own groceries.

David Henderson submitted requirements for a bank loan to pay miners time and a half for weekends to rebuild Buckeye Tipple. They would feed families for ten more days and then turn over the care and feeding of miner families to Jude and Elizabeth's grocery and clothing stores in Bluefield. They also approved Jackson Conor's job to also oversee construction, sales, and equipment purchases, if he could make the mine operational within sixty days.

***

Days later, Adele was dressed in a teal green dress fitted to accent her thin hips. She wore a matching pillbox hat and beige gloves for the cool mountain evening. Before leaving the house, Elijah had cautioned her to wear a shawl in the event her valet service took too long to bring her car around after dinner. When she drove up in her grandmother's Buick, Jackson stepped up to let her out before the valet took her keys.

"Don't you look lovely," Jackson said. He took her hand and wrapped it inside his elbow. They were waiting in line outside Fleming Steakhouse when David Henderson joined them.

"An extra guest wasn't on my mind," Jackson whispered in her ear.

The hostess brought them to an oak booth with bench backs covered in black leather. Adele slid into one side. Jackson and David waited until Adele was seated, then Jackson took the bench seat directly across from her. While David stepped away to greet another family dining nearby, Jackson held a sharp focus on Adele, looking away only to listen when the server brought their drinks.

"Are we all business tonight?" Jackson said.

"Yes, we are."

"Too bad. That shade of green brightens your eyes. What's behind them, Adele Dawson?"

David returned to his seat in the booth. "I think we can accomplish what we need to over drinks. You two stay for dinner if you'd like, but I want to spend time with my family."

Adele didn't dare look at Jackson for fear she'd catch his insipient grin.

"On behalf of the Flat Top Pocahontas Coal Mine company, I'd like to confirm Adele's recommendation that we hire you as mine superintendent." He reached across the table and shook hands with Jackson. "Welcome aboard."

David handed a folder of forms that included most of the work Adele had presented to the board. "There is one provision: that you live in the Bramwell home owned by the company. We offer multiple benefits to our leaders that offset the demands on your time. Frankly, we need you focused on rebuilding the mine rather than driving back and forth to Greenbrier County. And we've also included a revenue-sharing plan based on profitability, safety precautions you implement, and employee sustainability."

Jackson opened the envelope. "It may take a few days to read through this."

"Adele can fill you in on most of the details," David said. "I'll be blunt with you. You're the only one I trust to bring the mine back. The bank demands our revenue stabilizes in sixty days. So, if you'll take this job, you must strike while the iron is hot."

"Understood," Jackson said. He reached out to shake David's hand again. "I won't let you down."

"We're counting on that. Now, if you'll excuse me, I've got to make my wife happy again. Been away from her far too long."

Adele watched as David left, then turned back to Jackson. "Are you the one who made that happen? Or did David leave on his own?"

"David's a family man. So am I, or would be, if I ever found the right woman."

"That's for you and Cora to work out."

Jackson smiled as the waiter dressed in black with a white towel over his arm came up to them. "If you're looking for a special meal tonight, I recommend our Tomahawk rib for two. It is served at your preferred temperature with a crusted exterior and a rich buttery garlic sauce seasoned with thyme, rosemary, basil, and fresh parsley. Perfect for a cozy dinner."

"Oh, this is a business dinner," Adele interrupted.

"The steak sounds perfect," Jackson said. "And a bottle of Chateau Lafite."

The server smiled at Jackson. "Is this a special celebration?"

"It is," Jackson said. "This lovely lady and I are celebrating the beginning of a new life together."

""I'm his new boss," Adele stumbled.

"Of course, you are," the server said. "The younger, the better."

When the server stepped away, Adele crossed her hands in front of her. "Let's get one thing straight."

Jackson smiled at her. "Here it comes."

"I may be younger than you, but I am not your bride in waiting. I am the president of a coal mining company. And I am in a committed relationship."

Jackson grinned at her. "I wouldn't have it any other way."

When the steak arrived, the sizzling meat was so large, that it hung over the platter. The server placed the serving plate away from them so that the elongated bone pointed to the middle of the table. He then placed separate bowls containing herb-sprinkled potatoes and asparagus next to Adele. A dollop of butter filled with herbs melted on top of the hot beef. The chef had already scored the steak so that it could easily be divided into two plates.

Jackson grinned. "Served family style. Anything you want to tell me, Miss Dawson?"

"Yes. Say you'll take the job."

Jackson filled both glasses with red wine then raised his glass to her. "To a successful union." Adele tapped her glass to his. "I heard you have what it takes to manage the board of directors," Jackson continued. He sipped his wine, keeping a close eye on her, watching her mouth much too obviously as she lifted the glass.

Adele couldn't remember a time when her senses were more aware of the melting buttery herbs. With each tender bite, she tasted the sweet, sour, bitter, and salty sensations on her tongue. As good a chef as Tamasin was, Adele found it difficult to listen to Jackson talk about how long he had lived in Greenbrier County. She passively listened to his stories about the time he served in France, much too young to be a solder, but he and David Henderson served under the same commander. She didn't notice the waiter stopping at her table to refill her wine or water glasses. Somehow she fell into Jackson's laughter, admiring the joy in his eyes as he described the French countryside.

"For such a demure woman, you sure handle a mean steak knife," Jackson said.

"My word," Adele gasped. "I'm stuffed," she said, then noticed the bottle of red wine was empty. She leaned across the table to thank Jackson for being a complete gentleman when a woman brushed by their table and stood in front of them.

"I know you," she said to Adele. "Something's been bothering me ever since I covered your story in the *Bluefield Daily Telegraph*."

"Rebecca Parsons," Adele recalled. "Did the story ever run?"

"You didn't read it?" Rebecca accused.

"Is there something we can do for you?" Jackson asked.

"You're the man who this little lady hauled up from the pit," Rebecca announced. "We never really knew if you were going to make it."

"Appreciate your concern," Jackson said and turned away from the reporter.

"And here you are. Alive and well. With Miss Dawson." She turned to Adele. "May I ask, what compelled you to go into the pit after him? Is there a juicy story here?"

Jackson brought his napkin to his lips. He slipped out of the booth, then stood in front of the table, blocking Rebecca's access to Adele. "This is a private dinner, Ma'am. So, if you'll be so kind as to schedule another time, we may be able to offer a much bigger story."

Rebecca fumbled through her pocketbook and produced a page torn out of a magazine. "Like this you mean?"

"It's you, isn't it? Miss Dawson. Life magazine did a story about you." Rebecca leaned around Jackson, talking so fast, that neither Jackson nor Adele could respond fast enough. "When I saw you at the mine, I thought you looked familiar. You know, this picture made you famous. At least in Congress."

Jackson grabbed Rebecca's arm to pull her away, but she yanked herself back to the table. "You're the poster child for some Southern Tenant Farmers Association. Lobbyists used it to get funding for sharecroppers. So, who are you? A power grabber? A poor girl from the Bootheel or a mining company baroness? Whoever you are, you are hiding at least one identity from some very important legislators."

Jackson waived to the maître d'. "We're finished here," he said, blocking Rebecca from any further access to Adele.

Rebecca's voice grew louder. "It's a fair question. You see this woman's pitiful photo," she asked, holding up the picture of Adele and her sisters outside a dirty buttermilk painted shack. Chickens and filthy dogs stood on a dirt road next to a young boy. "Cover girl for the down and out."

"That's not who I am," Adele answered.

Rebecca studied the torn magazine photo. "No? It sure looks like you," Rebecca said. "How much did Life Magazine pay you to pose for this picture? Are you posing for another identity, ma'am?"

Rebecca looked at the magazine clipping, then held it up for other diners to see, all the while trying to force her way into Adele's line of vision. "James Madison's the photographer. These photos made him famous, too."

Jackson reached for Adele's hand and pulled her next to him. Then, he reached for her shawl, wrapped it around her shoulder, and held her tightly against his side. He pushed Rebecca Parsons out of the way while he led Adele out of the restaurant. His truck was parked less than two blocks away.

He opened the door and helped her climb in. "Stay here. I'll take care of the check," Jackson said tersely.

Adele bowed her head. Two years ago, she had been the woman in that picture. Unknowingly manipulated by Olga Beck, August's new wife, Adele believed she and her stepfamily were selected to document the lives of impoverished tenant farmers during the Great Depression. James Madison, the New York photographer, had been modest and kind while capturing their shanty home, the meager clothes they wore, a "radically artistic portrait," he had called it, of suffering. The story helped her win a grant from the Farm Security Administration to form New Madrid county's first co-op. That was before her grandmother summoned Adele to her dying bedside.

She sat in Jackson's truck and watched Rebecca Parsons being escorted from the restaurant by a brut of a man. The bouncer kept his large hand around the reporter's arm as he led her to her car. He didn't open the car door as much as he nearly ripped it off its hinges before shoving her inside. Then, before closing the now bent car door, he yanked the Zeiss camera from her pocketbook, opened it, and ripped film until it curled around his fist. She tried to explain. The bouncer said nothing but nodded at Jackson as he exited the restaurant. Jackson took large strides until he climbed into his truck.

His breath was hot, even in the cool evening weather. Beads of sweat formed around his eyebrows, but he said nothing until finally, he asked, "Am I building a mine, or will I be protecting you from your past?"

Adele opened the door to leave. "I will call the valet to bring my car around." Jackson reached over her and slammed it closed.

"We start with clear communication, or I don't take this job."

Adele held her hands in her lap. "What do you want to know, Jackson?"

"For one thing, what in the hell do you have over August Beck that he damn near kills everything that stands between you and him? And how did you ever manage to stay alive when you've lived like that?"

She looked at him to figure out whether he was mimicking or helping her. "People do what they have to," she answered. "We had a beautiful house on a farm when August moved Mama and me to Missouri. But then, floods, wheat failures, bad debt, his gambling, ate away at him. I don't know what made him this hateful. You would know better than I. He's from here. What made him so bitter?"

"He was raised bitter," Jackson answered. "Talk in town is that Irving saw something in August. Maybe with enough school, or enough college, he might have a decent chance at life if he was removed from such a bitchin bad family. You hang around church ladies enough; they'll tell you Auggie was the not-quite-son of a Dawson. What does that make you? You're blood. He's the outcast. Is that it, Miss Dawson?"

Adele felt exhausted. "I came here, trying to forget my life in Missouri. Reconcile what happened to my family for the last fifteen years. I wanted my sisters to have what I never did. All I've managed to do is bring hatred and destruction with me. I don't know where the reporter got that article."

"I don't give a damn about that reporter," Jackson interrupted. "What I saw in that clip is that there's common ground between you and me. I was that scrubby little boy. I scratched my way through the West Virginia hollers, Adele. I can rebuild your mine in forty-five days. And it will be better than any mine around. You might think I'm just someone David Henderson says you should hire, but I learned mining from the stripes on my back."

"So you're not angry with me?"

"Angry? Hell no! I'm sorry you don't trust me more than you do."

Adele smiled deep inside. "The reporter has it in for me."

"She's up to no good. I don't like her," Jackson said. "Said something about you being a cover girl? Wasn't Selma a Besame cosmetics' girl?"

"Jackson, I keep trying to get to the bottom of Momma's story. Elizabeth Radford has the answer. I need time alone with her."

"What you need is time with your other grandmother. Selma's mom."

The notion that Selma had a mother shocked her; it made her hair tighten. "What?"

"Birth parents. You never thought to ask about your mother's family?" Jackson said.

"Only once do I recall my mother saying anything about the Cassidys. Kettie, Quillan, Kenneth; they were her family. Are any of the Cassidy's still alive?"

"Gladys and Giles? They live up in Falls Mills. About four miles from here."

"Jackson, I have to visit her. She may have some answers. Like why my mother married the likes of August Beck."

Chapter 18:
Unraveling Decades of Secrets

"Tamasin, did you know my mother's mother is still alive?" Adele asked the next morning. "She lives a few miles from here."

Tamasin tossed a spoon angrily into the sink and pulled a hot pad from the stove drawer. "Not far enough, if you ask me."

Tamasin busied herself with breakfast for the girls. "Get yourself a dish a them biscuits n gravy," she told Adele. "Warms your heart and soul. Miss Collette, you staying afta school today for basketball?"

"Yes, ma'am."

"Hitch a ride back home with Miss Briana. She in the theater club. Drama, you know? Drama, drama." Tamasin flailed her hands. " Elijah pick you both up at 4:30. Don't be making him wait."

Adele waited for Tamasin to stop chattering.

"Look like it might get to snowing by the weekend," Tamasin continued.

Adele sat at the table with her sisters. "Snow?"

Briana shoved the last of her biscuit into her mouth. "Better than ice storms. Maybe Elijah will pull out the sleds."

"Maybe. If the snow tops ten inches. Might could happen."

"You girls, get on to school. Me and Faye goin' work on our alphabet today." As soon as the girls were halfway down the stone driveway, Adele turned to Tamasin. "I got the hint. But the woman I asked about is their grandmother, too."

Tamasin tossed a dish cloth from her shoulder into the sink. "Some storm doors best left sealed."

"You know that only makes me want to know more."

"Can't shove demons back inside once they get released."

"Tamasin, people in the area know a lot more than I do about the Cassidy family. What are you and Elijah keeping from me?"

Tamasin shook her head as she stepped into the pantry. She raised the lid to a flour canister and reached down through white powder, then pulled an envelope taped to the bottom. "I knows about what happened at the fancy eatery last night."

"You mean the reporter?"

"I wasn't talking about you and Mr. Conor. That a whole 'nother matter."

"She came at me from out of nowhere."

"Not nowhere. My Negroes seen her headin' your way. She been drinking at the bar, building steam. Showin' off that *Life* magazine picture."

Ever since arriving in West Virginia, Adele had come to understand that families of color had a way of communicating so intimately connected that weren't visible to her. "Tell me about my other grandmother."

"Gonna have to learn that you'self." Tamasin opened the envelope and pulled out a key. "I'll send Elijah up into the attic. Sit with him a spell. I warn you. Can't undo secrets once you open that door. Best be sure you got your breastplate on afore you open any locked door."

***

Adele straightened up the mess Benita left behind in the attic. She replaced empty boxes to the shelves and gently folded blue tissue paper that had once cushioned Mama's dresses. She stopped to pick up silver sequins, pulled away when Benita stuffed a gown into her suitcase. A brochure of what the girls thought to be a younger Olga had been torn, pieces crumpled on the floor. She stepped around the faded white columns. The paintings from Ludwig Kirchner and Paul-Hubert Lepage tilted cockeyed as if someone had examined them but quickly replaced them to the bins. The Otto Dix was missing.

Behind the green velvet curtain, she found the bank vault. Fresh scratches into the rosette appliques reminded her that Benita knew something big was inside the box.

Elijah met her on the back staircase, refusing to enter the attic through Miss Kettie's bedroom. "Thought you might be needin a bodyguard to sit beside you," he said.

"Stop, Elijah. Please. Just open the box."

She waited until his key matched the one she got from Tamasin. No gold, no money. Just brown legal-size envelopes, newspaper clippings, boxes of canceled checks, and a gold-plated Besame Cosmetics' accent chest.

"I don't get it," she said to Elijah. "What's the big secret?"

"Money. Greed. Power. Might be all seven deadly sins in this here box."

"Where do I start?"

"I s'pose Miss Kettie would want you to start with the Besame box."

Adele lifted the wooden container. It was much heavier than she expected. The lid had been secured with the Dawson family emblem seal. "You break that, you open up dirty family business. Gets to be too much, come get me."

When Elijah left the room, Adele picked at the seal until it broke into several pieces. Adele warmed wax sections in her hand as if someone might hold her accountable for breaking them. Finally, she sat on the floor and released the Besame secrets. It took her long into the night to unravel the puzzle, but it was all there, buried inside sealed contracts. It would be a long night, perhaps an even longer day tomorrow.

***

Her mother, Selma Marie Cassidy, eighteen-year-old daughter of Giles and Blanche Cassidy, was the first Besame girl. Adele opened a package of black and white photos to find three women wearing low-waisted dressed, bobbed hairstyles tucked under cloche hats. Their sensual stance included long geometric scarves and matching stockings. One woman held a long cigarette holder. Another held a strand of pearl beads as if caught in the midst of a twirl. Behind them a photo of the Linsly School for Girls stone entrance gate.

Noted on the back Olga Guttenberg, Selma Cassidy, and Elizabeth Frazier. Class of 1918. "Olga?" Adele questioned. The same Olga who married August Beck?

Another photo read, "Olga, Lizzy, and me at the Oglebay Golf Resort. Olga scored 73. Lizzy and me, 81." Another black and white photo. "Lizzy and me doing the Charleston, 1918. Olga sprained her back doing the Black Bottom."

"Mama, you and The Beast were friends?" Adele said out loud. "You never mentioned her. What happened? Nineteen eighteen. Two years before I was born."

A third faded black and white photo showed pictures of three couples dressed in formal wear standing under a floral archway. The back said, "The War Is Over! Senior formal, 1918. Olga and Auggie, Lizzy and Jude, Kenny and me."

"Wait!" Adele said. "Olga and Auggie were a couple in 1918?" If her stepfather and Olga knew each other in college, had he continued seeing her even after he married Selma?"

She opened another package of photos labeled "The Red Summer Triplets."

A rubber band held photos together into four bundles. The first bundle featured Olga demonstrating how to apply mascara. In one photo, she held what looked to be a golden box of caked mascara, and a Besame signature stamped on the lid. Even in the black and white photos, the lipstick looked bright red. In other photos, Olga lifted a brush to make long, lush eyelashes.

Adele choked at the vulgarity of Olga being even slightly seductive. She hated the thought of her step-father being romantically involved with the witch while he was married to Selma. When things got really bad at the farm, he'd be gone for days. Adele considered perhaps he wasn't just hunting deer. "What a floozy," Adele murmured.

A second pile showed a much younger, thinner version of Elizabeth Frazier applying various colors of lipstick. In each photo, Lizzy, now Elizabeth Radford, was demonstrating what might have been shades of red, pink, or peach if they'd been in color. Her lips curled up in a smooch. Yuck. Adele was immediately revolted by this lustful act, especially since Elizabeth could turn spiteful on a dime.

The third set of photos was wrapped inside brochures of Selma holding the Japanese fan. Mama was a one-of-a-kind beauty with a feminine mystique that obviously captured the photographer's attention. Here, she wasn't the woman who sacrificed her body to give Pa ten children. She was majestic; royalty. Her smile so enticing, it lured the viewer into a secret friendship. In another photo, Selma's eyeliner swooped up into an angle at the corner of her eye, making her look exotic, intoxicating, and yet unattainable. Adele realized the man standing in the background, looking approvingly at her, was Kenneth Dawson, her beloved father, protector, and hero.

Wedding pictures of Elizabeth and Jude Radford had been compiled into the fourth pile. Behind the cake-cutting picture, Adele noticed a smaller image of a couple caught in an argument. Another photo confirmed it was Olga pointing a finger into Auggie's chest. His face horribly twisted up as if to shout back at her.

"All of you were Besame girls?" Adele asked, trying to process the contents. Why then would these photos be locked up? What troubled the family so much that they would rather keep memories locked up? "Why not destroy them?" Adele whispered.

A legal-size folder labeled Besame Legal had been shoved down along the side of the bank vault. Brass fasteners had broken away, but a second wax seal closed it again. Adele picked away at the seal, then gently removed its content. Sacred ground. Sealed for a reason. She would write to Tommy and tell him all about these contracts later tonight.

She felt she was betraying confidence that wasn't hers to own. "I'm sorry, Mama. But I have to know."

After reading through the Whereas paragraphs, she learned that Besame had consolidated its product line under the creative leadership of one advertising agency, and that agency identified Selma Marie Cassidy as its American model. On page four of the contract, the agency would pay Olga Guttenberg and Elizabeth Frazier five thousand dollars each, in exchange for the irrevocable release of any claim to photos, products, and forever discharged releasee and its affiliates, successors and assigns, any obligations, promises, agreements, disputes, or causes of action connected with this release.

A separate envelope contained two documents from the West Virginia Judiciary. The first was an emergency personal safety order. The second, is a final protective order with a judge's stamp and signature. "Neither Olga Guttenberg nor Elizabeth Frazier shall have any written, oral, or in person contact with Selma Marie Cassidy. Neither may come within 100 feet of her physical body. "How did such a friendship turn sour? Mama? What did they do to you?"

A box with multiple Besame samples had been tucked beneath the envelopes. How old they were, she may never know. Lipstick in a compact, the shade of red she'd never seen except on her mother's photo. Eyeshadow, rouge.

Adele heard the front doorbell ring, but she was too far into the bank box to quit.

A yellowed brochure clipped to the protective order showed three women dressed in white satin low-cut gowns leaning seductively against a man behind the wheel of a convertible Bugatti. The man was dressed in a blue three-piece suit with a red polka dot tie and a red carnation on his lapel. "Fastest run through Moonshiner 28 wins an evening with one of these beauties. Two hundred runs get this Bugatti." Moonshiner 28s, Adele thought, was what Elijah had called daring men who drove through twisting roads under a cloak of secrecy to avoid revenuers.

"Oh, I bet Besame pitched a fit over that photo," Adele said under her breath. "Moonshine runners?"

Another legal document spelled out the contents of Selma Cassidy's reinstatement as the sole Besame model. In return, she would receive federal protection if she turned over evidence that the Besame girls were putting up a 'nice girl" image for the mobsters.

"Mobsters? Mama!" Adele stood abruptly, losing her balance. She halted any movement, hesitating to make any noise. Instead, she slowly sat back down and read on.

The Famiglia Vagabonda, composed of Black Handers, Comoristi, and Mafiosi, operating in Clarksburg and Fairmont, West Virginia, carried out a campaign of extortion in the Italian community. They were involved in gambling, narcotics trafficking, bootlegging, prostitution, kidnapping and murder. They had already killed twelve agents and a series of dynamitings carried out in West Virginia, Pennsylvania, and Maryland.

Big Joe Canetti, a member of the Famiglia Vagabonda family, was the man who coerced the three women to sit with him behind the wheel. Miss

Cassidy also must provide state evidence that would lead to the conviction of Frank Pisconeri, head of the Famiglia Vagabonda in Marion County.

"Oh, Mama," She gasped. "How did you get tied in with the mob? And dynamiting?"

She remembered Benita mentioning Olga liked to talk about her gangsters. This had to be Olga's fault. As a friend of the governor, Quillan must have called in some big favors to get mama out of trouble. Harold Hamburg, you were mama's Besame lawyer. Did you stand beside her while she turned against the famiglia? How did you protect her?"

Storm doors best left sealed. A voice from the kitchen sounding like her grandfather warned her to close the box.

She stood again and stepped back. "Elijah?" she called.

"Yes, ma'am. Be right there." She recalled the times he would sit outside Kettie's bedroom when she was most vulnerable, listening to her labored tuberculin breathing and knowing when she was gasping. He was still that close.

"Is someone here?" Adele asked.

"Your Uncle Irving just arrived, ma'am. Miss Tamasin escorted him to the library."

"I'm not ready for him yet."

"Ready or not, he here."

I'll be right there." Before she descended the third-floor attic, she locked the attic door. She placed the key in her skirt pocket, remembering that if Benita knew where the key was hidden, so did the others.

***

Adele combed her hair, put one of mama's barrettes named Radiance Spoon along one side of her head, and slipped into another skirt before descending the stairs. Irving's visit was unexpected. Though she suspected once he was back in the area, he might want rightful ownership in the Flat

Top Pocahontas Coal Mine. What she didn't know was whether Quillan had provided him any title to property in exchange for Irving going to prison. Now that I've just got Jackson signed up to be manager. All that work! Was it for naught? After serving thirty years in prison for killing August Beck's hot-headed father, he had a right to that claim.

Elijah held the library door in his hand. "You been up in that attic a long time I didn't hear no screaming."

"I'm getting closer to understanding why mama ran away. But the more I learn, the more confused I get."

"Maybe Mr. Irving might help."

"Mr. Dawson," Elijah said as he opened the door. "May I present Miss Adele Christina Dawson?"

Adele was stunned at the handsome man who stood to greet her. Looking very much like Quillan, she was immediately swept away by his warm smile. All the Dawson men shared a spirit of athletic gallantry. She saw glimpses of her daddy and her grandfather in Irving's face. When he reached out to shake her hand, she felt what thirty years of hard labor had done to him. A thick line cut through his left eyebrow. Rough scarred hands. Dark ruddy skin from years of pounding nails into railway lines. She was immediately in love with him. That, she determined, is what the Dawson men did to her. Even an eighty-three-year-old convict.

He stood waiting for her to sit. The Queen Anne library chairs had been placed in an oval setting. She led him over to two rocking chairs where she could hear everything he had to say.

"Welcome home, sir."

"Would you feel uneasy calling me Uncle Irving?"

"Uncle Irving," Adele repeated. It seemed unnatural, but she would try. He was out of prison on a compassionate release and likely needed a home.

"Pretty like your mother," Irving said. "My wife said she saw you at

Miss Kettie's funeral."

"I didn't know she was there."

"Unlikely anyone would have introduced you to her. People up Mingo County way still hold a grudge against me. My wife died soon after the funeral."

"I'm so sorry, Uncle Irving. Anything I've learned is from Elijah, Tamasin, and a few neighbors."

"I went to prison before your mother and father were married. Quillan and Kettie would bring my wife up to Hazelton once a month. Made sure I had some comforts. Auggie, he never visited. Didn't think he would. I tried to raise him right, but I guess that didn't happen."

"I cannot imagine what it must have been like for you. Alone. Away from family."

"Meeting the granddaughter of Quillan Dawson living in this home. Worth the trouble."

Elijah brought in plate of fresh ginger snaps, placed them on a side table, and poured a cup of sweet persimmon tea for both, then excused himself from the room.

Irving sipped his tea, then replaced the cup with its saucer. "You must be wondering why I'm here."

Adele held the teacup in her hand, wondering how much she would reveal in her response. Finally, she said, "You're family, sir. Uncle Irving."

"Thirty years makes a man think a lot about his family. Good things. Not so good things that might need to be corrected."

"It's a beautiful fall day. Do you want to sit on the porch?" Adele asked.

Irving nodded. "Don't get a lot of outdoors when you're in the big house."

She walked with him to the front porch and offered him the rocker she usually sat in when she wanted to feel close to her grandmother. Irving leaned back comfortably. "I made this rocker for Quill and Kettie. Wedding gift."

"Well, my goodness, it sure held up well. Fifty years or better."

"If you could extend some grace to my son, my foster son, I'd like you to know he has a good side, August does. The missus and I tried to instill a bit of Godliness in him."

Adele looked at Irving. No person can be all bad or all good, she thought. But her stepfather had an exceptional thirst for wickedness. How could Irving possibly offer any explanation that would earn August Beck a lick of grace?

"How did he get my mother to marry him?" Adele blurted. She had waited for nearly fifteen years to find the answer, and there it was, sitting right in front of her. A wounded tiger tossed into the arena of mountain madness. Noona had told her the answer was in the white steamer trunk. The steamer trunk held plenty of stories. But Noona hadn't mentioned the bank box in the attic.

"Selma has seen some hard times, too. She got caught up with a feisty crew of lawless girls after her mother and father put her in boarding school. Neither of them could stand the gossip about their little girl."

"It must have been hard for my mother."

"Broke my heart to see that pretty face all banged up by the Beck boys. And the talk around town filtered out of the mouths of Christians; there wasn't a place to hide that girl."

"So her parents put her in a boarding school."

"I reckon that's what happened. No one saw hide nor hair of her. Giles would shake out a kerchief of tears every time I saw him."

"Can you tell me a little about the Besame girls? Elizabeth and Olga?" Adele asked.

Irving chuckled sarcastically. "Olga. Gutter hag, that one. Raised by a hillerho. What'd ya expect?" He waited for Adele to stop snickering.

"Elizabeth got herself straightened out. Kind of a badass, pardon me, Adele. Served time, but Olga was a true cockatrice." Irving shook his head as if to shed horrible memories, then returned to his story.

"After prohibition and Amendment 18, Olga started running with the Black Hands in Marion County. Prohibitionists. They banded together with Frank Pisconeri and carried out a campaign of extortion throughout the county. Sent out threatening letters, punished those who didn't pay out. Didn't matter for what. Carved her lot as a lobbyist early on."

Irving placed his hand on a book, then pretended to outline his hand with his fingers. "If they decided it was your time to die, they drew a picture of a hand-painted black on the back of an envelope. It was the famiglia's way of letting you know they grew impatient waiting for you to pay their extortion. Olga and Elizabeth hung out with the boys in the back of Pete Fisher's barber shop on Water Street in East Fairmont. To be a gang member, you had to commit a murder for no good reason. Personal reasons did not count. Vics were usually an Italian businessman. Miss Olga, she made gang member too easily; no one ever ratted her out. We don't know who she killed, only that she earned a membership.

By the time one of her Vics received his third letter, he was marked for death unless he paid a much larger sum of money. Pisconeri dynamited at least ten resident homes before he took out the one marked with a Black Hand. Your father, Kenneth, knew about them and fought against organized crime. For a while, so did Auggie when he was running for state auditor.

Girl named Belle Lemmon got caught up in a love triangle between Big Nose Cenendre and Tony Corbi. When Belle chose Tony as her husband, she ended up naked, and stabbed seventeen times. Olga was one of Belle's friends, but Olga was street smart. She cozied up to August Beck. August protected her from the law and the Cenedre gang.

Adele sat stunned. Olga had led a deceitful life, but worse, August was married to her now as his wife. Which meant she had access to Benita. Olga had been alone with her sisters while Adele was in West Virginia caring for Noona. How, by the grace of God, had her sisters managed to stay out of Olga's way? She would never give them back to her stepfather now. Not as long as she had breath in her lungs.

"Have you ever heard of the Besame Girls?" Irving asked.

"I have."

"Then you should know that Olga threatened Selma with a Black Hands letter if she wasn't invited to be a Besame girl."

If Adele could put out a warrant for Olga's arrest, she would do it, right now! What kind of friendship was that? And how horrible for her mother to be so manipulated.

"When Besame canceled its contract with the Red Summer Triplets, Olga demanded the Famiglia Vagabonda dynamite the Dawson and Cassidy homes. Quillan and Kenneth somehow learned about the plan from some poor soul who likely died for his good deeds. Quillan called in the West Virginia State Bureau of Investigation, had the Vagabonda members indicted, but not before twelve more innocents were murdered, including the young little mouthpiece, Belle Lemons, who sold out Olga. Thought she was saving Olga's life, but the Cenendres already had good reason to stab her. Stripped her naked. Dumped her body on old man Beck's farm.

"Your mother was protected by the courts when she turned state's witness against Olga. Elizabeth cut her own deal. Olga pleaded guilty for extortion but never spent a day in jail. No tellin' why."

The thought of her mother running from gangsters did not fit into the scrapbook of knowledge she held in her heart. "Mama never let on."

Irving nodded. "Selma and Kenneth married and moved into this family's home, protected by the Dawson family." Irving pointed to the stone patio, "These walls, which I helped build, are enough of a fortress for a while. But your daddy couldn't live like that. A reporter came to Kenneth's state senate campaign and recognized your beautiful mother from the Vagabonda pamphlet. Kenny was rushing to get home when he was run off the road. Beat to a pulp."

"My daddy." She paused to take in his demise, the unrequited love he and mama shared. She felt bile raise in her mouth from the damage Olga had done to her father. The way the mobsters beat him stole him from her. "I read about that in my mother's diary," Adele confessed. "If not for her writing such intimate and sorrowful entries, I would not have suspected she was anything but the poor wife of a sharecropper," Adele said. "Olga called my mama a demon for trollop cosmetics. But she also said my mama was the cause for you going to prison, Uncle Irving."

Irving shook his head. "I went to prison for shooting my gun when my mouth couldn't pull the trigger. Old Man Beck killed my horse. His sons claimed they had their way with your mama. Lame braggarts got themselves moonshine impotence. Turns out Selma fought more than they expected."

Go, Mama! Adele said to herself.

"Your mother's parents swept her off to boarding school, but they were so terribly ashamed by the scandal that they disowned her. That's the real crime here, Adele. Her parents never showed up for Kenny and Selma's wedding. Claimed they had no daughter, not even when the Dawsons welcomed her into a family of great wealth. Five years later, when Kenny died, Quillan and Kettie told Selma she could stay in the house for as long as she wanted. Precious child, you were just four years old."

"She could have moved in with her parents, couldn't she?"

"I'm sorry to say they refused to acknowledge her. Said they had no child."

"How does a mother turn away her baby girl? Especially when she's in danger?" Adele felt the shame and unworthiness they forced on her mother. She recalled lying on top of Selma three years ago after Isaac was born. Curling her mother in her arms to keep angels from taking her mama to heaven.

"But why didn't mama move back home with Quillan and Kettie? They were her in-laws."

"Can't say as I know the real reason for that," Irving answered. "Shame kills happiness. Forces people to hide when they can't face the truth about themselves. Weren't even about Gladys and Giles. But they tormented your mama so. She had to leave."

"Her own mother disowned my mama," Adele repeated, trying to understand such a heartbreaking feeling.

Irving rocked in the chair for a while. Adele could almost see the theater of disaster after disaster rolling through his mind. His jaw tightened, pulsed. Then, he raised his head and took a deep breath.

"But what I do know is that my wife and I got August baptized in the Presbyterian church. At the time I went to jail, he was an upstanding young man. I heard he was running for state auditor. Miss Kettie must have thought he really had turned his life around. But you know what they say, 'once the Antichrist gets into a man's blood, the devil just lies in waiting for utter destruction.' Sure as heck, that's what got into my August."

Irving let out a few loud coughs, enough for Adele to recognize the sound of a miner's lung. "When you disobey the mafia, they don't forget," he went on. "Pasquale "Patsy" Corbi moved on to Chicago, but he remembered Olga, and he remembered Selma. When Patsy sent the Black Hands letter to Selma, August stepped in and offered to move her to a place so far away they'd never find her. I only had him for eight years. Not enough time to fix a bad habit. But of all the wrong things he did, my Auggie did right by Selma.

Irving continued. "So, Selma, her heart broken from losing her beloved Kenny, disowned by her parents, agreed to marry August. He wasn't a looker by any means, I know that, but he wanted children. Kettie said she'd help finance Selma's protection, but she made him swear that when you, Miss Adele, turned eighteen, he would return you to your rightful family."

"She was the most devoted, loving mother to me. How did she ever find the strength to love again when her own mother abandoned her?"

Irving shook his head. "Sometimes babies fill the void from disavowed parents."

"Mama was trapped," Adele said. "What happened to her disgusting parents?"

"Still living, far as I know, up in Falls Mills."

"I pass through on my way to the Bluefield campus," Adele said, then wondered why, if he was still alive, Giles never came to any of the coal mine board meetings.

"My grandfather purchased Flattop Mine from him. Did Giles also give up his board position? Maybe David didn't invite them to our last meeting?"

"Get a certain age, you let your banker stand in your place," Irving said. "Keeps them from having to reconcile you as Selma's daughter. Which brings me to another reason for my visit."

"I want to know that reason. But, my sisters will be home soon, and I'm not sure I want them to hear any more."

"Not much waiting left in this tired old body," Irving said. "I've been practicing what I would say for thirty years. If all I get is thirty seconds, I'll take it." He paused as if to force his mind to condense his comments. "I'd like to make it right between you and the Cassidy family. If you let me, I want peace in Giles, my friend's heart. We were school buddies. Served in the Marines together. Now I want to make sure Giles knows he's got grandchildren this side of the Mississippi. May I do that for you?" he asked, then leaned into the rocker, ready to stand. "And that brings an end to my stay."

"Wait. Why would they want to see us? Adele asked.

"Adele, Miss Blanche can be hard-headed. But this separation has torn Giles apart. He used to come up to Hazelton prison, check on me, you know? But all he'd do is cry over his beloved little Selma. Maybe if he met his grandchildren, his heart might heal a tad bit."

"All this time, I never heard one word about Mama's family," Adele responded. "I don't know, Uncle Irving. I have to give this some thought. Where are you staying?"

"With my daughter up in Bluefield. My baby girl. Already lost too much time with her. Don't take too long, Adele. I've got a ticker about to give up on me."

"No one told you about the money Quillan set aside for you?"

Irving laughed. "Quillan took care of my family while I was locked up. That's all I ever asked for."

"Two million dollars," Adele answered.

Irving leaned back in his rocker and shook his head. He put his hand over his chest like he wanted to keep his heart from falling out. "No, ma'am. That is not true."

"I don't know where it's kept. I do know my grandfather was grateful to you for protecting his family's honor," Adele said. "I will ask David Henderson and Eugene Bolworth to explain the details to you." She thought how rarely goodness popped into her life during the years she was on the farm. She understood now how siblings honor the other, either with silence or with an unexpected inheritance.

"How will I ever thank him?" Irving finally asked.

"Seems that's what made you such good brothers," Adele answered. "Never took the other for granted."

"And that's why I want you to know Giles," Irving said. "His heart for family is ripped with sadness."

Adele rocked in her chair. "I don't know that I really have much to say to a woman who shunned my mama, though."

"Mercy me," Irving said. "Sounds like I have a bit of patchwork to do. Next week, then?"

***

Later that night, Adele wrote a letter to Tommy, unraveling all the details about the family she never knew existed. She explained her anger at Giles and Blanche for abandoning her mother, scolding them for such heartless parenting. She also wrote about her Uncle Irving, how strong he looked, and explained how fragile he really was.

Three days later, she received a letter from Tommy.

> Precious Delly,
> I am in awe of you. The way you are uncovering your family history. Such anecdotes will give you a powerful connection to discover the women who have shaped you into the woman I love. Most of us give a listen now and then when it suits our mood. But you are the quintessential searcher. How heavy your heart must be to find a disastrous grandmother! If only I could be with you to warm you, holding you and your big heart as you bring your family together.
> I will give some thought to dangers of opened secrets and respond after my history class.
>
> Sweet baby Delly,
> I'm back from history, and it is late at night. I'm writing to you as I sit on the staircase of Harry Elkins Widener's library.

Inside are high ceilings, chandeliers, and so many hidden spots. Each time I find another low-lit chair, I think of the mysteries you have uncovered in your own life. Who would have thought you had grandparents that would turn away a woman with a heart as gorgeous as Selma Cassidy Dawson Beck? It's hard for me to write her name because I need room to add, "Blessed Mother of Adele Christina Dawson."

Come visit me please, I beg of you. I will take you to Annenberg Hall. It's difficult to eat in that dining room without gazing at all the luminescent or studying the beautifully carved windows. Its Gothic wooden trusses, and a ceiling so high, I wonder if it even ends. Enough of me and my love of Harvard.

Secrets, my love, are a disease all unto themselves. My father's health has deteriorated; I hate that I may lose him before I graduate. He must be careful not to let his skeletons slip out. A part of me wants to see him suffer. Another part is grateful for sending me to college. If you help your grandfather reveal his conspiracy, perhaps he will live long enough to share even more about wonderful YOU.

I must go home for Thanksgiving, but I will come to you during Christmas break unless you decide to thrill me with an unexpected visit to my gorgeous Cambridge. How lucky can a man be? I cherish and adore you. Love Tom

A trip to Harvard! How majestic, she thought to herself. Could she find time between classes, mining operations, and loving on her sisters?

Adele looked at his signature again. Tom. Not Tommy. Adele tucked his letter into her pocket and promised herself she would meet her grandfather, Giles.

Chapter 19:
Adele and Her Grandparents

B y sundown, strong winds whistled through the mountain and funneled their fury into the Bramwell valley. Clouds turned dark gray; moisture lingered like clouds on the ground. Adele and Tamasin ran back into the house from a grocery run, loaded with enough food to keep them prepared for days indoors. By mid-afternoon, snow blanketed the small town heavy layers of snow. Faye sat at the window ledge giving a snowdrift update as she sang songs Tamasin had taught her.

Adele huddled in the library with her sisters as they did their homework, stopping every half hour or so to bring in more logs from the backyard to feed the fireplace.

When Elijah claimed the snow would reach two feet, Collette, Elysia, and Deidre rushed into the kitchen and begged Tamasin to make sticky figs and pecan pudding. Tamasin giggled, and then offered to add a toffee topping. A pile of elderberry leaves hung over the sink. She rubbed them together, dropped them into a tea cup, then poured a cup of hot water over the leaves. She asked Elijah to be sure he brought down sassafras roots for her arthritic hands.

"Math and English first," Adele instructed. "Then, you can eat pudding till morning."

She and Tamasin exchanged smiles as Tamasin returned to the kitchen pantry. Faye served as chef, announcing to Collette and Elysia the food products Tamasin gathered for the pudding. "She found the F. I. G. S.

Coc'nut flakes. Sugar. F. L. A. R. And whipping cream."

It was as if a blanket of despair had lifted from the girls since Benita left. Adele giggled each time Faye provided an update. Tomorrow they would pull out snow sleds, but this night was a time to share the cozy joy of family, yummy winter desserts, and each other. If she could package this feeling and send it to heaven, she knew Selma and Kenneth would be so proud of the tiny world they were creating in Bramwell. Away from poverty. Warmed and sheltered. Filled with Figgie pudding, pecans with whipped cream on top.

As Elijah had predicted, at least three feet of snow fell to the ground. Drifts covered the library windows with breathtaking ridges of snowflakes. Adele was certain schools would close.

"Let's go sledding," she announced at breakfast. "We have our own mountain."

"Mighty cold outside," Elijah warned. "But I know where Miss Kettie stuffed long johns. Course it's all Kenneth's underwear."

Elysia and Deirdre pinched their noses, but Collette leaped from the table. "Show me. They all look the same to me."

"Oh, like you would know what boy's underwear looks like," Elysia teased.

"I've seen a few peckers," Collette snapped.

Adele dropped her fork onto her plate. "I don't want to hear another word about that. Climb into the underwear. All of you."

If there was a day to remember for the rest of her life, it was this day. The sun broke through the afternoon skies, warming their faces while the girls rode anything they could find from the back porch down to River Road. Garbage can lids, worn-out toboggans that likely hadn't been used since Adele's father and his brothers lived here. Elijah sat in the back of one toboggan behind Collette and Briana, showing them how to steer without breaking an ankle.

Around lunch time, Jackson walked up the driveway, carrying a shovel. He wore a wool knit cap that covered his black hair except for the sideburns around his ears.

"Thought I'd check on you, Elijah, and your band of snow bunnies. Make sure you have enough wood for the fire. Work on the mine is closed, at least for a few days."

He waved to Elijah. "Look at you, Old Man. Showing off our winter sports."

"We're not in the plains," Elysia argued. "We live in West Virginia."

Adele took a deep breath and giggled so hard it brought tears to her eyes. "Yes, Elysia. We all live in West Virginia."

Tamasin brought out hot chocolate with melted marshmallows and placed the thick mugs on a porch table. "Get yourselves warmed up, now."

Elijah was at the bottom of the hill when he smiled up at his wife. "Woman, you are my source of joy.." He nudged Jackson and invited him up to the porch. "Tamasin, where is your coat?"

"Stop your fussin'. Couldn't carry these here mugs with big coat arms." She turned to go back into the house when she slipped and nearly fell. Elijah and Jackson leaped to be at her side. Jackson got to her first. "Easy there, sweet lady. Don't want you twisting an ankle."

Elijah brushed Jackson off. "Jus' a little short of breath is all," Elijah said. "I gots ya, Sweet Woman. Make you a nice cup of elderberry."

Adele exchanged glances with Jackson. "Is she okay?"

Jackson flitted his fingers against his heart. "Just a little breathy. Dr. Luttrell checked on her last week."

"When? I didn't see him here?"

"He knows how much you worry."

"But she told you?" Adele argued.

Jackson sipped his hot chocolate. "Boy talk. Elijah and I go way back."

"If there is something I should know, you will tell me. Right?" she asked.

"Of course." A sliver of melted marshmallow rested on Jackson's upper lip. "I heard Irving paid a visit."

"Go like this," Adele said. She licked her upper lip as instructions to remove the white line of marshmallow.

"My, my. Do that again," Jackson teased. He handed her a napkin.

"You do the same," he said. He wiped his thumb across her upper lip, then licked his thumb. "Your mustache is much tastier than mine." She looked away to see if her sisters caught their exchange. Briana suddenly looked away, but she had a sly grin on her face.

"How did it go with Irving?" Jackson asked.

"Uncle Irving," Adele practiced saying, "and I are planning a trip to Bluefield next week. If the roads are clear."

"Good man, that Irving," Jackson said. "He's been robbed of family memories because of one low-life scumbag. Sheriff McKinley hated he's been locked up all these years. Tried to get an appeal but never found enough evidence to lighten his sentence. Now he just wants to fix what thirty years took from him. At least before he meets his maker."

Adele wondered how much Jackson really knew about August Beck's family, but she would save that discussion for another time. "He's that close to dying?"

"We all get there," Jackson said. "Sheriff McKinley made sure Irv's time was well spent."

"What does that mean?"

"Plant operations. He wanted to be prepared to work when he got out."

"Was he involved in coal mining?"

"He had my job before he went upriver," Jackson said. "The best at keeping men safe. If he was any healthier, he'd have my job. And you would be happy to give it to him."

"I haven't been to the mines for three weeks." Adele sipped her hot chocolate.

Jackson smiled. "You have to stop doing that."

"What?"

"That sweet 'stache. Drives a man crazy."

"When you're poor, there isn't money for warm marshmallows." She smiled. "I'm a bit out of practice."

"If you need a ride, I can take you to Irv's daughter's place,' Jackson offered. "She's not far from the Bluefield Inn. Know that place?"

Of course, she knew it. It was where she and Tommy spent their last evening committing themselves to each other. The thought of being this close to Jackson made her feel disloyal. "Thanks. I think I will drive myself. I may need a quick getaway."

***

It was a Tuesday between class work that Uncle Irving's daughter, Vivian, dropped her father off at the Stone House. Vivian had the same dark wavy hair as other members of the Dawson clan.

"You got plenty of cousins to meet," Vivian said sweetly. "We didn't want to overwhelm you at Kettie's funeral."

"You have good family here," Irving added. He waved goodbye to his daughter and climbed into the front seat of Kettie's black Buick. Even though it was unacceptable for a young woman like Adele to drive with a man in the car, Irving didn't complain about the impropriety. They drove up Route 52 across the state border, then turned onto Virginia Route 102 into Falls Mills. Adele had spent enough time in West Virginia now that she was getting familiar with the switchbacks and sheer drop-offs. Even so, she took curves slower than most drivers.

As they came into town, Irving pointed to a home surrounded by an iron gated fence. The front porch was a masterpiece of trimmings, its artistry obviously built by craftsmen. An oversized Victorian porch wrapped around a second-floor balcony that shadowed over a deep, white-walled entrance. Eleven curved steps marked the entrance to the front door. Adele parked on the street and looked at the gigantic home.

"This?" Adele asked.

"Quill paid Giles and Blanche handsomely for their shares."

"Wait. My grandfather bought out Giles and Blanche's shares, and they didn't have the decency to come to Kettie's funeral. I can't do this," Adele said.

"Giles knows you are coming."

"You told him?"

"I did."

"What if wild dogs guard the property?"

Irving laughed. "Blanche has a Yorkie."

She hesitated to find the right words. "This house is huge."

Irving placed his hand on Adele's arm. "You live in a bigger house. No different. Drive up now. The gate is open."

Adele drove the Buick to the center of the curved brick driveway. The house made her feel poor, undernourished. Penniless.

"You're a Dawson," Irving said, sounding so much like Noona. "She's the one who done wrong."

Adele nodded, then stepped out of the car. While she stood, familial anger progressed into hot rage, motivating her to the front door. Benita would be proud. Adele pushed her hands against her leather skirt, the one she wore to the showdown at Buckeye Tipple, to dry her palms. She twisted her coat's middle button, reminding herself she should sew it tighter when she got home.

At the top of the front stairs, she stopped to examine the etched glass windows between marble pillars. Run. No stay. Three minutes, then run.

Somehow her index finger managed to ring the doorbell. The chime sounded like she should be at Westminster Abby.

A woman not much taller than Adele came to the door. She smelled like fresh-sprayed French perfume. Her hair, though gray, was perfectly styled, her hands with cherry red fingernails poked out from a slit in a long brown cashmere cape. A teacup Yorkie, half-buried in the cape, yipped until the woman gently stroked the dog's tiny spine.

She pays more attention to a domesticated rat than she ever did to my mother, Adele thought. "Are you Blanche Cassidy?"

Adele caught a moment of hesitation in the older woman's face but then quickly straightened, haughty-like. "Who are you?"

"My name is Adele Christina Dawson."

There seemed to be another flicker of recognition in Blanche's eyes. She stroked the puppy's ears and blinked the moment away.

"What can I do for you?"

It was the way she said it that tore Adele's heart, as if she could just as easily toss stale bread into the garbage than greet her granddaughter.

"I believe Irving told you I would be here today?"

Adele felt Blanche's chill. A peasant at the door looking for a handout.

Two of the three minutes had already gone by. The spirit of Benita's ruthlessness showed up on the tip of Adele's tongue. Unable to take the cold shoulder any longer, Adele spat, "You condemned your daughter to a life of poverty!"

The puppy turned to nip at the woman's thumb as if she had squeezed it. "I have no daughter," Blanche responded. Her mouth turned into a tight straight line. She stepped away from the door to close Adele out of her life.

"You are the sorriest sack of blubber I have ever met. I am your granddaughter." Manners gone. Conviction stepped in. Adele was straight-up Benita, proud to be calling the woman what she was. "Your daughter needed you, and you turned her away."

God help her, she was screaming now.

"You should go to hell for what you did to Selma! How could you ever leave a daughter when evil bastards were hunting her down? What a bitch you are! What did my mama do to you? Threaten to end your perfect little prissy life?"

Adele took a breath.

"Selma was the most beautiful woman I've ever known. But she's dead now. You're fault, lady. Yours!" Adele pointed at Blanche. "How could you abandon her?" Adele stepped away from the door and took in the massive porch.

"God should have never given you a daughter as precious as Selma. How could a woman like you possibly know a mama's love? I should never have come."

Adele took a few more steps away from the door. A lifetime of her beautiful mother passed in front of her eyes. Mama and Delly dancing the jitterbug, Mama with bloodied fingers pulling cotton from thorny balls, Mama braiding field flowers to put on baby Howard's and baby Giles's graves, Mama dying giving birth to her tenth baby.

"And you have seven more grandchildren besides me!" Adele shouted at Blanche, hoping to stab one more blade of disgust at her.

Blanche's upper lip curled. "Your precious Kettie has her own ghosts, too."

Adele stumbled, trying to get away. As Blanche closed the door on her, Adele felt her mama whisper, "I'm sorry, Delly. I made so many mistakes. This is not your battle."

Uncle Irving was standing by the car. His hand in his pants pocket, stoic as her daddy used to be when he wanted to scold her but chose instead to worship her. Adele eyes turned blurry; she didn't know how she would step off the porch or drive. She ached for mama. She choked from the tears that flooded her throat, making it nearly impossible for her to breathe without coughing. She was sorry August turned out to be such a moral rogue. By the time she got to the car, her heart was fully engulfed in pain; she was not able to see the door handle. Her hand slipped. She wiped the back of her hand against her nose, then on her coat. She tried again to open the door. Irving stepped near to help.

"Let me," he said. "Please forgive me, Adele. I thought it would be different."

Irving looked up at the house as a man came running toward them. He nearly fell off the porch leaping too many steps at a time. "Wait. Please wait."

"Giles," Irving said.

Adele would not speak with a man who would disown his daughter. His wife decorated a glorious home while their daughter slaughtered the neighbor's pigs. God, she was grateful she hadn't exposed her sisters to this nightmare. They would never ever have to feel such shame. Mark my words, B's. Never, Ever.

"Please, if you'll give me one minute," Giles was saying. "We shouldn't have put Selma away. It wasn't my fault."

Adele looked at the man who could not even admit he'd harmed his daughter. "Mister? Whoever you are." She looked him square in the face. "You're a yellow belly." She tasted salt as it dripped onto her upper lip.

Irving was still holding the door for her. She sat down behind the wheel, fumbling to find the keys. She wrapped her fists around the steering wheel and sobbed heavily.

Irving closed the car door, leaving her alone inside the car with her grief. He stood beside Giles while the men said their goodbyes. Giles offered his hands up prayerfully. He grabbed Irving's forearm, pleading, shaking his bowed head. Finally, when they came to some understanding, Irving walked around to the passenger side, slipped inside the car, and closed the door. Giles stood in the driveway.

"I hoped Blanche would show remorse," Irving said. They sat in silence until he offered her a handkerchief. "Prison dreams are just that. A man writes the script over and over but forgets to tell the actors how it should go."

He handed Adele the keys. "Giles said he would meet us at the Soda Shop if you'd like."

"The man wants to shake off his guilt with a milk shake?" Adele asked.

Irving shook his head. "Just wants to get to know you."

"Uncle Irving?" Adele said. "Plenty of broken hearts need to be reconciled in this family. I'm sorry I ruined your dream. Another time, but not now."

Irving patted her knee as she put the car in first gear. "At least you still have emotions. That's a start."

***

When she arrived home, she pulled out her stationery and wrote to Tommy, telling him how excited she was before meeting her grandmother. Selma's parents were still alive, only to learn how they disinherited their daughter. She explained the look on her smarmy grandmother's face when she mentioned Selma's name. Now, she wanted nothing to do with them.

Briana moved about the living room as Adele pulled out her fourth sheet of paper. "That's some kind of missive," Briana said. "Fast as you're writing, you must have walked into a hornet's nest."

Adele signed the letter with love, then sighed.

"I met our grandmother today," Adele said. "She refused to acknowledge me."

Briana sat down beside Adele. "We have a grandmother. What is she like?"

Adele considered how she might close any history of Blanche Cassidy. "Her nose is twisted so badly she can hardly breathe. Her long fingers cast spells and will turn you into a skunk." Adele felt good creating this horrible vision. "She has a scrawny little rat for a pet."

Briana giggled. "Really, Delly? She's perfect for our family."

Adele pushed herself away from the desk and took her sister's hands in hers. "She made me feel poor."

Briana thought for a few minutes. "Delly, when you came here, you wanted to learn about your family. Are you angry they aren't like us?"

"I never thought mama's mother would be so joyless."

Briana leaned over to hug Adele. "We have a good life here, Delly. You got us out of hell. I will forever be grateful that you sent for us."

Chapter 20:
Threat of Another War Heats Up Coal Production

On Tuesdays and Thursdays, Adele went to the coal mines, hoping she would never have to admit how much she enjoyed watching Jackson supervise the mine reconstruction. She told herself it was her job, as the mine owner, to oversee the rebuild. No child apprenticeships, but if a woman wanted to work the coal mine, Jackson was instructed to hire her if she could lift twenty pounds of coal. It never happened.

Adele and Elizabeth had arranged for local churches, restaurants, and freemasons to bring in hot dinners to support workers, teachers, and families. Often, chefs got competitive over family recipes for sassafras short ribs, pork chitterlings, and famous pepperoni rolls.

But on this Wednesday, Adele finished college classes early. Rather than going home first, she drove to the Buckeye Tipple to see if Jackson and Elizabeth Radford needed more supplies before the end of the month. She and Jackson had discussed a timeline to close the tent community and send families back home for warmth. The board had given her 60-days to get the mine functional again, though she and David told Jackson forty-five days in case they needed a cushion. Good thing they did. She had fifteen days left to generate revenue, or she'd have to take another business loan from the bank.

As she drove onto the site, she recognized most of the cars and mindlessly tried to match worker to vehicle. She'd need to confer with Jackson on the unrecognizable trucks. With a clipboard in her hand, she nodded to several familiar faces as she made her way over to the general contractor's tent.

"Hey!" Jackson greeted. "What gives with a Wednesday visit? I would have showered."

"Something said I needed to come in today." She stood near the gas-fired space heaters.

"Never one to mess with a woman's intuition," Jackson responded. "Look," he said, pointing to a canvas map with thumbtacks of empty tents. "We're far enough along that these families could leave. Each tack shows an empty tent where a family has moved into a neighboring town," Jackson explained. "We will ramp up to nearly 2,000 workers by December. Elizabeth tells me this morning that we'll have to step up our relocation efforts. The Army wants their tents back by mid-January."

Coal mining executives, he explained, believe something big is about to happen in Europe. "Radio commentators on the German occupation of Czechoslovakia speak of the Nazi invasion. Adolph Hitler calls it an act of mercy. Mercy, my ass."

"Irving, Giles, and I talked about the conditions Allies imposed on Germany," Jackson continued. "None of us believe Hitler will put much stock in paying back that five-billion-dollar debt. For now, the Allies continue to hold the War Guilt Clause against Germany, but I'm not sure Mr. Hitler cares much for the Allies' politics of loan paybacks.

"Supply and demand, Adele. That's the business we're in. If war is imminent, we will stockpile our culm and then fire up the coke ovens as soon as we can," Jackson said. "Our men are committed to exceeding production quotas in the next ninety days. We can still ship raw coal to Pittsburgh, but we need to retain enough here to burn and add another shift of workers. Demand is going to hit our backyards, too."

Adele struggled with the thought of her uncle and grandfather working together in her mine. "Irving and Giles?" she asked.

Jackson grinned. "Couldn't skirt through that fast enough. Could I? They have wartime knowledge, and they have contacts in Washington, DC. Giles served alongside your grandfather, and he has been interpreting news stories coming out of Hungary and the War Department.

"Our equipment is outdated. I've had to train some of our excavator crews to become tool and dye apprentices. We need parts. Giles knows the dynamics of how to pack explosives into seams without creating another disaster. He understands our needs for coal cutters, conveyors, and telemetry. Not much that man has forgotten."

Adele was still shaken by the confrontation with her mother's parents. "Do you know what Giles did to my mother?"

"He's been forthcoming about that."

"And you still hired him?"

Jackson stared her down. "This is business, Miss Dawson. Didn't we agree I would run the mines?"

Adele heard heavy bootsteps near the tent's entrance. Elizabeth Radford opened the flaps and stepped inside. "Thought I heard your voice," Elizabeth greeted. "Miss Dawson! This man you hired to run the mines has been a Godsend, It seems all of America is transporting steel, iron, and military goods to Europe. Most of it is shipped out of Pittsburgh, so that's where we have focused our distribution lines."

Adele recalled the financial warnings she'd heard from her board of directors. "Elizabeth and Jackson, nearly everything we own is tied up in getting our mines operational again," Adele argued. "When do we start making shipments?"

"Trains still run through here every day," Jackson said. "I have to call the dispatch at N&O railroad and tell them when to make regular stops."

"And that is?"

"Next Monday."

Elizabeth sat at the edge of Jackson's desk and folded her arms. "When Washington says, Ship steel to Great Britain, we'll give Pittsburgh all we can spare. Washington predicts Pittsburgh will need nearly 100 million tons of steel. Coal fired into steel turned Pittsburgh into the city of blast furnaces."

Adele tried to make sense of the volume of coal needed. Maybe she should quit college at least for a few months.

"Irving oversees transport, marketing, labor relations, and record-keeping of all anthracite engineering," Elizabeth reported. "He wasn't here during the 1922 coal strike," she said, raising her her hands mimicking handcuffs, "for obvious reasons, but he's been studying employment and accident tables for coal mines submitted to the Bureau of Mines. Dust explosions used to take most of his time, but the Department of War wants him to become an expert on chemical and gas warfare."

"Washington wants to hire him away from us?"

"No, no, he would stay here but likely travel to DC once a month. We need him," Elizabeth said. "He's our insider mole. We wouldn't be this far along if he wasn't advising us."

"How much longer will he live?" Adele asked. "He's out on a compassionate release."

"That's what the DOW likes about him. He's on a short timeline, so he works fast." Jackson opened a notebook filled with formulas, handwritten notes, and diagrams. "On the other hand, Giles predicts our production capabilities will increase eight hundred percent in the next four years. Ham radio chatter is calling for an increase of strip mining since Germany far outpaces the world in steel production."

"Strip mining?" Adele said. "You mean open-pit mining? It destroys landscapes and wildlife. Kettie warned me not to get into destroying the environment. We're not going in that direction."

"I agree. West Virginians don't like anything that warms rivers or makes them filthy," Jackson responded. He waved to Irving as he ducked into the tent. "Fill your daughter-in-law in on strip mining."

"Got nothing good to say about it," Irving said.

"Good man," Adele answered. "You and Kettie feel the same."

"But," Irving went on, "if we get pulled into another war with Germany, strip mines will push commodities out to Europe a lot faster than going deep. It all depends on how much steel production will be needed. Demand will outpace supply."

"Are we drilling deep or staying shallow for a drift mine?" Adele argued.

Irving pushed his arm out. "Drift. Straight in," he said. "Building roof stability as we go. Cleanest coal on the continent, right here on these mountains."

Adele felt uplifted from the energy Jackson and Elizabeth were showing. Having Irving onboard meant the mines would benefit from the Dawson's knowledge of mining.

"Come look over my shoulder at Giles's designs," Jackson said. "Giles built Flat Top Mine into one of the cleanest mines in the nation," Jackson offered. "Like I said, we're using some of the same equipment he used. Cuts down on labor and parts. The guy is an engineering wizard.

"And he's coordinating our rebuild with our partners at Mill Creek, Booth-Bowen, and Klondike. Giles met with the Dean of Engineering at University of West Virginia. Got us some interns with innovative ideas for coal gasification, explosives technology, and secondary recovery of petroleum products."

"Just tell me, are employees safe coming back to work?" Adele asked.

Jackson exchanged smiles with Elizabeth. "It helps that Mrs. Radford here makes the best apple and cherry pies. Tends to make them feel safe."

"You know what I mean," Adele countered.

"For those living in town, we still have ghosts to burn off. But we're working with the West Virginia Department of Mines," Jackson offered. "They make surprise and scheduled visits, and any time we cross off a milestone, they're here."

"Leadership team meets every Wednesday afternoon. Should have started fifteen minutes ago," Elizabeth said. "I don't know what's taking Giles so long to get here, but if you can wait, I know he'd like you to see how he's making a difference."

"I'm not sure if …"

Elizabeth interrupted. "Giles wants to atone. Give him a chance. How many times have you asked for a second chance?"

"We meet in this tent, so if it doesn't go well, you can slip out between tent stakes," Jackson teased and winked at her. Adele hoped Elizabeth hadn't seen Jackson's flirtation. She didn't want to get into an argument with Cora.

"If you make it through the first sixty minutes of department reports, I'll open up one of the pies in the fridge," Elizabeth coaxed.

They heard a commotion from the entrance to the tent village that continued to get louder. Foot scuffles drew near. Then, they heard a loud shout, "Get. Off. Of. Me!"

"Men don't scream like that," Jackson said. He pushed away from his desk and opened the tent door. "What the hell?"

Giles entered, forcing a woman he held with one arm behind her back into the command tent. She was wearing steel-toe mining boots, brown corduroy trousers, a baggie flannel shirt, and a plain kerchief around her neck with a monogrammed "STFU" letters. A brown Tractor Supply hat had been stuffed on her head, making her ears look oversized.

"Just dug up some trash," Giles said. "Caught her snooping around the excavators. And these were in her hand," he added. Giles tossed brochures onto Jackson's desk.

FAIR LABOR RELATIONS ACT RAISES MINIMUM WAGE TO 25 CENTS/HOUR. DEMAND HIGHER WAGES NOW.

The brochures featured black and white photos of children and women working in a cotton field, Latino women shelling pecans, and young girls at a manufacturing center, each sitting behind a sewing machine.

"We already pay workers 50 cents an hour," Adele argued. "Why is she here?"

"Let me go, Giles!" the woman shouted back. "You violate my first amendment rights."

Adele thought she recognized the woman's voice but could not believe the woman would be spying this close to the mines, nor how she got beyond the guard gate. Adele looked at her farmer attire and unruly hair poking through the ball cap. "Do I know you?" Adele asked.

"Oh, please. Don't be coy," the woman barked back. Giles tightened the grip on her arm, forcing the woman to arch her back even more.

Giles looked at Adele. "I'm sorry I haven't been a better grandfather to you. I'll make it up to you," he said, squeezing the woman's arms until she winced. "This is your stepdaddy's wife," he said.

"Olga! What the hell are you doing here?" Adele asked.

Elizabeth closed the folders she was reviewing and stepped in front of her once best friend. "You bitch." She raised her hand and struck Olga across the face. "How dare you show your face in my town!"

Olga lost her balance and fell sideways into Giles' arms. "What was that for?" she demanded.

"Get her the hell out of my town," Elizabeth ordered. "She's a spy, sent over here by the unions, you can be sure of that!"

"Don't gloat!" Olga tutted back. "I still have family up the road."

"Not buying it!" Elizabeth shouted. "I served three years in Ossining because of you. Selma died under your husband's *protection*." She emphasized protection as if the word was spittle. "And you come rolling in here thinking it's all peachy to check up on us?"

Giles forced Olga to sit in a chair next to Jackson. "How can I possibly believe curiosity drove you to our coal mine?" he asked, looking down at her.

He opened the top drawer of his desk, pulled out a short cartridge Italian Beretta, then placed it on top of his desk. "Say your peace. Then get your goon self out of West Virginia." He kept the nozzle pointed at Olga, his finger on the trigger.

"I've got no business with any of you. It's her I'm here to see." Olga nodded at Adele.

Adele sputtered. "I have nothing to say to you. Shoot her, for all I care."

"Then you would not know the location of your precious darlings," Olga countered.

Adele fell silent. There wasn't a word Olga had to say that would make Adele want to listen, except something about her family. She kept a low voice, not wanting to give Olga any concession. "Precious darlings? "You mean my sisters?"

Giles lunged at Olga and wrapped his fingers around her throat. "What have you done to my grandchildren?"

Jackson waved Giles away, but not before Giles left fingerprints on Olga's throat. "Let her talk."

Olga smiled wickedly at Giles. "So now those toadstools are your grandchildren? After you disowned their mother?"

Giles lunged at Olga again, gripping her until her cheeks turned red. "I'll kill her. Let me have her."

Jackson pushed Giles back once more. "If anyone gets a turn with this old bag, I say Adele should have the first cut."

"You wouldn't dare," Olga taunted. "She knows I'm just the message carrier."

Elizabeth squared her jaw and faced off with Olga. "You're still a mobster, aren't you? You stupid smut bucket. I paid my dues to society, but you got all cozied up with the mob. Even after the Dawsons paid August to keep Selma safe."

"Paid?"

"Oh, the things August will do for money. He's as crooked as a politician's back," Elizabeth answered. "Anything he didn't specialize in, he learned from this bitch."

"How much, Olga?" Adele asked.

"Five bricks," Giles answered. "Between the Dawsons and Cassidys."

"My family paid August Beck five hundred thousand dollars to start a new life with Mama?"

"Over time." Olga threw her head back defiantly. "Selma knew some money was coming in, just not that much. She would have spent all of it on little Miss Prissy here. Auggie and me, we loved getting those Besame dividends. Should have been mine in the first place. I was the real Besame girl."

Adele leaped toward Olga, wanting to tear her apart. But Jackson grabbed Adele and pulled her back before Olga could respond. He grabbed the gun and poked it into Olga's side. "You're in no position to pick another fight," he growled.

"I say I am," Olga snapped. "I've got a message from Mr. Auggie," she continued. "A letter. You'll find it in my satchel."

Giles raised the satchel from the floor and held it up to Olga's face. "Take it out."

"You've got my hands tied," Olga answered.

"I'll get it," Adele snapped. She flipped the satchel's lid open and dug through handkerchiefs, a compact mirror, and a coin purse until she found a brown envelope. When she raised it, she held it up to Giles and Jackson, pointing to the hand's outline in black ink.

"Seems we've got a copycat here," Adele snipped. "Not very original."

Immediately, Irving stepped beside her. "Drop the letter, Adele."

"She's faking it," Adele said. "It's just an envelope."

Jackson snatched the envelope from Adele's hands. He examined the envelope's front and back. "It's a diversion. Where are the girls?"

Olga sneered at Jackson. "I guess you'll have to open the letter to find out."

"Both of you, drop the letter." Irving tossed his glove on top of the envelope. "I've seen this in Germany. Might be poisonous dust inside. The Kaiser infected livestock with anthrax."

Olga cackled. "Your stepdaddy has asked you several times politely to release the girls and come home. He won't be ignored again."

Adele crossed her arms, not sure whether to step back and follow Irving's lead. "He showed up at Kettie's funeral with a skinning knife. Blew up the mine. How is that considered polite?"

"You scared him. Chased him away, Adele. You and your band of gunslingers."

Elizabeth shoved Irving away from Olga. "Listen, you stupid bitch, I won't be an accomplice to your extortion schemes any longer. What's in the letter?"

Olga smiled. "Like I said, I'm just the messenger."

"Stay put." Jackson grabbed the envelope, the gloves from Irving, and stepped outside the tent, far enough away that no one but he would be impacted by the powder. When he returned, his face was ashen. He opened the palm of his hand to show the contents. A lock of blonde hair soft as a child's hair and small bloodied fingerprints. He got in front of

Olga's face. "What has Beck done?" he demanded. He leaned down to her face, his eyes fierce and threatening. "I will see you in hell if he, or you, have hurt Adele's sisters."

Olga shrugged, feigning haughty superiority. "The letter is actually a request for donations to the Southern Tenant Farmer's Association," she said. "I wouldn't call it extortion since you'd be giving to a non-profit. We need funds to support our protest. Landowners are keeping federal subsidies rather than paying sharecroppers government-issued subsidies. Nothing sells a news story better than young lassies freezing in a ramshackle tent along the roadside."

"Dear God, if he as much as scratched one of them, I will kill him. How much is he demanding?" Adele asked.

"Well now, that depends on how much love is in your heart," Olga answered. "Six girls. Round it up to fifty thousand for each."

Adele lunged at Olga. "I have hated you," she said as she kicked the chair out from underneath Olga, making her fall sideways to the ground. "From the minute Pa brought you into our house. You will not ever steal again from my family." She fought off Jackson as he tried once more to pull her back, but Adele had years of focused rage pent up into this single battle.

Elizabeth pulled Olga from the chair and started kicking her former friend. But in the process, Olga twisted free. She rolled sideways, then climbed up on her knees and grabbed the handgun from Jackson's desk. She steadied herself and pointed the gun first at Jackson, then at Irving. Finally, at Giles.

"I guess I'll be off now," she said, forcing herself to stand. She backed out of the tent's front entrance, but Elizabeth lunged at her again. Olga fired the pistol, creating a reverberation that echoed throughout the mining village. The bullet whizzed past Elizabeth's shirt and burned a hole in her sleeve. Elizabeth grabbed her arm from the bullet's heat.

Jackson rushed to tackle Olga, forcing her to fall into the gravel outside the tent. Olga should have put up a bitter fight, but she seemed to suddenly become a quiet victim as workers gathered around to help. She sneered as if Adele and Jackson.

Irving stepped out of the tent and placed his foot on top of Olga's face as he thanked his employees. "You never know how many friends you have until you come back from prison." He waved away several men who had rushed to the source of gunfire.

"Call Sheriff McKinley. I want this bitch arrested," Adele demanded.

"You're giving her just what she wants. A bloodied face. Bruises," Jackson said. "Makes a gallant protestor photo. For all you know, there's a photographer waiting for us to emerge."

"She wouldn't dare," Adele snapped.

"You'll never know, sweet thing," Olga spat at her. She tried to push Irving's foot away from her face, then struggled to stand, but Irving pushed her back down to the ground. Olga was a middle-aged woman whose anger was being strategically dismantled. Adele looked down with pity, until she realized Olga was a decoy, just as Jackson had suspected.

As if to confirm Adele's suspicions, Olga wiped blood from her mouth. She drew lines of her own blood across her forehead, wiped splotches of blood onto her sweater, her knees, and finally drew bloody circles around her eyes. "I cannot wait," she said, "until you find your sweet little sissies … are with their daddy."

Rebecca Parsons stepped out from behind the tent and aimed her camera. "Heard there might be a gunfight," Rebecca laughed. "Miss Olga, you didn't disappoint."

"Like a loose bowel, that woman," Jackson snorted. "Can't expel you fast enough."

Elizabeth pulled out a handkerchief from her purse. She stepped outside the tent, kneeled to block Rebecca Parsons and her camera, and spit into the cloth. Roughly, she wiped away splotches Olga had painted so sloppily, pausing to spit again into the hanky to keep it moist. "I have a better idea."

Giles leaned down and helped Elizabeth raise Olga to her feet. "I hear the old mobster, Patsi Corbi moved his operation to Baltimore," he said. "Am I thinking what you're thinking?"

Elizabeth and Giles helped Olga stand, but each kept a tight grip on her. "Ship the bitch to Baltimore. Couple of gangsters still want a piece of her ass," Elizabeth sneered.

"What has Pa done with my sisters?" Adele interrupted.

"I guess you'll never know," Olga said, her smile contemptuous.

"Take her back inside the test," Jackson said. "No cameras. No witnesses."

Adele picked up her belongings. "Elizabeth and Giles, you have a long history to reconcile with this woman. I have to find my sisters."

"Wait," Giles said and stepped in front of Adele. He cupped her face in his hands. "I am so proud of you. I'm ashamed I wasn't there for you growing up."

"Giles, I have to find my sisters."

"August likely took the girls to the old Beck farm," Giles said. "He's drawing you into union-striker country. Hatfield and McCoy types. They barbecue coal owners for lunch."

"I know some folks up there," Jackson said. "But we're going to need help." He motioned for several miners. Adele overhead him explain that he was headed up to Beck's farm near Gilbert Creek.

"Gilbert Creek? Are you nuts?" one of them said.

"Maybe. We could use some help. August Beck kidnapped his girls."

"Same som'bitch that blew up the mine?" one asked. He spit a wad of chewing tobacco onto the ground.

"That's him," Jackson answered.

"Never done learn his lesson, does he?" another miner said. He spits a wad, intentionally trying to outshoot the previous miner's spittle. "Boy's gotta pay for what he did to my family."

"Gonna get ugly," Jackson said. "I need every one of you healthy and back here tomorrow morning."

One of the men pounded a fist into the palm of his hand. "Let's go get us a varlet."

"Please let me come," Giles said. "I have some unfinished business to settle. These boys harmed my daughter."

"Giles, you have to stay with Elizabeth," Jackson argued.

"Irving is here," Giles argued. "I wasn't there for Selma. Let me help."

"Someone's got to stay with Olga," Adele said.

Elizabeth rubbed her arm and placed the gun on her lap as she took a seat behind the desk. Olga was tied to a chair in front. "My friend and I have some unfinished business," she said, rubbing the gun barrel back and forth in front of Olga's nose. "If you come back in one piece, I will keep her alive before I turn her over to some friends of mine up Baltimore way."

Adele turned to Irving. "Please send a message to Sheriff McClain,' Adele said. "Ask him to first stop at the house. See if the girls are still there. Maybe Olga is bluffing. If not, the Sheriff has to head up to the Beck farm. Quickly."

"You have no idea how much I want to be there," Irving said. "Settle more than a few bloody scores with those bastards."

"You just served thirty years, man," Jackson said. "No more heavy lifting. Tell the Sheriff to send his deputies to Bramwell first. If the girls are gone, he should coordinate with the Mingo County sheriff. Sheriff can't barge into another county without giving notice."

"You want a story?" Adele said to the photographer. "Come with us."

Rebecca Parsons grabbed her camera and reporter's notebook. "What's the story here? Is somebody gonna die?"

Chapter 21:
Save My Sisters!

Giles, Jackson, and Adele stood in front of Jackson's truck to build an attack plan. "I don't want my granddaughter in harm's way," Giles said. He turned to Adele. "I just found you, and I don't want to lose you again."

"I wouldn't miss this for anything," Adele responded. "I hope you never find out what he's done to my family."

"Can you handle a shotgun?" Jackson asked.

Adele thought about all the times she'd shot coyotes from taking down livestock. "August taught me how to shoot."

"Damn. He will use that knowledge against you."

"Then we have to outsmart him," Giles said.

Jackson reached out his hand to Giles. "If I don't have another chance to thank you, I want to do it now." After they shook hands, Giles turned to Adele. "Thank you for letting me come with you."

Adele turned her cheek away from Giles when he tried to hug her.

"I don't deserve your love," he said. "But today, I hope to gain your respect."

***

Jackson opened the truck door for Adele. Giles climbed into his own shiny black Chevy sedan. They rerouted their way up Route 10 long enough to stop at Jackson's family home. Straightaway, Jackson opened both barn doors, unlocked his gun cabinet, and returned to the car with four shotguns and a pistol. He stopped to give Giles one of the guns.

"No need," Giles said. "I've got my own in the back."

"Man after my own heart," Jackson responded.

For nearly two hours, they traversed mountain roads, trailing each other but keeping a safe enough distance to avoid arousing suspicion that a posse was coming for August Beck. Knowing his calculated way of exposing his victims, he likely had already alerted half of Mingo County to send a signal if anyone saw a Mercer County truck winding up to Gilbert Creek.

Adele sat in the front seat and pondered her immediate future. She could run full boar into her stepfather, push, kick, and punch him, demanding he return her sisters. Likely she would be gunned down before she made it ten steps from the truck.

Whose blonde hair had he cut and shoved into that threatening envelope? It had to be Faye's or Briana's. The others were dark or red. Had he harmed them? She thought about when her sisters introduced her to the B's Club up in the barn loft. She did not know their secret society, mainly because she was so busy with her own drama. What a fool she had been, ignoring the girls so she could pamper her dreams. Dreams to become a professional agriculturalist. Farm owner. Irrigation specialist.

Now, she owned a mine. Nineteen years old, and she owned a mine. Doesn't that just beat all? You fight to achieve your dreams. And it's another dream God gives you. Whatever was happening with the girls, they were scheming, too. She knew her sisters so much better now. They were standing up for each other, maybe driving August crazy with their chatter.

She watched Jackson grind his jaw, knowing he was likely developing his strategic kill shot.

"What does a gunslinger think about on his way to a fight?" she asked.

"How not to get shot," Jackson answered. He downshifted to get around a bend.

"Do you think about family? Friends? Dreams you never achieved?"

"Can't afford to."

"Will you tell me your plan?"

"No plan."

Adele sighed. "Then, what am I doing here?"

"I don't know." Jackson glanced her way but then turned the wheel sharply around a curve to avoid hitting a squirrel. "What are you doing here?"

"You can avoid hitting a squirrel while planning a shootout?"

"Squirrel meant no harm."

He tightened his jaw again. Pulsations so precise, it looked like he would break a tooth. Adele knew he was grinding out a plan that would neutralize August, perhaps his brothers and cousins, anyone from Mingo County who simply loved to shoot people and still save her sisters. It wasn't looking good.

She tried to remember what Noona had told her about Beck's farm. Not much, since it was Irving who had taken his horse out to resolve her mother's kidnapping. Outbuildings. Horses. Not a real pleasant place. Maybe something like the pinewood home in New Madrid County, where she and her sisters grew up.

Jackson stopped the truck on a roadside carve out that overlooked the Guyandotte River. Giles pulled up beside him. Right behind Giles, three more trucks stopped and parked. Ten men in all, Adele counted. "Please, Lord, keep these men alert and my sissies safe."

Rebecca Parsons pulled up behind everyone in her rusty Studebaker. She pulled out her reporter's notebook. "Ok, what are we doing here?"

Jackson shook his head. "Keep her away from me. No pictures of my men."

Adele walked through the grass to be at Rebecca's side. "We are here to rescue my sisters. It might get bloody,"

"I love bloody," Rebecca interrupted.

"You might get shot if you get too close," Adele continued. "If you miss something, I can fill you in later."

"So, it's a kidnapping rescue, then?" Rebecca asked as she jotted notes.

"Might say that," Adele answered.

***

Fall rains muddied the Guyandotte River, making it run above-expected flood levels. Swirling tides splashed up against concrete pillars. Trellises supported an arched bridge in the middle of the road that ran at least 500 feet on either side of the bridge. If they moved any closer, their vehicles would be exposed from both sides of the arch.

Jackson and Giles pointed to the bridge and then to the houses tucked against the riverbanks where August would have placed his stakeouts. Free-roaming cattle grazed along the riverbank. A steep mountain road tucked between the houses led up to Beck's farm.

"We're ripe for getting picked off," Giles said. "Is there another way across the river?"

Jackson shook his head. "Another bridge thirty miles upriver, but it will be sundown before we get to the Beck ranch."

"Maybe we could pile into one or two cars," Giles responded. "Reconnoiter on the other side. Circle back in town and come to the farm through back roads.

"He knows my truck," Jackson said.

"He doesn't know my Studebaker," Rebecca offered.

"I can't involve you in anything illegal," Jackson answered.

"I'm a reporter. Not a judge."

A large cattle truck came barreling toward the bridge, forcing the group of men to move even further off to the side of the road. The driver did not use his hydraulic brakes; they would have created a loud whooshing sound. Instead, the eighteen-wheeler came to a quiet rolling stop.

Sheriff McKinley rolled down the window and leaned out, a wide grin across his face. "Girls aren't in Bramwell. So, I thought you might need a decoy to cross the bridge," McKinley said. "Heard tell the Becks might be shipping cattle to market. Thought we'd go pay him a visit."

Jackson stepped up onto the running boards and gripped McKinley's arm. "Amen, brother. Glad you joined us."

"I'm not here for a shoot-out. Just a concerned citizen. Sheriff Stevens up Mingo way is sending troopers out to the farm. Thought maybe y'all might need to get there first."

Giles, Jackson, and Sheriff McKinley talked through their plan. Jackson and Adele would go in first to sweep the buildings and locate the girls but would take no action until the cattle truck arrived. No gun shots, just contain the situation until the Mingo sheriff arrived.

Rebecca drove the Studebaker, Adele in the front seat while Jackson hunkered down in the back. When they had crossed the bridge, Rebecca turned up Bull Bottom Road and parked the car in the woods, about 500 feet from Beck's house.

"Stay near the car," Jackson told Rebecca. "This isn't your fight."

"But it's my story."

"Actually, it's my story," Adele argued. "I will wave when it's safe for you to come in."

Jackson wrapped the shotgun sling over his shoulder, tucked his pistol under his belt behind his back, and secured his skinning knife around his ankle.

Jackson leaned close to Adele and whispered. "Once I find the girls, I'll whistle twice for you to come forward. Keep the girls calm. Remember, our number one goal is to get the girls out. We are not here to harm August Beck unless he fires first."

"He's a hunter, Jackson. For all I know, he's watching us right now," Adele warned.

"I'm not walking into his trap," Jackson assured her. He double-tied his boot laces and disappeared into the mountain foliage.

Adele listened for any sound that might give her a clue to the girls' whereabouts. She heard voices but couldn't make out anything more than gibberish. Perhaps it came from the two homes near the river.

Rebecca pulled out her reporter's notebook. "What are you thinking?" the reporter asked.

Adele put her finger to her lips.

"Are you scared?" Rebecca whispered.

Adele nodded but frowned at Rebecca for treating this rescue as a news story when it was a dangerous mission to save her sisters. Had August tied and gagged them? Were they scared? She counted on Collette to be brave and innovative. Briana would comply to a fault. Faye would be sucking her fingers.

When she heard two sharp bird calls, she turned to Rebecca. "If you're scared at any time, you should leave. No one will fault you."

Rebecca tapped her pen against her notepad. "This is too good to miss."

Crouching along the side of the road, Adele began making her way up toward the house. As she crept, she thought about how this place started Mama's life into a downward spiral. The dirty Bull Bottom Road. Tall weeds on both sides of the road that just as quickly served up camouflage for a rattle snake as it could for a skunk. Neither delivered a great outcome. Still, she crept forward.

As she neared the top of the road, she saw the tops of several outbuildings emerge. She counted: a barn, two-grain silos, a coop wrapped with chicken wire around the sides and top, and a shop with stacks of lumber next to sawhorses. She eased her way close to an electric power pole. The dingy main house sat back from the road. An overhanging porch tilted to one side. The swing on the porch was moving. Someone had just been there.

Jackson stood behind one side of the barn and looked at her, frowning. She gave him a quizzical look. His hands, crossed in front of his belt waved ever so slightly as if to tell her to turn back. That's when she saw the tip of a double-barrel shotgun pointed at his head. The gunman was hiding behind the barn, waiting for her.

She took a step back. Jackson seemed to nod, affirming her retreat. With the next step, she felt something tug at her ankle. When she looked down, she saw a tripwire stretched behind her heel. Just as she tried to kick loose of the wire, a block of chopped wood swung straight at her head. She tried to duck, but it immediately knocked her off her feet. She saw a glimpse of a man walking her way, but then the sunlight went dark.

When she could open her eyes again, she was lying on a bed of hay, her arms tied behind her back. The other end of the rope was anchored to a wooden stall. Behind her, a hose looped down from a window dripped a steady stream of water into a trough. Round clods of horse manure in the back of the stall kept her from moving. Or taking deep breaths.

"You bitches never learn," she heard a man say. "Just like your mother. Poking your nose into business that ain't yours." He was sitting on a dirty green farrier's bench. Shavings of horses' hooves cluttered the ground.

"Where are my sisters?" Adele asked. Her head ached. Her shoulder felt dislocated.

"With their daddy."

"Who are you?"

"Not that it matters to you. Auggie's little brother. Friends call me Hash."

"You're the one who kidnapped my mother?"

"Long time ago. You're not still sore over that? Cause I got a gun pointed at your pretty little head to help, you clear up that problem."

Adele remembered how much her mother had fought to prevent August's brothers from having their way with her. "Well, Hash, was that your booby trap that knocked me out?"

"You liked it, didn't you? Guess I'm smarter than I look."

She wondered what had happened to Jackson. Where was he, and where were the girls?

"Why am I tied up?" Adele asked.

"Easier to hand you over to the sheriff."

"Great idea," Adele answered. "I can't wait to give him evidence your brother tried to blow up the mine." She tried to move to relieve pressure on her shoulder. "And my sisters? Where did you say they were?"

"Safe. Away from you."

She let her head rest on the hay, tired of the conversation.

Hash stood up and began unbuttoning his shirt. "You're not falling asleep on me, are you?"

"No, Hash. I'm not falling asleep."

"Because I got a few dance moves I'd like to show you. Your momma liked them."

"What a bore," Adele answered. She could feel the knotted rope behind her. Her fingers started working to untie herself.

"You?" He kicked hay into her face. "You? Calling me boring?"

She coughed to get the dust out of her mouth, shook her head to remove strands from her face and eyes. Her shoulder screamed when she moved. And now, her cheek was starting to swell from his assault.

"Don't think I came here by myself," Adele said. "Others are right behind me."

"You mean J-Man? He and Auggie are chatting in the house."

She wondered how Jackson let August get the best of him. All those guns. Not again. That doesn't sound like Jackson at all. He should be on to August blindsiding him. She could feel the knots loosen. Almost free.

"Did you bring the money?" Hash asked.

"What money?"

Hash walked around the horse stall. Adele rotated on her hips to follow him. She must stay prepared for his next move. "The donation, bitch." He kicked her in the lower back. "Three hundred thousand."

"I don't have that kind of money," Adele cried out.

She released the last of the knots but held herself curled in a ball, awaiting his next move. Was this how the Beck men managed to accost her mother? Ambushed her and then tried to have their way with her? Oh, how they must have humiliated her mama.

Hash unbuckled his belt and dropped his pants. "I guess I'll just have to go dig for it." He dropped to his knees and pulled her legs towards him.

He was heavier than he was strong. His rough hands scraped her legs. His ragged fingernails cut into her skin. You might have caught my mama off guard, Adele told herself, fighting him off her. She could smell his stale beer breath. Rotting wheat. He had her pinned down. She twisted and banged her bad shoulder on the ground, willing it to pop back into place. What was it that made the Beck men think they had to neutralize a woman to have their way?

When her shoulder reached the maximum pain she could endure, Adele leaned back, pulled her knees up into a ball, and thrust her feet into his chest. Again. Geez, it hurt. He leaned in to grab her legs. She kicked up into his face. The next kick went into his groin. Her sudden movements loosened the rope. He doubled over, coughing.

Quickly, she twisted free and scrambled to get away from him. She stretched the rope between her hands and tightened it around his neck, pulling as tightly as she could. Hash gurgled angrily. He shook his head from side to side, his arms flailing to reach her. If she could hold on, he would pass out. He was stronger. He grabbed her hands and pulled her down to the ground just as she heard a shotgun rack. Please let it be Jackson.

"Let her go, Hash," she heard August say.

"She's a bitch, just like your old lady," Hash argued.

"A bitch?" August argued. He drew the shotgun over his head and brought the gun butt down hard on his brother's face. "I loved that woman." The gun thudded against Hash's temple. "Don't you ever talk about her like that!" Thud. Thud. "Never. Ever."

August reached down for Adele's hand and helped her stand. "It wasn't supposed to go like this, Delly. Didn't you get my message?"

Adele brushed hay from her clothes. "You mean the extortion demand?"

"Olga said you agreed to meet me," August said. "I asked her to convince you to come home."

"No, August," Adele said. "Olga's message didn't sound anything like that. She had a Southern Tenant's brochure with bloodied fingerprints and a lock of hair."

"Oh, that," August said.

"What does that mean, 'Oh that?' You knew?"

"She stirred up her old gangster boys. Vagabondas are in jail. But a fraction of them thinks they can keep the Famiglia alive. They're in the house waiting for me to bring you in."

"For what?"

"Sign some papers. I told them you'd never turn the mines over to them. But when they threatened to bleed out the girls, I sent Olga to bring you here."

"I don't have that kind of signature approval. I would have to threaten two-thirds of the board to sign the mines over."

"Not the way they see it," August answered. "Ivan Mills seems to think you have authority."

"Ivan is dead."

"Faked his own passing," August said. "The Committee recruited him after your daddy died. They've got Jackson inside too."

Gangsters didn't bring Jackson inside just to serve refreshments. They were hurting him. "Was Jackson in on your plan to explode the mine?" she asked.

"Ivan, Olga, and Hash, they're the architects."

"But you were there."

"And it was me who was trying to save your life. Limit the explosion to property damage. Kill the mine, you know? No one was supposed to get hurt. Then you had to get all righteous. You took matters into your own hands. Come home and get your degree from MU. Like you planned."

Hash grabbed his head and rubbed his scalp. If he could stand, he might warn the intruders. He scowled at August. "You just chose the wrong side, brother," Hash said.

"Where are the girls?" Adele asked her stepfather, ignoring Hash's threat.

"In the house."

"We need to get them out, Pa."

"Collette's got a filthy mouth," August responded. "Worse than Benita. Where'd she learn to talk like that?"

"Where do you think, Pa?"

"I never talked to the girls like that."

Adele couldn't resist shaking her head. "When it comes to hard times, they come through for each other," Adele responded. "They call themselves the B's Club."

"Band of bitches, those girls," August responded.

"Because they band together? If that's all you see, then you're missing out on what they can do. What's it going to be, Pa?" Adele asked. "Are you turning me over to them? For what? To be murdered, beaten?"

The sound of an eighteen-wheeler rolled up the driveway, releasing compression popping sounds as the pressure in the cylinders slowed the pistons. August raised and cocked his gun, but Adele put her hand on the barrel to lower it. "They are here to help. Here's what we're going to do."

***

August tied and gagged Hash to the horse stall and then stepped outside to greet the driver. With the truck blocking the view between the house and barn, Adele ran up to the passenger's side. August and Sheriff McKinley exchanged a few words, and then August pointed to the corral as if to advise the driver where to park and wait for the cattle to load.

Adele stepped on the truck's running board and hung onto the door handle while the truck pulled away from the house.

"What's the situation, Adele?" McKinley asked.

"Thugs are inside holding the girls, but I don't know in what room. And Sheriff, one more thing. Ivan Mills isn't dead. He's inside. He's one of them."

"I'll be damned. Best lawyer your granddaddy ever had," McKinley said. "How in the hell did they turn him?"

"Money, extortion, bribery. Who knows?"

McKinley looked around the farm, studying it as if to modify his plan. "Do you know if the girls are injured?"

"Olga made it look like they'd been bleeding. Count on the girls to have a trick or two up their sleeves. Ivan Mills wants this to look like a messy union turnover."

"He misses the Hatfields and McCoys?" McKinley said sarcastically.

"Where is Jackson?" Adele asked.

"Last I saw, he was held at gunpoint."

McKinley shook his head. "He allowed himself to get captured," he stated as if he knew all along Jackson's plan.

Adele had completely misread Jackson's move. He had sacrificed himself to protect her sisters. She needed him to be safe. If there were injuries, she would hold herself responsible. A gunslinger and bodyguard; that is what he was! She would observe him and try to read his signals.

"Alright, Miss Dawson, here on out, you stay out of the way. Stand over by the grain silos. That's where we'll send your sissies. Troopers and I will take it from here."

Dressed in muddy overalls, Sheriff McKinley looked every bit the part of a cattle trucker here to pick up his load. August led the Sheriff over to the shop, then, a bit more dramatic than necessary, searched his own pockets as if to try to find his wallet. He smacked his forehead like he remembered his wallet was inside the house. Adele thought to herself, good acting, considering they were trying to make out that the sheriff was a cattle buyer.

August and Sheriff McKinley walked into the house like it was another ordinary day of doing farm business. Curtains inside the house moved ever so slightly. August held the door for McKinley as if he might convince the kidnappers that he had convinced this farmer bumpkin to come inside the house and complete paperwork before loading up cattle for the stockyards. McKinley tucked his right hand behind his back to conceal the handgun. At least ten troopers in shotguns and tactical gear crouched low to the ground, surrounding the house.

Adele slipped behind the first of two silos, trying to stay within sight of the house. She heard the Sheriff shout, "Police. Put down your guns."

"Girls, stay hidden," she silently coached, as if they might be able to sense her warning. "Don't come out. Stay down."

The back door opened, not in the heat of battle but quietly. Jackson ran out of the house, holding Faye in one arm. Deirdre clung to his left arm, and Elysia tagged along behind Deirdre. When Elysia tripped, Deirdre grabbed the back of Elysia's shirt and yanked her to her feet.

Jackson dropped behind the silo to be sure the girls made it safely into Adele's arms. His leg was bleeding; his cheek, badly bruised, his lip was cut in several places.

"You're hurt!" Adele said. She tore a piece of her skirt into shreds and tied a tourniquet around his leg.

"Always ripping your clothes off for me. Check on the girls," Jackson ordered.

Adele called the freed sisters into a huddle behind the silo. She ran her hands down each from shoulder to toe, looking for wounds or bruises. "Where were you hiding?"

Elysia started sobbing and spoke between sloppy wet breaths. "Briana pushed us into a stand-up wooden closet."

Faye broke out in tears. "Bri got M.A.D. She said no talking."

"We hid behind some man's smelly boots," Deirdre added. Her eyes grew wide. "They have Collette tied up in the kitchen. Briana's in the attic. Nita hid her there."

"Benita is here?"

Faye nodded. "Her bossy self is back."

"Did anyone hurt you? There was blood on a brochure."

Deirdre shook her head. "Olga Beast cut the head off a chicken. She's good at that whack, Delly."

"Then what?" Adele coached.

Elysia stepped in, adding power and more drama to the story as she looked up to Jackson. "She made Deidre and me hold the head while the chicken ran away. Then she pressed a piece of paper to our hands."

Adele hung her head, not sure what to do next. Laugh, cry, and hug her sisters. The bottom of her heart was turning black with disgust for Olga and August. Her stomach churned, her back and shoulder ached. She looked at Jackson and thanked him for fighting for her. For taking on the hate and greed from people she had never met. An uncontrollable frenzy built in her. Goons inside became so irrational, adopting a cause for which they likely had no connection. A meaningless love of gunfights caught her sisters in the line of fire.

She thought about the Besame contract and hoped there might be unpaid royalties that the board couldn't gain access to. "I'm going inside," Adele finally announced. "Somehow, I'll pay the ransom money."

"Nothing good comes of that," Jackson said. He stood with the bandage around his leg and tucked his gun into his belt behind his back. "Guys like this, come back for more."

"What they want is money," Adele argued.

"Ivan wants a signature, Adele. Do you not see that?" He put his hands on her shoulders and looked desperately into her eyes.

She felt a strong desire to kiss him. She could feel the intensity of his grip on her shoulder tighten as if he wanted to share an intimate moment, but then he pulled away.

"I haven't figured out who is calling the shots yet, Ivan or some dude who taps his fingers, counting. Spot him right off. He can't look straight at you unless his fist is headed for your jaw. They call him Jugs. Big ears like handles on a jug."

"I can't leave the girls in there, Jackson."

"Leave that to me." Jackson leaned in and kissed her forehead. "I got this." Limping, he ran back into the house. As soon as the door opened, she heard another round of gunfire.

Adele spun around and slapped her hand against the side of the grain silo. "Listen girls; I'm going to try something else. Do you know how much I love you?" Faye leaped up into her arms and hugged Adele. Adele winced from the movement in her shoulder but found comfort in Faye's embrace. Elysia and Deirdre stretched their arms around her waist.

"Stay right here. I will come back for you," Adele said.

***

Adele walked steadily up to the Beck home, a pinewood structure with dirty spider webs where shutters had once hung. She knew about houses like this. Shame lived here. It was the place her mother had been kidnapped and taken prisoner when she was a teenager. The house seemed to drag Adele into a world left behind, where wild white yarrows were trampled. Dogs barked at the slightest twitch. Despair smelled like a moonshine mill. No, her sisters would not be subject to this life ever again.

The draperies shifted. They were anticipating Adele.

"I'm coming in!" she shouted. She stood squarely in front of the door. "I will pay your demands. Don't shoot." She counted to five, then opened the door, hoping she had given the kidnappers enough time to lower their guns. She listened to the door's rusty squeal; walked inside, knowing she would likely feel the brunt end of their weapons. She had to make the gunmen think she had control of the one thing they wanted most: money.

Three bodies lay on the floor. Another body in an armchair, his blood staining the worn beige fabric to a dull liquid purple. His ears bulged nearly half the size of his head. *Jugs.*

"Look at you. All shot up." She felt Kettie Dawson written all over her.

Her eyes scanned the room. Jugs would not look at her. He tapped his fingers against his thumb, one after another. Ivan peeked out from behind a desk turned sideways in the back of the room. Sheriff McKinley had established a tactical position in the kitchen behind the counter. The palm of his trigger hand wrapped around the gun butt, steady.

Adele crossed her arms. "So, this is who Reverend Whitfield sent? He would never support your approach."

No one said anything. Grown men, most of them bleeding, stared at her, dumbfounded.

She breathed herself into being large. "I want to see Collette and Briana."

"Did you bring the money?" Jugs demanded.

"I have the money. But like Olga said, it's going to the Southern Tenant Farmers Union."

Jackson slipped into the kitchen, his eyebrows raised, mouth opened wide. He held up his hands and mouthed the word, "What?"

Adele examined the thugs to be sure she could afford to look straight at Jugs. "You have my word; I will pay," she said to him.

Jugs tapped his fingers. "How do we know?"

"Because I know what it's like to open a coffee can and find out someone stole a year of savings. I irrigated wheat fields, picked cotton until my fingers bled, and then watched my stepdad hand ninety percent of our earnings over to a man who kept our subsidy." She looked to Jackson, who indicated she should keep talking while he moved in for a better shot. "I sold celery and carrots to the neighbors so that we could buy hay for the cattle. I believe in the Southern Tenant Farmer's mission."

Jugs stood behind the couch and pointed his gun at her. Blood dripped down his wrist onto the sofa, creating a red river down to the seat. "You a communist?"

Adele shook her head.

"Then, you expect us just to drop our weapons?"

"Yes, I do. This isn't your battle."

Jugs lumbered away from the chair to pull Collette out from behind a half wall. A checkered bandana blindfolded her; the cloth had grown damp from her tears. "I will keep this one at my side until you make the final payment."

"I can outwait you, Jugs," Adele answered. "You're bleeding out."

"You think I'm kidding?" Jugs taunted her. His eyes shifted, unable to focus. Movement outside caught his attention. "The oldest. She got free. Which one of you cretins let her go?"

The hand holding his pistol began to shake, perhaps from the loss of blood. Adele didn't dare take his bait. She held his gaze. Another gunman said, "Hiding in the attic. I found her and tied her up."

"Not well enough. She just broke free," Jugs shouted. "That twit is right outside the window. Running to the barn. You can't keep track of a sixteen-year-old?" he yelled at his men.

Adele thought she recognized the shenanigans of twin sisters taunting the men. Oldest trick in the Book of Twins. Benita was outside, running a decoy for Briana.

"Your men are hurt. I'd say they want to go home." Adele held softly, but she enunciated every word like Kettie had taught her. "I think you do, too."

"We didn't come all this way to give up without getting paid," Jugs argued.

"Who hired you?"

Jugs looked over to Ivan Mills. Ivan ducked behind the desk.

"That sonofabitch," Jugs answered.

"Ivan, is this your doing?" Adele asked. "What did you promise them?" She was stepping aside from any logical boundary. At any time, this fragile truce could blow up in her face.

"We have the girls," Ivan said from behind the desk. "You're in no position to negotiate."

"I am not hiding behind a desk, Ivan. And, I have money."

She saw Jackson move behind Sheriff McKinley in the kitchen. On Jackson's heels, Giles tiptoed to a wall where neither could be seen anymore. Damn, now she'd drawn her grandfather into the gunfight. He might even the odds, but Giles was in Germany the last time he held a gun.

"Collette, step away from Jugs now," Adele said, aware that her only weapon was her steadfast voice and the Dawson family bank account. "If she takes a bullet, I pay nothing."

Jugs released his hold on Collette long enough for her to raise the blindfold from her eyes. He pushed Collette toward the door. She stumbled, trying to find her way, then stood.

"Wait outside," Adele instructed. No emotions. "Get away from the house."

"Okay. They still have Briana."

Adele nodded at Collette and waited for her to leave.

Jugs moaned. "Girl escaped. Thanks to my brilliant colleagues."

"Jugs, I don't have a gun," Adele said. She held up her arms to prove she came in without weapons. "I'm not here to fight you. I will ask Sheriff McKinley to arrest Ivan, though."

"What's your point, bitch?" Jugs responded.

"Take your men and go home. Anyone who harms my sisters or me will get arrested too. It's a long ride to the closest jail. A man could die on the way."

She waited. Jugs's eyes shifted. His bloodied fingers tapped out a symphony. He leaned his head back and shut his eyes. The cords of his neck pulsed as if his heart was trying to determine whether to pump blood to his brain or his fingers.

A bedroom door opened. Two men came out. One man's shirt was bloody. The other's face and hands were covered in blood. They raised a third man from the floor and helped him out the door. None of them looked back to see if Jugs would object.

"We're done, man," one said. "Not enough to get killed over."

Jugs looked to be on the verge of saying something to the men deserting him, but his arm dropped, weakened from his blood loss and the weight of the gun. Sheriff McKinley was immediately beside him, pulling the weapon free. Within moments, McKinley had secured Jugs in handcuffs and was leading prisoners out of the house. As she watched them leave, Adele caught sudden movement in the back of the living room.

Ivan stepped out from behind his desk. He glared at Adele and snapped his six-shooter, keeping it trained on her. "Woman!" he shouted. "Everything I did was for your grandfather. Not you. There's no revenue if you're running the mine."

She had no time to understand why he carried such a grudge against the Dawson family.

"I say she does," Giles retorted. "Drop the gun, Ivan."

Adele dropped to the floor as shots were fired. A bullet whizzed past her. Again, more shots.

When the gunfire ceased, she looked up to see Ivan's shadow lumbering toward her. His face wretched with anger, his eyes fiercely dark, the gun pointed at her head. His finger was still on the trigger. Another shot and blood spewed from the back of his head.

She rolled into a ball, needing to take a breath; her lungs were frozen.

Ivan dropped the gun on the couch, fell forward, and landed next to her on the floor. His deadly eyes still open, staring at her as he let out a harsh whoosh of his last breath. Her legs shot into involuntary action, forcing herself to crawl backward. For the last fifteen minutes, her shoulder had not screamed at her. It was on fire now.

Giles, her grandfather, was instantly beside her pointing his gun down at Ivan's head. Adele could smell the gunpowder residue from his weapon. A faint circle of smoke lifted from the barrel.

Giles reached down and pulled the gun from Ivan's hand, tossing it towards Sheriff McKinley. "He's gone," Giles said. He lowered his weapon to help Adele stand. "You okay?"

"Maybe. My hands are still shaky."

"That was a daring negotiation you pulled off, boss," Giles said. "Next board meeting, I'll remind members not to argue with you."

She smiled at his recognition. "Thank you, Grandpa," she said. She took the hand that he offered her to get up off the floor. Standing, she leaned into him and hugged him.

"Grandpa," he repeated. "I can do that." Giles seemed to be twenty years younger. "Get that shoulder looked at," he added.

***

Sheriff McKinley finished rounding up the gunfighters and made them climb up into the cattle truck. Jackson had slipped out without her knowing.

Adele finally found him limping toward his truck. "We need to rescue Olga from Elizabeth's surveillance," she said when she caught up to him.

He re-tied the tourniquet around his leg. "I told you not to go in," Jackson barked.

"I was the only one who could stop this," Adele responded, surprised he would be testy with her now that the kidnapping was resolved.

"You could've been killed," Jackson continued. "I called Sheriff McKinley for a reason."

"I had hoped a peaceful approach might help. It did," Adele argued.

"You brought logic to a gunfight?"

"Olga provoked her renegades. There should never have been a gunfight," Adele said.

Jackson leaned into her. "You don't like gunfights? Stay out of Mingo County."

"I don't understand you, Jackson Conor. You need medical help."

"Go rescue Elizabeth," Jackson snapped. "Benita said Olga got away. The sheriff will drop me off at the hospital."

Rebecca Parsons ran up to Sheriff McKinley as he was backing the truck out of the Beck farm. "Hey, what happened in there? Can I get your side of the story?"

"Tell you what, Miss Parsons," Adele answered. "We're on our way to the hospital. If you can get Mr. Conor to talk, you'll have one hell of a story."

***

Adele left Jackson in the front seat of McKinley's cattle truck and headed to the silo to find her sisters. The girls were playing tag as if it was just another day of sister play. Benita stopped chasing Collette as Adele grew closer.

"How did you get here?" Adele asked the oldest twin.

"I really did try to go home," Benita said. She brushed dirt from her hands. "Olga showed up at the train station when I was about to leave. That's when I knew something bad was about to happen. Sheriff McKinley was about to arrest her when he got the call to come here. I don't know where she is now."

"Thank you for coming back," Adele answered. "You and I have a lot to talk about."

Benita shrugged. "I guess we do. Seems I'm always spitting apologies."

Adele grinned. "What are your plans now?"

"I don't know, Delly. I've messed things up pretty much with you. Olga's going to jail, I guess. Pa's going to need me back to work the farm."

"What about all those things you stole? Quillan's military coins. Family memorabilia?"

"I dropped all that off with Tamasin. She said she'd put everything back in the attic. Figured you'd be seething. I shouldn't have taken them."

Adele opened her arms for Benita. "Nita. Please come home with me."

Benita hugged Adele harder than she'd done before. Adele felt a river of anxiety drain from Benita's shoulders.

"What about the Southern Tenants march?" Benita asked. "I can't stay in Bramwell when I know families need help."

Adele wrapped her arm around her sister. "Sassy as you are, you have a calling to defend the helpless. I promise at the right time, you will carry the funds to Reverend Whitfield."

August Beck was immediately at Benita's side. "It's no bother for me to deliver it in person."

"No!" Benita and Adele said in unison. Benita added, "This is for Delly and me to do."

"But you're coming home with me," August argued. "We will plant winter wheat next month. Can't do this without your help."

"I'm going to stay with Delly until Christmas," Benita responded. "The next time I leave here, it will be a proper farewell. I need my diploma. And a college degree, too. You going to pay for that, Pa?"

"What will happen to the farm?" August asked. "When I sell, a big part of that revenue will go to you."

"When YOU sell?" Benita taunted. "Focus on Olga. She's going to need a really good attorney," Benita answered. "I might know one in about eight years."

Chapter 22:
Christmas, 1938

It was the first Christmas Adele and her sisters had seen a gift under the tree from anyone but a charitable organization. Ribbons and bows took the place of cards that read, "from your friends at New Madrid Charity."

Benita and Briana decided to limit the gifts to just five each, giggling that they should be so bold to suggest five when they were lucky in the past to receive one basket of bread for the entire family. Their rule was that each gift had to meet Benita's criteria. One gift for themselves, one for a Secret Sister Santa, one for a friend, one for the church orphanage, and one book for the family library. Adele agreed to provide $10 to each sister for Christmas shopping. She went by train with her sisters to Bluefield, now a monthly excursion, for Christmas gifts. Collette appointed herself to oversee the Secret Santa assignments.

Adele crumpled newspapers and stuffed them into shopping bags to hide evidence of what each sister had purchased.

The girls had been to the Corner Shop, where they saw a picture of children sitting around a noble fir tree, decorating it with popcorn, cranberries, tinsel, and balls. So, on the Saturday before Christmas, Elijah drove the girls, each decked in long stocking caps, mittens, and new winter coats, up to Bushy Mountain Christmas Tree farm to cut down their first tree.

Elysia and Deirdre clapped snow off branches as they plowed

between rows of bushy green evergreens. Collette pulled together fallen limbs to make them into wreaths. Adele carried Faye on her shoulders. Benita and Briana argued over which tree was tallest but still would fit at the base of the staircase. Elijah sat on a bench at the base of the mountain until they agreed on which one to cut down.

The next morning Adele gathered baking pans for cookie making. Benita and Briana joined the Presbyterian church's high school youth group as they cooked and fed Jewish refugees who had escaped Germany's occupation of France. The Presbyterian church had volunteered to provide a safe passageway for these families as they traveled from Cuba to New York, trying to connect with families. Collette, Deirdre, and Elysia joined the youth choir singing carols for children at the Bluefield Sanitarium.

Adele and Faye remained at the house with Tamasin, determined to help bake ginger snaps, fudge, and tea-time tassies. "You gots to press your thumb into the tassie dough. Halfway, girl," Tamasin instructed. "Leave room for the Karo and pecans."

Tamasin was gradually getting stronger from her elderberry and vitamin regimen. Adele understood better now why Elijah tended the herb garden. Dr. Luttrell offered new hope from a tuberculosis vaccine, but he also encouraged Tamasin to spend time sitting outside, even if she was wrapped in blankets. Take in all the sun treatments you can, he'd said. Adele opened all the shutters in the kitchen, making sure Tamasin got her vitamin D.

Collette, Deirdre, and Elysia baked gingerbread cookies under Tamasin's tutelage. The following Sunday, they hosted a Sunday afternoon party for children in the neighborhood. Faye held a tray filled with Christmas cookies. Tamasin limited the number of marshmallows for each cup of hot chocolate.

Adele and Faye were cleaning up the kitchen when the doorbell rang.

Faye answered the door since Adele's hands were covered in flour and cookie dough.

"Jackson!" Faye squealed. He stepped into the parlor and lifted her into his arms. "Merry Christmas, young lady! You did a mighty fine job lighting the trees outside."

"Lijah made the lights shine," Faye squealed. "L I T E," she spelled.

"My, aren't you the smartest," Jackson answered.

"I'm ready for kindergarten."

"Well, I guess you are. Is your big sister home?"

The last time Adele and Jackson had seen each other, he had brushed her off on his way to get a bullet removed. Adele rinsed flour from her hands and stepped into the parlor. "Merry Christmas," she said, hoping not to show how happy she was to see him.

Jackson stepped back out onto the stone porch and produced a huge poinsettia. "I took a chance I might find you here."

"That's very kind of you. Do you have time to come in? Tamasin is a bit crabby with me, teaching me how to fill these tiny pies with pecans."

"I arrived just in time." Jackson pecked Tamasin's cheek. "Is it the herbs or Dr. Luttrell's breathing treatments that make you look so radiant?"

"It's the Lord's birthday," Tamasin answered. "Ever body shines brighter these days."

Social pleasantries weren't Jackson's specialty, Adele thought, but he was mighty pleasant this morning. He had something on his mind.

"May I have a word with you, Adele?" he asked. She washed her hands, thanked him for the poinsettia, then offered him a small plate of Tamasin's tassies.

"Let's go into the library," she said.

Jackson was clearly uneasy with the formality of a library setting. She knew he was a kitchen table kind of guy, but she sensed he needed some privacy. He struggled to find words, then finally spoke. "Miss Cora and I have elected to make our wedding vows."

Adele straightened in her chair, hiding her sudden loss for words. Finally, she said, "I didn't know you had formalized your relationship. I would have sent a congratulatory note."

"Frankly, neither did I until I took a bullet. That's when Cora says she came to realize how much she loved me. She said she wanted a ring for Christmas."

"Smart man to accommodate such a request."

"She says the only person I will take a bullet, for now, is her. I guess I shouldn't have put myself between you and the felons up at Beck's holler."

"I have to admit; she has a point!" Adele leaned back, realizing how comfortable she felt in her grandmother's favorite chair. "You made good on your promise, Jackson, to rebuild the mine. Now it is the envy of West Virginia. You made that happen. We will meet Britain's cry for coal now with the Nazis invading France. I hope you are giving our miners a holiday break."

"So, no hard feelings?" Jackson asked.

Adele pondered his question. "Why would I have hard feelings? You and Cora have been together since I've known you."

Jackson stood up and reached for her hands, offering to bring her to her feet. "I don't know if this is the right move for Cora and me. Especially since you and I have feelings for each other."

Instinctively Adele's hand flew up to her chest as if to question his observation.

"I know it, and you do too, Adele." He placed his hand on her neck, touching her throat with his thumb. "You can't deny me that. Down in the mine together. At the old Beck house. You and I belong together, Adele. You have to know I will always be at your side, protecting you."

He leaned close to her. "You have to know I am in love with you."

Adele stood, stunned by his revelation. She checked the buttons on her sweater to be sure she wasn't as exposed as she felt. Jackson had brought to light the feelings she could not let her heart admit. Jackson had befriended her when a rogue journalist came after her. He demonstrated unfailing determination to put the mine back on its feet in record time. He'd been with her through gunfights and snowball fights. He had given her courage that she might not have achieved on her own. He demanded nothing but honesty from her. But now, he pushed a raw, provocative emotion she had refused to admit. Was there enough between them to turn her back on Tommy, the love of her life? She had just turned twenty years old. What did she know about dangerous love when all she'd known was Tommy?

Jackson kissed her cheek like a man who wasn't sure of his boundaries. "Mull it over, Adele. If I'm right, you know how to find me."

He leaned down to kiss her forehead. "Merry Christmas, boss," he said and walked out the door.

Adele knew she had an exotic, almost forbidden connection to Jackson. He affirmed her as his strong woman boss. Against advice from Tommy and mining engineers, she'd gone down into a pit to rescue him. He was ruggedly handsome, fearless, a rule breaker that made her cheeks blush when he was nearby. Charming, appealing, aggressively defending her against bullish people. But something inside her said some of his behavior might be a little too opportunistic.

If she let him into her life as a love-mate, what would that say about her leadership skills? That she was available for certain favors from some minors? If a relationship with Jackson changed, she would likely have to fire him. Or the board would ask her to resign. She trusted Jackson to maintain fair governance over the miners, keep morale high as the economy boosted, and meet quota without any lives lost. That respect earned him the best pay in the county and a bonus for meeting 1938 goals. She could depend on him to meet Europe's demands.

Jackson hadn't been gone for more than 20 minutes when she heard the whistle from the Norfolk and Western curving around the Bluestone River, then stop at the train station. Everything in her body said, "Tommy is on that train." His letters brought comfort, especially when he said he would be with her for Christmas. But there was nothing like having the man in person, his arms around her. Both she and Tommy had experienced significant life changes. He'd started college at Harvard. But look at her?

Every day, she proved her worth as she stood up to organized vigilantes, keeping the mine in business. Accounting, she discovered, was second nature, a gift her stepfather had discovered in her years ago. She hated to acknowledge any compliment from August Beck for fear he would exploit her. Like when he demanded she cook the books for him to present a better portfolio to bankers. Nope. No longer. In the reinvention of Adele Christina Dawson, he no longer served an important role. She had developed an intuitive sense of opportunists.

As she stood on the piazza watching for Tommy, she began to understand why Quillan built this house on a hill overlooking the small town of Bramwell. The train's steam engines puffed fresh white smoke clouds as water poured from the tender to the locomotive. A tugboat on the Bluestone River meandered through town, slowly pushing a barge to the Bramwell dock where it would offload supplies. Wreaths hung on the bank of Bramwell corner railings. The Presbyterian Church parking lots provided sprays of light on children needing to be picked up after caroling through town. David Henderson was working late again. Pocahontas Coal Mine offices had closed for a two-week Christmas break.

She leaned over the rail, checking to see if an office light was on. She saw the silhouette of what looked like a woman moving in the office. Odd,

Adele thought, since she and the office manager were the only two women employed, and the office manager had gladly used her Christmas bonus to visit family in New York. She watched for movement, but there was none. As soon as Tommy arrived, she would check that out. Or should she go now?

The church bus slowed as it stopped in front of the Corner Shop, momentarily distracting her. Children climbed down and gathered in a semi-circle to sing O Little Town of Bethlehem. Despite snow clouds moving in, she could still hear Collette's tone-deaf voice pierce through the melody, "Yet in thy dark streets shineth."

"That's my girl," Adele said, smiling. "Let em know you're there."

She wrapped a coat over her shoulders. Who was in the office at this hour? She wanted to find out, but she also wanted to be present for Tommy when he arrived.

She saw Jackson's truck pull up into the Corner Shop and walk inside. About ten minutes later, Cora, Elizabeth, and Jude Radford drove up to the restaurant. Jude helped his wife and daughter out of the car, then held the restaurant's door as they walked in. Cora bounded inside, a happy bride-to-be on her way to be with Jackson. Before joining the family, Elizabeth turned and looked up the hill. She brought her hands together prayerfully and mouthed "thank you" to Adele.

Perhaps it was Elizabeth she'd seen moving around the office. It made perfect sense. Adele nodded once to acknowledge her friend's sign of gratitude. Adele would need Elizabeth's support as the mine set out to meet the 20-ton order they had just received from Great Britain. West Virginia coal produced very little smoke, making it ideal for the carburizing coking process that turned coke to steel. Under Jackson's direction, the mine would export steel that helped Great Britain transition from a volunteer army to a full-blown military defense army against Hitler's advancing storm troopers.

If there could possibly be better news, it was that the love of her life was on his way.

***

"What took you so long?" Chase had been pacing in the dark parking lot of the Pocahantas mine offices. He chewed on a Cuban cigar, showing off that he could still get them from Havana even though several of the Allies were boycotting the country. In his long brown duster, some would think he looked like a German military officer. Smugly, he rather enjoyed shaking up the community. Make the people of Bramwell think Nazis were preparing to invade the United States.

"You look like a thug in that coat," Olga snapped. "When will you learn?"

"Learn what?" Chase snapped.

"Fit in, Chase. You stand out. Too easy to remember. And why call a meeting now?" Olga asked. "Not many of us still alive. Except the yellow bellies," she said glaring at him, "who couldn't get their asses down to the Beck farm."

"Bloody mess," Chase murmured. "But what d'ya know, Miss Dawson has opened up a golden door for us. Her time's run out. Mrs. Cassidy will see to that."

"Now, what'd she do?" Olga snorted. "Olga's tone showed how annoyed she was that Chase had invited Blanche Cassidy to meet this close to Christmas.

The door to the manager's office was open. "Well, well, if it isn't the Lesser Committee," Blanche welcomed. She was sitting at Adele's desk, leaned back in a leather chair, petting a miniature Yorkie. The dog licked her fingers as if to calm her. Blanche patted the arms of the chair. "You know this belonged to Giles before Quillan bought us out. I could use this in my home."

"Why are you here?" Olga asked. She pulled a flask of cognac and two jiggers from her pocketbook and filled them. She handed one to Chase and toasted him. "Forgive me, I thought there was just the two of us," Olga said. Blanche reached into the third drawer of the desk and produced a small cut crystal glass. She placed it in front of Olga.

"Story around Tazewell that Miss Dawson was seen coming out of the Bluefield Inn some weeks ago," Blanche said. "With a man from down St. Louis area. She's not married that I know of."

"Probably Tom Thompson," Olga explained.

"So, you know about her indiscretions?" Blanche asked.

Olga sighed. "Old news, Blanche. She and Tommy have been friends for ten years or more. They act like newlyweds."

Blanche stroked the Yorkie. "And that's what brings me here today. Adele is still here. Nothing any of you have done dissuaded her. I'd say she's starting to become a tiny legend. What are you going to do about that, now?"

"I'm taking her out tonight," Chase answered much too boldly. He reached in his overcoat pocket and produced a double-barrel Remington derringer.

Blanche huffed. "Not tonight. This town is abuzz with celebration."

"She will not be alive in Bramwell by Christmas. I promise you that."

Olga interrupted. "There's a better way. She'll marry Tommy and move to be with his family near St. Louis. Kettie put a clause in her will that Adele must remain in the Bramwell area. Or, the funds go to

Kettie's charities."

"Kettie did show a preference for the Cassidy Family Foundation." Blanche raised the dog to her face and rubbed noses with the Yorkie. "I wouldn't say that's the only foundation Kettie liked. So we're still leaving too much to chance."

Chase pressed his cigar butt against Adele's mahogany desk, leaving a burn mark on the corner of her desk. "People are distracted this time of year. Lots of dinners, and holiday exchanges. It's time for us to spread a little boycott of our own on the Dawson family. My Famiglia boss is impatient. I have three days to get her gone. Are you in or out?"

"You won't get Auggie's support on this one. We've got a tenant farmers protest early next year." Olga sipped from her cognac. "Auggie will come after you. He's been unequivocal. Leave the girl alone."

"But Olga, dear. You are still under contract!" Chase hissed.

Well, I just broke the contract."

"And you cleared this with Wheeling?" Chase asked.

"While you were out shooting tin cans, Dinky Winky, the Familigia was getting killed."

Chase reached for the Remington. The nerve of this bitch to poke fun of his genitalia.

"You're not from Bramwell, are you?" Olga wiped a ring of lipstick from her cognac glass and snickered. "The likes of you won't fare well in this town."

Chase stood abruptly. He fastened two buttons on his coat duster and slid the weapon back into his pocket. "Don't ever come running to me to do your dirty work. Never again."

"But Miss Olga Beck, that's precisely what we're doing," Blanche argued. "I came to your aid only a few months ago. Got you away from E-Liz-A-Beth Radford when she would have just as soon left you in that cold, dirty tent. What neither of you seems to understand is that I need Adele gone. Now."

Olga poured another glass of cognac for herself and put the flask back into her purse. "I'll stay for one more day. But no one must know that I helped."

"That's the Christmas spirit," Blanche answered, sarcasm dripping like sour milk. She put the yorkie on top of Adele's desk. "Doesn't Olga have a servant heart. Yes, she does," Blanche said rubbing her nose against the yorkie. "Never asking to be noticed for her good works."

Olga swallowed the last of her whiskey. "You've been warned. Best I can do."

The puppy suddenly bent sideways and nipped at her master's hand. Blanche looked up through gray furrowed eyebrows at Chase and Olga. Her eyes were ice cold. "Cowards. Both of you. I'll show you how it's done," she spat, her grin derisive.

"You?" Chase chortled.

"Tonight. Stone House. And if you doubt me again, I won't bother with a hitman."

***

When it was dark, Collette, Deirdre, Elysia and Faye turned the candle lights for the windows and turned the Christmas candle lights on. Elijah flipped the switch for the driveway, lighting the white lights that encouraged friendship, and new relationships, and served as a reminder to share the joy of Christmas. Adele hoped the lights would provide enough light for Tommy, and what was taking him so long?

She stepped back inside the house to stoke the fire when Elysia moved from one window to the next, watching movement outside. "It's Tommy! Elysia squealed. "Tommy's here."

Adele rushed through the kitchen to open the door. She ran out to greet her beloved friend. Tommy dropped his suitcase and a grocery bag, then opened his arms to hold her close. Adele kissed his ears, his cheeks, and then his lips until he finally stopped spinning long enough to plant her feet back on the ground.

"I have missed you," he said, spending much too long, for Adele, looking at her lips until he finally kissed her, gently then hard. He put both hands on top of her head. "Let me look at you. You're not taller, not fatter. But why are you lovelier than ever before?"

Adele and Tommy held each other; bodies pressed together until Adele feared his coat would melt from their heat.

"Your letters. They were amazing," Tommy whispered. "I felt so close to you. But I need you right here."

"How did you get away from your mother so quickly?" Adele asked.

"She can't quite get over that you're an heiress," Tommy answered.

Adele nodded. "Sometimes, neither can I." She also was starting to feel the winter freeze. "We're still standing outside when I have a perfect fire to warm you."

"Not yet," Tommy argued. "I told my mother she had to accept you because we were getting married."

"Married!" Adele cried.

"You do, don't you? Want to be my wife?" Tommy looked worried. "Delly, I thought about this from the day I left here. On the train ride up here, I ran every scenario through my mind. What if you met someone else? What if you said 'no.' What if your ignorant stepfather pulled off another threat? I cannot go through this life not knowing who is here to protect you. Then, as soon as I saw you come running, I knew I couldn't wait one more second."

He reached into his pocket, then knelt on the cold ground and took her hands in his. "Marry me, please, Delly?" He opened a black velvet jewelry box and held the ring out for her to accept his proposal.

Adele stared at the large diamond mounted on a gold band. She looked at him, looked at the diamond, then back to Tommy. "What about college?"

"You're asking me that while my knees are freezing?"

She laughed, feeling an abundance of burdens suddenly lifted. She would have a life partner, a confidante in the middle of the night. She would have an advocate, her best friend, at her side.

"Is that a yes?" Tommy asked.

"Yes! Yes!"

Tommy pulled the gold diamond setting out of the box and placed the ring on her left hand. "I have loved you since you peddled celery on my street. I saved quarters from my newspaper route. I don't even like celery, but I had to be home when you and your sisters came by. Now, the carrots and green beans," Tommy added, winking at her.

Adele bolted into his arms, nearly knocking him down while he tried to stand. "My sisters are getting so impatient. Look at them standing on the porch waiting for us." Despite the winter chill, she felt completely warm. "Come inside. We've been making cookies. And Tamasin set aside a dozen of her tassies for you."

"Your kiss would have been enough." Tommy handed her the paper bag. "This is for our Christmas meal." He picked up his suitcase and wrapped one arm around Adele's shoulder as they walked inside. "Fiancé," he whispered. "Precious." He kissed her forehead. Even in the cold, she felt the warmth of her smile melt away any fear she had of turning Jackson away.

"Okay, we saw that," Benita greeted. "Did she say yes?" she asked Tommy.

Tommy's smile was contagious as if he couldn't stop grinning at Adele. He squeezed Adele's shoulder and looked down into her eyes. "She said yes."

"She said yes!' Briana clapped.

Benita elbowed Tommy. "We're going to be a two-lawyer family. Welcome home." She leaned close and kissed his cheek.

Collette jumped down two steps at a time and then ran into Tommy's arms. "I knew it. I always knew you'd straighten up."

"Me?" Tommy laughed.

Deirdre and Elysia each took one of his hands. "How soon will you come live with us?" Deirdre asked.

Adele exchanged looks with Tommy. "We have a lot of planning to do," Adele answered. "But that will certainly be one of the items on our list."

Faye waited outside the circle of girls. Elysia reached for Faye's hand and pulled. "Delly and Tommy are getting married!"

Tommy squatted to be eye-level with Faye. "Is that okay with you, Punkin?"

"Are you going to be my new daddy?" Faye asked.

"Even better, Miss Faye," Tommy said. "I'm going to be your new big brother."

Faye's eyes moved back and forth as if trying to find a place in her mind for a brother.

"I know you have a little brother," Tommy said. "Can I be the one who lifts you up," he said, raising Faye to his chest, "and hug the bugs out of you."

Faye tucked her head against his shoulders and wrapped her arms around him tightly. Tommy kissed her cheek, then set her back down, but didn't let go of her hand.

Together, they walked from the parlor into the kitchen, helping Faye climb up onto a chair. He handed a large brown sack to Tamasin. "I stopped at the butcher's shop on the way here. I say we start a new tradition this Christmas. Standing rib roast."

"' Bout time you gets here," Tamasin said. Black as she was, the glint in her eyes sparkled diamond white. "Miss Adele and me be holdin' back cookies hopin' they wouldn't spoil."

Tommy stepped up to Tamasin and opened his arms wide. "I have missed you, woman."

"Don't you be womaning my woman," Elijah said. He stepped into the house and reached out to shake Tommy's hand. "Good thing you brought that roast, Tommy. I was afraid I'd hafta go out and shoot us another pheasant. Saved me the trouble."

"Well, now, I'm not saying a pheasant is out of the question," Tommy bantered. "There's always New Year's Eve."

***

After dinner, the girls dragged up stories about growing up in New Madrid, explaining to Tommy how they hoped to finish decorating the Christmas tree, now that he was there, Deirdre grabbed Tommy's hand and walked him beside the grand staircase. "That tree looked a lot bigger in the field," she said.

"Well, let's get some more lights on it," Tommy offered. When the doorbell rang, Adele heard Elijah explain to the visitor that the family was not receiving right now. The woman's voice was insistent she see Adele now.

"Excuse me, Miss Dawson," Elijah said. "Mrs. Cassidy wishes a word with you."

"Mrs. Cassidy?" Adele asked, grimacing. "What's she doing here?"

Tommy touched Adele's hand. "Who is she?"

"She's my mother's mother."

"Your grandmother?" Tommy asked.

"My mother's very estranged mother. She lives not too far from here."

"I've never heard you talk about her."

"That's because she disowned my mama at a terrible time in her life."

Tommy showed concern and lowered his voice. "And you've met her?"

"Boy, did I," Adele answered. "It was not pretty."

"Do you want me to come with you?"

"No. Help the girls decorate this tree. They wanted to wait for you."

Adele loved that Elijah hadn't brought Blanche Cassidy into the library; instead, he left her waiting outside in the cold.

"I hope you'll forgive me for dropping by unannounced," Blanche said when Adele opened the door. "We got off to such a bad start. I wondered if you could find just a few minutes for me to see my grandchildren." She held out a plate of decorated sugar cookies.

Adele looked at the plate, then at Blanche. "I don't have anything to say to you. I'm sorry you stopped by," she said, then reached to close the door.

"Wait, I deserve that," Blanche answered.

"Yes, you do. And so much more." Adele reached once more to close the door.

"I've not been kind to you, I realize. But it's been so long since I've heard such adorable laughter. May I come in?"

"No, you may not," Adele snapped. It was the first time Adele regretted how heavy the door was to close. Blanche shoved her foot into the doorway.

"Giles is in Washington, DC," Blanche said sternly. "The UK has admitted 10,000 child refugees. Kindertransport, they call it. The children are," she cleared her throat. "Jews."

"They are German children," Adele corrected. "I heard about it on the radio."

"My dear, if you were listening to the radio, you would also know the children are orphans. Prime Minister Chamberlain could not stand against Adolf Hitler. Thousands of children tucked away."

Adele heard her sisters laughing with Tommy and ached to leave this ridiculous woman to herself.

"Chamberlain has prevailed upon President Roosevelt with huge demands for steel." Blanche's eyebrows furrowed as she wrapped her hand around the heavy door. "I've been studying your production numbers. You will need to more than double in the next 30 days."

Blanche was forcing her shoulder into the narrow space. Adele held firm, but Blanche was advancing. "Step back, Mrs. Cassidy."

So that was the light on in the office. Blanche was digging through files in an office for which she had no permission to access.

"Illegal entrance!" Adele accused. She kicked at Blanche's foot, spun around, and quickly pressed her back against the door, not caring whether she injured Blanche's foot or crushed her fingers as the door finally snapped closed.

"Tommy?" she called, desperately needing backup. She pressed her feet to the floor, even as Blanche wiggled the doorknob.

She heard what sounded like a large dish smash on the kitchen floor, immediately followed by the smell of smoke. What in God's earth happened to Tamasin?

"Tommy?" Adele called again.

"In the kitchen!" he shouted. "Tamasin's been hurt."

'I can't. Blanche is trying to break in."

Adele stepped away from the door for an instant, then leaped against it once more, finally hearing Blanche cry out in pain. Adele might find blood in the doorframe tomorrow, but she sensed Blanche would not give up.

From the kitchen, she heard the girls scream and began bolting down the long hallway. Briana's cry was loudest, followed by a cacophony of her sisters. Her sisters never screamed unless they were mad at Benita. A thousand images. Benita's at it again. What broke? Where's Elijah? Tommy? A gunshot. Then a howl like the sound of a wounded wild animal.

She spun around the wall and ran directly into the chest of a man holding Deirdre, her head pulled backward, her red hair twisted in his fist. She struggled to stay on her feet as he tugged her hair from side to side.

"Miss Dawson! We meet again." In his other hand, he held a small pistol. Two barrels, one on top of the other, pointed at her chest.

Odd, Adele thought, how quickly the mind shoots images of past events, reminding her of Jude Radford's comment months ago about his son Chase's ruthless taste for blood. In the background, she saw black smoke coming from the kitchen and then the sound of water splashing against the walls. A puddle was forming around Chase's feet.

"You're Elizabeth's boy," Adele accused. Where was Tommy? Did the girls get out of the house? A neighbor would see smoke and call the fire department. How long could she hold off?

"You're something of a pain," Chase said. He waved the gun between Adele and Elysia.

"Don't point that gun at my sister," Adele said. "What do you want?"

"Seems obvious, doesn't it? It's not personal."

"What's not personal?"

"Well, I don't know," Chase derided her. "This?" he said, pointing the gun at Deirdre's head. The puddle around Chase's feet flowed close to the library. Why was he wasting time? Was the house on fire? Blanche was outside somewhere.

"Dee, I'm going to take care of you, you know that, don't you?" Adele said. "Remember how we used to play chess in the library?"

Chase's grip on Deirdre's head made it hard for her to respond. But Deirdre blinked her eyes as if she would try to help. Adele knew her sister was in pain, the way the creep tugged on her hair. Even so, Deirdre whipped her foot out, then quickly stabbed the stiff sole of her shoes back against Chase's instep.

"Run!" Adele called to Deirdre. Immediately she tucked her head down and rammed herself into his chest, forcing him to slip and fall. She fell on top of him, punched his face, and then pushed the Remington out of his hands, causing it to slide down the hallway.

"Not so fast, little lady."

Adele felt a hard kick into her side. She rolled over in pain. Blanche stood over her, kicking her in the back. "You might be my granddaughter, but I," Blanche grunted. "am your assassin."

Adele was unable to move. Her stomach felt like something inside had ruptured. Her back screamed at her to remain still. She was lying in a pool of water, unable to figure out how to stand and fight back. She curled into a ball, then climbed up onto her knees, knowing she was badly injured, but damned if she'd let a pitiful excuse for a grandmother get the best of her.

"Get up," Blanche ordered. "You and I are going for a car ride."

"No, you aren't!" Adele heard her sisters yell. Benita and Briana rushed out of the kitchen and tackled Blanche. Blanche slipped on the wet floor, and grabbed for the wall to regain her balance when Collette and Elysia leaped on top of her.

"I've never punched a fat woman before," Benita said. "But you," she said, throwing punches into Blanche's face and belly, "are trying...to hurt...my sister. Get in here Bri," Benita coached.

All five sisters, Deirdre now included, leaped, then came down on their knees into Blanche's face, legs, arms, and knees. "Is this allowed?" Collette asked.

Chase reached down to pull Deirdre from the pile.

"Hell, yes!" Benita said. She jumped and landed with both knees this time into Blanche's leg until the girls heard a bone crack. "Touchdown! Might have scored this time," Benita cheered.

Badly as she felt, Adele loved the thrill her sisters were getting out of beating up the evilest woman she'd ever met. Adele had been their big sister, protector, teacher, nurse, and surrogate mom for so long; it was wonderfully healing to have all of them breaking the woman who disowned mama. Still kneeling, Adele tried to stand and offer her own kick, but she could barely breathe, let alone throw a punch.

Another shot rang out into the air. "All of you, get off my boss," Chase said. "Whole lot of you are crazy."

"Kill 'em all," Blanche groaned. "That's an order, dumbass!"

"All of them?" Chase asked. He walked around the circle, as each girl slowly rolled off Blanche. "I kind of like choosing which one goes first," he scoffed, pointing a gun at each girl's head. "You," he said, pointing at Benita. "The mouthy one. I get extra points by making you watch what I do to your sisters."

When he stood to take his first shot, Adele felt the woosh of another bullet whiz by. Chase dropped to his knees, the gun still in his hand. He pointed the Remington at Adele's head, but before he could pull the trigger, another bullet pierced his forehead. He fell back against his knees, then rolled over, his dead eyes staring up to the ceiling.

"Do all your boyfriends end up taking a bullet for you, Miss Dawson?" Tommy asked.

Still kneeling, Adele looked up as the girls leaped into his arms, kissing him. "Hang on, girls, I need to check on my fiancé." Adele, still crouched on all fours smiled over at the woman who had attacked her family.

"Blanche, meet your granddaughters."

Briana and Collette were the first to give Adele a look of horror.

"She disowned our mama when she was barely sixteen. Sent her away and wrote her out of any inheritance."

Benita leaped up to her feet. "Oh my God. You bitch!" she screamed. She kicked Blanche' broken knee and spat on her stomach. "Do you know what a woman she turned out to be? Awesome. Beautiful. Not a bit like you."

Briana broke out in tears. "How could you? If only you'd given her a chance."

"All right, ladies," Tommy broke in. "That's enough. Just keep a gun pointed at her until the sheriff gets here."

"My pleasure!" Benita scoffed. "Please, bitch. Move. Give me a reason."

When Tommy knelt beside Adele, she noticed blood pooling on his arm. "You're shot."

"It's Tamasin's blood," Tommy said. "Elijah's tending to her."

Tommy reached his arm around Adele to help her stand. "We're going to do this slowly," he coached. "Lean on me and I'll get you to the hospital."

"I'm not going."

"Yeah, you are," Tommy insisted. "Already disagreeing with her soon-to-be husband."

"It's our first happy Christmas here." Adele complained.

Briana piped up. "The speakerphone in Grandma Kettie's bedroom. It goes straight to Doctor Luttrell's office." She ran to the grand staircase but stopped after taking two leaps. "That was fun, Delly! But I don't think we should do it again for a while."

"Besides, who works at a hospital on Christmas Eve?" Collette asked.

Adele leaned against Tommy as he helped her hop into the kitchen.

"How bad was the fire?"

"I've seen worse," Tommy whispered. "This was amateurish."

"Like you're such an expert in house fires," Adele teased. "What took you so long?"

"You were in good hands with your sisters. They couldn't wait to rip Blanche to pieces. I put a tourniquet on Tamasin's leg, then battled the fire. They came at us from all directions, Delly."

Tommy supported Adele's back until she bent down into a chair. He leaned over her, winked at her, and smiled. "We're going to have a few visitors, baby. Sheriff McKinley just pulled up the driveway."

He felt her left arm, then the right arm for broken bones. "How's this?" he asked, touching her stomach.

"Sore. Very sore."

"That's the first place Dr. Luttrell will check."

Adele looked around the kitchen to see the extent of damage. The floorboards were charred, as was the door to the pantry. A partially burned log hung between the curtains and kitchen where Chase had set the house on fire. Curtains were completely burned. The walls were blackened like someone had smudged them with smoke.

"It all can be fixed," Tommy said, as if reading her mind.

"How's Tamasin?"

"Now that is one tough woman," Tommy blurted. He pulled up a chair and turned it back to face Adele. "Broken glass cut her foot. Her arm is scorched a bit from putting out the fire. Elijah took her to the hospital. Tamasin doesn't argue with her man, like some woman I know. And Love."

Adele leaned in to kiss him, but when her stomach muscles protested, she sat up straight. "Did you see those girls? The way they tackled Blanche?"

"I'm sure I'll hear about it," Tommy said. "Elijah and I were putting out a fire when Benita said she had to save her sister from a fat lady."

"What's going to happen to you, Tommy? There's a dead guy in the hall."

"That's up to Sheriff McKinley. But I'd call it self-defense given the carnage lying in the hall. And then there's Mrs. Cassidy. Briana is still holding a gun to her head. That girl has a fresh new sense of power."

When the sheriff knocked on the back door, Tommy waved him in, then stroked Adele's hair. "Are you okay for a few minutes while the sheriff and I check on Mrs. Cassidy?"

"Get her out of here. Arrest her."

It was while Tommy and Sheriff McKinley were removing Blanche into the squad car that Doctor Luttrell arrived.

"Goodness, child! Miss Kettie lives and breathes! By the looks of things, she'd be mighty proud of you, but it's time to stop this nonsense."

"I cannot agree more," Adele said. She sat up straight while he squished his fingers around her head, feeling for bumps and cuts. He held her arm in one hand while he rotated her shoulder, then the same on the other side.

"Lean back against this pillow," he said, and listened to her stomach.

"You know I've heard more than my share of gurgles from this family, but I'm not hearing one now." He sat in the chair where Tommy had been and took her hands in his.

"I'm very serious about the future of this family. You're it. This town needs fresh blood. A new direction. We're not a fighting town, but we will fight for our own."

"Yes, sir," Adele said.

"You're going to be plenty bruised for a bit. And I see that bright shiny ring on your finger. Is that new?"

"This afternoon."

"And that's your husband-to-be out there?"

"It is." Adele grinned. "We've known each other since grade school."

"Well, I met my wife in first grade. Can you beat that?" the doctor asked.

"You win. Fifth grade for us."

Dr. Luttrell nodded and patted her arms. "You cough up any blood, you come to the hospital right away. Rest now. It's Christmas."

"I'm here to tell you that's exactly when she plans to do," Tommy said as he and the sheriff stepped into the kitchen.

"You put an end to a long train of violence, Adele," Sheriff McKinley said. "Blanche is from up Wheeling way and has somehow kept her part in organized crime a secret from Giles. We've been tracking her for a long time but never found enough evidence to convict her."

"How long will she be in prison?" Tommy asked.

"Let me put it this way. You two will have grandchildren before she's released."

Epilogue

Adele climbed outside of Tommy's Packard and stood at the top of River Road looking down onto the farmland that her stepfather once owned. The pinewood home, once paralyzed in aged wood, now leaned so far into the wind, it could collapse at any moment. No more sun-bleached bonnets on the wall. Only one stray dog sat on the porch, waiting for his master to come home and offer scraps. She wondered if that master was August Beck.

Roofers stepped sideways on top of the original farmhouse that Pa, she, and Mama had lived in before floods and the Depression forced them to flee. Olga stood outside barking orders to hurry it up. The finishing crew would be there in the morning.

"Come on, Delly, it's in the past," Tommy said. "She can't hold a candle to the home you live in now."

"I want him to walk me down the aisle," Adele responded.

"You're not serious. Not after all he's done to you?"

"He needs to acknowledge that he is giving me away."

"You were never his to give away, baby."

"He doesn't know that yet."

***

They had come back to New Madrid so that the only priest either of them had ever known would bless the start of their lives together. Adele and her sisters stayed in the home of Selma Beck's best friend, Grace

MacPherson. Isaac was three years old now. While he was reluctant to greet his sisters, Deirdre, Elysia and Faye played with him until he brought them toys to entertain him.

Catherine Dawson, Tommy's sister stopped by in her new Cadillac. "My goodness, it's all us girls back together again," she said. She stroked the long set of white beads tied in a knot.

"That's us," Benita sang, using a voice an octave higher. "Just us girls." She had taken a seat on the couch next to Adele to make it clear to Tommy's snooty sister that no one would get near Adele without Benita's say-so.

"So, what's it like in West Virginia with all those cowboys and such?" Catherine asked.

"It's a shoot-out every day," Benita responded. Both she and Adele snickered.

Catherine twisted the beads. "My mother said you already had enough bridesmaids."

"Six," Adele said. "You know, the alphabet."

"No law against having seven, don't you think?" Catherine asked much too coyly. "Tommy deserves to have his kin represented, too."

Adele looked to the ceiling; she raised her fingers to her face as if to be deep in thought. She looked to Benita, then said, "No."

"Well, apparently those cowboys sure twisted your nose. Be careful you don't drown when it rains," Catherine said. She stood, grabbed her overcoat, and walked out the door.

The next day, the church was full to the brim with townsfolk wondering what in the world happened to Adele Christina Dawson Beck. Some said she was getting even. Catherine Thompson wore a burgundy gown, the same design, and color as Adele's sisters, the bridesmaid that was never chosen. She sat on the aisle next to Tommy's parents, immediately behind August and Olga, and yes, damnit, Adele thought.

August brought Olga to the wedding. An insult since Adele and Tommy paid for everything.

Father MacDougal started the ceremony by saying, "This is a sacred ceremony, designed by the church, between two people who wish to start their lives together with Christ as the center of their family. If you are here to celebrate that union, Our Father and I applaud you." He looked directly at the Thompson family. "But if you are here to critique the bride's dress or looking for gossip about the family, our Father in Heaven and I know the sins of your heart. Please leave now."

Silence sliced families in half with a blow that would make the purest sinner squirm. Adele could see Catherine's neck tense, desperately trying not to look at her father.

The groomsmen stepped to the altar. Adele peeked through an opening in the church's bride's room. She gasped when she saw Tommy. His black hair glistened under the church's candlelight. Dressed in a pinstripe double-breasted suit, he couldn't be more handsome. "I am absolutely in love with you, Mr. Thompson." Tears filled her eyes as she watched him take deep breaths to calm himself. Finally, the organist began playing Wagner's "Wedding March. "

Briana bent down and straightened the train on Adele's wedding gown. "The B's have grown. Now it's the BTs with Tommy joining us." Adele squeezed her sister's waist and kissed her cheek.

"I'll look after the girls now," Benita said. "You need to be a wife. At least until we all get back to West Virginia." She tried to smack Adele's behind, but her hand got lost in layers of ivory lace. Briana, Collette, Deirdre and Elysia followed all wearing matching gowns. Faye held a basket of flowers and dropped them one at a time. She looked up at Tommy halfway down the aisle and shouted, "I love you, Tommy."

Women snickered.

"I love you, too, Punkin," Tommy answered. He motioned for her to come and stand at his side.

Holding Faye's hand, three-year-old Isaac, Adele's brother, carried a satin pillow with ribbons holding rings for the bride and groom.

Adele stepped out of the bride's room and reached for her stepfather. August Beck was a handsome man, and yes, he'd been the worst of the worst to her. But she needed him to heal. He took one look at her and bent his head. Tears dripped down his face as the organist played the Bride's Chorus. Father MacDougal signaled for the congregation to stand.

"I can't do this, Delly. I don't deserve a daughter as beautiful as you on my arm. I never have."

"Give me away, Pa." Adele looked straight forward at her groom.

They walked down the aisle together. August sniffling the entire way until at last, they stopped in front of the altar. James Thompson tried to offer Adele a look that said, "I know the color of your underwear," but Adele returned an incipient grin because she knew he would serve time in prison for attempted rape and child molestation if she and Tommy had their way. It seemed the congregation was trying to hold their tongues until they could drip stories at the beauty parlors of the millionaire who came back to marry a Thompson. August patted Adele's hand and whispered, "You have given New Madrid a new matriarch."

"This matriarch lives in West Virginia, Pa." Adele didn't bother to see if he winced.

"Who gives this woman in marriage?" Father MacDougal asked when they'd reached the altar.

"I," August started to say, but then cleared his throat. "Her mother in heaven, and I do."

When he had been seated, Tommy reached for Adele's hand and whispered. "You are gorgeous. God will give us peace, Delly girl."

About the Author

 Carolyn Palmer Hartley's work crosses multiple disciplines. She is the lead co-author of Amazon's #1 bestselling The Caregiver's Toolbox (Rowman 2015) and creator of the historical fiction Buried Sunshine series. Her stories, published in literary and consumer magazines, are influenced by seldom-remembered events that changed the way we live and care for each other. Her characters are driven by social justice. They come alive in early chapters; then, later explain how they got into, or out of complex situations. Most plots and twists come to her in the early hours of the morning while she's working out, swimming, or listening to music. Carolyn also was a healthcare journalist for several national medical societies and consumer magazines and is the acquisitions editor of JMerrillPress. She is mom to three beautiful women, one son, and Nana to nine athletic grandchildren.

Acknowledgements

R eaders are my lifeline. I owe my career, my fascination with people's choices in life to readers like you. I am blown away by those who have invested time in reading my books; some of you I've never met, but you changed my life. You posted reviews on Amazon, social media, or online booksellers. You are the reason Adele Dawson thrives in the Buried Sunshine series.

I am grateful to a select group authors and scriptwriters, inspirational friends. You critique manuscripts, and offer a solace of encouragement: Jay, Terresa, Millie, Laura, Scotty, Don, Charlotte, Vonnie, Debbie, Sue, Cathy. Thank you to my sisters in Christ; Sherry, Gwen, Carol, Kathie, Ginny, and Susan, for your prayers, encouragement, and love. You listened and shared the best glasses of wine and French 75s with me. My sisters in love: Mimi, Megan, Cameron, MaryeJo, Joan, you lift me up. To Ellie Maas Davis, I am deeply grateful to you for your sharp editorial pen – for carving a tighter manuscript. Huge thanks goes to William Petty, my email pal and major contributor to bramwellwv.com. Your vetted content continues to provide insight into the history of the majestic village of Bramwell. Thank you, Louise Stoker, Bramwell mayor for providing access to so many brilliant folks in your town; to Jackie Shahan for the tour of your incredible home, which I truly believe is the centerpiece for Kettie Dawson's home. The Mining and Engineering department at West Virginia University holds a treasure trove of historical videos, textbooks, and information. Thank you for allowing users like me to access them.

Finally, I am grateful for my daughters, Kristen and Laurie, for your unimaginable love, kindness, and generosity, and to Chris, my husband, who built an incredible office/guest house for me to bury my mind in a soundproof world surrounded by shiplap. You are beyond patient with me. I cherish you.

Bibliography

Research is the backbone of historical fiction. I am indebted to those who provided pathways of knowledge, details, and information that influenced *Reconciliation's* content. To learn more about coal miners' challenges and their lionhearted spirit, I encourage you to read any of these invaluable resources.

- Corbin, David A.; *Life, Work, and Rebellion in the Coal Fields: The Southern West Virginia Miners*, 1880- 1992. University of Illinois Press, 1989

- Richards, John Stuart; *Early Coal Mining in the Anthracite Region (PA) of America*. Arcadia Publishing, 2002

- Freese, Barbara; *Coal: A Human History*. Penguin Books, 2004

- Green, James; *The Devil Is Here in These Hills: West Virginia's Coal Miners and Their Battle for Freedom*. Atlantic Monthly Press, 2015

- Bailey, Rebecca J.; *Matewan: The Coal Mining Massacre America Forgot*. West Virginia University Press, 2008

- Jeanette Walls, *The Glass Castle*, Scribner, 2006

- Giardina, Denise; *Storming Heaven*, Ivy Books, 1987.

- McNab, Chris; Coal Mining Operations Manual, The Quarto Group, Hanes Publishing, UK 2020

- Smithsonian Institute, National Museum of American History, Workers and Managers Exhibit.

Videos

- West Virginia Coal Mine Wars: 5 Things to Know. West Virginia University Libraries
https://www.youtube.com/watch?v=Y3qeG3TYE-0

Book Club Discussion Points

1) Prosperity came to a screeching halt for many Americans on Black Tuesday, October 29, 1929. In the next few years, children competed with adults for jobs. Families with several children would barter then in exchange for canceling a debt. How is that different today in several international cultures?

2) American gangsters found lucrative businesses during the roaring twenties. By 1926, powerful gangs like Al "Scarface" Capone and George "Bugs" Moran turned city streets into war zones. Was it hard for you to accept that Selma Cassidy got caught up in criminal activities?

3) Of the official bad guys in *Redemption* and *Reconciliation*, who would you most like to see an end to his demise?

4) Adele often has to make tough family decisions, such as whether to return to college, oversee the coal mines, take care of her siblings, and be a wife to Tommy Thompson. Do you see your life different from hers?

5) Do you believe Adele married the right man? Or do you see Jackson coming back into her life?

6) How would you have accepted Tamasin and Elijah if you inherited a large home?

7) Why did Adele allow August Beck to walk her down the aisle for her wedding?

8) Olga represents some pretty unsavory politicians, and like some, she is never imprisoned. Do you think we offer pardons for some individuals while we don't for others?

Made in the USA
Coppell, TX
01 August 2022